Praise for Meghan MacLean Weir's

THE BOOK OF ESSIE

Finalist for the 2018 New England Book Award

"An incisive novel."   —Publishers Weekly

"A page-turning tale."   —Minneapolis Star Tribune

"Weir does a fine job of portraying Essie initially as a teen whose
mind-set is reflexively strategic, and increasingly as a young
woman with an elegant intelligence and a beating and quite
breakable heart."   —WBUR

"[A] propulsive debut novel."   —BookPage

"Every once in a while, a novel comes along that is both time-
lessly beautiful and unbelievably timely. The Book of Essie is such
a story. Meghan MacLean Weir has given us a young heroine
who is at once authentic and courageous—and a tale that is
wonderful and mysterious and relentlessly surprising."
                                                  —Chris Bohjalian,
                              bestselling author of The Flight Attendant

Meghan MacLean Weir

THE BOOK OF ESSIE

Meghan MacLean Weir was raised in the rectory of her father's church in Southbridge, Massachusetts, and later moved with her family to Buffalo, New York. Her memoir, *Between Expectations: Lessons from a Pediatric Residency*, chronicles her years in training at Boston Medical Center and Boston Children's Hospital. She continues to live and work as a physician in the Boston area. *The Book of Essie* is her first novel.

www.megweir.com

THE

BOOK

OF

ESSIE

———

THE
BOOK OF ESSIE

Meghan MacLean Weir

———

VINTAGE BOOKS

A DIVISION OF PENGUIN RANDOM HOUSE LLC

NEW YORK

FIRST VINTAGE BOOKS EDITION, MAY 2019

The Library of Congress has cataloged the Knopf edition as follows:
Name: Weir, Meghan MacLean, author.
Title: The book of Essie / Meghan MacLean Weir.
Description: First edition. | New York : Alfred A. Knopf, 2018.
Identifiers: LCCN 2017032041
Subjects: LCSH: Teenage girls—Fiction. | Celebrities—Fiction. |
Families—Fiction. | Domestic fiction.
Classification: LCC PS3623.E4324496 B66 2018 | DDC 813/.6—dc23
LC record available at https://lccn.loc.gov/2017032041

Vintage Books Trade Paperback ISBN: 978-0-525-43607-2
eBook ISBN: 978-0-525-52032-0

www.vintagebooks.com

Printed in the United States of America
10 9 8 7 6 5 4 3 2 1

For my family

And the king loved Esther above all the women, and she obtained grace and favour in his sight more than all the virgins; so that he set the royal crown upon her head, and made her queen.

ESTHER 2:17

Then Esther the queen answered and said, If I have found favour in thy sight, O king, and if it please the king, let my life be given me at my petition, and my people at my request:

For we are sold, I and my people, to be destroyed, to be slain, and to perish.

ESTHER 7:3–4

THE

BOOK

OF

ESSIE

———

Esther

On the day I turn seventeen, there is a meeting to decide whether I should have the baby or if sneaking me to a clinic for an abortion is worth the PR risk. I am not invited, which is just as well, since my being there might imply that I have some choice in the matter and I know that I have none. I listen in, though, the way Lissa and I used to before she went away. It was Lissa who discovered the vent in the wall of the laundry room, who realized that you could eavesdrop on everything that was said in the production office if you climbed onto the dryer and put your ear up against the filigreed bronze grate.

The winter Lissa broke her leg, she was fourteen and I was nine. I remember she chose an orange cast that Mother hated and the doctor laughed and said something about Lissa being a firecracker and Mother frowned but didn't dare to disagree, not with the cameras rolling. I could tell she was worried that the color was too bright, that it would bleed on-screen or at the very least be distracting. It lasted only a second, the withering look she shot my sister as the fiberglass was unwrapped and wound round and round the crack above Lissa's ankle. But even at nine, I was well versed in Mother's methods of wordless communication. I knew exactly what to look for, just as I knew to look for the flash of defiance in Lissa's eyes that was my sister's only reply.

The doctor signed the cast when he was done and so did all the nurses, then Lissa and I were given Popsicles for the ride home. They were orange, to match the cast, but Mother made us throw them in the trash as soon as we reached the parking lot. She said the sugar would ruin our teeth, but I think really she did it just to punish us, to remind Lissa that she shouldn't count on the cameras for protection, that they might delay the consequences of her actions but would never entirely prevent them. She needn't have bothered. It was the first lesson any of us learned.

That cast was the reason it became my job to climb up and report everything the grown-ups said, because Lissa couldn't do it herself without breaking the only good leg she had left. It's possible that without that orange cast, Lissa would never have told me about the vent at all, since trusting me was a risk. She might have kept the secret to herself, ferreting away this little piece of knowledge the way she used to hide the choco-late bars she stole from Stahl's Sweet Shoppe when she stopped in with Becca Twomey on their way home from school. Lissa never bought anything, but Becca was allowed to spend her allowance on whatever she wanted; in any case, that was how it seemed.

Lissa and I, on the other hand, were allowed chocolate only on birthdays and Easter. I always wondered, after she was gone and I found the box of unopened candy under her bed, why she bothered to steal it at all, why she took such a chance. If she had been found out, it wouldn't have been only Daddy's paddle she'd have had to contend with. Mother's silent punishment would have been much worse. It meant something, I realized, that Lissa could sneak the Milky Ways into her bag without Mr. Stahl noticing yet never bring herself to open them. Eating the choco-late, I saw much later on, would have been the thing that made the stealing real.

———

The dryer is running and slightly warm when I sit on it. It's a pleasant sensation, but the clang of some sort of metal clip getting thwapped against the drum covers up the sound of the producer speaking on the other side of the wall, so I turn the dryer off. Once the drum has stopped turning, I can hear well enough to make out what Candy is saying. The name fits her. Sweet as sugar but hard enough to break a tooth on. She has been with us since before I was born, since that first Christmas special when Matty was not quite three and my parents had just been told that there would be no more children.

Daddy had spent so much time on television by then you'd have thought it would have come naturally, but Mother said he was as nervous as a pig in a bacon factory the day the new crew started filming. Up until then, the cameras had only been at church, where they were entirely under Daddy's control. Could he tell then that the balance of power was subtly shifting? In any case, Mother had to force Daddy to let the crew into the house and even then he did this thing where he scratched his wrist incessantly anytime the cameras were pointed at him. Candy's team did their best to edit this out, to use the close-ups of his pensive expression and his clear blue eyes, but there are a few shots where you can see him moving his fingers back and forth compulsively, as if possessed, like an addict scratching at invisible bugs burrowing just beneath his skin.

Mother stole the show, though, so it didn't matter. She cried real tears when she revealed their struggles to conceive, their disappointment. She was candid when she confessed that they had always wanted a big family, a brood, a flock to tend and raise up in His grace and light. After all, if children are a gift from God, surely Daddy was deserving of more than just a single blessing since he had made it his life's work to speak His truth and praise His name even in these darkest days. She sighed and reached out and took my father's hand then, stilled it, and held it tight to keep him from scratching. With her eyes turned up to the ceiling, the tears welled at first but did not fall. Then Mother looked directly at the camera and breathed something about accepting God's will and those fat drops rolled right down her tastefully rouged cheeks as if she had control over gravity itself.

That hour-long special probably would have just been a one-off since Daddy said the focus should be on his ministry, not on his family, but on Christmas Eve they found out that Daniel was on the way and people called it an honest-to-God miracle and there was no stopping after that. Nine months later when my brother was born, ten million people tuned in to see it happen. Not the actual moment, of course, but everything leading up to it: the praying, the hand-holding, the reciting of bits of verse. Then he was lifted, slick and shrieking and still streaked with blood, and Daddy let loose a heartfelt alleluia and a regular television phenomenon was born.

On the other side of the wall I hear Candy say, "Are you sure?"

To her credit, there is no judgment in her tone—none that I can detect, in any case. Her face might be an entirely different matter, but I cannot see it. I can imagine, though, the near silent signs of disapproval: the slightly downturned lip, the light tap of a perfectly manicured nail on the polished wood surface of the table. Candy has no children, after all. We are all the family she's got. It's possible that this feels personal, though I doubt she would ever admit it.

"I watched her repeat the test myself."

This is my mother's voice, smooth and velvety and utterly composed. You would think she was discussing which muffin recipe she might bake for an upcoming church fair, parsing the relative merits of currants and pumpkin spice. She almost sounds bored. The words fall evenly from her lips, with a hint of a drawl that I recognize as an affectation. Like her modest light blue suit and single strand of pearls, this voice is something that has been carefully chosen; cultivated, even. The vocal coach comes once a week on Tuesday mornings and stops by on an as-needed basis to deliver special lozenges if Mother's throat is sore, which is more often than you would expect. She is forever sipping tea with honey and telling people how exhausting it is, running the household all by herself since Daddy has to conserve his energies for more elevated pursuits. Except she doesn't really run the household; Candy does. But no one would ever dare tell Mother that.

In the early days, when it was just Daddy's church services that were being broadcast and before Mother herself was properly a star, they used a voice double for close-ups of Mother standing in the front row during hymns. As the voices of the congregation swelled behind her, Mother would hold her hymnal open at her waist, never looking down at the page but instead keeping her eyes glued to the stained glass window above and behind the altar. She had each and every song in that book memorized, knew even the page numbers by heart. The organist would play a few bars of introduction and then Mother's mouth would open and shut in rhythm with the music, soundlessly I knew, but it looked for all the world like she was really singing, as if the music itself had her in its thrall.

Then the camera would zoom in even closer and in the version that TIL would broadcast, one voice would be heard rising above the others, a voice like an angel's, or so Daddy liked to tell his parishioners during coffee hour. This sort of compliment always made Mother blush demurely and shake her head so that the gaggle of old women who followed Daddy around at events like this would transition directly from talking about Mother's voice to remarking upon how modest she was. No one knew that the voice was not really hers, that it belonged to a music teacher in Cincinnati named Tracey Goldberg. No one knew that Tracey, raising three children all on her own after her husband skipped town with a waitress from Des Moines, had not even read the nondisclosure agreement Candy had handed her, had not stopped to think what sort of lies she would be helping to perpetuate, since signing that single piece of paper meant that she would never again have to worry about how to feed her children.

These days they still dub in Tracey's voice for the singing, but even the speaking voice that Mother uses now, a voice that she probably thinks of as entirely her own, is a complete work of fiction. This used to make me angry, especially when she was yelling. I used to yell back, to try to push her into revealing her true self, that sharp twinge of Appalachia, the dropped consonants, the seemingly arbitrary vowels, but she never did. Eventually I began to suspect that maybe she had no true self remaining, that it was not just covered up but had been destroyed entirely.

"You watched her?" Candy asks, and here there is a hint of amusement.

I know she is picturing me on the toilet, skirt hiked up and underwear around my ankles, holding the stick with just the tips of my fingers as I try to pee on it without getting any on myself. As if such a feat were even possible.

"I watched her."

In truth Mother had turned away once I began to shimmy down my cotton briefs. She hasn't seen my bum since I was potty trained, I don't think, and just the idea of that much flesh probably embarrassed her. But she heard the stream of urine, heard me place the stick on the edge of the sink beside her, watched as it turned blue. A mother's worst fear, or so some people say. But not my mother's.

"And she told you she was afraid she might be pregnant?" Candy asks.

How would that conversation have played out? I wonder, and once again I consider it. First off, I would have had to catch Mother alone with no risk of interruption, no easy task given the number of people who walk freely through our house. Then I would have had to make sure she was listening, truly listening, and not just nodding her head and gazing vaguely in my direction the way she often does. No, a conversation would have been too risky. There was too great a chance it would have gone according to her plan instead of according to mine. So I bought the pregnancy test and left it in my bathroom where I knew she would find it. Actually, I bought three, though I left the money on the shelf rather than going to the register. The first I used to confirm what I already knew. The second I left for her to find. The third I hid underneath my mattress in case denial kicked in and she threw the second away.

"No, I found a pregnancy test in her bathroom where she had stashed it and I knew right then that something must be wrong."

From my perch on the dryer I almost laugh out loud. I find the notion that Mother does not realize that I know she goes through my bathroom drawers almost tragically comical. But more than that, this proposition that she possesses some heightened intuition, that she picked up on some subtle clue and swooped in just in time to play the hero, is blatantly absurd. The pieces to this puzzle should have been apparent to her all along.

"And the father?" Candy is asking.

Here Mother is silent. There is the sound of papers being

shuffled. Has she really brought notes to this meeting? She couldn't have. She wouldn't want there to be anything in writing, anything that might be tracked. The papers must be for something else, or maybe they are even blank, just there for effect. Maybe she is playing a part even within that room, just as she does outside it.

Finally, Mother answers Candy's question without really answering it at all. "We don't have to worry about him. He won't say a word."

Of course he won't, I think. He has the most to lose.

"Well then," says Candy, who has lasted as long as she has by learning when to stop, when not to push. She can tell that this is information that Mother does not plan to share. "Let's run through our list of options. Gretchen?"

At this I sit up straighter and turn my head so that my ear is pointed up toward the grate. I am curious to see if there are any options besides the ones of which I am already aware. I hear Gretchen clear her throat. She is younger than Candy and Mother, who are roughly the same age. Brown hair, sharp features, mousy, though that descriptor applies more to a tendency to twitch and scurry rather than to her actual appearance. Her face, taken by itself, is actually rather pretty. Gretchen works in media relations or publicity or whatever it is you call it when your job is to make a fairly unremarkable family universally recognized and adored.

At this, she and the others who came before her have been surprisingly successful. Recently I've tried to dissect this improbability, but when I was growing up, I never really wondered why the show became so popular. Contrary to what some left-wing bloggers might say, this wasn't because I am at all conceited. It was because I lacked perspective. Mother said we were Called to lead by example, and the capital *C* hung in the air like something holy. So I believed her. I didn't know any better.

Other families had enjoyed their fifteen minutes of fame, their moment in the spotlight, only to have their shows canceled after a few seasons when the parents divorced or the child who was adorable at age four became positively homely at seven or failed to outgrow a lisp. Or maybe, for no discernible reason at all, the audience simply grew bored and advertising revenue dried up. Then the camera crews would pack up their things and retreat, leaving the house feeling empty, the living room just slightly too large, the rooms eerily quiet. Or so I always assumed.

I took it for granted, I guess, that we were special, we were chosen, or at the very least odd enough to be intriguing to those who continued to tune in season after season, year after year. Because they did tune in. They watched Daniel take his first steps, saw Matty cut his knee when he fell off his bike and cried along with him when he got stitches. They saw Daddy and Mother move to the new house, the one the church built for us, the week before Jacob was due. They marveled at Mother's cool exterior, the calm she exuded in the eye of the storm created by those whirling dervishes who were her many sons.

For by then she was vastly outnumbered. Daddy, Matty, Daniel, and Jacob had been joined by Caleb. Then came Elizabeth, the girl my parents and the nation as a whole had been waiting for. Then triplets, two more girls and a boy, who were born much too early and whose short existence was chronicled and broadcast live from the private room in the neonatal intensive care unit where their three isolettes stood under constant guard. Looking weary but dogged, Mother would lift the thick quilted coverings that encased these strange plastic pods to reveal the closed eyes or purple waxy toes of Mary or Ruth or Zechariah, each of them with tubes disappearing into their mouths and plunged into their belly buttons, dependent upon the machines that pushed air into their tiny undeveloped lungs or dripped sugar and fat into their blood.

Those weeks the show got the best ratings it ever had, though some said the exploitation of such sick, helpless infants went too far, crossed some invisible line drawn in the sand. Mother was not one to apologize, however, and though people started petitions and vowed to boycott the funeral episode, no one actually did. That month a photograph of those three miniature caskets lined up side by side in a sea of roses made it onto the cover of *Time*.

There was a break, then, from the making of more babies. It was just as well. After the triplets, the fans had lost their stomach for such things. Apart from a few miscarriages, after each of which the doctors again said that Mother would never be able to bear another child, the show shifted its focus to Matty and Daniel, then ten and eight, who begged Mother to let them go to the public school rather than be taught at home. They asked for and received a puppy, a golden retriever named Blister, who shed on the carpet but redeemed himself by learning to catch a Frisbee and retrieve a ball. These were some of the most boring episodes, but there was a war on at the time, one of those unnamed conflicts in the Middle East, so the mundanity of it all was probably soothing. Anyway, this sort of thing carried them through until Lissa was nearly six and I was born, wholly unexpectedly, another miracle of a sort, a reward for those fans who had stayed loyal for so long.

It was not only the folks who watched Daddy's sermons from the comfort of their couches, or the locals who called out "Pastor Hicks" and waved every time he walked down Main Street, who were tuning in. It was not only those who flocked to his church by the thousands who let the episodes fill up their DVRs. Others as well, some devout and others less so, watched with morbid fascination the seeming contradiction that we epitomized. Our family rejected materialism and popular culture and yet we also produced it. The show, which by then had been called many things but was currently airing with the title *Six for Hicks*, paid for the SUVs Mother and Daddy drove, the lake house, the "spiritual retreat" that was actually a villa in Saint John. It paid for the car seat I rode home in from the hospital, the muslin blankets I was swaddled in when I slept. It paid for my first backpack when it came time for me to go to school, Mother having by then completely abandoned giving lessons in the living room, not just because her time and energy were better spent promoting our brand but also because marketing said that what our audience wanted at that point was a character who was "normal."

The show paid for everything. And now it would pay for a solution to my "problem," one chosen from a list that Gretchen, on the other side of the wall that I am leaning up against, is about to run through aloud. She starts with the obvious, though I can tell that it makes her uncomfortable. Just forming the word with her lips in all likelihood feels sinful and she probably just wants to get it out of the way.

"Well, there's an abortion, of course. She'd have to cross state lines to reach a provider, and such a trip would certainly not go unnoticed. An impromptu college visit to New York or Boston might work. Or maybe even something abroad, though safety might then be an issue. The trip to Cuba is already on the books. A contact of mine knows a doctor there who will work for cash and promise discretion."

"I'll consider it," Mother says, and I feel the air go out of my lungs. My skull begins to buzz. She makes this statement as if it is nothing to her, a choice of deli meats at the supermarket counter: thinly sliced roast beef or ham. She speaks as if she has not spent the last twenty years railing publicly against abortion and organizing protest marches on the front lawn of the only Democratic official within a hundred miles, even though as comptroller he has nothing to do with health services of any kind.

An abortion is not anything I have ever wanted, but then again, I never wanted any of this, and for the first time, I consider how it could erase what has happened and maybe even turn back time. As I feel the last of the heat leave the dryer beneath me, I allow myself to hope that there is some part of my mother that cares about my future above her own. That I will at least be offered the choice.

But Gretchen is already talking again, and I know that despite what Mother says, she will not really consider it. Not because she is so staunchly pro-life, a position that I now realize is just another carefully crafted aspect of her public persona, but because her empire would come crashing down if we were ever caught.

That sort of crash almost occurred when Lissa left and refused to have the cameras follow her. All season they had aired tape of Lissa looking at colleges, but when she left for Northwestern just shy of her eighteenth birthday, she made it clear that she was going there alone. There were a few unflattering articles written, but Mother found a way to squelch the rumors that Lissa was a girl gone wild and after those last shots of Mother and Daddy carrying boxes into her freshman dorm, Lissa was never seen on film again.

Every once in a while a grainy photo will show up in some tabloid rag, but for the most part she has proved remarkably adept at avoiding the paparazzi. That or they have taken pity on her, which I suppose is entirely possible. Back when the triplets died, people used to cry that those babies were never asked if they wanted to be on television. They said it was a travesty. But none of us were asked, Lissa told me before she left. I guess they were afraid of what our answers might be. So in the end, Mother had to let Lissa go, had to fall back on leaking details to the press about phone calls that had never happened, trips home that had not been recorded due to Lissa's desire to remain off camera and Mother's equally important desire to respect her daughter's wishes. But the truth is, when Lissa left this house, she never came back. Not once.

Gretchen drones on about the possibility of a fictitious mission trip overseas once I begin to show, with footage limited to a few carefully edited interviews, angled to mask the baby bump. All the while I would be hiding out poolside in Saint John. The cook and housekeeper at the villa there had been heavily vetted before they were hired, and of course nondisclosure clauses were included in their contracts. They would never tell. I could give the baby up for adoption anonymously. Alternatively, Mother and Daddy could adopt the baby, if we wanted to keep it in the family. I could have a brand-new brother or sister, and there would be the obvious and added benefit of their appearing to have come to the rescue of a child in need. Mother dismissed this idea before Gretchen had even launched into the particulars. There was too much of a chance that the child would look like a Hicks. Even a slight family resemblance might trigger exactly the sort of rumors they were trying to avoid.

"What else are we left with?" Mother asked.

"A wedding," Gretchen answered. "Essie could get married, quickly. I could throw something together by the end of the month. We'll have to come up with a reason the ceremony can't be put off, a sick relative on his side or yours whose dying wish is to see the young lovebirds take their marriage vows."

"What happens when the baby is born too soon?" Candy asked. "At least some of our viewers can do simple math."

"I know a private midwife who will go on record that the due date is whatever we need it to be, then make a statement that the baby came early. Essie will deliver at home so we can limit the number of variables. But even if there are complications and she needs to go to the hospital, I've got contacts there as well, one obstetrician in particular that I know we can trust."

I hold my breath at the sound of a chair creaking as Candy or Mother pushes back from the table. Gretchen would not dare to do this until formally dismissed.

"Candy?" says my mother.

"I have to admit, there's something appealing about just having it over and done with. But remember what happened to Bill Lennox when his daughter got her abortion? It was just supposed to be a few pills she took at home to induce a miscarriage, but she ended up hemorrhaging. It was all over the news. His bid for the governorship was over before it even started."

"I agree," says Mother. "It's just too much of a risk."

"So a wedding it is." Candy sighs with finality. "And just who do you think the lucky young man should be?"

"Give me a day," Mother tells her. "I'll let you know by tomorrow."

With this, I scramble down and toggle the dryer to resume its cycle. I slip out through the back hall and step into the sunroom. There's an empty watering can on a shelf beside Mother's large overgrown jade and I pick it up, tilt it over the pot. I face the windows overlooking the yard until I hear the door open behind me, then I turn and smile at Gretchen, who quickly lowers her eyes and shuffles off toward the basement stairs that lead down to her office. After Gretchen comes Candy, who embraces me expansively and kisses both of my cheeks. She looks back at

Mother, who tilts her head to the side in an act of dismissal, and makes for the basement stairs as well.

Mother gazes at me appraisingly in a distant, slightly cold way.

"How are you feeling?" she asks.

I replace the empty watering can and stand awkwardly with my arms folded in front of me.

"Fine, thanks," I tell her.

"How was the library? Did you find the book you were looking for?"

I nod and remind myself that the first lie, the one that started everything, was told this morning when I fabricated a school paper I had to do research for. Now I need to stay calm and see it through. I am breathing faster than I should be and so I lower my arms to grip the edge of the shelf behind me and will my voice not to shake. I try to sound as casual as I can without raising suspicion. "While I've got you in private," I say, "I was wondering if I could ask you to add Mr. Richards and his family to your prayer list for this week."

"Why?" she asks, her eyes narrowing. Typically this is the type of thing we discuss freely in front of the cameras. Most people in town like to hear their name mentioned on the show for all the usual reasons: the birth of a child, the death of a distant cousin, the onslaught of some minor affliction that he or she needs the Lord's help to rise above.

"No reason," I say and drop my eyes to the floor. "It was silly. Forget it."

What is essential at this point is that I remain silent while Mother considers whether or not to take the bait. I grind one foot absently into the rust-colored floor tiles, twisting my heel back and forth. This is a habit of mine when I'm hiding something, which works particularly well in this case because I am hiding something, just not the something that Mother thinks.

The best lie, Candy always says, is the one that is ninety-nine percent truth. It's easier to sell.

"I will not forget it," Mother says brusquely in a tone that is meant to be noble. "If the Richards family needs my prayers, then they will have them. I do, however, need to know what exactly I'm praying for."

"Well," I say softly, "I heard that Mr. Richards might lose the store. He went to the bank for a loan, only his credit is so bad, the bank wouldn't give him anything at all."

Mother narrows her eyes, says, "And how did you come by this information?"

I shrug, then tell Mother more of what is true. "Lily told me. It was her father who had to turn Mr. Richards down. Please don't say anything to Daddy or anyone. Even Lily wasn't supposed to know."

Mother swallows and nods. "Mr. Richards always was a proud man. He wouldn't want anyone talking behind his back or knowing his business. Still, I'm glad that you told me. What they need now is the power of prayer and that's just what they'll get."

She tugs at the bottom of her fitted blue brocade jacket.

"Yes, ma'am," I say. "I'm sure that will make a world of difference to the three of them."

Mother moves toward the door and then turns back as if something has just occurred to her.

"Roarke Richards is about your age, isn't he?"

"He's one grade ahead," I answer. "I don't know him that well, but I've seen him at school."

"He's always seemed like such a polite boy," she says thoughtfully.

"Yes, ma'am," I repeat. "That's what everybody says. Do you want me to bring some of your muffins to school on Monday to give to him?"

Second only to her praying, Mother believes her muffins are the most surefire cure for all the ills in the entire world.

"No, no." She shakes her head. "I think I'll bring some by the house instead."

Mother leaves the room then with a clicking of heels upon tile and I lean back, exhausted, and allow myself a ghost of the first real smile I've had in weeks. As she goes, I realize that she's forgotten my birthday, but I don't even care. Her sudden heartfelt interest in the Richards family is the best present I could get.

Roarke

Dad's still at the shop when I get back from baseball practice, but Mom is home. She's sitting at the kitchen table with that woman, the one from church who somehow got famous for acting holier-than-thou, which in and of itself is nothing special, but she does it on TV. It's been a long time since I've seen the lady, and even then it was only from a distance. All spring I've been ditching church to coach JV since practice starts right after the late service lets out and there's no way I'm getting up for the early one. I could probably get home and still make it in time if I hustled—that's what the players all have to do—but I told Dad that I need to be there early to set up and he didn't push. Baseball may not be his favorite sport, but it's the only one that's got any chance of helping pay for college. Dad appreciates that a strong recommendation from the coach could really help my prospects. Working with the younger kids is basically community service. That's the sort of shit that makes an applicant stand out. The guidance counselor told me that, though she didn't say it in quite those words.

I walk into the kitchen and scan for cameras, but there aren't any. She's come alone. I wonder if maybe she left them because she didn't want there to be any witnesses, but as soon as I think it, I know it's crazy. Still, there's something off about the entire family and it doesn't really have anything to do with them being on TV. Right now, for instance, Celia Hicks is creeping me out and there's not a single television camera in sight. Maybe it's all the smiling they do, the plastered-on look of it, their mouths split wide open, teeth bared, like animals being led to slaughter. Not Celia Hicks, though; never her. Her teeth are always covered. Mom would call that sort of smile ladylike, but I think she probably hides her teeth because she has the sharpest fangs of all.

Before they notice me, I take the opportunity to really look at her. From where I stand I can see the spot near her hairline where the makeup thins and gives way to normal skin. The sort of skin that is filled with pores, with imperfections. Her hair is dyed. I see that now. I'm not an expert on women's hairstyles, but for some reason I find it thrilling that just behind her ear there is one fine wisp of gray. I stare at this rebellious strand of hair as if just by looking at it I might be able to spot her other flaws. She must have them. I know. No one can be that perfect.

Mom looks up, startled. She's actually holding that woman's hands. Their fingers are intertwined across the table and I can tell that Mom's been crying. Not Pastor Hicks's wife, though. I'll bet she never sheds a tear without capturing the moment, to milk it for all it's worth.

"You're home," Mom says, entirely unnecessarily.

"I'm home," I repeat, not because I'm being sullen but because I'm still trying to get my bearings, to know what's the right thing to say. There's a tin of muffins on the table, clearly an offering from Celia Hicks, and I try to come up with some reason we deserve them.

Typically we fly below the radar. We sit in the back row, or slip in right after the service has started—that is, if we're not skipping out entirely. We do belong to the church, of course. Everyone in town does. The folks from the surrounding towns as well. Even Lev Gottlieb, who everybody knows is Jewish, plays his trumpet at Easter every year. He's coming back from Juilliard specially next month. The way I heard it, his parents got into some sort of mess with the Health Department. They own a deli on the corner of Main and Pine. But once Lev agreed to play with the brass section during the Easter Extravaganza (broadcast live!), those troubles went away. Lev has been playing for them ever since.

"Roarke," Mrs. Hicks says warmly and pulls her hands away from Mom's. I'm embarrassed to see that Mom seems visibly crestfallen when Celia Hicks lets go. "It's so very nice to see you," the woman continues. "Your mother has just been telling me about Columbia. Congratulations. That's quite an accomplishment, young man."

I look at my shoes and produce the expected response: "Thank you, ma'am. I'm not sure it will work out for me to go, but I'm real grateful to have been given the chance."

There's no way I'm going to Columbia. I don't need a financial aid letter to tell me that. Even with help, there's no universe in which we could afford it.

"Well, that's such a nice way of looking at it." Mrs. Hicks turns back to Mom. "You've raised a fine boy, Suzanne. No doubt there."

"We think so," Mom answers, and then, when it seems that more is expected, she says, "Essie is getting quite grown up herself. I saw her just last week when I was picking up Roarke after school. She's the spitting image of her daddy at that age."

Mom went to high school with Pastor Hicks before he left town for college and then seminary. Celia Hicks, on the other hand, is an outsider, though most everyone seems to have forgotten that and for some reason she doesn't seem happy to be reminded that Mom knew her husband long before she herself met him. Her lips press into a thin, hard line. It lasts only a second, then the expression softens and once again it's the face we all know from church or else from television. The face that would have you believe that this woman is so pure, both inside and out, that her shit don't stink.

She nods. "The girls always did take after Jethro, and the boys take after me. Though people say that Caleb's eyes are the exact same shade of blue as his father's."

Of the boys, only Caleb seems to be around with any regularity, having just finished law school. I've heard rumors that he's considering some sort of career in politics, which shouldn't be a problem what with all the money the family has to throw into a campaign.

"Oh, I see that. I definitely do." Mom is agreeing with her, though I'm fairly certain that she's never seen Caleb Hicks's eyes up close.

Both women stare at me for just a beat too long. Even with all the smiles and compliments, it's clear that I'm intruding. I cough and shift my bag onto my other shoulder. I'm still in my baseball uniform.

"I think I'll hop in the shower. It was a real pleasure to see you outside of church, Mrs. Hicks."

They wait until I'm nearly all the way up the stairs before they start to talk again, and by that time I'm too far away to hear anything they say.

———

The next day I see Essie Hicks everywhere I go. It's strange, because I haven't really noticed her all year. We didn't go to the same elementary school, but I remember that when she was a freshman, it seemed as if every corridor I turned down had a film crew in it, just waiting to catch the perfect shot of her walking casually down the hall. Her hair was longer then. Light brown. The same color as her freckles. She wore barrettes with flowers on them, or sometimes birds or ladybugs. It was like they were trying to make her look younger than she was, to preserve that innocence that made her so popular with the press. Or maybe she just liked ladybugs. I never got close enough to ask.

Blake Preston got close, though. He's the only one of my friends who's actually talked to her directly, but not because he walked up and said hello like a normal person would. It's because he failed ninth-grade math and ended up repeating it the year Essie started at Woodside. Blake sat behind her in class and instead of paying attention to Mrs. Nixon, he would spend the entire period trying to tie pieces of Essie's long hair into knots without her noticing. It became a game. Every day he kept track of how many knots he'd tied before she finally moved forward in her chair. Eventually she turned around and told him to cut it out or else. And Blake did, he told me, because he could tell that she meant it, no matter how sweet she seems when she's on TV.

The cameras don't follow her in school anymore, so I guess it's possible that I've passed Essie on the way to physics every day and just never noticed. But I don't think so. And I don't think she's been in the third-floor hallway on any other day when my American Government class lets out. But today she's standing there, tugging at the ends of her shoulder-length hair, listening to Lily Gaines talking about how she's certain that she failed their Spanish quiz and how if she gets anything less than an A, she'll never get into Vassar. It seems crazy to me that anyone would pay attention to such self-absorbed whining, but Essie manages to keep her eyes on Lily's flapping, berry-colored lips. Then, as I pass close by them, she glances over at me and our eyes meet and she gets this little wrinkle in the center of her forehead like I'm a puzzle she's trying to solve. Just as I'm about to stop and ask what her problem is, her eyes move back to Lily and she says, "Vassar would be crazy not to take you. I one hundred percent know that you're going to get in."

Lily probably will get into Vassar next year; not that I care one way or the other, but there's a building there named after her grandmother and I know enough to know that this is how things work. It's amazing the things money will buy. Lily and I went on one date last year when I was a junior and she was a sophomore, so I know that her house is the sort of place you would call a mansion. Her dad has some high-up job at the bank; he may even be in charge. I didn't go inside the house, though, just caught a glimpse of the chandelier shining down on the polished white marble floors in the entryway. Still, I can pretty much imagine what the rest is like: high ceilings with soft recessed lighting, window treatments instead of curtains, a double-door fridge that's probably filled with nothing but tofu and Vitaminwater. It's the sort of house in those magazines that Mom likes to buy and then flip through and clip out pictures from. She puts these into a box labeled *Inspiration*, but as far as I know they've never actually inspired her to do anything more than buy another magazine and add more pictures to the box.

I took Lily to the movies, something with Theo James, and she talked about how hot he looked every second he was on-screen. It kind of made it hard to concentrate, even for me, and I'm someone who can tune out an awful lot. Also, she ate almost the entire bag of popcorn even though she said she didn't want any when we were at the concession stand. That sort of thing drives me insane. So all in all, not a stellar evening. But then when we got to her front door, there she was, standing with her eyes closed and her berry lips turned up toward me. It was impossible at that point for me to do anything other than kiss her, not unless I wanted her complaining to all her girlfriends about what an awful time she'd had.

So I did, for about fifteen seconds. I know because I tapped out the seconds on my leg while my other hand brushed the curve of Lily's chin. The way I saw it, it had to be more than a peck or else I risked going through with the kiss and having it not count at all, of still having her feel slighted. But it also couldn't be a full-blown make-out session or else she might invite me to come inside, up to her room, that sort of thing. It would force my hand, make me tell her no. Or even if it was just front-step kissing, too much would mean I was a douche if I didn't ask her out again, which I honestly had no intention of doing. So fifteen seconds seemed about right. Interested but still gentlemanly. Then, later that week, I told Blake and Sam Wells that I'd gotten back together with this girl I'd been seeing over the summer, hoping that it would get back to Lily and I would be off the hook.

Strictly speaking, this girlfriend was a work of fiction, but it was a ploy that I made use of on and off until the end of junior year. It got somewhat harder to pull off after I got my license and risked being dared to actually produce said girlfriend in the flesh. Before I could drive, all I had to do was invent little snippets of our conversations in order to be convincing, and if my parents didn't feel inclined to drive me all the way over to Bridgeton to see her, it wasn't really my fault that we hadn't gone all the way. After I bought Little Jimmy, a blue second- or thirdhand hatchback with a dent in the passenger-side door, it became harder to lie.

So for three months at the beginning of senior year, I dated Gemma Moore. Her mother was a member of the New Light altar guild and the year before last their family spent Thanksgiving with Pastor Hicks. Gemma was prettier than Lily and wore less makeup. She had a round face and hazel eyes and a mess of dark yellow curls that she pulled back with some rhinestone-studded clip I would knock loose any time I slipped my fingers up into her hair. I was surprised by how much kissing was involved with dating Gemma. Her plain clothes and long skirts had not really hinted that this sort of thing would be open for discussion, but shortly after Gemma's parents invited Mom and Dad and me to join them for Sunday dinner, Gemma started sneaking over after school to hang out before my parents got home. I never asked where her parents thought she was, but I knew it wasn't in my bed sighing gently as we listened to Florence and the Machine and I tried to unhook her bra one-handed.

For one fleeting moment I wonder if Gemma has anything to do with the reason Esther Hicks was looking at me so strangely just a minute ago. I look back through the jumble of bodies pushing me along the hall, but Essie's back is turned. Lily is still talking. Then the two disappear around the corner, and there is an instant when I think that I might run back, grab her arm hard and shake her and ask just what she's playing at. But of course I don't. If I did, I'd have to explain why I care about Esther Hicks at all and I don't know what I'd say.

Mom was in a tizzy last night when Celia Hicks finally climbed into her giant black SUV and backed out of our drive. At dinner she must've said a dozen times how nice it was for Celia to stop by. It was the first time I'd ever heard Mom call Pastor Hicks's wife by her given name. Each time Mom said it she lingered on the *e* a little longer, as if relishing her newfound alliance, until the name became practically indecipherable. Dad grunted something in response, seeming preoccupied, and generally just let Mom prattle on. It was only when she pressed him—"You'll come, now, won't you?"—that he looked up in a startled way and Mom had to explain all over again that they had been invited to the Hickses' house for tea on Thursday. Dad frowned and actually looked over his shoulder to see if there was someone else that Mom might've been talking to instead of him. Then he swallowed his mouthful of hamburger and said, "I suppose there's no way out of it." And Mom was off talking again at lightning speed.

So what I want to say to Essie is that she and her parents should just leave us the hell alone. Are you allowed to say "hell" to a preacher's daughter? Probably not, but I don't care. I'd tell her that Mom doesn't need Celia Hicks to come swooping into our kitchen in a fog of expensive perfume. Mom doesn't need her attention in order to feel worthy. Dad doesn't need to be forced into his only suit, which has gone shiny at the thighs and elbows, to sit stiffly in the Hickses' parlor on a sofa that I know from the show is overflowing with matching pillows and has lace doilies draped over its arms. It will only embarrass him to have to endure that tea with your parents, I would tell Esther, so they should just stuff their Christian charity and their attention where the sun don't shine. We don't want it.

Except that apparently Mom does, desperately. After school, she does nothing but talk about the fact that they've been invited to tea at the rectory. She's in an absolute flutter about having nothing to wear. Dad's suit is already laid out with a matching shirt and tie even though the tea isn't until tomorrow. She's shining Dad's shoes when I get home and there's a smudge of shoe polish on one cheek where she must have wiped it. She looks thin and suddenly very old sitting there with the shoe in one hand and the brush in the other, and I'm overcome by how deeply I love her despite everything.

"You're here," she says brightly and I realize that she is not just stating the obvious: she is truly surprised and grateful for my presence.

I slouch against the doorframe as her wrist begins to swing back and forth again, bringing the brush lightly across the shoe leather.

"I kind of feel like hot dogs tonight, if that's okay," I tell her. "How about I start the grill and take care of supper? It looks like you've got enough to do."

She smiles at me with an expression that tells me I am all she has ever wanted in this world. I am all her hopes and dreams come true. The look paralyzes me for a heartbeat and I feel panic rising up like acid in my throat at the knowledge that two simple words would forever wipe that look away. Then she drops her gaze to the shoe again and tells me not to forget the potato salad on the bottom shelf of the fridge, and I feel the panic fade.

Outside, I throw the dogs on the grill and then move back into the kitchen and get to work setting the table. Without even thinking, I switch on the television to fill the quiet, something I do when I'm home by myself and the place feels too empty. Usually I change it right away to whatever college football game is on, but today I run outside to check the hot dogs before I get a chance to flip the channel. While I turn each dog carefully, I hear a commercial droning on about some skin-care product that will make the years of crow's-feet practically melt away. Then when I come back inside, she is there as well, as she has been all day long. Esther Anne Hicks is staring at me from the television screen with that same look she had earlier at school and I think for a moment that she can actually see me, that she is looking out of the television and into my kitchen, where I stand wearing my mom's flowery apron and holding a barbecue fork raised in the air like a sword.

This is ridiculous, of course. Esther Hicks cannot see me, I remind myself. I take a step forward and then another until I am standing right in front of the TV. Her eyes flick away from the camera and back to whoever is interviewing her. A banner in the bottom left corner of the screen tells me that this conversation is being broadcast live. She must've left school and gone right to the studio, or wherever it is that they're filming. For all I know, there's a special room in the Hicks mansion just for this. Maybe they change the backdrops and the furniture to give the illusion of variety but make the journalists come to them.

"This year has been a busy one for you, hasn't it, Essie?" the woman asks.

She is young and vaguely familiar. Pretty, though it looks as if she's trying to hide that fact. Her hair is pulled back in a ponytail and her collar is buttoned all the way up to her neck. Still, even in pants and the uptight blouse, you can tell that her body is smoking hot. Or so Blake would say.

"It has, Libby. It certainly has," Essie answers. "But of course very rewarding all the same."

"And you are really planning to graduate this year, a year early?"

Essie nods. This is news to me.

"I'm hoping to have enough credits to do it. I've taken extra classes each of these past three years at Woodside, some through independent study, a few others online by correspondence. It'll be tight," she says and here she smiles, a look that is utterly captivating even to me and I usually don't go in for that sort of thing, "but I think I might be able to squeak through and leave high school behind in just a few months' time."

"Well, you certainly sound driven. Your parents, I know, are very proud."

Essie blushes and drops her eyes; her lashes tremble and then she looks up again.

"And what are you planning to do next year?" the woman asks when Essie remains quiet. "We haven't seen you going on any college trips yet."

"Oh, no." Essie laughs, a tinkling sound so unlike the cackles of the other girls at school. I wonder how I never noticed her laugh before. I must have heard it on TV, even from the next room, while Mom watched *Six for Hicks* or the entertainment news. That laugh is almost enough to make me trust her, but not quite.

"College is not really in the cards for me right now," Essie is saying. "Next year, maybe, or the year after that. Goodness knows I appreciate how important education is, especially for young women. But before that, I really feel that I want to do some good in this world. That's why I'm planning a yearlong mission to help raise literacy rates for children of color in inner-city schools."

And there, just like that, she loses me. Even with the laugh. She is seventeen years old and thinks that she can walk into some poor community and tell the people who have lived there their entire lives precisely what they are doing wrong and how things should be done instead. I blink at the screen and wonder if she's ever even talked to a real live black person, since Woodside—and the entire county, for that matter—is not exactly known for its diversity.

Reggie White, our shortstop and a dude who fully appreciates the irony of his name, is the only black kid in the whole school and I know that he's never spoken to Essie. He makes a point of avoiding her, in fact, given some of the shit her father's said about African Americans in his sermons, which of course are watched by millions and so inform the national conversation on race more than any small-town preacher should. Of course, Pastor Hicks would say that he does not mean the White family when he speaks about how the blacks in our country are inclined toward violence, or lust, or having babies out of wedlock.

"You're not anything like those people," Pastor Hicks once said to Reggie's father.

"The worst part," Reggie said from inside the batting cage as he told the story, "is that he meant it as a compliment, that he really believed he was being kind."

Remembering this, I frown as Essie goes on about the power of the written word to raise children up out of poverty and I can see that the lady on the television is eating this whole literacy thing up. I half expect her to start fawning over Essie's qualifications. *You took both AP and IB English Literature? The Chicago public schools are going to be so lucky to have you.*

Instead she's saying, "So you might be leaving home before too long. What do you think will be the hardest thing about that?"

Essie looks squarely at the camera and there is that expression again, the crinkling of her forehead that I noticed in the hall at school today.

She says, "Probably the hardest thing is that I'm pretty sure I'm in love. It will be difficult to let that go."

Before I go back outside to take the hot dogs off the grill, I think how Esther Hicks in love is not something I would've seen coming. The next thing I think is that this dude had better run while he still can.

Liberty

When Esther Anne Hicks tells me that she thinks she's in love, it's all I can do not to laugh. Mama never approved of people who broadcast their business all around town, and even though broadcasting other people's business is now literally how I pay my rent, this is one of those moments when I can imagine her eyes rolling all those hundreds of miles away. I'm not sure which is more pathetic, this lovestruck-teenager act or the bullshit literacy project Essie is peddling. It's a toss-up. They both make me want to cut the feed and get up and walk away. The fact that what is expected of me right now is a sympathetic smile and not a lecture on white privilege or entitlement makes me hate myself even more.

I hear myself saying, "This special someone. Is there any chance you want to tell me his name?"

Or her name, I think, but I know that saying something like that would only get me fired. There is a seven-second delay on live television, which is enough time to bleep out expletives or black out the screen in case of wardrobe malfunctions but not enough to censor any worldview that stands in opposition to the megalomaniac who owns TIL and her sister stations. That's what pink slips are for. Maybe someday I'll be able to pull a stunt like that and get away with it, but as things stand now, I'm not holding any cards. Any outlet that makes a habit of real journalism won't touch me. This job was the only one I could get.

Essie blushes and shakes her head. "I don't think I should say."

"Well, I can certainly appreciate your desire for privacy. Especially given how very public your life has always been."

Essie shrugs. It's a practiced move. She says, "I've been very lucky. To share my life with so many people, to share the work that our family does both in the church and through our many charities, well, that's a blessing that is sent to us straight from God. We owe everything we are and everything we do to those who watch and share this journey with us."

Amen, breathes Mama from just behind my ear. *At least she knows enough to give credit where credit is due.* She is referring, of course, to the Almighty. Whatever differences in opinion Mama and Essie Hicks might have when it comes to definitions of vanity or avarice or sloth, the God they worship is still the same. I actually stop listening while Essie is speaking. I don't have to pay attention to know what she is saying. The line she is feeding me is one that I delivered many times myself. But that was a long time ago.

When I see that Essie has finished talking, I shift forward in my seat and ask the only sort of hard-hitting question I am allowed: "But as a teenager, as a normal teenage girl, you must sometimes wish you could get away from the cameras even just once in a while and let loose, maybe go a little wild."

Essie's upbeat expression fades and suddenly she looks pale and older than her seventeen years.

"It doesn't do any good to wish for things you'll never have."

I blink, uncertain how to follow this departure from the cheerful persona the girl has always put forth in public interviews. I scramble for something to say, but Essie is already talking, laughing.

"Besides, I'm not sure I'd know how to go wild. My idea of fun is curling up with a good book."

I realize that I have been holding my breath to keep from panicking and I let the air out of my lungs. Well, *didn't you just beat the Devil around the stump*, I hear Mama say.

After this, the interview dribbles on and then comes to a rather lackluster end. Essie promotes an upcoming episode of *Six for Hicks* that follows her brother Matty and his family on an African safari. She actually hasn't been in any episodes since last fall while the overseas ministries of Matty and Daniel have been featured instead, but she promises that folks will be able to see plenty of her as she heads toward graduation and her literacy work next year.

Then the lights dim and the camera is switched off. Candy, the woman who accompanied Essie to the local studio, excuses herself to use the restroom and I begin to pack up my things. As soon as Candy leaves the room, Essie is standing close beside me.

"I need a cell phone," she says urgently.

"You can borrow mine." I reach into my bag and begin to fish around.

"No," she says. "I need one to keep, at least for a while. I need to be able to reach you without using my own phone, in case they check it."

"In case who checks it?"

"My parents. Production. Any of them. I have a story. If you want it, I need to be able to call you. Hurry. She'll be back any second."

I motion for Margot, my camerawoman and assistant, and whisper, "Give me your phone."

She looks confused but hands it over. Essie checks it to make sure the ringer is silenced and drops it into the pocket of her coat. Margot starts to protest, but I raise a hand to quiet her.

"Don't call me. I'll call you," Essie says. It's the sort of phrase that I imagine is used a lot in spy films, but mostly it makes me think of Nelson Mandela, someone Esther Anne Hicks probably knows nothing about. I don't think *Long Walk to Freedom* is on the approved reading list for girls like her. It certainly wasn't on mine. She continues, "I'll give you a series of exclusives, but I'm going to need something from you in exchange."

"What do you need?"

Essie shakes her head. "Not here. Not now. We'll discuss it when I call."

"Exclusives covering what?"

"Can't you guess?" she asks. This time her smile contains none of the sugary sweetness she used when the cameras were rolling. "I'm getting married. You'll get an exclusive on the big day."

———

"Shit," I say, rubbing my eyes. "Did that really just happen?"

I am driving too fast, I know, but I need to get out of this piddly town and back to the city before I start to melt. I floor it and my hybrid rewards me with a wholly unsatisfying surge in speed. We are almost to the highway. On our left is the New Light megachurch, where Essie's father tends to his mayonnaise-colored flock. It is both gaudy and industrial at the same time, a combination that makes the building particularly unattractive from the outside. Inside must be even worse, since then you would be surrounded by the congregation, a group of people for whom smiling while passing judgment has become a sport. Or so I assume. I've never been to a service there and I hope I never have to attend one. Steering clear of overpowering religious leaders is part of the spiritual cleanse I've been undergoing to make up for my first eighteen years.

One more turn and we are on the highway, though it looks identical to the country road we just left behind. To both the right and the left of us are cornfields, and the road runs straight and flat for another hundred miles.

"I can't believe it either, but is that any reason to try to break the sound barrier in a Prius? Spoiler: it's never gonna happen," says Margot. She is holding on to the center console so tightly that her knuckles are starting to turn white. I ease off on the gas a little and Margot relaxes. She asks, "When did little Goody Two-shoes have time to fall in love?"

The teenage-puppy-love thing I'm not particularly interested in, per se. Sure, it helps my case to break a story, even one as devoid of journalistic interest as this one. Sid is always saying what did he hire me for if I'm not the same firebrand that I used to be when I was fourteen. As if anyone really wants to hear that it's all been downhill since eighth grade. What hooked me was the look in Essie's eyes, the promise that there is more behind those blue irises than the mindless sheep she has always appeared to be.

"An exclusive," Margot is saying. "A whole series of interviews leading up to the wedding."

"The wedding hasn't been confirmed," I say, and now I'm starting to have doubts that any of this is real. "There's no way her parents would let her get engaged at seventeen, let alone married."

"You don't know that," Margot says, and I can hear the hope in her voice. If I know anything about her at all, it is that she is already spending the money in her head. Margot has been known to burn through her paycheck with little regard for the need to pay bills or buy groceries, which is a large part of why her wife handles their finances these days. "What about that other TV family, the one with all the kids? They married them off pretty young."

"And then they got canceled," I remind her. "If there's one thing the Hicks family knows how to do, it's go the distance. Conservative enough to appeal to the Bible Belt, but not so backward as to alienate the East Coast viewers. They've found the sweet spot, I'll give them that. No, Essie will do whatever 'Save the Children' crap she was peddling and then she'll get her ass into college. I guarantee it. Especially since they didn't get to air the college episodes they had planned for Elizabeth when she dropped off the face of the earth."

"Maybe they'll let you do a series of interviews anyway," Margot, ever the optimist, tells me. "The more airtime you get, the better."

"Tell me something I don't know." I sigh.

This is the sort of rhetorical statement that Margot has a tendency to take seriously, so she says, "The state with the lowest highest point is Florida, where Britton Hill rises to only three hundred forty-five feet above sea level."

"Thank you," I tell her, deadpanning, "I'm sure that information will be very useful at parties."

———

We get back to the city just after eleven. I drop Margot off and then drive the seven blocks to my apartment. Mr. Danziger has left his Weber cooling in my spot again and I have to get out of my car and drag it back onto the patio before I can park. I shoot his door a withering look as I climb past his landing to the third floor. Mike is asleep on the couch, presumably overcome by the act of waiting up for me. I can't really blame him. There's a constitutional law book open on his chest. If I'd been reading that, I'd probably be asleep as well.

I bypass the living room and head straight to the kitchen and open an IPA. I take a sip as I sink into a chair across from Mike and remember the summer we found this chair on the side of the road and he insisted that we carry it home even though home was fourteen blocks away. This was before we had a car. When it still felt strange that there was a *we*. Back then we weren't living together, not really. I was technically still living in Barbara Lawrence's spare room, as far as my parents were concerned, though even then Mike's apartment was where I was spending most of my nights.

Small-town girl in the big city; they almost didn't let me come. None of the Bells had ever moved away. I practically had to bribe my parents to let me leave home for college and then, after graduation, I had to get a lawyer to gain access to the account where the money from my book had been deposited. It could have gotten uglier than it did, I suppose; at least my parents were still speaking to me after that. Now, not so much. It was the living in sin that finally broke them. Not when it happened, of course, but when it hit the papers.

I was surprised, actually, by the vitriol, which I realize is entirely hypocritical. After all, hadn't I been one of those mudslingers in the first place? Weren't the profits from such bitterness and name-calling precisely what I would eventually use to pay my half of the rent for Mike's, for *our*, apartment? So I shouldn't really regret the book, or the blog, or even the flaming dumpster fire of a podcast that defined my life from age twelve until about eighteen. But I do. I regret it every day. I am lucky to have that money, little though it is. There is some part of me that does acknowledge that. But it doesn't feel like luck. It feels like a pittance given in exchange for my near perpetual humiliation. I deserve it, though. I deserve everything I get.

For Whom the Bell Tolls made a surprise appearance on a few best-seller lists. That it was written by a fourteen-year-old gun-toting, gay-bashing hick named Liberty Bell pretty much summed up the entirety of its appeal. The number of people who bought copies because they were legitimately interested in my thoughts was most likely outweighed by those who did not read it at all. Some probably bought the book in error, thinking they were ordering the famous novel, but others bought it to send me a message that the people I hated so much for being different were capable of kindness in the face of hatred, of turning the other cheek. Once it was publicized that the profits were being placed in a trust to which I would only gain access when I turned twenty-one, there was a movement among liberals to order copies online to be sent to an organization that would shred them.

Volunteers used the strips of paper to make a giant papier-mâché replica of the actual Liberty Bell, the one in Philadelphia. Even at the time, I had to admit that it was pretty well done. Then the giant, painstakingly assembled paper bell was placed front and center at a ceremony welcoming a busload of Sudanese refugees. The headlines boasted something about literally creating love from hate. In the picture accompanying the story in the *Gazette*, the men and women making the thing wore T-shirts that said *Free Libby* or sometimes *Liberty for the Bell*. They had financed my escape long before I realized that an escape was something I needed.

The book, the blog, all of it was why I was given the job I have, but it is also why it has been impossible for me to find another. No one wants to be associated with the sort of person I used to be. No one, that is, except for Sid, my boss, and the asshole that he works for. That kind of crap is what they've built their fortunes on. They churn it out day after day, year after year, and their faithful viewers don't know any better than to lap it up, chunks and all.

Mike was also sleeping the first time I saw him, I remember.

His hair was longer then, but really his face looked no different than it does now, jaw slack and mouth slightly open, a small pool of spit forming at the corner of his lip. He looked like buzzard bait, dozing there like that. There was someone sitting across the table from him that day in the library, another freshman who had torn up little bits of paper and rolled them around between his fingertips until they were pressed into hard round balls. I recognized the kid from my European Literature class, his pimply face scrunched up in a look of concentration as he lobbed his miniature grenades at Mike, trying to land one of those balls right in the corner of Mike's mouth.

When one of them hit Mike square between the eyes, he lifted a hand as if waving away a gnat, but he didn't wake up. The kid, who I remember talked incessantly all semester about how James Joyce was his personal hero, hesitated, waiting until he was sure Mike was still truly and deeply sleeping, and then started throwing the paper balls again. The floor was littered with them when I walked out of the library several hours later, but by that time Mike was gone.

We didn't formally meet until that spring. He stopped by my dorm room looking for my roommate, and when I told him she was in the shower, he said that he would wait. I stood, blocking the doorway, not sure what was expected, then stepped back to let him in. He flopped gracelessly onto Lara's bed and leaned against the wall. I had never been alone with a boy before and I had the sudden urge to run. Looking longingly at the door, willing Lara to return, I moved back to my desk and tried to continue working on my blog.

"Writing something?" he asked.

My back was to him and then suddenly he was at my shoulder. I could feel his hand on the back of my chair. I sat up straighter and closed my laptop, but not before he saw. I felt him back away across the room.

"You're her," he said in disbelief. "You're Liberty Bell. Lara never told me."

"Why would she?" I challenged, ready for a fight. "There's nothing to tell."

He was sitting on Lara's bed again, but this time with his feet on the edge of the shaggy pink rug she'd put down on the floor beside it. He was still skinny then, all elbows and knees, a collection of sharp edges. He folded himself forward and leaned his arms on his legs as if pressed down from above.

"I grew up hearing about that day," he breathed.

I said nothing, and in the time it took for his words to register, Lara burst into the room, wet hair streaming, wrapped in a yellow robe. Mike stood and Lara hugged him even though she was naked underneath the thin layer of cotton. He pulled a pair of tickets to some concert from his back pocket and handed them to her and she hugged him again and said thanks and then all at once he was gone.

"You feeling okay, Libs?" she asked and dove into the closet in search of a perfect pair of shoes to match the dress she wanted to wear that night.

"Fine," I said. "I just need a break. I think I'll go for a run."

I pulled on a pair of sneakers and burst out of the building and into the cold air, my heart still racing, because I knew exactly which day Mike was talking about. I ran toward the lake, but before I even got to the edge of campus, I had to hightail it to a trash bin to throw up. I stood there, retching, long after my stomach was finally empty, hands like a vise on the painted black metal rim of the can. I was shaking.

Mike stirs on the couch and I say, "Hey," then, "Thanks for waiting up."

He rubs his eyes and blinks at me.

"You know I need my beauty sleep," he says.

I rock forward out of my chair and move a pillow so that I can slide next to him, nestling my head on his chest. I can feel his heartbeat, deep and slow like the ticking of some ancient clock.

When I am settled, he curls one hand onto my head and asks, "How was it?"

"Didn't you watch?"

"Of course. But how did it feel to be in the same room with her? Esther Hicks, in the flesh."

"She was very professional," I say, not sure where to start or how much I really want to tell.

"She's done this before."

I know that Mike does not mean it unkindly, but for some reason I feel it as a slight that he clearly thinks of Essie as having more experience on camera than I, even though I realize that of course she does. It's been her entire life. I, on the other hand, nearly a year out of journalism school, am continually frustrated that I have so little to show for it. Puff pieces, mostly. This one was no less puffy, but since Essie hasn't been seen on camera in a while, there's a chance that it will get picked up by the national media and aired again. Even if there are no follow-up meetings, today's interview still ranks as the pinnacle of my adult career to date. Pathetic.

"Did she say why she asked for you specifically?" Mike wants to know.

I shake my head. "I didn't get a chance to ask. Maybe next time."

I have to buy Margot a new phone tomorrow, I remind myself. Maybe I can expense it.

"Next time?" Mike asks.

"She's offered me more interviews," I say slowly.

"Isn't that a good thing?"

I shrug. "I didn't really get the sense that she had run it by her people. It might come to nothing."

"Well, even so, I think you did great today."

"Really?"

"Sure," he says. "I hardly recognized you with all that makeup on. You almost looked pretty."

I punch him in the stomach and he throws his hands up in surrender. Then he lifts my head so he can kiss me and I let him for a little while, taking comfort in how solid he feels, how familiar.

Eventually I pull my head back and say, "I feel sorry for her."

Mike sits back and laughs sardonically. "Sure. Poor little rich girl, with her mansion and her private jet to fly her down to that big place they have in the Caribbean. She's really suffering."

"None of that money is hers," I remind him.

"But I'm sure it will be someday. Money like that can buy anything. That idiot brother of hers is leading in the polls and he hasn't even officially declared. What qualifies him for the House? He was practically at the bottom of his class in law school."

"He *did* go to Yale," I say, nudging him playfully with my head.

"And how do you think he got in there in the first place?"

Yale had turned Mike down, so I know it's best to drop it. I lean against the arm of the couch and stretch my legs out straight onto Mike's lap and say, "She's not like that, though."

"You think you can tell what she's really like by how she acts when she's on camera?"

"No, but there was a moment after." I stop, consider whether to tell Mike about the wedding, and decide against it. Instead I say, "We were alone for a few minutes after the interview. She just seemed different then. It reminded me that she's a real person, not just that little girl we've all been watching on TV."

"That doesn't mean she deserves your pity."

"Why not? Isn't she just as much a product of her environment as I was of mine? Isn't that why you forgave me for all the things I did?"

Mike sits up straighter at this and looks right at me. "First of all, I never pitied you. Let's be clear about that. Second of all, I had nothing to forgive you for. You didn't do anything to me. Besides, you were just a kid."

"Isn't that exactly what she is too?"

"Esther Hicks is not a child," Mike says then. "She's a virus. Her entire family is. They've infected the country with a special brand of intolerance that masquerades as a religion."

"She's done nothing that I haven't done," I say softly. "She's just had more success."

"You were different. You couldn't help it."

"Don't you dare think that what happened to Justice is an excuse," I tell him, and my voice is louder than I mean it to be. "As if she somehow lets me off the hook."

"Well, you're trying to do what's right now. That's what matters."

"Maybe Essie is trying too."

I want Mike to back down, but his voice is bitter when he says, "By giving you more interviews? Her generosity is overwhelming."

"She's just a kid," I try again. "She's grown up inside a bubble. And she just seemed so small, so vulnerable. She has no idea at all how the real world works."

Esther

For the first time in my life, Mother is doing what I want and not the other way around. She doesn't know this, of course, and her not knowing is the only hope I have that this might work. It's only when the Richardses have left the house late on Thursday afternoon that I am sure my plan has actually been set in motion. Until then, I was limited to watching Mother's face for some sign of confirmation, but of course the last thing I could do was ask.

When Mr. and Mrs. Richards pile into their ancient station wagon, Mother comes into the den, where I am reading. I don't look up right away. It wouldn't do to look too eager. I wait for her to clear her throat and only then do I turn *Wuthering Heights* over in my lap.

"Esther Anne," Mother says, and I know that she is hooked. She only uses my middle name when she is about to tell me something that she knows might cause a fight. "I've been thinking a lot about your situation."

She says this as if my "situation," as she put it, has nothing to do with her, at least not directly, as if it is not in any way her fault. Mother sighs and looks vacantly toward the window. I can tell that she is not really looking out at the fragile splendor of the cherry tree, which is in full blossom, but is instead considering whether enough time has passed for her to replace the drapes. It takes a while before she continues, but I wait as patiently as I can, tracing a finger over the embossed *B* of *Brontë* until she turns her face back to look at me.

"I've considered all the options and I really believe that the best course of action is for you to get married, quickly, before you're too far along."

I keep my face still but force my eyes to widen, provide just the right measure of shock.

"If that's what you think is best," I say as reluctantly as I can.

"I do," Mother says, and her voice carries just an edge of brusqueness. It makes me want to stab her through the eyes.

This is the life of a child she is deciding. The life of two children, actually, since technically I am still one myself. I hate her for the calculation in her eyes when she looks at me, as if I were a rat she is training to run through a maze.

"Did you tell?" I ask.

"Darling," she says too sweetly, "I've told no one. I promised that I wouldn't and I shan't. Not Daddy, not anyone. It is our secret. We will get through this thing together."

For some reason it makes me feel better to hear the lie, as if it makes everything entirely justified.

"Who will I marry?" I ask in a voice that I hope conveys just the right degree of shyness.

Mother sighs again and stands. It seems this heart-to-heart is already over.

"Soon, dearest. It's almost decided."

The next day after school there is a baseball game and I ask Mother if I can stay to watch. Sporting events are still cleared for filming. It's just inside the school that's banned. Well, not entirely, but it requires special clearance. When I first started at Woodside, the crew followed me everywhere I went, even into some of my classes. But then Veronica Richter, who was a year ahead of me, put an end to that, complained that it was a violation of her right to privacy and created an environment hostile to learning. She wasn't the only one who objected, but she was the first. Now they can film me at the bus stop or walking to school but not inside the bus or the school building itself; that is, except during specially staged events like the school concert and the discussion group in my fake English class, the one where we're reading *Wuthering Heights*.

It made Veronica pretty unpopular for the second half of her sophomore year, but she didn't seem to notice, or else she just didn't care. She has this ability to float above it all, which made it kind of surprising that she was bothered so much by the cameras. I like to think she was just doing me a favor after finding me locked in the girl's bathroom one morning before U.S. History when I was trying to avoid my crew. She was giving me the sort of space I could never have gotten on my own, even if I had been brave enough to ask. If that really was the reason she lodged the complaint with the principal, then it was one of the nicest things anyone has ever done for me, which is weird because Veronica Richter is not even my friend.

Mother looks surprised, but she agrees. It's not often that I'm willing to go to games of any sort, so it's possible that she just wants the footage and doesn't even know that Roarke Richards is the captain of the baseball team. I need to talk to him before this goes any further, to warn him, or just try to explain. But the truth is, I have no idea what I intend to say.

The day drags on. I see Roarke between first and second period and then again just after lunch. He moves easily through the halls. People move aside to let him pass, a fact of which he seems entirely unaware. His dark eyes are always elsewhere, his smooth jaw set. Both times I see him I try to catch his eye, but he is always in motion and he never looks my way. Why would he? We've never even really met. I've seen him at church, of course, but his family tends to slip in and then out again. They don't stay for the hand-shaking-and-coffee-cake-crumbling torture that starts after the service ends. God Is Love, proclaims the bright felted banner on one wall of the refectory. My Sunday school class made it when I was eleven. The lopsided *v* in *Love* is entirely my fault. Beneath the words are two outstretched felt hands, palms held toward the gathered, in a way that gives the impression that they are pushing or shooing instead of welcoming in. I understand why the Richards family might choose to avoid coffee hour. It's all gossip and backstabbing as far as I'm concerned.

So Roarke and I have never talked at church, and we've certainly never talked at school. It's not a very promising relationship. Especially when I consider that spring break is just around the corner and that means I need Roarke to propose by the end of next week, Sunday at the latest.

It is the first really warm day of the month, and although I've worn a sweater, I take it off sometime in the fifth inning. The sun beats down on my back and arms as I sit squeezed between Lily and Tabitha Riker on the bleachers. I made sure to chat with a sufficient number of people before the game so Lincoln, who is my cameraman today, could get enough shots of me moving through the crowd while the light still holds. I waved to Reggie White, hoping that he'd come over since footage of me talking to an African American would really get Mother's knickers in a twist. I know she'd never allow them to use it, but imagining her trying to explain to the editors why the footage needs to be cut without saying the word *black* made it worth the try. Reggie ignored me. I can't blame him. I would ignore me too if I were him.

Instead I talked with Bobby Shaffer, who is a year behind me but tall enough to look good in the shot. I leaned against the chain-link fence that separates the crowd from the dugout and smiled, allowing my eyes to drift over to Roarke while Bobby talked, my gaze shifting in a way that I knew would be obvious when the footage is reviewed. I am nothing if not helpful.

Now, while I sit with Lily and Tabitha, Lincoln gets some shots of the game itself, including one good one where Roarke hits the ball far into the outfield and then almost makes it home before retreating to third base. After this, Lincoln waves and indicates that he and his sidekick are going to pack up and leave. I wave back and watch them trudge off to their van and then, after stowing their equipment, finally drive away.

By the time the game is over, I really need to pee. But I know that if I run over to the bathrooms, Roarke will probably be gone when I get back. I say good-bye to Tabitha and shoot a look at Lily, who is getting kissed by Mason Clinch. Weaving through the crowd, I head straight for Roarke, not caring what this will look like to anyone who is bothering to watch. He is bent over and riffling through his bag when I reach him.

"Roarke," I say. "I'm Esther Hicks. I don't think we've ever been formally introduced."

He stands up and I extend my hand, which he eyes suspiciously but does not take. I drop the hand self-consciously to my side and pick at the fabric of my skirt.

"What do you want?" he asks.

The bluntness of the question surprises me and I realize that I still have no earthly clue what is the right thing to say. For all that I know *about* Roarke, I don't actually know him, not really.

For instance, I had assumed that he would probably dislike me, but the tone of his voice tells me that it runs deeper than that. In the end, this is probably a good thing. It means that we are on the same side. But it also means that it's going to be harder than I thought to make him realize this, that it might take some time, and time is something I just don't have.

I decide to try. "Lily says she heard that you're probably going to be valedictorian." His expression doesn't change, so I say, "Lily Gaines? I thought you knew her."

The way Lily tells it, she and Roarke practically did it standing up on the front steps of her house and then he never called her.

Roarke still doesn't say anything, so I continue on with, "I'm actually graduating this year myself. I've been taking some extra classes."

He raises his eyebrows and then he says, "So you're saying you might be valedictorian instead?"

I shake my head and take a step back. This isn't going at all the way I'd planned.

"No, no. I'm not eligible. And even if I were, I'm sure you'd still get it. Have you decided where you want to go to college?"

"I haven't heard back from all the places I applied, but I'll probably end up at State."

I tilt my head and pretend to be confused. "Really? I always pegged you for the Ivy League, or at least someplace in Chicago."

Roarke throws his duffel over his shoulder and says, "You get what you get and you don't get upset."

It is a throwaway comment, the sort of phrase a kindergartner would use, but it is also a way in.

"Why don't you?" I say.

"What?" he asks me, surprised.

"Get upset," I say, and then, "You should get upset when things aren't fair. You should do something to fix them."

"Is that right? And just what is it that you're doing to fight all the injustice in the world?"

I think how best to answer, but since Blake Preston is walking toward us, I take another step back and simply say, "You'll see."

I give a half smile and turn. I can feel Roarke's eyes following me as I walk away.

———

Not perfect, I think, but it will have to do. I walk home quickly, stopping in the bathroom off the front hall as soon as I walk in the door. Then I head upstairs to change. My foot is on the second step when I hear the voices coming from the production office. It is unusual for anyone to be in there at this time unless there is an evening taping. Candy should have gone home for the day. Even Gretchen, who makes a habit of staying late to showcase her work ethic, usually takes off in time to eat dinner with her disabled brother. I retrace my path and tiptoe to the laundry room, climb onto the dryer, and kneel with my ear toward the vent. I hear Mother's voice, then Suzanne and Leroy Richards each say something in return. Mother is moving even faster than I could have hoped.

"I just wanted to follow up on the lovely chat we had yesterday," Mother is saying. "I was so sorry to hear about your troubles with the bank and with the store. We have always been proud patrons of Richards and Son's Sporting Goods. In fact, I think that's where Jethro and I bought all the boys their very first hunting rifles."

"It was, ma'am," Leroy Richards says.

"And I was so very impressed to hear about Roarke getting into Columbia," Mother continues. "It would be a shame to put such an opportunity to waste."

"There's nothing wrong with going to State," Mr. Richards says sharply.

"Oh, I agree, of course. Our own Caleb went to State before continuing on to Yale. It can be quite a stepping-stone toward bigger and brighter things. But you said yourselves that the store is in danger. If it goes under, then even the tuition at State will feel like a million dollars when those are dollars you just don't have."

"We'll make do," Leroy tells her, and I can hear the anger in his voice, anger that is entirely justified under the circumstances— but it is not only anger. He sounds offended and dangerously close to walking out of the room.

"I know you will," Mother says in her most soothing tone. "But you shouldn't have to. Shouldn't have to just make do, that is. Fine Christian folks like yourselves, you should be able to put your brilliant boy through school and not give it a second thought. A boy like that, captain of the baseball team, future vale-dictorian from what I hear, the hardest decision you all should be having to make is just which of the many fine schools he's been accepted to is the most deserving of him. Not the other way around. You shouldn't be waiting on the mercy of some financial aid officer to decide your only child's fate."

Mother knows far more about Roarke Richards than I have given her credit for. I wonder if her spies have uncovered all of the Richards family secrets. But clearly they have not, or else she would not be bargaining for Roarke to stand with me before the altar.

"What else can we do?" Mrs. Richards is asking, and I hear the hopelessness in her voice, the utter lack of imagination.

"Well, now that you ask, I do have an idea. I'm sure it will seem rather extreme. Shocking, even."

Mother pauses and I can practically see Suzanne Richards leaning forward against the table, see her fingers fluttering over the wooden surface as she longs to take my mother's hand. She is seeking salvation, with my mother playing the role of savior, a role Mother is all too willing to embrace.

"Go on," Mrs. Richards says breathily.

"I don't know if you're aware of how seriously our ratings are flagging. It's a travesty, actually, with all the good works that Matty and Daniel are doing overseas right now. I so wish we were reaching more people with their message of hope."

"What on earth has that got to do with Roarke and college?" Mr. Richards asks. He is still annoyed, but the edge in his voice has gone. She has him interested.

Mother says, "We need something to keep the viewers invested, especially the young people, because we all know that they are the ones most in danger of straying, most in need of the example that we strive to demonstrate. Essie has plans to graduate early and spend next year in Manhattan. She's already corresponded with some principals as well as with the chancellor of the New York City schools. She wants to teach poor children to read, bless her heart. Perhaps you saw her on television yesterday? No? Well, I know you don't have daughters, but I'm sure you can appreciate that there is no way I can allow her to go to a place like that unchaperoned."

Mother is rewarded with a "Goodness me, of course not" from Mrs. Richards.

"But we've also been told by our production team and marketing researchers that it's important to viewers that Essie be able to find her own way in this world. They are most engaged with her when she is acting on her own, exploring."

Here Mother sighs, and I wonder if Suzanne Richards has

now overcome her shyness and reached out to take my mother's hand.

Mother says, "It has been suggested that if Essie were married, if she had a trustworthy young man looking after her, then maybe we would feel more comfortable letting her go. Now, at first I said no, of course. She's too young. It was out of the question. But the more I thought about it, the more sense it made. Who better to look after her than a husband? Who better for her to share this new adventure with?"

"I didn't even know that Essie had been dating," Suzanne Richards says.

"She hasn't," Mother tells her. "But why should a little thing like that stand in our way?"

"Our way?" Mr. Richards asks.

"Our way," my mother says again. "I would very much like for your son to marry my daughter. It's not romantic, I know, but I'm certain that they would grow to love each other. In the meantime, your family would be generously compensated for what I realize is an incredibly unorthodox proposition. I intend nothing tawdry, I assure you. They could live as friends, if they so desire. I'm certainly not in the habit of pimping out my youngest child."

I close my eyes. The most disgusting thing about this is that Mother believes what she has just said.

"Now, let me just get this straight," says Mr. Richards. "You want us to tell Roarke that he should marry a girl who is practically a stranger just so you can help your ratings and he can babysit her in New York?"

"And so he'd get to go to New York as well, don't forget. We'd pay for Columbia. That would be written into the agreement. And we'd pay off what you owe on the store and on your house. Then, if the young people remain married for at least five years, enough to get Essie safely through college after taking next year off, both you and they would be given an additional incentive, with another bonus given for every five years they remain together after that."

There is a scraping of chairs and I sense that my mother has stood, not Suzanne or Leroy Richards, who are both no doubt still somewhat dumbfounded.

"It's a lot to take in and I've kept you too long as it is. I don't expect an answer now. Go home and think it over. Do you have a lawyer? Excellent. We'll meet again soon, and if your answer is yes, we'll let the suits hammer out the details the next time we talk. Let me show you out."

I consider hiding in the laundry room until they've gone but decide that seeing them in person can only help my cause, make this all seem real and less like some fantasy cooked up by an overbearing parent. I slip into the hall and away from the production office so that it will look as if I am just coming down the stairs. When I hear the door open, I turn and skip back down the last few steps and then come up short, as if I'm startled.

"Mrs. Richards. Mr. Richards. What are—?" I stop there, as if remembering my manners, and instead say, "It's a pleasure to see you. Roarke hit quite a triple in the game today. I hope you'll tell him hello for me."

I smile and do my best to look like daughter-in-law material, the sort of girl you dream your son might willingly bring home someday, instead of the knocked-up used goods that I know I am.

Suzanne's eyes dart toward Mother and then back to me. "Your mother has just been telling us about a plan of hers."

I can't let her say any more than that or else I'll be forced to either storm up the stairs in protest like a normal teenager or come out directly in support of arranged marriages. Neither seems like a good idea at this juncture, not when what the Richardses really need is some time to sit with the idea, time to think about the money. Once they've done that, I very much suspect they'll stop caring what I think or how strange all of this must seem.

Instead I giggle, a little too maniacally, so I stop abruptly and then say, "Oh, Mother's always making plans. She's where I get it from, I guess. Did she tell you I might get to go to New York City next year? I've only just begun my research, but apparently the high school graduation rate there is less than seventy percent. Can you imagine? And since it's been established that early childhood literacy greatly impacts school performance well into adulthood, isn't it obvious that someone has to step up and teach these children to read? Inspire them to dream of a better life for themselves and for their families? Each and every one of those children should have an opportunity to change this country for the better. They only need someone to help them take those first steps and learn the value of hard work and perseverance."

I am talking too fast, and moreover, what I am saying is complete and utter nonsense. Mother looks aghast, but Suzanne Richards, so sweet, so in need of hope, nods at me with tears in her eyes.

"Bless you, child," she tells me and then she and Mr. Richards leave.

When they are gone, Mother leans back against the door and faces me.

"Well," she tells me, "that just might have worked. I think we may find you a husband in time after all."

———

That night I sit on my bed and retrieve the phone I practically stole from Liberty Bell's camerawoman from where I have hidden it beneath my mattress. I turn it on, and while I wait for it to power up, I press it between my hands to steady them. It is still too soon for me to promise anything, I know, but I can't wait any longer. I scroll through Margot's recent calls and there she is, under Libby B. I hear a door close down the hall as my parents shut themselves into their room. The house is still. Growing up, it had never really been quiet, not like this. Lissa would be yelling at Caleb to turn down his music or at Jacob to stop bouncing his ball against the wall between their rooms.

Mother would say, "Boys will be boys, Elizabeth. Just ignore it." She was always Elizabeth to the others. She was Lissa just with me.

The boys were always allowed to be boys. That was a precedent that was set early on, when even Daniel and Matty were still around most of the time. They would come and go from college, but they were usually home on weekends to drop off a hamper filled with dirty laundry or to eat an entire refrigerator-ful of food. They had the run of the house. They were kings of the castle. They were not ever once told no. It was different for Lissa and me. We were made to do the chores that our brothers skipped out on, no matter what their reason. We picked up the slack. We covered. We bent ourselves to their wills.

The quiet is unsettling, even though Lissa has been gone for almost four years. It still sounds alien, that vacuum where there should be something. What? I don't know. Just something. But instead there isn't anything at all.

I press the Call button and Liberty Bell picks up on the second ring. I do not even give her time to say hello before I speak, knowing that when I do, things will be set in motion that I will have no power to stop even if I wanted to. The same thing happened when I went to the library. Even when I was standing there, I almost walked away. My voice is barely more than a whisper and I cannot say all I need to say here, in my room, with my parents so nearby, but still I am afraid that I will lose my nerve if I don't speak right away.

I hear a buzzing of traffic and loud voices when the line connects and I ask for the one thing that might end the quiet, fill the emptiness I feel inside.

"I need you to find my sister, please."

Liberty

I am half a block from my apartment when she calls. I weave through the Friday-night crowds outside O'Leary's Pub and try to step away from them and into the street, but someone is throwing up near the curb. Mama would say he's airin' the paunch and shake her head with disapproval. Once, when Lee Sherman puked in front of the post office, she actually made the sign of the cross in the air and turned and walked in the opposite direction. Mama never did care for excess, especially when it came to a man who didn't know how to hold his liquor. As I break out of the throng, I begin to jog. I can barely hear Essie over the voices behind me and the fact that some driver chooses that exact moment to lay on his horn only makes it worse. I let myself into the small square entryway of our building and fumble with my keys, the phone cupped between my ear and my shoulder.

"Don't hang up," I tell her as the rest of my belongings clatter onto the floor. "Balls!" I exclaim, then quickly apologize as I pick up my things and eventually get my fingers on the correct key. It sticks in the lock at first, of course, because our landlord doesn't know the difference between a screwdriver and his own dick and also because he's counting on my getting annoyed and finally fixing the deadbolt myself. I lean my weight back while holding the handle to pull the door tight and only then can I get the key to turn. Inside, I sit on the stairs and extract a notebook from my bag, rather than tackling the two flights up to my apartment.

"Sorry about that. I was just outside. I didn't hear you. What was it you said?"

The voice that comes through the phone is small and I am reminded once again of just how young Essie is. It is what I was trying to explain to Mike when I got home last night, though I didn't exactly do a bang-up job of it.

"My sister," she says. "I need you to find her."

"Elizabeth? She's still at Northwestern, isn't she? She's supposed to graduate in May."

"That's what the papers say," Essie replies.

"But it's not true?"

I hear a sigh. "It may be true. I don't know. I haven't spoken to her since she left."

"When was that?"

"When she left for school. We haven't spoken since she left for college her freshman year."

My pencil stops then and I hold it just above the notepad that is open on my knees. I am confused.

"But she was in your Christmas card, I'm sure of it. She's been in the stills used to promote the show every season even after she moved away."

"But her image is not to be used in the live video," Essie intones as if she is reading, "out of respect for her wishes to remain off camera. That's what the PR statement says, or something like it. But she wasn't even in those photos, not originally. She was Photoshopped in."

"Why?" I ask.

"You don't really care about the answer to that, do you? It's too obvious. She's in the photos because if she were missing, then people would start asking the really interesting question."

"Which is?" I say, even though I already know the answer.

"Why doesn't Lissa want to come home?"

I start writing again and as I do, I say, "And you don't have any idea why this might be?"

"I have one idea, but I hope I'm wrong," Essie tells me. "Find her. Tell her that I need to talk to her and that I hope she'll talk to you."

"What if she doesn't have anything to say?"

"Then at least ask her if she'll come to see me. We'll figure out the where and when once we confirm the pre-wedding interview schedule."

"So there's definitely going to be a wedding, then?" I ask.

"There has to be," Essie answers. "The show must go on, or so they say."

All of a sudden I am scared for her. "Essie, they can't *make* you get married. I hope you know that."

"Oh, they're not making me do anything. Not anymore. From here on out, I'm calling the shots." Her voice is angry. "I don't want you feeling sorry for me. Not for one second. Tell me that you understand."

I open my mouth to say one thing and reconsider, then close my lips tightly for a moment. The truth is, I know exactly how she feels. So I tell her, "I understand. About that anyway. But I don't understand what it is I'm supposed to be doing here."

"You're helping me the same way that I'm helping you," she says. "If you want to get the interviews, then you'll find Lissa. You get her to talk to me if not to you. Then, if I'm right about why she went away, there will be just one more thing that I'll need you to do."

"And what's that?" I ask, and this time I have no idea what it is she's thinking.

"I've read your book," she tells me, as if this is an explanation. "I think it may be time to write another."

———

I climb the stairs in a rush once the line goes dead, taking them two at a time and grossly overestimating my fitness level. My chest is burning when I burst through the door and find the apartment empty. Mike must still be out with his law school friends, celebrating or else drowning their sorrows after today's exam; both activities look about the same. Just as well. I don't need any distractions. I put the kettle on to boil and then pull out my laptop. It's been a while since I've read anything about Lissa Hicks that was not directly circulated by the publicity team at *Six for Hicks*, but this had never bothered me. She was in school. She was trying to fly under the radar. It was exactly what I would have done in her position. It didn't mean there was anything amiss.

Even if what Essie says about Lissa not having been home since starting college is true, that still doesn't mean there's a story there. A teenager hating her parents for putting her on television thirteen episodes a year and then reaping the profits is hardly shocking in and of itself. In fact, it's barely noteworthy. All teenagers hate their parents. There's no real outrage in that. Now, if she were trying to sue them for damages, for mental anguish and suffering, like the tightrope kid from *The Circus Is in Town*, then that would be a different matter. Then there would be a paper trail, legal documents to beef up the narrative, instead of just a rich and whiny teenager angry about all the ways that Mom and Dad have completely and totally ruined her entire life.

Also, how old would Essie have been when Lissa left? Twelve? Thirteen? Probably there had been some fight that she was not privy to at the time. A boyfriend of Elizabeth's that her parents didn't approve of, which would basically have been any boyfriend of any kind. Maybe she was experimenting with pot or alcohol or Molly, the usual things, maybe even with more hard-core drugs.

Even if she has track marks between her toes, I don't particularly care. That's her business. Not that it wouldn't be a hit with Sid. We all know scandal sells. But I don't want any part of it. Still, if Essie wants me to produce her sister so they can have a heart-to-heart, I'll do what I can. As far as I'm concerned, Elizabeth is probably the most normal family member that Essie has and it sounds like that girl could use a little bit of normal in her life.

I do a quick search and come up with nothing. Apart from the official promo material from the show, there are only a few pictures of Elizabeth since she left home. One shows her sitting on the grass outside the library, the wide stone building and its tall arched windows framed by the blue sky behind her. Her head is bent over a book, her brown hair falling forward and partially covering her face. I used to sit in practically the same place myself, last year when I was at Medill. Most of the other journalism students steered clear of the undergraduate hangouts, but I always liked the view from that particular patch of lawn. I check the date. Fall of her freshman year. So she was at Northwestern three and a half years ago. Tell me something I don't already know.

Aside from that picture there are a few other close-ups that were published in the Enquirer and other papers of that kind. There is very little text accompanying them, nothing to place the shots in time or space apart from the date of publication. They are all from that same year. Then nothing.

I reread every article I can find that mentions Elizabeth and was published over the last six years. There's a good amount to sift through from her junior and senior years of high school, pieces about whether or not she would be allowed to attend the junior prom (no) and then a flurry of online activity when it was announced that she would be going to her senior prom with a boy named Carter Banks. He was probably chosen by her parents to escort Elizabeth to the dance. I doubt they've kept in touch, but it's all I have to go on, so I take a chance and google his name. Unlike Elizabeth, Carter Banks has a fairly typical online presence, which is to say that within minutes I know far more about him than I ever knew about my best friend growing up. Most important, I know that he is enrolled at the University of Chicago, my alma mater, which gives me options.

It's Friday, meaning that the registrar's office at the university will be closed through the weekend. Still, stopping by on Monday and sweet-talking my way into a copy of Carter's schedule is not entirely out of the question. It's what I did my junior year when some senior got too handsy with my roommate Samantha. She never reported it and in her head I know she didn't even think of it as assault, though as the one who walked in on them, I can say with the utmost clarity that an assault was exactly what it was. Since she wouldn't let me take her to the school counselor, I figured the best I could do was help her avoid the asshole until he graduated that spring.

I played the Libby Bell card with Darlene, the woman in the registrar's office, said that the senior was stalking me but that I couldn't report it without risking it hitting the papers. Her eyes teared up a little as she took my hand, but I think that had more to do with how much I look like Justice, even now that I'm older and my sister isn't. I could tell that Darlene was the sort of woman who would have taken Justice's death particularly hard. People will do practically anything if they think it will keep me safe. They all feel guilty that when it mattered most for Justice, no one did a thing.

So the registrar is one option. Darlene still works there, and she still sends me a card on the birthday that I once shared with my sister, but she won't be in for two more days and I don't want to wait that long. Then I find Carter Banks's name in an orchestra program listed under percussion, and with just a little more searching, I learn that there will be a performance of *Carmina Burana* next weekend that is being rather graphically advertised as "Orff with Their Heads."

I smile for the first time since I started reading, not because I find the pun amusing but because now I know how to find Carter Banks. It's better than nothing. Blearily I rub my eyes and shut my computer. It is after midnight, so I leave Mike a note and riffle through a pile of clothes until I find some pajamas that smell clean enough. Then I fall into bed. Just as I'm pulling the covers up around my ears, I hear him moving around in the kitchen, but I am asleep before he comes into our room.

———

The next morning I get up early and head to the campus security office. The fall of my sophomore year I interviewed a guard named Azzam Ghazali for the school paper after several students' cars were broken into. It was my first real assignment as a journalist, or at least that's how it felt. I know that if I had met Azzam even six months earlier, we would not have become friends. I was raised to believe that there are different kinds of people and that this world can best be navigated by recognizing folks for what they are and not expecting them to be what they are not.

For instance, as Mama had told me more than once while I was growing up, Lee Sherman was a drunk. There was nothing that would change that; it was just how he was made. So instead of asking the Mississippi to reverse direction and head back up north, it did infinitely more good to fill a Crock-Pot with stew and drop it off on Lee's front stoop. Then at least he would eat that week. There was no harsh judgment in her voice when Mama talked about Lee. His actions may have sometimes attracted her derision, but the man himself was always forgiven. Nor was there any judgment when she told me that the congregation of Reverend Nance's church were not really Christian, that they were just going through the motions but they had none of them answered God's true call.

"Don't you think I know a Christian when I see one?" Mama would ask, and Justice and I would nod because Mama was famous for her looking eye, for being able to tell with just one glance the truth that was inside. She knew when a cow was ready to calf even before Topher, the ranch hand, who told people he'd been raised by a dairy cow called Etta Place and that the cattle were practically family as far as he was concerned. And Mama knew when Lou Ann Laramie had been beaten one too many times and was fixing to shoot her husband. That's how she got there first and took the rifle out of Lou Ann's hands. Mama told Mo Laramie that if he laid a hand on his wife again, she would come back and save Lou Ann the trouble and just shoot him herself.

"People may not have the power to help what they are, but you two best be able to separate the good from the bad. If you can't, then you're liable to pack a pound cake when a shotgun is required or the other way round."

She said this to Justice and me as we brushed the horses the day after Easter, the last one we would spend together, though at the time there was no way of knowing what would happen in December of that year. This memory is rooted firmly in time only because I wanted to skip the talking and get back to the house, where Mama had promised we could have pie for breakfast. I complained of having to go out in the cold at all while the visiting cousins slept in. Still, even with a thin crust of snow covering the ground and the wind whipping across the flat prairie as it stretched for miles in all directions, inside the barn it was warm. I leaned my cheek against Jasper's withers and his muscles twitched as if I were a fly in search of blood, then he turned his head around with a baleful expression to urge me to start brushing him again.

In the next stall, Mama ran a currycomb over Milo's back. Justice had named him when he was born, which made him for all intents and purposes her horse, but Mama had said that she would take care of Milo if Justice agreed to work on the knots that had gotten tangled up in one of the lead lines. Knots were one of Justice's specialties. Her fingers were small and strong, the opposite of my own clumsy ones. So Justice sat outside Milo's stall on an overturned bucket, her quick deft touch unraveling the line.

As she worked, she said to Mama, "Pa says that Ham's son Canaan was cursed because his father sinned, that the child takes on the sins of the father. And that God made all their descendants black as punishment so that his transgressions would show up clearly on their skin."

Mama did not stop working on Milo when she answered, "Don't you two go around thinking less of someone just because he was born ignorant or shiftless or colored. It is our Christian duty to protect them from themselves so that the Lord might have mercy on all our souls."

I remember thinking how good Mama must be, how righteous, to preach love even for those who were black or brown, while knowing how badly Pa would punish her if he heard her talk that way. Even now, long after coming to realize the prejudice in such a loaded statement, I still think Mama was brave to say what she did. She was trying to teach us as much about love as she knew how.

———

Azzam has moved up through the ranks since his years watching over the BMWs and Audis in the student lot. I place a coffee from his favorite diner on his desk in offering. He embraces me warmly, then motions for me to take a chair and we both sit. There is a picture of his son dressed in a shirt and a crooked tie, smiling shyly into the lens, placed prominently on a bookshelf next to the watercooler.

"My friend," Azzam says, "you cannot be here just to visit an old man. I can tell. It is not possible that a television star such as yourself has time for the likes of me."

I wrinkle my nose and say, "You saw it, then?"

"Saw it? I DVR'd it and will watch it often."

I laugh and say, "Please don't do that. But I may have another chance to grace your television screen before too long. That is, if you're willing to help."

He spreads his hands wide and his lips stretch out into a grin. "When have I ever refused the call of Liberty?"

I clap soundlessly at his pun, since it is one of his favorites.

"I knew I could count on you, patriot that you are," I say. "I need to know when and where the orchestra practices next."

"As you wish," he tells me and turns toward his computer and pulls up the schedule for campus events and security assignments. "Shane is unlocking Mandel Hall for them at ten. Does that help?"

I lean forward and kiss him on the cheek. "You know, I think it just might."

———

Walking across campus, I catch sight of the tower before I can see Mandel Hall, and I remember how when I first visited, I was convinced that God must live here, the buildings were so beautiful. I think that this conviction, which I told my parents had come to me in a dream, was the only reason I was allowed to leave home for college. That and I told them I would be studying early Christian religion, which of course I did, among other things.

I wait by the fountain and flip through the Facebook pictures of Carter Banks that I've saved on my phone. He's wearing the same jacket he had on in his most recent selfie when I spot him crossing the courtyard.

"Carter!" I yell and raise my hand in a wave.

He smiles uncertainly, likely trying to work out where we've met and if we've hooked up and whether it might be better to run away. I am already jogging closer and extending my hand.

"Hi. I'm Libby. We don't know each other, but I'm hoping you can help me with something."

He stuffs his hands into his jacket pockets and lifts his shoulders against the wind.

"Shoot," Carter tells me.

"I recently spoke to Esther Anne Hicks. I believe you went to prom with her sister, Elizabeth?"

He says nothing and his face is a blank, no confirmation or denial.

"I was wondering if you might still be in touch with Elizabeth. Essie wants to find her and she asked me to help look."

"Shouldn't she just ask her parents?"

"Maybe she did already, or maybe she doesn't think that's an option. I don't know. I just know that she needs to find Elizabeth. Are you still in touch or not?"

But Carter is already backing away.

"Essie didn't send you," he snarls. "Why can't you all just leave those girls alone?"

"She needs to find Lissa," I call out, and he stops at my use of the nickname. "Please."

"Is Essie in trouble?" he asks and he moves a step closer.

I shrug. I don't know what else to say that might convince him to trust me so I try, "How could she not be?"

Carter clenches and unclenches his jaw as he deliberates. Then he takes out his phone.

"One call. That's all you get. I'm not going to take you to her. I'm not even saying I know where she is, do you hear me?"

I nod. "Thank you."

"Come on," he says and motions me to follow him out of the courtyard and into a line of students carrying violin cases or rolling cellos. Once we're inside and out of the wind, Carter dials.

"Hey, Liss," he says. "I'm sorry to do this, but there's a woman here who wants to talk to you . . . No, don't hang up. She says that Essie sent her. I haven't told her anything. She doesn't have your number, but I'm going to hand the phone to her, if that's all right." He looks up and mouths the words Go ahead and holds the phone out to me.

"Elizabeth?" I say, then, "Lissa?"

"Who told you that you could use that name?"

"I'm sorry. Elizabeth, then. It's just that it's what Essie called you when we last talked."

"Why on earth should I believe that you've spoken with my sister?"

"My name is Liberty Bell. I met Essie a few days ago when we filmed an interview. Maybe you saw it?" I'm met with silence, so I say, "Maybe if I text you a link to the video and Carter takes a picture of me on his phone . . ." I trail off, uncertain how to finish.

"That's not necessary," she tells me. "I recognize your voice now. What is it that you have to say?"

I step away from Carter and turn my back. "Essie wants to know why you never come home. She wants to see you."

"That place stopped being my home a long time ago."

"She wants to know what happened, why you left, or at least why you won't come back. She seems to think that something drove you away."

"Why? What did she say?"

"That's it. That's all she told me. She said that I should find you and get you to talk to me or else get you to meet her at one of the pre-wedding interviews so that she can talk with you yourself."

"Who's getting married?" Elizabeth asks.

"Your sister. At least she says she is."

There is a pause, then Lissa says, "Tell my sister she's crazy. Nothing happened. I'm not in any trouble. I just want to be left alone."

I take a chance since it worked on Carter and say, "But what if she's the one who's in some kind of trouble?"

There is another moment of hesitation as Elizabeth considers this. Then in a cold voice, she says, "I told you. I don't live there anymore."

Roarke

I ran into Essie Hicks at the baseball game yesterday, which is why I can now say with the utmost certainty that the girl is even crazier than she looks. I'm not sure who I would say this to but that's entirely beside the point. Not Mom or Dad; they've been acting truly nuts ever since their fancy tea at the rectory a couple days ago. Also, they aren't home, so I can't say anything to them at all. I thought they might show at the game if Dad finished early at the store, but no such luck. Then this morning they were out the door while I was still trying to convince my brain that it was time to wake up and start moving. They yelled something about talking to their lawyer as they left but didn't answer when I asked them what it was about. Then they were gone.

So I'm alone and there are a few hours to kill before I have to head to baseball practice. Mom left nearly a full pot of coffee, which is good, because I was up half the night thinking about Essie Hicks, though I can't really explain why. Something about the way she looked at me makes me feel like she thinks she knows me. That in itself is not a surprise. Girls are always looking at me like that, like they feel they have me figured and are just working out how to fix me. Their solution usually has something to do with kissing or else giving me access to what's underneath their shirt. But yesterday, with Essie Hicks, there was a moment when I thought she might be right. Maybe she *does* know me. Maybe she knows me better than I want to admit.

I go for a run and then hop in the shower. When I get out, I can hear Mom and Dad moving around downstairs. Their voices are loud and so I hang out upstairs, waiting for them to finish whatever argument they're having. Eventually, though, I am out of excuses and besides that I'm hungry. I wait for a particularly impressive bit of shouting to die away before I trudge heavily down the stairs, making enough noise that they will hear me coming.

Just as I expected, by the time I enter the kitchen, it is silent. Mom stands at the counter putting together some sandwiches. Dad's pouring the last of the morning's coffee over some ice.

"Son," he greets me as he nods. He takes a long gulp of his drink and I can tell that he's stalling. Finally, he says, "We need to talk."

Mom's still standing with her back to us, facing the counter. She places a piece of bread on top of the sandwich she's putting together and leaves her hand there, hovering above the crust.

"Suzanne?" Dad calls over to her and she jumps a little.

"Coming," she says after letting out a sigh.

In a few swift, practiced movements she cuts the sandwiches and places them on a plate, which she sets in the middle of the kitchen table. Dad and I sit.

"Help yourselves," she tells us unnecessarily. We've never had to be told to dig into food before. But no one moves. After a pause, Mom sits down. I look from my dad, who is dunking one of his ice cubes beneath the surface of the coffee with his index finger, to my mom, who is staring at her lap.

Since I am generally of the opinion that it is best to get out ahead of things, I take the initiative and say, "I didn't do it, whatever it is."

Mom ventures a small smile, but I can see that the effort pains her. Dad clears his throat. I wonder how long we are going to sit here before one of them says something. I don't have to wonder for too long, though, because after a painful and heavy silence, Dad says, "Roarke, I think you know that the store has been struggling."

This isn't news. Our station wagon has four bald tires that should've been replaced a year ago. It's a miracle that the car made it through the winter without an accident. But it's not just our store. The whole country is in a recession, though the talking heads on the news say that the numbers are improving. Whatever that means. Still, I know we're not rich, which is why I'm not counting on Columbia. Even with financial aid, we don't have the money for me to get back and forth or pay for room and board. I'm fine with State. I really am. I tell myself this every day.

Dad takes another sip of his iced coffee and continues, "We've been riding a thin line for a while now, waiting for things to turn around."

"They still might," I say hopefully, because this is beginning to sound worse than I had thought.

"That's true. They might. But not in time. We're going to lose the store, the house. We're going to lose it all. I had been working out just how to tell you, but there's no easy way to tell a boy his father is a failure."

There's a silence during which I know I'm supposed to say something reassuring, but my throat has squeezed shut. I can't make any noise at all. It's the shock, I guess, the reversal, the notion that for the first time, it's not me who's failing him.

Instead Mom says, "Leroy, please."

He stands and leaves the room. Mom wrings her hands in front of her on the table and I'm struck by how raw they look, how broken. Her red skin is cracking at the knuckles. They're the hands of someone much older than my mother actually is.

"Is that it?" I ask, expecting her to say it's okay to take my sandwich up to my room, but she shakes her head.

More time passes before she speaks. Then she says, "We've been offered a way to keep the house, the store. It would mean enough money for us to stay above water, avoid bankruptcy. It would mean more money than I thought we'd ever see in this lifetime. You would get to go to Columbia."

I can tell from her tone that it's not only this, there's something more, something I should be afraid of, but foolishly I begin to hope.

"What is it?" I ask when she does not offer an explanation on her own.

She looks down at her hands as if aware of them for the first time and then buries them in her lap. Her eyes, when they find my own, are pleading. It's the look that gets me, that makes it finally sink in, and suddenly I'm terrified.

"You would have to marry Esther Hicks."

I know there must be more to this, background of some sort, but I don't wait to hear it.

"No," I say. "No way. Not in a million years. I'll get a job. I won't go to college. I want nothing to do with that family."

I pass my dad on the way through the living room but don't stop. I'm already up the stairs when I hear him say, "What did you expect? We knew it was too good to be true."

———

I leave for practice without saying good-bye. I'm angry, I think. Though really what I'm feeling is more complicated than that. It's impossible to put a name to. They were willing to trade me, in exchange for money. So what I feel is shame, but I also feel powerful. I wonder if this is how all of those countless girls have felt over the millennia, loaded into trucks and sold into slavery. I saw a show about that on the History channel the other day. There were some boys mixed in there too, though not as many, for the obvious reason that even most pedophiles prefer to think of themselves as straight and it's generally men who are pigs when it comes to sexual arrangements. It's men who trust they will suffer no consequences for their actions, while women suffer no matter what they do.

I think about where Essie and I would live—hypothetically, of course, since I'm not really considering it. There's plenty of room for me in the rectory. That place is an actual mansion. Even if I had to sleep in the garage, it would be about a million steps above the stained concrete bunker where they locked up the girls on that TV show. Maybe I shouldn't be complaining. Compared with my family's cramped three-bedroom split-level complete with its leaky roof and cracked foundation, the Hickses' house is practically Versailles. But we wouldn't be living there, I remember now, since I'd be at Columbia. In married housing, presumably, if that even exists. It'd have to be a large apartment, huge by New York standards, what with the space needed for the camera crew and hair and makeup and that sort of thing. I assume that would be part of the bargain. I'd be sold not into slavery but into celebrity, which I realize on some level amounts to pretty much the same thing. I think this and then I stop myself, since the idea is no less insane than it was an hour ago and my internal dialogue sounds too close to an actual debate.

I'm glad when Blake slides up next to me and claps me on the back. I can use the distraction. But instead of taking my mind off things, Blake seems to know what I was thinking, because he says, "Dude, why on earth was Esther Hicks all up in your business yesterday? I never got a chance to ask."

"No reason," I say, because it'd be too ridiculous to say it out loud. But then, maybe just to see how it would sound, I venture, "She probably wants to marry me."

I'm careful to say this in a way that makes it clear that I'm joking, the sort of joke that goes over well with Blake. It's just the right blend of vanity and assholery. Totally up his alley.

I'm rewarded with a laugh and then he says, "Man, what I wouldn't give to get with her, that prissy little preacher's girl."

"Maybe on a temporary basis, but don't you think it would be a bit much in the long term?"

Blake tilts his head to the side and taps a finger against his pursed lips. "I don't know. I think I could make it work. I like my creature comforts. Hot tub. Maid service. No one yelling at me to pick up my goddamned underwear because there would be someone whose actual job it was to pick up my goddamned underwear for me."

"But you'd have all those cameras following you around all the time. And you definitely wouldn't be allowed to say 'goddamned.'"

"So? I can talk pretty like the rest of them if I have to. Besides, in case you haven't noticed, I'm incredibly photogenic. I bet I'd be a huge hit with the middle-aged women in Omaha."

I roll my eyes in response to his overinflated ego and then point out, "I don't think they have a hot tub."

Blake looks outraged. "Well, that right there is a deal breaker if I ever heard one. I guess I'll just have to hold out for Morgan Lily. She was pretty hot in her last movie."

"I didn't see it," I tell him and nod to Coach Willis, who is motioning for us to join him.

Practice starts, and though Blake keeps trying to make me guess Morgan Lily's bra size, at least he doesn't mention Essie Hicks again. When she shows up about ten minutes before practice is due to let out, I refuse to look over in her direction. I concentrate instead on the ball in my hand and on Reggie White's mitt as I throw and catch, throw and catch, repeating the motion over and over until my arm is moving independent of my brain. It's soothing, the stretch and snap of my muscles and the solid poof as the ball hits my own mitt, finding its center, returning home.

It's not until we are jogging back to the dugout to pick up our bags that I answer Blake's questioning glance with a nod of acknowledgment. He sidles up to me and purposely knocks his shoulder into mine.

"Check it out, Roarke," he whispers.

"What?" I ask, though I know he could only be talking about Essie.

"I think you're in."

I shake my head and grimace and stoop to gather my things. I want more than anything to just run home and get out of there, but I know I'll have to face Essie one way or another, and since there's no way around it, I figure it's best to wait until everyone else has left. I help Coach Willis stow the equipment in the athletic building, and when we've finished cleaning up, there's a moment just before I step back outside when I half expect the field to be empty. Instead Blake is leaning against the chest-high fence talking to Essie. The panic that I feel is like a thick tar that nearly blacks out my vision and makes it hard to breathe. I blink a few times before I can see normally again and swallow. My legs are like waterlogged bags of cement, but I force them to run. I'm sweating by the time I reach Blake and Essie and I untuck my shirt to fan myself.

Blake smiles widely, clearly enjoying my discomfort. He and Essie both are silent, waiting for me to say something, but I just glare at Blake and wait for him to take the hint. Finally, after an uncomfortably long pause, he grins at Essie and reaches out to take her hand and lifts it gallantly to his lips.

"Esther Anne," he says, "always a pleasure."

I can hear him laughing as he walks away. I wait until he's out of earshot before I growl, "What do you think you're doing here?"

"I just thought that we should talk."

"About whether I want five kids or maybe seven?"

The chain-link fence is still between us and Essie turns away and leans against it so that her back is to me but off to one side. I can still see most of her face.

"I see your parents have broached the subject."

"They have. My answer's no."

She turns back and grips the top of the fence. Her eyes are burning, but behind that look I can tell that she is scared. "Don't say that," she tells me.

"Why on earth do you think I would marry you? The first time we ever talked was yesterday."

She shrugs and suddenly she looks smaller, completely unthreatening. I remind myself that this is how they lure you in. Then they pounce and strike to kill.

"It's not like I'm expecting you to love me," she tells me sadly.

I'm almost sorry for her in this moment. Almost, but not quite. So I say, "I could never love you."

"I know," she answers, and this time, strangely, she does not sound sad at all.

"So why, then? Why should I say yes?"

"I think first of all, it's easier if you don't think of it as a marriage," she suggests.

"What should I think of it as?"

"A business arrangement," she says simply. "An alliance. A pooling of resources for the greater good."

"Whose greater good?"

Essie lifts her chin, a quick birdlike gesture, as if she is working out how much to trust me, or debating whether she should fly away.

After she has come to a decision, she tells me, "Ours. Yours and mine."

"You don't think you have enough already?"

"Enough of what?"

I wave my hand in the air, back and forth, taking in the entire space around us. "Everything." I stop then and drop my hands. "It doesn't make you special," I say quietly.

"What doesn't?"

"Not being poor."

"I know it doesn't."

She's looking at me, and though I don't want to give her the satisfaction, eventually I look away.

"My parents want me to, but I suppose you know that."

"I know things are difficult for you financially," she says slowly.

I snort. "Of course you do. You think it makes me an easy target, don't you? How could I possibly say no to everything you're offering?"

"Did they tell you what we're offering?"

"No, but I think I've got the gist. Money, fame, a chance to get out of this stupid town."

"And you don't want those things?"

I turn and lean against the fence as well. We are almost back-to-back. I can feel Essie's eyes moving over my face.

"I want to get out of this town, yes. The other two I can do without."

"But there's no getting out of here without the money," she reminds me.

"So I'm caught, then? I'm out of options? You think I'll just willingly fall into your trap?"

"No," she says. "It wouldn't be like that."

"How would it be, then?"

"I told you. A business arrangement."

"So no sex?" I see her stiffen and so I continue, hoping that the words alone might hurt her. "No kissing. None of that sort of stuff."

"No sex," she tells me defiantly. "But there would have to be a certain amount of kissing, just for the cameras. Lily tells me you're fairly good at that. I didn't think it would be a problem."

"You didn't think it would be a problem? Do you have any idea how insane you sound?"

I turn back and see the tears in her eyes.

"This could work," she whispers. "We could both get out."

I feel a surge of pity, wonder if maybe Essie is the one who is trapped. But even so, why should it be my job to save her?

"I'm sorry," I tell her. "It wouldn't work."

Her breath rattles out of her narrow chest and she sucks in another. For a moment it is silent and I can almost feel Essie letting go.

Then she says quietly, "Is it because you're gay?"

Without thinking, I spit out, "What did you call me?" and start to walk away.

I want to run, but running would be an admission and I can't risk that. So I walk. My hands are clenched and my temples throb as the blood rushes, pounding in my ears. Essie runs along the fence until she comes to an opening and her feet stomp up beside me.

"Roarke, wait! I didn't call you anything. It was just an observation. You're gay. I've known that for a while now."

"You don't know anything," I hiss angrily, and it's not my voice, it's my father's, and the realization is enough to make me stop. I sway slightly, feet planted on the ground.

Essie doesn't hear the venom or else she ignores it and just keeps talking. "I know you made up a girlfriend somewhere so you wouldn't have to keep dating Lily. I know you're a good kisser but you always keep your eyes closed, probably so you don't have to think too hard about what you're doing."

"You don't know anything," I say again, but this time I can hear the break in my voice, the weakness.

"I know what it feels like to want to be anywhere but inside your own body."

I think of all the times Essie has smiled into the camera, batted her eyes, said exactly the right thing. I have seriously underestimated her. Reluctantly I realize that under different circumstances, Esther Hicks is someone I might be able to like. But that still doesn't mean I want to marry her.

Suddenly she takes my hand and forces me to look at her. "I'm not like my parents. I don't think the way they do."

"You sure had me fooled."

"Thank you. That was always the intention. And it's why I think this actually might work."

I'm silent while she tells me, "It wouldn't just be some money. It would be a lot of money. And it would be ours. Yours and mine. Then when we get divorced, we split it down the middle, fifty-fifty. You can do anything with it that you want."

Slowly, I say, "My parents said they would get to keep our house, the store."

Essie nods, but it's clear that she's not really interested. "There's more than enough in the offer, as far as I can tell, that they won't ever have to worry. But you're eighteen, Roarke; you should really have your own lawyer. I'll text you the contact information for the woman who represented Liberty Bell when she sued her parents."

"I'm not going to sue my parents."

"Well, if you have your own lawyer, then you won't have to. You'll see to that up front."

"Before your long walk down the aisle?" I ask, and she nods. "I suppose that will be televised as well."

"That won't be part of my parents' demands, but it is part of mine. I want it broadcast live."

"Why?"

"I have my reasons. One of which is to rake in as much cash as we can if we're going to go through with this thing." She pauses and looks at me shyly. "Are we going to go through with this thing?"

I look at Essie and the craziest thing is that she doesn't seem so crazy anymore.

"How much money are we talking about?"

"For exclusive wedding interviews and pictures, not to mention the ceremony itself? We should be able to bring in at least five mil, maybe ten."

I choke and Essie lifts a hand as if she is ready to smack me, but I recover just in time. "Five million?" I gasp.

Essie is calm as she looks at me. "I told you it would be a lot of money."

I'm feeling dizzy, so I sit down on the grass and lean my head between my knees. Essie sits beside me, close, so that our legs are almost touching.

"How did you know?" I ask, unable even now to say the word.

"That you're gay? I've been watching you for a long time," she says. Fifteen minutes ago I would have found this statement creepy, but now it seems like the most normal thing that has come out of her mouth so far. She looks down as if she's embarrassed and tells me, "Also, I know about the summer you were sent away."

My stomach twists. Essie moves her hand so it's next to mine, the fingers just barely touching. It's weird but also comforting. I don't move away.

"So we would, what? Have separate bedrooms?" I ask.

"Naturally," she says. "And you'd be welcome to have whatever . . . company you choose."

Completely against my will, I smile. There's still a chance that all this is a trap, but there's a part of me that feels relief. "You mean guys."

Next to me I feel Essie smile in return. "I mean guys. I told you, I'm not like my parents."

"I'm beginning to see that," I say. "And I'd get to go to Columbia."

Essie sits up and shifts away from me so that she is looking into my eyes, her expression earnest. "You could go anywhere, do anything, be whoever you want to be."

"Except when I'm on camera."

This stops her and she sits back slightly and then says, "Maybe the cameras wouldn't be with us for very long."

"What would that feel like, do you think?"

Essie closes her eyes and a dreamy look comes over her. "Different," she says. "Wonderful." Then her eyes snap open and she fixes her gaze on me again. "But I can't get there alone."

She holds this look until I flinch and turn away, then lies back on the grass and runs her fingers over the tips of the narrow blades. She's right. Her plan might work and, what's more, it's strangely beginning to make sense.

"If I say yes, then we're in this together. We're partners. We make all decisions together from this point on."

Essie sits up and nods. I can tell that she's trying hard not to smile.

"What?" I ask.

"I think you just defined marriage almost perfectly. As for the rest of it . . ." And here she leans forward and kisses me gently on the lips, then pulls away and says appraisingly, "I can work with that."

Esther

I give Margot's number to Roarke in case he needs to reach me, tell him to text first and that I will call back as soon as I can get away. We walk together as far as Locust Street and then stop on the corner. There is a swish of curtains from behind Mary Bettencourt's kitchen window. Roarke does not notice, but I am fairly certain that Mother is getting a phone call as we speak.

"I don't want you to be alarmed, but we have an audience," I tell him. "If it doesn't make you too uncomfortable, it might help if you kiss me on the cheek before you go."

Roarke looks around and sees nothing because there is nothing to see. No one out with his dog or walking to the mailbox anywhere on the street. The Bettencourts' curtains hang undisturbed, but I know that Mary is still able to see us through the slit between them. There is no way that she is not watching. Lissa once said that ninety percent of the gossip in this town originates with her. Walking home from school, there are two ways Roarke and I could have come, two paths we could have chosen, but only one of them led us past this house. He followed me left without asking when it would have been just as easy for us to go straight up to Elm. Already he is proving to be an excellent partner.

He clears his throat before he speaks. "I haven't said yes yet. But I'll call the lawyer. I'll go to the meeting. I want to see it all spelled out before I sign."

"I understand. And I agree. There's no sense in going into this blind."

"After all," he continues, "you know my secret."

"So you should know all of mine? I'm an open book. You can watch my entire life on reruns if you want, relive the braces phase. Or the day Daddy took me bra shopping in order to make him seem more relatable, to show his congregants that he is just like them, that he gets as uncomfortable about female undergarments as the next guy."

"I think I missed that episode."

"You're lucky. I'm told it was painful to watch. Just imagine how painful it was for me to live through. The disgusting thing is that his likability rating did spike right after that and it stayed high for about a year. From that point on, they decided to just work in one truly embarrassing thing for Daddy to do each season to keep him down-to-earth."

"And he's okay with that?"

"He does what Mother says. She is the 'keeper of the house.' I guess that means the show falls under her purview. He would never interfere, just as she would never dare contradict him at church or out in public."

"I see."

"That's not how I want things to be for us. I told you. Joint decision making in all things. If that's what you want."

"If I say yes."

"If you say yes," I reassure him.

"So I just go ahead and kiss you now?" he asks.

"On the cheek. That's what Mother would say is allowed. If we announce our engagement, there will probably have to be some kissing on the lips, but it's nothing you haven't done before. I'm sure you could be very convincing," I tease.

He sighs and once more looks over his shoulder, then leans

down and kisses my left cheek. After a few seconds of contact, he straightens and starts to pull away but then reaches out to run his fingers through my hair as if he wishes he could do more.

"Nice touch," I tell him.

"Normal people don't live like this," Roarke mutters through his teeth.

"If we do this, you won't be a normal person anymore. You'll be rich. The rules are different for them."

"Don't you mean that the rules are different for you?"

I take a step back and begin to turn away. "I'm not rich. My parents are. But I think it's time that changed."

I wave longingly toward him and then move in the direction of my house. Earlier today I bought a charger for Margot's phone and I want to plug it in. Niles Jenkins, who runs the only electronics store in town, looked at me suspiciously when I bought it. He knows Daddy is a vocal critic of Apple's CEO and boycotts any company that actively supports, or is run by, "the gays." I told him I accidentally broke Lily's charger and was just replacing it, that I didn't think Daddy would mind because the Bible says "thou shalt not steal" and breaking the charger was the same as stealing it in a way. He nodded thoughtfully and I paid cash.

I expect Mother to be waiting for me when I get home, but I do not expect her to be waiting quite so close to the front door. I almost run smack into her as I walk into the house and instinctively I back away, as you would from an unfamiliar dog.

Her eyes flash, but she waits until I shut the front door before she says, "What did you think you were doing?"

"What are you talking about?" I ask innocently.

Mother places a manicured hand on one hip and tells me, "You were seen with Roarke Richards. He kissed you in public, for heaven's sake!"

I think, Women must likewise be dignified, not malicious gossips, but temperate, faithful in all things.

Instead I say, "He kissed my cheek, which you previously indicated is within the bounds of decency."

"For someone you are dating, yes."

"Am I mistaken in assuming that you intend for me to marry Roarke Richards? Isn't that why his parents came to the house last night? Isn't that what you meant when you told me you had found a husband for me after all?" My mother says nothing, so I continue, "Except you hadn't. I ran into Roarke after baseball practice and it turns out he was going to tell his parents no. He's a person. You can't just expect him to go along with what his parents say because that's what you raised us to do. Not every family is like that."

Mother gives me a measured look and says, "I trust that the problem is taken care of?"

I swallow and try to sound confident when I say, "It is."

"All right, then. I'll give it a few hours and call Suzanne. I'm thinking we should aim for an Easter wedding. With any luck, we can have the details hammered out after church tomorrow. That will leave one week before spring break. It should give us just enough time to stage some scenes of you two falling in love before you leave for Havana."

"I think Roarke should come with me."

"On the trip? I don't think so."

My face falls. With Mother it is better not to put up a fight. Instead I say, "I just thought it might be nice to show that Roarke is involved in our mission. It's not as if we won't be chaperoned. But if you think it's best for me to go alone, I understand."

I begin to climb the stairs and have nearly reached the top when Mother says, "I'll think about it."

I turn back to thank her, but she is already gone.

When I get to my room, the first thing I do is text Libby that she needs to tell her lawyer to be ready for a meeting tomorrow, assuming that Roarke decides to follow through. It will be Sunday and short notice. There's a good chance that she won't come. But I think if Libby communicates to her just how important her help would be, both tomorrow and in the future, and how appreciative we would be, there is more of a chance that this lawyer will say yes. I'm sure she will understand that this means a hefty paycheck. I hope it is enough. Now all I can do is wait.

———

The next morning the gospel is from Matthew. The passage, where Jesus is tempted in the wilderness after fasting for forty days and forty nights, is one of Daddy's favorites. Every year during Lent he opens one of his sermons with the line spoken to Jesus by the Devil: "All these I will give you, if you fall down and worship me." He is dressed simply, without robes, in a light gray suit and a blue tie the color of a robin's egg, when he climbs into the pulpit beside the altar. He faces the congregation, and on the large screen on the wall behind him you can see that the tie exactly matches the color of his eyes. Mother must have chosen it. He wears a darker blue for photo shoots when he is standing next to her, to compliment her own eyes, but at church at least she knows that he stands up there alone.

He looks out calmly over the sea of more than a thousand faces. With Easter approaching, attendance is on the rise. Even the back pews are full. That's where Roarke and his family usually sit, but today they are front and center. Mother saw to that. As soon as Suzanne Richards arrived, Mother captured her arm and held tight to Mrs. Richards's hand, leaning her head in conspiratorially, flashing her perfect white teeth at everyone who greeted her as she and Suzanne Richards walked down the long center aisle. Leroy Richards and Roarke trailed behind, looking somewhat lost, while Mother guided the entire family into seats in the row just behind our own.

I can practically feel Mrs. Richards trembling as Daddy prepares to speak. The sun brightens behind the stained glass and casts rainbows over the white altar cloth and Daddy turns to look appreciatively at the window depicting Jesus's ascent into Heaven.

"We're not quite there yet," he says with a smile as he turns away from the window to again face us. The screens throughout the nave project his image for those too far away to truly appreciate his boyish dimples. "Soon, though," he promises and lifts his hands, palms forward, to quiet the laughter.

Then he looks grave and his mouth forms around the words uttered by the Devil as Jesus stood starving in the desert, his lips cracked, his skin burned, his belly hollow and aching to be filled. Then Daddy's voice changes and is filled with sympathy as he says, "Each one of us gathered here knows what it is to want." Behind me there is a restrained susurration as the flock affirms what Daddy has just said, a whisper only. They understand the need for buildup, that the shouting should come only at the end.

"And when I say that word, when I speak of *want*, you know that I am not talking about trinkets or baubles or even about the new Halo that comes out on Xbox in three weeks."

He is rewarded by another tinkle of laughter and points into the crowd and says, "I know that feels like *want* to the teenagers out there, but it isn't. Real want comes from someplace deeper, someplace baser. Someplace that speaks to the Devil himself, and that is why it can be so hard to resist, to cast him off, to stand in the light as God intended."

There is more about what temptation looks like in the modern world. Amazingly when Daddy talks about fame and fortune, he does so without a trace of hypocrisy and the crowd leans in toward him and then falls back when he throws a hand out, fingers splayed, as if the Devil himself were insinuated within the masses and needed to be cast out. When Daddy's hand shoots out, heads all around me are thrust back, chins raised, mouths open, and a moan rises up, quietly at first and then growing in volume until the whole church is keening. Hands are joined together and somewhere to my right a man stumbles into the side aisle and begins speaking in tongues. He falls forward and is caught up in a sea of arms, embracing him, drawing him back toward the surface.

Above the din, Daddy's voice rises in intensity and my heart beats faster and I feel the familiar pull, the desire to surrender myself to the spectacle. Today, though, I also feel Roarke's eyes from just behind my left shoulder and then Daddy is beseeching God Almighty to protect his flock from sin, from pride, from adultery and fornication, but most especially to protect us from the filth of homosexuality, since that path leads to the flames of Hell. My eyes move from Daddy to the cross and the shame burns across my chest. Roarke's hands are on the back of my pew, his knuckles white, and I place my own hand on top of his in apology, but I know that it is not enough and I do not blame him when he pulls his hand away.

I turn and try to catch his eye, but by then Daddy is announcing the anthem and Mother is pushing me toward the stage in front of the choir. I am confused for a moment and then remember that I am expected to sing. I hurry to take my place between the musicians, careful not to trip over the wires running to the instruments. There are several bars of introduction and the organ's chords rise hauntingly from the pipes above us and are joined by the cello first, then the guitars. The violins come in last, just as I take a breath and begin the song. The text is based loosely upon the Beatitudes, and when I sing the section about those who are persecuted for the sake of righteousness, my eyes find Roarke and he meets my gaze with a look that is blazing with defiance and I see him nod, a gesture that is meant just for me, his answer to my plea.

———

After the service, Mother ushers Suzanne and Leroy Richards into the refectory and personally serves them coffee and cake. Roarke looks around the room and it occurs to me that he may have never been inside this space, never penetrated this far into the fortress. There are children everywhere. They laugh and scoot under the folding tables laden with snacks and sweets. The purple cloths billow as their small bodies crawl from beneath one table to the next and small hands sneak up in search of cookies and then disappear again.

Mother is introducing Suzanne Richards to my brother Daniel and his wife, Hillary. The youngest of their five children is among those under the tables and the other four are presumably lost somewhere in the crowd. Not far away, Jacob is talking with Daddy while Jacob's wife, Lucie, bends down to wipe chocolate off one of my nieces' cheeks. Jacob and Lucie met while they were both at Sewanee, which was a bit liberal for my parents' taste, but the campus looked lovely on camera and the young courtship played well with the crowd. Together they run the church's music program, with Lucie serving as organist and Jacob as choirmaster. Their three girls are always dressed in matching outfits, and today is no exception. This time it is a frilly concoction of pleated pastels that is my sister-in-law's idea of adorable but which makes the girls, who have been known to pull the legs off frogs and other small animals, look like they might have murdered nursery rhyme characters for their clothes.

Matty, my oldest brother, is all the way on the other side of the hall, still wearing a beaded necklace presented to him by members of the tribe in Kenya that he and Daniel recently visited for filming. He looks ridiculous, and I am reminded of the summer we visited Wall Drug and Mother bought the boys enormous Indian headdresses and he and Caleb went whooping through the parking lot all the way back to our van. The memory actually belongs to Lissa; I was still in a stroller then. But over the years she told the story so often that I came to believe that I myself had seen how the feathers shivered when Matty dragged them through the air. That day my sister had wanted a simple dreamcatcher on a chain, but Mother shook her head and called it gaudy and said Lissa shouldn't be trying to draw attention. It wasn't becoming of a young lady. Lissa said she had responded by picking a chewed piece of gum off the armrest of a bench and popping it in her mouth, but I don't think that part of the story was true.

As Matty talks, his wife, Lilith, is nowhere to be seen, but I suspect she is in the kitchen, directing the volunteers. Their three boys and two girls are standing in a group of children who are not much younger than I. Matty says something in Swahili and the crowd that has gathered around him claps and he takes a bow. I roll my eyes and feel Roarke come up beside me.

"The gang's all here," I say.

"Not all," he answers.

I shrug. "I think people stopped expecting Lissa to show up a long time ago."

"I meant Caleb," he says. "Is he somewhere campaigning?"

I let out an exasperated sigh. "He hasn't officially announced that he's running for anything." I pause, then tell him, "He and Naomi are visiting her family. It's her aunt's fiftieth birthday."

"What are their kids' names again?"

I turn to him and say, "You're really doing your homework, aren't you?"

"That's what most girlfriends expect."

I nod appraisingly and tell him, "Millicent, or Millie, is the oldest. Actually, I got to name her. They had narrowed it down to a list of three and Naomi let me pick. Naomi's the closest thing I've had to a sister since Lissa left. Anyway, after Millie came Nathan, or Nate. And there's one on the way. They're right on schedule. One kid for every year of marriage. If they hit the jackpot and have twins, then they'll catch up to Matty and Daniel in no time."

"Is it a contest?"

"Of course. Everything's a contest. Especially when it comes to this. Go forth and multiply. Mother and Daddy made it clear to all the wives beforehand that they were expected to breed."

"Those must have been interesting conversations."

"They were," I agree. "I thought Naomi would faint from embarrassment. She always strikes me as being kind of frail, but she's certainly held up her end of the bargain, or so it would seem."

"And you really all just sit around the living room and talk about things like that?"

"Oh, no. Of course not. Mother sits down with the girls in private and I listen in. If I didn't, I'd probably be as brainwashed as the rest of them. I have Lissa to thank for that. She taught me that I need to look out for myself."

"How did she do that, exactly?"

I think for a moment that I would like to explain about the library, about how Lissa would have approved of that sort of insurance, but it is too soon. I like Roarke, but I'm still not sure how much I can trust him, so I say instead, "She left me behind. And she never came back."

Roarke does not say anything, but he reaches out a finger to touch my hand. I wonder if he is doing it just to shore up the story of our romance, but when his finger hooks around my pinky, I realize that he really means to comfort me. I smile shyly, grateful for his friendship at least, even though it can never be more than that.

"Is the lawyer coming?" I say.

He nods. "I didn't even have to ask twice. It was like she knew I would be calling. She's already made some changes to the contract. She'll be here by the time the meeting starts at three."

"That's good. Remember that it's fine to get whatever you can for your parents, but that you're really there to get as much as you can for yourself."

"And for you. We'll be partners, after all."

He begins to slide his finger up my arm, stroking it gently, and this I know is deliberate. I can practically hear the heads turning. I drop my eyes and move half a step away.

"You're enjoying this," I accuse.

He shrugs. "Hey, I wouldn't be saying yes if I didn't think I'd be able to have some fun."

"Well, you've certainly given them something to talk about. Well done."

"Just imagine what would happen if I kissed you," he teases.

"I don't have to imagine. I know. There would be at least two heart attacks, probably Hester Perkins and Evelyn Cook. Those two are really on their last legs. Not to mention the rash of fainting, some of it legitimate but most of it for show. It would be a madhouse."

Roarke smiles and stares at me without speaking.

"What?" I ask finally.

"It's funny. I think I'm going to really like being married to you."

The meeting takes place at church since the production office is not big enough to accommodate everyone. It is clear that Daddy has been brought into the loop, although I have no idea when Mother would have done that. Not when I first told her I was pregnant, that much I know. She would have never brought Daddy a problem until she had solved it to her satisfaction, would have never risked letting the decisions be taken out of her hands. In fact, there is a good chance that Daddy does not even know about the baby. I think about the times we have sat down to dinner together or passed each other in the hall. Surely if he knew, he would look at me differently. There would be a flicker of disappointment or else disgust. Or maybe it would be the opposite. Maybe he would be pleased—not consciously, of course. Still, he has given enough sermons on the dangers of fornication to not feel at least a little vindicated by my situation. He would be gloating, and I've seen no hint of that.

At first I am not sure if I will even be allowed in the room, but as the others gather, Mother eventually twists her head to motion for me to follow. It is the same room the confirmation class uses and there are posters they have drawn or painted decorating the walls. Daddy sits at one end of the long polished table with Mother to his left and the family's lawyer to his right. I claim the other seat next to our lawyer rather than sit next to Mother. Roarke is diagonally across from me with an empty chair between him and Mother, and his lawyer is on the other side. Suzanne and Leroy Richards look anxious as they sit, but their lawyer looks the most nervous of all in his ill-fitting suit and crooked tie. He is clearly out of his depth. Roarke's lawyer, on the other hand, looks entirely at ease in her tailored burgundy suit and practical heels. Her hair shines as if she's just stepped

out of a shampoo commercial. She makes sure to introduce herself and shake everyone's hand.

Daddy opens the meeting by thanking everyone for coming.
Then he says, "Esther's mother and I are thrilled that Essie has
found someone so worthy to share this next phase of her life with
and the years beyond. Roarke, we welcome you to the family."

Daddy has told me nothing of his happiness. In fact, I'm nearly
certain that before today he did not even know Roarke Richards's
name. I narrow my eyes, but Roarke manages a "Thank you, sir"
and Daddy continues, "Now, given the special circumstances of
our family business, so to speak"—he pauses for laughter and
Suzanne Richards manages a croak—"it is understandably a bit
more complicated than the two lovebirds just saying their *I do*s.
This contract here outlines our proposal and the various remu-
nerations. I trust you've had time to look it over."

The Richardses' lawyer nods obediently, but the lawyer sent
to Roarke by Liberty Bell indicates that she needs a few minutes to review the contract since she was driving while the last
round of edits were being exchanged by email. I take a copy
as well despite Mother's raised eyebrows and run through the
major points. For Mr. and Mrs. Richards there is the promised
assistance paying off their mortgage and the cumulative debts
on the store. Additionally, they have been offered $250,000, half
of which they will be given up front and the other half of which
they'll get only if Roarke and I stay married for five years. After
that, a stipend of $10,000 a year has been written in for the dura-
tion of our marriage, as long as Mr. and Mrs. Richards remain
married themselves.

Roarke, on the other hand, has been offered more, which is
entirely reasonable, since he is the one who will actually have
to be married to me and spend his life on TV. He gets tuition
and costs for Columbia as well as $250,000 up front and another

$250,000 at the five-year mark. Then the stipend is $50,000 a year for a long as we stay together.

"What about children?" I ask.

Mother looks sharply at me and Daddy says, "What about them?"

I speak slowly and say, "If I'm not mistaken, the boys' wives have each been given incentives of one hundred thousand dollars for every live birth and twenty thousand for every pregnancy that ends in miscarriage as long as the miscarriage is documented on the show."

Roarke's lawyer presses her lips together, probably to mask her disgust. At the other end of the table, Suzanne blinks like a catfish caught on a line. Daddy looks sideways at Mother and whispers gruffly, "Is this true?" She nods once and Daddy glances over at their lawyer and mumbles, "Add it in. Anything else?"

Beneath the table, I pull out Margot's phone and type discreetly. I see Roarke jump as his own phone buzzes and he glances into his lap, then whispers into his lawyer's ear.

She bobs her chin, then faces my parents and says, "My client would like five hundred thousand dollars up front instead of what's currently being offered and the rest of the terms remain the same."

Daddy pushes his palms down on the table and says, "You can't be serious," but Mother slides her hand over his and says, "Five hundred is fine. Why don't we just send Lucas out to revise the contracts and get them ready to sign?"

Roarke

I feel the air rush out of my lungs when Celia Hicks gives me an extra $250,000 as if it's nothing. Gives us, I should say, and I look over at Essie where she sits across from me, hands folded beneath the table, eyes lowered, waiting patiently. Soon the revised contracts are being passed down the table. My eyes can't focus on the words, but Delaney Phillips, my new best friend of about thirty minutes, seems more than up to the task of reviewing the updated document. She places a hand on my shoulder when it's time to sign, and I feel as if the pen that moves across the page is being held by someone else. My parents sign each copy when I've finished, then they're passed to Essie and Pastor and Mrs. Hicks. The contracts are notarized and the copies tucked into briefcases, after which everyone files out of the room. Once in the hall, Mom hesitates uncertainly, but Celia Hicks, who has been fawning over her all day, does not even say good-bye before she goes clicking down the hall in her heels.

Mom's face falls, but Essie steps in then and hugs her, saying, "Would it be all right if I called you Mom?" and I see my mother melt at the attention, confirming for me what I long suspected—she had always wanted a girl. She and Essie leave the church hand in hand and Essie walks us all the way to our car. Pastor Hicks had retreated to his office, lawyer in tow, after shaking my father's hand and then, after a moment's hesitation, shaking my hand as well.

Essie closes the car door for my mom as my dad climbs in behind the wheel and then she crosses the narrow strip of grass to join me on the sidewalk. I'm standing with Delaney, who says to her, "The extra money was your idea, wasn't it?" Essie doesn't answer, and instead of being offended, Delaney laughs and begins to walk away. "I'll be in touch. Don't agree to any media appearances without letting me vet them. You both did very well today."

Delaney pulls away in her Mercedes and I hear Dad start the car to signal that it's time to go.

I ignore him and instead say to Essie, "So, what happens next?"

"Besides living happily ever after? I'm guessing we have to shoot some footage of us falling in love. I'll have my people call your people," she says, laughing, and she starts to move away.

"You're really enjoying this, aren't you?" I call after her and she turns back and throws her arms out to either side.

"You've seen my life up to this point. You, Roarke Richards, are one hundred percent the most interesting thing that has ever happened to me."

———

Essie is right about the love story. It seems this is part of what we need to sell. A lot of thought has gone into choosing the locations. Nothing early on is shot outside or near a window, since we're supposed to have started dating in winter, when there would've been leafless trees and snow on the ground. Instead we go to a private art gallery and several restaurants. We hold hands at a small indie movie theater several towns over. Essie is fitted with hair extensions since she cut her hair sometime in December. I'm invited over to the rectory to "meet" her parents and have dinner, a scene that is just as awkward in real life as it's meant to be on film.

We are on schedule to finish this background footage by the end of the week. On Wednesday, just as we're getting ready to film our first "real" kiss, Essie asks me to come with her to Havana.

"I'm going next week for spring break," she tells me. "It's a mission trip. We'll pay your way, of course, or the show will. It's really the same thing. The flight from Miami to the island is chartered, so it's no trouble to add one more person. I know that there's no baseball practice. I already checked."

For some reason this annoys me and I say, "If you want to know if I have baseball practice, ask me. You don't have to go around doing reconnaissance behind my back. We're partners, remember?"

"You're right," she says. "I'm sorry. Will you come?"

"I've never been on an airplane. Heck, I've never even left the state except riding on a school bus to get to baseball games."

"What about Columbia?" she asks me.

I shrug. "Never been. But I figure it's got to be better than here."

"So that's a yes?"

"Yes, Essie. I willingly submit. I'll fly with you to a tropical island on a private plane paid for by your ridiculously rich family so we can take long romantic walks on the beach."

"The cameras will be coming."

"Then I better bring plenty of sunscreen. Make sure I don't end up looking like a lobster on TV."

Just then the director, a guy named Graham, finishes talking to the cameraman and walks over to us and says to me, "Just like we talked about, okay? Count to three silently and then kiss her."

We're in a planetarium, sitting side by side in the cushy seats and looking up at the blank ceiling, where there should be stars. I'm told they will be added in later, but for now the camera lights shine in our faces. I hear Graham say "Action" and turn my head sideways to look at Essie. I'm already holding her hand. I count the way that Graham has instructed and then I lean over and kiss her. Essie's lips are soft and smooth, without any lipstick. Pressing my lips up against hers is not entirely unpleasant and I close my eyes and reach a hand across to brush her cheek.

"Cut!" Graham shouts. "Again, and this time don't block her face with your hand."

By the fifth take we are both getting punchy and after a few good moments of usable kissing, I purposely brush my hand up against her boob. Essie bats it away and punches me in the arm.

"What?" I ask innocently. "They want it to be realistic. What's more realistic than a teenage boy trying to cop a feel?"

"Again," Graham says wearily. It's clear that when he went to film school, he thought he was going to be the next Scorsese and now he is wondering where he went wrong.

———

Dad picks me up that night, and instead of driving home, he takes the car to the quarry. In summer, kids hang out in the clearings along the edge and a few years ago one of them died while jumping off the ledge into the water below. The police guessed he must've hit his head on the rocks on the way down based on where the blood had spattered, meaning he was probably dead before he hit the water. You have to get a good running start if you're going to make it. Everyone knows that.

I didn't know him, but I went to the funeral. The whole town did. They talked about what a tragedy it was, that a life with so much promise had been cut short before it had even started. What they didn't say but we all knew was that he jumped after his girlfriend dared him to. That she dared him to jump and called him a coward only after he tried to strangle her and accused her of cheating on him with a senior from the next town over. That he was drunk out of his mind at the time and that everyone who knew him best said that if he hadn't jumped, he very probably would have killed her later that night, because that was the sort of guy he was.

No one said this out loud, though. Instead his girlfriend stood between the dead guy's parents and cried as if she really was heartbroken. And maybe she was. Who knows? People are funny that way. They remember only what they want to and manage to forget the rest. At the very least I'll bet she felt responsible and having her dead boyfriend's mother's arm around her waist would've only made that worse.

You would think people would've stopped coming to the quarry after that, but again, memories are like sand: they can shift or else be filtered, and by the end of the summer it'd become customary to shout out his basketball number when making the jump off the rocks. That's still how it's done. The jump doesn't count unless you manage to keep your shit together enough to yell out "Forty-three!" Kids'll probably keep doing it long after anyone remembers what the number means.

Dad doesn't know any of this, except the part about there being a kid who died. He even knew him, which is more than I can say. Our store doesn't stock his shoe size and the boy had to have his sneakers special-ordered. Dad probably had to run his fingers over the dead boy's feet to measure him. Sitting in the car as Dad kills the engine, I shiver at this thought and watch my father's hands fall from the steering wheel into his lap. The moon is bright enough to turn the granite blocks that mark the start of the trail a milky white and without saying anything, Dad gets out of the car and starts in their direction.

It's a good ten-minute walk to the edge of the quarry, but the path is wide and flat and I have made it before in less light than we have tonight. Another tradition is to bring a flashlight but then refuse to turn it on, no matter how frightened you get. I once asked why I should bring a flashlight at all and Greg Meyers, who was a couple years ahead of me and captain of the baseball team the year I first made varsity, told me that only an idiot would wander off into the woods without one. The irony of that statement, made as we both stumbled in the dark, was entirely lost on Greg, who really was a fantastic baseball player but maybe not the sharpest tool in the shed.

The path is wide enough for Dad and me to walk side by side, but for some reason I stay just a few steps behind and am content to let his dark shape take the lead. Part of me wants to see if he really knows the way. There's a turn in the trail right near the end that breaks off from the main path to the nature center and it's this narrower spur that spans the last few hundred feet to the edge of the cliff itself. Dad takes the turn as if it's second nature and it's only then that I realize that kids have been coming here for far longer than I ever bothered to consider.

When we break out of the trees, Dad ignores the edge and takes a seat on a well-worn log that's been rubbed so flat and smooth it's practically a bench. After a moment of hesitation, I sit beside him and wait for him to speak. The distant wall of the quarry reflects the moonlight back toward the sky and shimmers like the set of some low-budget sci-fi movie.

Beside me I feel my father's body slowly relax, then he says, "This is where I asked your mother to marry me."

"I thought you proposed at her college graduation."

"I did. That was the time she said yes. But I asked her here first, when she was just seventeen."

"I didn't know that."

Even without looking, I can feel Dad's shoulders lift and then go slack.

"She said no. I guess I figured it didn't count."

"So why're you telling me now?"

"Because she was right to turn me down even though she didn't want to. We were too young. We had no business getting married. If we had, neither of us would've ever finished college. We would've never gotten jobs that paid enough money for us to save up to start the store. I'm not saying we haven't got ourselves into a mess now, but things were going real well there for a while. That store put food on the table, it kept a roof over our heads, and it did that for long enough that we got you very nearly raised."

"Are you trying to tell me that I shouldn't marry Esther Hicks?"

Dad shakes his head. "No. I'm trying to tell you that I'm sorry it has to be this way. And I'm trying to thank you for what you're doing for us. I'm saying I'm incredibly lucky you grew up to be so much like your mother, who did the right thing even when it went against what her heart was telling her. I know that's how this must feel for you and I want you to know that I'm grateful."

"It won't be so bad," I say. "She's different than I thought she'd be."

"Good. I hope you two get along real well. Still, it's not at all what I wanted for you," he says.

And all of a sudden I'm angry at being forced to comfort him in this after everything he's done, however long ago, so instead of telling him again how fond I've grown of Essie, I force myself to say, "I thought it was exactly what you wanted for me. I thought this wedding was the thing you were most afraid you'd never get. You must be incredibly relieved."

———

On Friday we wrap up filming early in order to get to an interview with Liberty Bell. I've never heard of her apart from that
one segment with Essie that I saw on television, but Essie says
she grew up as part of a cult or something and that it got her sister killed. The members of the cult were big on conspiracy theo-
ries and living off the grid and preaching the overthrow of the
government, that sort of stuff. Not Libby herself, of course, who
was only a kid at the time, though later she took on the mantle
and made a name for herself on the conservative blogosphere
and even wrote a book. Essie says she dropped out of that whole
world shortly after she started college, stopped blogging, disappeared from social media. Most people thought she just grew up,
decided to focus on school, but that wasn't how Essie saw it. She
thought Libby had broken free.

"Is that why you like her?" I asked then.

"No, but it's why I trust her" was Essie's short reply.

When we do meet, Liberty Bell is the opposite of what I'd
expected, which is to say that I don't immediately hate her the
way I thought I would. By this time, I've read all about the mas-
sacre at Black Rock. One of the pictures on the Wikipedia page
is of a girl being carried away from the visitor center, where the
militants had holed up for the better part of that winter. She
reaches her arms over the shoulder of an FBI agent in full tac-
tical gear, face tear-stained, teeth bared like a wild animal. It
must've been taken just after Liberty's sister, Justice, died. She's
not named in the caption to the photo, but it's those same eyes
that greet me when I walk into the studio. She has that vaguely
feral look of a person who always knows where the nearest exit
is, who will never be entirely at ease.

She walks across the room to greet me and extends her hand.
"Mr. Richards, so nice to finally meet you. Essie has told me
you'll be attending Columbia in the fall. Congratulations."

"Thank you," I answer. "Call me Roarke, please. Mr. Richards is my dad."

She smiles, and in this expression there is no trace of the polished persona she projects for the cameras. Instead she is genuine and kind and I don't flinch when she places a hand on my arm and leads me over to the set. She introduces me to a short woman who's setting up the cameras whose name, I'm told, is Margot. Margot has close-cropped purple hair and wears heavy boots, men's cargo pants, and a T-shirt that reads *Nevertheless, She Persisted*. I notice a delicate silver ring in her left nostril. She nods at me but doesn't stop what she's doing.

"This is where you and Essie will sit, and I'll be here." Liberty Bell indicates a modern-looking couch and, across from it, a sleek matching armchair of the same red leather. "I think it's best if you're there, to Essie's right, just as you'll be when you're at the altar. Does that sound okay with you?" She actually stops then and looks at me for an answer instead of breezing on. I manage a "Fine" and then she's leading me past the set and through a door to a room labeled *Hair and Makeup*.

Up until this point, I've been spared having my appearance fussed over—probably because the show couldn't afford to have the footage look too staged. But I guess these lights will be brighter. They need to make sure I don't look washed-out. Anyway, since this is my official debut, I understand that they want to take extra care to make sure I look presentable.

Essie is already sitting with her hair in curlers while a pale and emaciated-looking woman brushes a cream-colored powder over her face and neck. Libby leaves me and I'm guided to a chair of my own. I sit facing a wide mirror mounted to the wall and submit to tugs and prodding as a gorgeous dark-skinned woman with no hair at all begins to make me into a more acceptable version of myself. I'm actually surprised by how quickly I'm transformed as her fingers shape and smooth my hair, then brush foundation over my cheeks. It's not that I look any different, not really, but somehow the makeup blots out more than just my imperfections. It makes me feel like I'm covered in armor and impenetrable and I begin to see the appeal.

Before I know it, I'm sitting on the red sofa next to Essie. Her brown hair falls in loose curls that just brush her shoulders. Her lips and cheeks have been painted with the faintest hint of matching pink. Her freckles have been banished for the occasion. She wears a sleeveless dress made of some slippery fabric, silk or satin or whatever. It's a pale blue not unlike the color of her eyes, with narrow pleats that fall straight from the high-collared neck down to the narrow waist. The dress manages to look at once old-fashioned and fresh. Her round pearl earrings match the button just below her collar and as I take in this small detail, I realize for the first time just how beautiful she is. It feels almost like a betrayal, how I never noticed this until now.

———

We've already gone over the questions like a million times. I told Delaney not to let me know how much money we're getting paid for this series of interviews because I was afraid it would make me nervous, but now, all of a sudden, I wish I had asked. Essie signed off on it, though, so it must be something obscene, the sort of money that, before last week, I didn't believe was real. As the lights grow hotter, it occurs to me that there's a very good chance that I might be sick.

"Breathe," Libby instructs me and leans forward in her chair. "You can do this."

She says it sincerely and I'm overwhelmed by the ridiculousness of the entire situation, that a girl who saw her sister murdered is somehow comforting me. It's Libby's eyes that bring me back into myself and I do breathe then, a big breath in and out again, and the flushed dizzy feeling dissipates and I tell her that I'm ready whenever she is.

Libby sits back in her chair and crosses her ankles and adjusts her skirt. Then she says, "I'm here again with Esther Anne Hicks, younger daughter of Pastor Jethro Hicks and his wife, Celia, and a star of their family's hit show, Six for Hicks. When last we sat down, Esther hinted at some very big life changes. Essie, thank you so much for joining us again."

I know that the shot is framed to be just the two of them, so I sit frozen with my hands flat on my thighs, careful to keep my elbows folded close in to my sides, away from Essie and safely out of view.

"Thank you for having me," Essie says.

"Now, I think we all know that when television personalities such as yourself come to interviews like this one, you have a certain product to promote. So I honestly never expected that you were serious when we spoke last and you said that you thought you were in love. I thought that someone must have put you up to it, that it was some sort of publicity stunt. But it seems I owe you an apology. For the man in question is in fact real and he's as adorable as he can be. What's more, he's here with us tonight."

As the camera backs away to include me in the shot, I force my face into the expression we agreed was my best chance at looking both irresistible and entirely wholesome at the same time.

"Essie, would you like to introduce us to your boyfriend?"

Essie giggles, again just as we rehearsed, and Libby asks, "Is something wrong?"

"No, of course not, it's just that it still sounds strange when you say it out loud."

" 'Boyfriend'?" Libby asks, and Essie blushes. "Well, even so, now's no time to be shy, not with the poor young man sitting right there beside you."

Essie turns to me and takes my hand and then says to Libby, "You're right. I'm so sorry. Libby, this is Roarke Richards. I'm so incredibly blessed to have him here with me tonight and to be able to tell you that he's not only my boyfriend, he's my fiancé. Just last night he proposed and I said yes!"

She holds up her left hand and turns it this way and that so Libby can appreciate the ring. We'd discussed making the announcement later in the interview, but Libby suggested dropping the bombshell right out of the gate. That way, once I did speak, people would be hanging on my every word.

Now Libby is turning to me, saying, "Well, it seems that congratulations are in order, Roarke. Is it all right if I call you Roarke? Do you think you can tell us how you feel?"

I look from Liberty Bell to Essie where she sits beside me, hands now folded calmly in her lap, and I'm surprised to find that I'm not lying as I deliver my line: "I feel like the luckiest person in the entire world."

Liberty

The boy is doing well. Better than I could have hoped. He is good-looking, which helps. Easy on the eyes, Mama would say, and she would be right. When I think of teenagers, I picture baggy jeans, greasy hair, and bad skin, but the young man Esther Hicks produces to play her one true love has none of these. For that I breathe a sigh of relief. Farai can work miracles with her paints and her brushes, but even she can't turn a pimple pincher into a Hemsworth brother, and a Hemsworth is exactly what we need if we're going to sell this.

Luckily, Roarke needed very little touching up. His eyes are dark and smoldering, a nice contrast to the Hicks brood's obvious Aryan tendencies. They make you wonder if Essie has left the fold in search of a bad boy, if Roarke might be her own private rebellion. But the bad-boy image stops there, with his eyes. The rest of his face is safer. Strong jaw, good cheekbones, the kind of chiseled looks that even Farai cannot conjure from nothing, but in this context, with his pressed trousers and brand-new Oxford shirt, they are bland, unthreatening. He is the sort of boy any mother would be happy to have her daughter bring home. Esther could not have planned this better if she tried.

I say this because I do not for one minute believe that these two children are in love. Which is fine with me. It's more interesting, really.

Essie called midweek to see what progress I had made in finding Elizabeth. I told her that I had tracked down Carter, that I had spoken with Lissa on his phone.

"I asked her why she cut off contact and she said that nothing had happened, that she just wants to be left alone," I reported.

"But she seemed okay?" Essie asked hopefully.

"She seemed fine," I assured her. "I think Carter is a good friend. He was looking out for her. I'll bet she has real good people in her life. Maybe she just wanted to be out of the spotlight. You and I both know how suffocating it can feel. She probably wanted to leave that, not you, behind."

"You'll keep trying, won't you?" she pleaded.

"Of course, if that's what you want," I said.

"Yes. Thank you. Delaney will be finalizing the schedule and payments for the interviews I promised in the next couple of days. Can you make sure Lissa knows where I'll be?"

"Carter will probably send the information along to her if I ask. I'll also do some more digging around on campus. Maybe we'll run into each other and she'll have a change of heart and want to talk."

"All right," Essie said then. "I guess I'll see you soon."

Something in the tone of her voice reminded me of what I'd said to Elizabeth, about Essie maybe being the one who is in trouble despite her claims that she is the one who is in control, so I said, "Or you can call, anytime, whenever you need to talk, off the record or on. I hope you know that I'm here if you need me."

"I do. I just haven't decided yet what it is I need."

"But you'll let me know?"

"I will. I just need time. And I need to talk to Lissa before I do something that can't be undone."

There is no hint of the Essie who steals phones to call reporters at one in the morning, who makes cryptic statements and then hangs up, in the girl sitting across from me now. The girl sitting on the red couch next to her newly proclaimed fiancé is wholly two-dimensional; she is a projection only, like light cast on the surface of a still pond or the first hint of dawn in winter as it breaks behind the barn. She smiles when it is expected. She says all the right things. She is the exact combination of humble and sarcastic that gives the impression that she might actually be real. But she isn't. She's a fabrication. A meticulously constructed and lifelike illusion, but an illusion all the same.

Both Essie and Roarke answer their questions seamlessly. How they met, when they first noticed each other staring across a crowded high school hall. It's not a particularly interesting story, but they make it compelling with the looks that they share, the shy little smiles, the fingers that reach out for each other as if they can't help themselves. We pause at the appointed times so that some shots of the two of them together can be cut in before the interview airs later tonight. When we're done, they both look exhausted, Roarke especially. Or maybe it is just that the room seems dark now that the brighter lights have been turned off. There are shadows in his face that I hadn't noticed before that make him look older than just eighteen. Still attractive, but also weathered. There is a story inside him as well, I sense, and I wonder if I will ever get to hear it.

"That was great," I tell him, and I mean it. "You're a natural in front of the camera."

"Yes, well, I've had some practice this week," he says, and he and Essie share a laugh that isn't forced at all.

They really seem to like each other, I'll give them that. But love is an entirely different matter. Love takes time. It takes energy. And when exactly are these two supposed to have put in that sort of legwork, I would like to know? I've seen the clips that the Hickses' production team sent over and they are charming, but there's no real substance, no uncertainty, no fighting, no moments when you can see that it would be easier for them to walk away but then they don't. They choose the harder path. And they choose to walk that path together.

Still, they are fond of each other and maybe that's enough. Maybe that is the sort of affection that should serve as the basis of a lifetime commitment. Maybe everyone else has been doing it wrong, expecting too much only to be disappointed. I certainly shouldn't be giving advice, but if I were asked, I guess I would say that the key to any relationship is a shared vision for where you both want to be. No frills. No fuss. Just a road map for you both to follow so no one gets lost along the way.

———

That first day, when Mike so casually walked into my room and then walked out again, the furthest thing from my mind was that I could ever love him. I already knew what he thought of me. I had heard it in his voice. They were words I had heard before. Whack job. Loony. Conspiracy nut. Crazy cultist. I had been called all of these things and some of the harsher four-letter words besides. If you ignored the profanity, the rest of the name-calling was well deserved, though at the time I would have defended my beliefs as fiercely as a mountain lion protecting its kill. I would have gone for blood. This was easier to do from the privacy of my dorm room, of course, where I could read only those comments on my blog posts that I wanted to and ignore all the rest. In person, it was more difficult. In person, I sometimes heard my own words as I was speaking them and realized how cruel they were, how hurtful, because there was no way to avoid the pain visible on the other person's face.

So I expected Mike to keep his distance. After all, despite my own tendencies to always seek out a fight, in my experience, most other people weren't so inclined. They just wanted to go about their business quietly, sleep through class, hang out with their friends, and drink too much on the weekends. And Mike did his share of all that, I know, but he also started to read my blog and comment on it. He was writing the sort of comments that I used to just skip over, but now that they were attached to an actual person who had stood in my actual bedroom, I found them difficult to ignore.

He clearly didn't agree with anything I wrote, but he was funny about it. When he called me narrow-minded and bigoted, he did it in a way that made me laugh. He created a Twitter account just so he could troll me, but instead of being angry, I found myself thinking about ways to bait him, to draw him out. He would never let comments about gays being responsible for 9/11 go unanswered, for example, or those blaming the Jews for killing Jesus. But he had a way of deflecting rather than resorting to name-calling that allowed us to have a conversation even though we were as close to polar opposites as two people can be. I had never really spoken about such things directly with an unbeliever, not without eventually being told that Hell was preferable to having to spend an eternity in Heaven with the likes of me.

It was months before I saw Mike again in person. I was carrying my tray into the dining hall when I heard my name called out above the din.

"Liberty Bell, in the flesh!" He was practically yelling. My cheeks burned and I began to move away, but then Mike was sliding over, making room, and gesturing for me to join him.

I stayed long after I had finished eating and Mike did too. His friends were engaged in some good-natured sparring about Second Amendment rights and I watched in bewilderment as they volleyed back and forth without the exchange devolving into a shouting match. What's more, they actually listened to what the other person had to say. When the two girls across from us, whose names I had already forgotten, stood to leave, they kissed each other on the lips before walking out separate doors. Instinctively my body stiffened, but I didn't look away.

Beneath the table Mike pressed his knee against mine and whispered, "It's shocking, I know. They look like actual human beings, but they're lesbians in disguise."

He was laughing at me and this time, in person, I did get angry.

"Stop looking at me like that!" I yelled.

"Like what?"

"Like you think you know me. You don't know anything about me, anything at all."

I was running then, weaving past the other students trickling out of the dining hall. My sandals slapped the damp flagstones and I headed for an arch at the other end of the courtyard, simultaneously wanting to hide and at the same time hoping that Mike was following. I had not quite reached the arch when he caught up with me, grabbing my hand and spinning me around. His face fell as he took in my tears.

"Libby, I'm sorry. I thought that was what we did: poke fun. You've never gotten upset before."

"It feels different in person, that's all."

I heard him sigh. "Of course it does. That's always been my point."

And I knew that Mike wasn't just talking about the two of us or even about his lesbian friends, who are now married and have a baby. He was talking about all of it, about everything I'd ever said, every person in every group I'd ever targeted and tried to hurt in the name of that same God who said "Do not repay evil for evil or reviling for reviling, but on the contrary, bless, for to this you were called, that you may obtain a blessing."

Mike didn't kiss me then. That would have been too easy and my transformation was anything but that.

Instead I said, "I have to go."

My skin felt hot and I was dizzy as I stumbled back to my dorm. There was a buzzing in my ears that I knew was Mama's voice. Before then it had always been so clear, but at that moment I couldn't make out a single word she was saying. Mike followed a few steps behind me until I barged through the door to my building. I could feel him even without looking back, but he didn't come any closer. He had just followed me to make sure I was safe.

I took down my blog later that week, deleted everything, and canceled my Twitter account. I barely went to class. It was a miracle that I didn't flunk out of school entirely, but I rallied toward the end of the semester and managed to pull through finals, though at the time it didn't feel like much of a success. The seasons had changed again by the time I caught sight of Mike walking across the quad; summer had come and gone. I had been home as well, a painful few months during which I began to see my parents, our family, and our church as Mike might see them, as anyone who was not us would see them. I still loved my parents, very much, but I was also deeply ashamed. I began to wonder what would have happened if I had seen it earlier. I began to wonder if Justice would still be alive. I decided that I would not go home again.

———

Roarke and Essie tell me they'll see me in Havana and then Margot and I drive home. I don't say much during the ride and eventually Margot falls asleep, slumped against her door. I keep my eyes on the ribbons of white reflective paint on the highway and let each slide into the edges of my vision, blur, and disappear into the night. Margot comes up when we get back to my apartment and we eat the dinner that Mike cooked and watch the interview when it comes on. The editing team has done a good job. I open my laptop and watch the internet explode. Within an hour the story is trending on social media under the hashtag #Essie&Roarke4Ever. By the time I go to bed, Google suggests *Essie and Roarke Wedding* when I begin to type in her name.

———

The next day I track down Carter as promised. He does not look happy to see me, but I tell him that Essie has asked me to give Lissa the list of interview times and locations so that she can come and talk with Essie in private if she changes her mind.

"No one else from the family or staff will be there. It's my people only. Essie gets dropped off. That was part of the deal."

Carter nods. "I'll let her know. But tell Essie not to get her hopes up."

"Why shouldn't she? You don't think her own sister wants to talk to her?"

"I'm not saying anything. This is totally off the record. But that entire family is a special kind of fucked-up."

"All except for Lissa, you mean."

Carter blows his breath out of his mouth in a quick puff of air and says, "Lissa's probably the most fucked-up of them all. I love her, but that girl has problems. How could she not? But you didn't hear that from me."

"Well, tell her it's important. Essie seems to think Lissa can help her make some sort of decision."

"What decision?"

"No idea. But she needs to make it before the wedding, or so

I gather. Remind her that Essie was just a kid when Elizabeth left home. She's still a kid as far as I'm concerned. Whatever happened inside that house, none of it is Essie's fault."

"Okay, I'll tell her."

"And if she changes her mind about me, I'll be in the library every day this week between ten and one until I leave town on Friday. I'm meeting Essie in Havana for an interview on Saturday. Lissa is welcome to join us at that one too, but I figure one of the studios on that list would work better."

Carter nods and as he walks away, I see him take out his phone and dial.

———

On Monday and Tuesday nothing happens. I spend the hours in the library working on my laptop, churning out the print pieces to go with this last interview and then revising an article on feminism in evangelical communities that will likely never see the light of day. Tuesday afternoon Margot and I go shopping for sunscreen for the trip and then stop into the office to meet with Sid. He talks about the number of hits the video has received, the number of times my articles have been shared. He's pleased, his face plethoric, and he wheezes as he walks around the room outlining his vision for what the approach should be when we are in Cuba.

Wednesday is disappointing as well. As I'm packing up to leave the library, I think I see a girl who could be Lissa sitting across the reading room, watching me. I notice her just out of the corner of my eye, but when I turn, there's no one there.

I almost skip the library on Thursday. Sid has given me another, unrelated interview, and though it won't take long, I still need to pack. But when I walk into the reading room, Elizabeth is sitting at my usual table, waiting. I slow down for the staff to check my photo ID and then cross to where she's sitting. She looks nothing like the girl who was pasted into her family's holiday card only a few months ago, though it is hard to put a finger on exactly what has changed. Her hair is different: shorter, darker, with a streak of crimson on each side that neatly frames her face. But it's not just the hair—even her face itself is changed somehow, though each individual feature is just the same. I wonder if this is what she always looked like when the cameras were off, like someone I would have wanted as a friend.

She greets me with an ironic smile but does not stand. Her chair is pulled out from the table and her legs are crossed. She is slumped back to give the impression that she is at ease, but I can see even as I am walking toward her that every muscle is wound tight.

"You found me," I say as I sit.

"More like you found me," she counters.

"I hope Carter passed along the other piece of my message as well."

"I have the interview times, if that's what you mean."

"It is. Essie is really hoping that you'll come."

Elizabeth looks down and changes the subject. "This boy that she's marrying, do you think he's good for her?"

"If you're asking whether I think he's a good person, then the answer is yes, though I only met him once. But he was kind to her, respectful. She says she's happy that this wedding is happening and she said it without any cameras rolling, so I have no reason not to believe her. But if you're asking if I think she loves him, if he loves her, then no. I don't. Not even a little."

"So my parents have staged it, then," Lissa says. "Typical."

"Maybe. Or maybe it's Essie who's pulling the strings."

Elizabeth shakes her head. "You clearly have no idea how things work in our family."

"No, I don't. But Essie does. She seems to think she's running this show, and from what I've seen, she's a smart kid. Who's to say she hasn't figured out how to get her way despite everything?"

"Mother would never allow it."

"Maybe your mother doesn't know."

Elizabeth considers this for a moment and pulls her chair forward slightly. When she speaks, her voice is bitter. "Nothing in that house happens without her knowing."

"Like what? What happened? What did your mother know?"

Elizabeth tilts her head to the side and practically sneers, "You think this is when I open up to you, bare my soul, tell you all my secrets? Believe me, I wouldn't even if I could. You are exactly like them, a hypocrite. I don't trust you, no matter what my sister says."

"I'm not asking you to trust me. If you don't want to talk with me, that's fine. But at least talk with Essie. She trusts me, for some reason of her own that I don't think I'll ever really understand. I want to make good on that trust. The only thing she has asked of me is to find you and to bring her sister back to her."

Elizabeth shakes her head. "The sister Essie thinks she remembers, that girl doesn't exist. Maybe she never did."

"I don't think that's true," I say, leaning partway across the table. "I'm sitting right across from her."

"It only looks that way because you haven't been paying attention. Elizabeth Hicks was a fictional character I walked away from a long time ago."

"We have something in common, then, whether you want to admit it or not."

"Do we now?"

"You may not believe me, but I'm not the person you think I am. I know what people think when they hear my name. I even thought about changing it. But that wouldn't have solved the problem. Just because I want to leave the old Liberty Bell behind doesn't mean she ceased to exist. She's still inside of me. But she's trying to be better. Every day, she's trying. I'm sure you can relate to that."

"Maybe," Lissa says grudgingly.

I watch her fidget. I can practically feel how much she wants to leave. I know that we have gotten closer, but it is still not close enough.

"As much as I don't like to think about the person I used to be, the place I've come from, there isn't anything I wouldn't do to be able to talk to my sister again."

This is a desperate move and I know that Elizabeth sees it for what it is, but despite this, something inside her loosens and she says, "Okay. Tell Essie that I'll come."

She stands and picks up the woven bag hung across the back of her chair and slings it over her chest, then pulls out the piece of paper that Carter delivered to her for me. She points.

"I'll come to this one," she says and nods once as she turns to go.

On a hunch I ask, "How much did they give you? How much not to talk?"

"I really can't say."

She is looking at her shoes. They are scuffed, but they are also expensive.

"Of course you can't."

"But if I could, I would tell you that I don't exactly need to work for a living. Not unless I want to, that is."

"You do want to, though, don't you? You don't strike me as someone who would want to sit around for the rest of your life."

Elizabeth tilts her head slightly. "Actually, I've already got the perfect job lined up. I start right after graduation."

"Congratulations," I tell her. "Where will you be working?"

She smiles as if genuinely amused and answers, "Planned Parenthood."

Then she walks away.

Roarke

Around the third or fourth time the plane hits turbulence, I begin to seriously rethink my life choices. It'd seemed like a good deal, this whole thing with Essie. Crazy, of course, but once I moved past that and accepted the crazy, I knew there was really no way that I could say no. I know why I was taken in. It's not just the money itself but also everything that it represents, the opportunities and what it made me feel I was worth. Yes, I was really that shallow. But I hadn't realized that until now. Once we boarded and stowed our things, though, there was nothing to do but sit and wonder how I got here.

The plane lurches again and I think about how if I die now, my parents won't get a penny of what they were promised. I have to legally marry Essie for the deal to take effect.

"Just relax," Essie urges.

I look out the window, but we're deep within a bank of clouds and there's nothing to see. In the aisle seat beside me, Essie drops her eyes back to her book and lifts one hand to cover mine where it grips the armrest between us. She gives my hand a reassuring squeeze and then withdraws it to turn her page. I close my eyes and try to loosen the knots in my shoulders and the back of my neck.

Yesterday, while I was packing, Blake appeared suddenly in my doorway. I was halfway under my bed, reaching for my duffel bag, and when I straightened, he was standing there, watching me. Naturally I jumped.

"You're a little on edge for someone who's blissfully in love, aren't you?" he asked sarcastically.

I finished pulling the bag from underneath the bed frame and then sat on the narrow chair in front of my desk. Blake threw himself belly-down on my bed as he had so many times before.

"What gives?" he asked. "I had to find out that my best friend is engaged by watching him on TV?"

"Sorry," I muttered.

I should've had more of an explanation ready, but in truth I was hoping I could slip away without having to talk to anyone before I left. I even turned off my phone shortly after the interview, afraid that what made sense when I was sitting next to Essie would start to unravel once my friends started picking at the threads. I didn't want to have to explain something that I only half believed in myself.

"I don't understand," Blake told me. "You hate them."

"I never said that," I protested.

"You didn't have to. Why do you think I teased you about Esther coming to practice that day? I did it because I knew it would bug you."

"The actions of a true friend."

"Damn straight, I'm a true friend, which is why I'm here to tell you that you can't go through with this. I don't know what she has on you, but it can't be enough for you to throw your life away."

I started tossing clothes into my bag, not wanting to look Blake in the eye. "She doesn't have anything on me. She's not like that. Maybe her parents are, but not Essie. We understand each other. That's as good a place to start as anything. Listen, I think you should go. I really have to pack."

"So you love her? That's the story you're sticking to? Really?"

"It's complicated."

"I'm sure it is," Blake replied and stood to leave, but he stopped in the doorway and turned back and said, "There were some reporters down at the diner asking about you."

I felt my stomach drop. "What did you tell them?"

"I didn't tell them anything. But they talked to Lily and to One-Eared Pete and some of the underclassmen."

I stood facing Blake with the unmade bed between us.

"Don't ruin this for me," I said quietly with what I imagined was just a hint of menace in my voice.

"Oh, I wouldn't do that. After all, who am I to stand in the way of true love? I just hope you understand that we're not finished here. Someday you'll tell me what's really going on."

"Someday," I echoed, "I may actually figure it out enough to be able to explain."

That seemed to appease Blake and he left then. I didn't say anything to Essie about Blake's visit when we met at the airport this morning. It wasn't that I didn't want to worry her while we were away. It was more that I didn't want her to think of Blake as her problem, or any sort of problem at all. As my friend, he deserves the truth—maybe not right away, but eventually. Until then, there's no reason for Essie to be thinking about Blake at all.

So I keep my eyes closed because even if I did want to talk with Essie about what I should tell my friends, the plane is not the place to do it. I feel like I have to shout to be heard over the engines and this isn't the sort of conversation either of us would want witnesses to. There are about fifty others on board. We flew commercial to Miami and then changed planes to this chartered jet that will take us on to Havana. There are real flights now that the embargo has been lifted, but not that many and it can be hard to get enough seats together. At least that's what Essie said.

Some of the people are from home, like the young woman named Gretchen who's sitting across the aisle from us. She works for Essie's mom, something to do with production of the show, but it's clear that she has also been assigned to be our baby-sitter. There are a handful of others from New Light, but no one I know particularly well. Everyone else on the plane converged in Miami from their own hometowns, with some coming from as far away as the Pacific Northwest. This trip is an annual event, ever since the border opened, and I'm one of only a few who are going for the first time.

Essie said her father saw the opportunity even before the embargo was lifted, making sure to get in before any of the other evangelicals managed a foothold. Back then you could travel for "cultural exchanges" and Jethro Hicks himself went on many of the earlier, smaller trips. When trade did resume, tourism spiked and the average Cuban household began to have some surplus cash lying around. Much of it went to things like rice and toilet paper, but some of it went to Essie's dad, or to his church at least. Even some of the Catholics converted. Anything American had a certain shine to it and they were eager to join the flock.

Pastor Hicks would say that he was reaching out to those who were most like Jesus. They were poor. They were humble. They had long turned the other cheek under the reign of the Castro brothers, or something of the sort. But Essie said he made quite a bundle out of the licensing agreements to broadcast his sermons on one of the newly established cable stations. He made even more for his role as administrator and fund-raiser for the boarding school we were going to visit on this trip.

"That doesn't make you mad?" I asked Essie as we sat in the

airport in Miami a little away from the others and waited for our next flight.

She shrugged. "It used to, when I first realized, but then I realized something else."

"What?"

"There's no one who is not, deep down, truly selfish. Naomi taught me that, and she's right. Of course, when she said it, she meant Lissa. I went through a phase after Lissa left when I refused to sit up straight in church and it was ruining all the shots. I wouldn't listen to Mother, so she sent Naomi, who said I had to let Lissa go. That part I ignored, of course, but over the years I've found that the general rule 'Everyone is selfish' applies in other situations as well. I'm not saying there aren't good people in this world and I'm not saying there aren't people who run charities who are less selfish than Daddy. But everyone, to some degree or another, if they're being really honest with themselves, is selfish way down deep."

"And that made you feel better?" I asked, surprised.

"Sure," she answered. "It meant that even if Daddy does what he does for all the wrong reasons, that doesn't detract from the results. The school wouldn't exist without Daddy, without his name and his image generating interest from donors. They write checks for lots of different reasons. Maybe they're generous because they're trying to make up for being cruel to someone earlier in the day or even years ago, or maybe they want to be able to tell their friends how pious they are. Maybe they're even trying to buy their way into Heaven. It doesn't matter. The children at the New Light School have a roof over their heads because my father makes people afraid of the very worst versions of themselves, of the secrets they keep wrapped up inside."

"I thought he always said he wanted to help people embody the best version of themselves." I was pretty sure something of that sort was printed on the brochures.

"Isn't it basically the same thing?"

Essie looked pleased as she said this and not at all bitter, which I found strange. That the world has a tendency to reward the wicked is something I've always accepted, but it doesn't make me happy. I didn't know how to say all of this to Essie, though, so instead I said, "I'm not sure."

"Well, there's no reason to let it get you down. You're here, in this place, because my parents are the sort of people that they are. If they aren't good people, strictly speaking, does that mean you can't enjoy this trip, learn something from it, maybe even make the world a little bit nicer, a little bit better along the way?"

I saw then that this was a conversation Essie had had before, with herself, probably many times over the years. Maybe it was her way of staying sane.

"Sure," I told her. "I guess that makes sense. It's a nice way to look at it, in any case. So is that how you've managed to stop being angry, by rationalizing everything they do?"

"Don't get mad, get even," Essie said then, looking out the window and over the tangle of taxiing planes on the hot pavement below. There was a pause and then she giggled, maybe to indicate that she was joking before she went on, "Isn't that how the saying goes?"

"That's the saying," I agreed, then asked, "Just how are you planning on getting even?"

And Essie turned her face away from the window to look at me and smiled sweetly, transparently. "I already did. I decided to marry you."

―――――

Not long after this we boarded the chartered jet, and though Gretchen tried to steer Essie into the seat beside her, Essie dropped something—on purpose, I think—and Gretchen had to step out of the way to let her pick it up, opening a path for Essie to move into the aisle next to me.

"It won't be much longer," Essie reassures me as we hit another patch of bumpy air. She speaks without looking up from her book. "We'll be descending soon."

She turns a page and I wonder for a moment if she's really reading or if it's just another act, if this too is for show since Essie knows that Gretchen will be reporting back on her every action, her every word. I shake my head and turn again toward the gray light coming through the window, feeling exhausted by the impossible task of deciphering Essie's motives. No matter how often she claims that her life is an open book, the only thing that's really clear to me is that it's anything but that.

We land without fuss and walk down the stairs that lead off the plane and onto the tarmac, where we're ushered through to customs. The official there stamps my stiff new passport, expedited for the bargain price of I don't know how much, and gives me half a nod. On the other side of this desk there's a driver holding a sign that says New Light and we gather in an awkward clump. I'm already sweating. From the small, open lobby of the airport, we walk out again into the bright light of the sun high overhead, lined up like obedient schoolchildren, past a throng of street vendors selling cold sodas and woven hats, and onto an air-conditioned bus. The cool air hits my face almost as if someone has splashed me with water. I throw my backpack onto one of the overhead racks while the driver loads the larger bags into the compartments underneath the bus.

This time, when we sit, Gretchen is successful in forcing Essie to a seat up near the front. I claim a spot a few rows behind, next to a boy not much older than me who introduces himself as Brady. He's a sophomore at Bob Jones University in South Carolina and is on spring break, but he has arranged to get some sort of class credit for this trip. He's never met any of the Hicks family except for Essie and he eagerly tells me how he talked to her a few times during the trip last year. He continues on with his biography, dropping hints about the other mission trips he's been on, and it takes me some time to work out that he's doing this because he wants me to like him, to approve. He's treating me like some kind of royalty and it finally sinks in that I am for all intents and purposes now almost a Hicks myself.

Brady keeps spouting gibberish for pretty much the entire ride to the hotel, but as soon as it becomes clear that he isn't paying any attention to whether or not I'm listening, I tune him out and watch a pair of motorcycles weaving through the traffic, through the mix of Studebakers and old Chevrolets. Then the bus pulls slowly up a long drive lined with towering palm trees and past the sign for the Hotel Nacional de Cuba, toward the twin turrets ahead. Winston Churchill stayed here, Essie told me, and Hemingway spent time drinking at the bar. I try to imagine what it looked like then, back in the 1940s. Probably not much different than it does right now. The lobby is cool in comparison to the heat that was bouncing off the pavement and I run my eyes over the warm tiled floor and the dark beams in the high ceiling. This seems a bit upscale for a mission trip, but I'm no longer surprised. I'm still looking up at an elaborate chandelier when Essie takes my hand.

"I told Gretchen to bring our keys outside when they finish checking in."

We leave our bags with a bellhop and Essie leads me through to the rear of the hotel and out onto a veranda that runs the length of the building. There's a fountain and some gardens and, beyond that and far below, I glimpse the sea. I stop to take in the wide expanse of blue, but Essie pulls impatiently on my hand.

"There's someone I want you to meet," she says.

We wend our way past groups of cushioned chairs that are arranged around low round tables, all looking out over the grounds. A peacock wanders by, dragging his long tail feathers behind him. He perches briefly on the fountain's edge and then awkwardly hops down and continues along his way.

"Esther Anne, as I live and breathe!" a voice booms out and Essie releases my hand and breaks into a run.

A dark-skinned gentleman with wild-looking gray hair throws his arms around Essie and then looks me over carefully. He stands beside a small bar that's the same dark wood as the beams in the lobby.

"So, this is the boy?" he says.

Essie nods and extends her hand to wave us through introductions. "Hector, this is Roarke; Roarke, Hector." Then she explains, "Hector has been working here for as long as my family has been coming. His granddaughter Beatrice will be starting at Fordham in the fall. Maybe we can have her over for dinner sometime after we're settled."

Hector smiles at this and then tells me, "When my son wanted to take his family over to the States because they needed to see medical specialists for their youngest, Esther's parents helped with the paperwork and a recommendation for a job."

There's something about Essie's smile that makes me wonder if she wasn't the one behind this act of generosity, if maybe she hasn't been pulling the strings for longer than I suspected, but there's no way to ask her. And anyway, she would tell me that it doesn't matter, that the result is the only thing that counts, not whatever happened behind the scenes.

Hector retreats behind the bar and begins to crush mint for

two mojitos—minus the rum, of course. He catches Essie up on his son's family and their five children. Juanita, the baby, has just undergone another heart surgery at Boston Children's Hospital and is expected to do well. When a group gathers around the bar, Essie kisses Hector on the cheek and we leave him to the other guests. We walk, glasses in hand, until we can see down the rock face at the back of the property to the esplanade that runs along the shore. Musicians sit along the rock wall with their backs to the ocean, their horns to their lips, but the wind carries the sound away.

"That's the Malecón," Essie says. "It was originally built to serve as a protective barrier for the city, but now people mostly use it to feel close to the sea."

We watch a fisherman cast his line, young people walking hand in hand. Behind them the blue of the ocean stretches out to the horizon.

"I've never seen anything like it," I say. "It's beautiful."

"Oh, it's spectacular all right. But I think I prefer the sort of things no one else realizes are beautiful, or that they don't appreciate for what they really are, the things other people walk right by."

"Like what?" I ask.

"Like you," she tells me, and I worry for a moment that she wants to kiss me even though there are no cameras, but then she looks away.

———

We drive to the school the following morning and at first the bus is mired in traffic, but as we move past the outskirts of the city, the brightly colored buildings give way to a lush green that stretches as far as I can see. Dogs nap in the warm strip of dirt that lines the highway. Children kick a soccer ball in a yard, using a laundry line as a goal. Beside me, Essie reads, but I keep my eyes on the landscape. I've never seen colors so vibrant and I realize how much of my life up until this point has been painted in various shades of brown or gray: the dry close-cropped grass in the small square yards of our neighborhood, the endless ribbons of cement, even the muted fields of corn or soy. None of it has looked like this.

After about an hour, we pull through a high iron gate into a courtyard in front of the school. Immediately, small faces pop up in the windows of the nearest classroom building, arms waving back and forth in greeting. The children smile broadly as they stream out of the buildings. Essie is quickly drawn away by two young girls in knee socks, and not long after she disappears into the crowd of people, a boy of perhaps eight or nine reaches out to take my hand. Once everyone is assembled, the principal welcomes us and then the first- and second-grade students step to the front to sing a song.

We spend the rest of the day building squat cinder-block enclosures behind the dormitories. When they're finished, they will hold low-odor composting toilets that have been donated by the manufacturer—or at least that's what we're told. Later, we eat lunch on the ground with a group of students and they teach us a song about a man who lived with seven cats. After that, we work on the outhouses some more until it's time to drive back to the hotel. There's a buffet of different Cuban dishes that seems to stretch on for miles, but I'm so tired that I barely taste my food and the moment dinner has ended I go to my room and fall asleep.

———

The next morning I knock on Essie's door just before we're supposed to meet for breakfast.

Her voice comes from behind the heavy door. "Just a minute!"

A toilet flushes. She's wiping her face with a washcloth when she lets me in. She's still in her pajamas and her hair's a mess.

"This is what I have to look forward to, huh?" I tease.

Her face goes pale and at first I'm afraid that I've broken some girl rule by joking about her appearance, but then she runs back into the bathroom and throws up. I hear the toilet flush again.

"Laugh all you like, but you might be next," she says with her back to me while standing at the sink. She reaches for her toothbrush and goes on, "I must have eaten a bad mussel or something. How do you feel?"

"Fine," I tell her. "Do you want me to tell Gretchen you're too sick to come today?"

Essie finishes up in the bathroom and shakes her head. "No. I'll probably be fine once I get something in my stomach. I feel better already. See?"

She throws her hands up and wiggles her fingers as if she has just finished a dance routine.

"Not quite camera ready," I say skeptically. "Why don't I give you a minute to get dressed? And maybe brush your teeth again."

I step back into the hall and wait while she pulls on shorts and a T-shirt and then we go downstairs. After breakfast, we spend the day back at the school. Brady and I finish the toilet enclosure we started yesterday and then wander back to the central yard to ask what we should do next. We find Essie and a group of the older schoolchildren, paintbrushes in hand. Where there had been a blank white wall that morning there is now an intricate mural, bold bright colors wrapping around one another and spiraling outward from a central image of a white star against a background of red that echoes the one found on the country's flag.

"That's amazing," I say.

Essie shakes her head and waves her brush in the direction of the two oldest students. "Elena and Fernando are amazing. I'm just doing as I'm told."

"There's a first time for everything," I tell her and laugh.

Essie smiles back at me, but then her face goes ashen and I think for a moment that she's going to faint. It lasts only a few seconds, but it's long enough and something clicks that I should've seen before.

"I think I need some shade," Essie says, then sets down her paintbrush and wipes her hands across the bottom of her shirt.

I follow her to a patch of grass underneath a tree. She doesn't look sick now, only pale and tired, and I try to remember clearly what she had to eat the night before.

We sit for a while before I work up the courage to say, "You didn't eat the mussels. I didn't realize that until just now."

Essie shrugs. "It must have been something else, then. What does it matter?"

I pull up a blade of grass and twirl it between my fingers. I can feel her eyes on me, but I can't bring myself to meet them. I don't want to let her see how angry I am at being treated like a fool.

"You're pregnant," I say then, and I don't even need to look at Essie to know it's true.

Esther

My heart is pounding even before Roarke manages to say the words.

I ask, "Does it matter?"

It is a stupid thing to say, but I am trying to buy time, to think of some reasonable explanation for why I didn't tell Roarke before. Now that he is sitting next to me and we have come to this point, I realize that there is no excuse that will make what I did okay.

"Does it matter that you're pregnant?" Roarke says in disbelief. "No. Not to me. That's what I would have said two weeks ago. I barely knew you. So how could it have possibly meant anything to me if I found out then? You know what? I take that back. It would have mattered even then, because two weeks ago I would have probably felt more than a twinge of satisfaction that the prissy little preacher's daughter had gone and got herself knocked up. Cosmic karma, that's what I would have called it."

"That's not what happened," I say, my voice trembling. "I didn't go and get myself knocked up."

"Whatever happened, it amounts to pretty much the same thing, doesn't it?" He stands up and then turns back and leans over me before going on, "It all makes sense now. I feel so stupid. I should have seen it before. I'm the perfect cover-up. You needed a husband. My parents need the money. It's a shame that

I'm not straight. Then you could have screwed me too and convinced me it was mine."

I rise to face him then, scrambling to my feet quickly, and he has to jump back to avoid having my head knock into his nose.

I say, "I wouldn't have had sex with you and tried to pass this baby off as yours, even if you were straight. I wouldn't do that."

"Forgive me," he tells me, bowing slightly. "I guess I'm just a little behind on what you would and wouldn't do. So you were just going to blackmail me, then? I keep your secret or else you tell the whole country that I'm gay?"

"No," I breathe. My voice is barely a whisper. "No, of course not."

"You know, you actually had me fooled. Your whole 'I'm different from my parents' routine was convincing. But you're not any different. You are all exactly the same."

"I'm not," I manage, but I can hear the desperation in my voice.

I stumble backward until I bump into the trunk of the tree that we are standing under. Its bark is smooth, but there are deep cuts where someone has carved his or her initials. I run my fingers along this groove to anchor myself, to stop this feeling of falling, but it is no good and I feel like I might throw up again.

Roarke raises a finger and points it at me. His words, when they come, are slow and accusing. "You are, all of you, manipulative, self-centered, egomaniacal phonies. You use people up and you toss them aside. There is no amount of money that could ever convince me to marry you. Not now."

I am silent. It is over. I can hear it in his voice and I know that there is nothing I can say to change his mind. What's more, I do not blame him. Not even a little.

Roarke starts to walk away and I almost let him, but then I say, "They had a meeting. Did you know that? They had a meeting to decide what they should do. Mother didn't talk to Daddy, not the way that normal parents do. She talked to Candy and to Gretchen. I was a public relations nightmare. I wasn't her daughter. I wasn't even a person. I was a problem to be solved."

"You think that makes it acceptable, what you tried to do to me?"

"I didn't say that."

"What you did to me wasn't any different, except that instead of being the problem, I was the solution, wasn't I? I was your way out, your path to legitimacy, your Hail Mary. I was the only way that no one was going to call you a whore."

I feel the tears start to gather and I tell him, "Now you're just being mean."

"Maybe I am mean. After all, you don't really know me. Maybe mean is who I really am."

"I don't believe that," I say, and now the tears begin to fall. I bite my lip to stop them while my throat makes an ugly snuffling sound. In the branches above my head, a bird jumps from branch to branch. "Libby will be here in a few days. What am I supposed to tell her?"

Roarke shrugs and begins to walk away and this time I let him. As he goes, he turns his head to tell me, "That's not my problem, is it? None of this is my problem. It never really was."

———

Roarke does not talk to me for the next four days. If Gretchen notices, she doesn't let on. In fact, she is probably relieved that we are not trying to make out or sneak into each other's rooms at night. During this time, we finish the construction projects at the school and move on to a local church where they have plans to raise a guesthouse for visiting clergy. I doubt very much that the lengths of wood we nail together into a frame could be considered up to code, but we do the best we can. I suspect they will take it all apart and start over as soon as we are gone, but it looks good on camera since Jesus was a carpenter. Daddy would say that segments like this lend an air of humility to the show, but he says it while wearing a three-hundred-dollar tie, so I'm not entirely sure he knows what the word *humility* really means.

Liberty Bell flies in on Friday with Margot. Roarke has not officially said that the interview is off, but probably only because he hasn't said anything at all. I ask him if he wants to come in the car with me to pick up Libby from the airport, but he pretends not to hear.

At first Gretchen objects to my being driven out to the airport alone, but when I remind her that Mother is paying her to make sure Roarke and I behave appropriately in public and in front of the other missionaries, not to babysit, she leaves the lobby and heads toward the pool. I stare blankly out the window as the car moves out of the city. I am not nervous about seeing Libby. In fact, I don't feel anything at all. I am numb. I feel almost exactly the same way I did when I first realized that I was pregnant.

It's odd, I think now, how calm I was. I should have felt some panic. I should have cried or stomped or beat my fists against my bed and buried my face in my pillow in a soundless scream. But instead I felt almost relieved, that it was decided, that now at least something would have to happen, that my life would not go on just as it always had. Roarke's not speaking to me is like that. It is not the way that I wanted things to happen, but then again, none of this is what I wanted. If he won't marry me, then I am still one step closer to all this being over, even if I don't yet know precisely how it will end.

Margot chats excitedly in the front seat from the moment she slides into the car. She knows some Spanish, which she inflicts upon our driver, who looks at me pleadingly in the rearview mirror for a while before he gives up and starts to answer Margot's questions using the smallest words he can.

Libby speaks so quietly that I almost don't hear her when she says, "She promised that she'd be there. The interview at the Hyatt. Lissa says she'll come."

Her eyes flicker toward the driver and it is clear she is concerned that he might be under orders to report anything he hears.

"I'm looking forward to the pool," she says after a pause, her voice louder than it needs to be, her smile like something drawn on her face. "And dancing. Please tell me we're going out tonight."

"You feel free," I say to her. "There's no way that Gretchen will let me go."

But Gretchen does let me go, much to my surprise, primarily because she gets to tag along and it seems that Liberty Bell has been her hero since she was a little girl, that there was a time she absolutely lived for Libby's blog. I never pegged her as quite that type. It must have been wishful thinking, but I always thought she was exaggerating her fanaticism to please Mother, that she talked about "the gays" and "the immigrants" at her first interview just so she would get the job. I guess her bigotry was real.

We claim a group of tables at a club recommended by the concierge. As soon as we arrive, a married couple in their sixties who are with our group, Lyle and Martha from Grand Rapids, immediately head toward the dance floor. Martha's hips move like a much younger woman's and it is clear that she has danced to music like this before. Probably she listened to Buena Vista Social Club with her book group while discussing *The Havana Quartet*. I laugh as Lyle struggles to keep up.

Then Libby leans forward to Roarke and tells him that he and I should be dancing. She calls me his fiancée.

"She's not my fiancée anymore," Roarke says, but it is too loud and Libby doesn't hear.

She waves him toward the dance floor and he grudgingly stands, having decided that this is easier than protesting, and leaves the table. I scurry to catch up.

"This doesn't mean I've changed my mind," he tells me as he puts his hands on my hips.

I do not answer, but I let him lead me haltingly around the floor. Occasionally we bump into other couples and Roarke looks embarrassed, but eventually we find our own rhythm. I feel his arms loosen and his waist relax as he gives himself over to the music. He spins me out, then back again and Libby gives him a thumbs-up from the table.

By the time the song has ended, I have nearly forgotten that he hates me, but then he asks, "Why are you smiling? What could you possibly have to smile about?" and I remember.

"I'm happy," I say. "This right here is my very last moment of happiness and I'm going to enjoy it. Tomorrow my world may come crashing down, but tonight, well, tonight is mine. I'm not going to let anyone take it from me."

I cannot read Roarke's expression in the dim lights, but I feel the tension return to his shoulders. He breaks away from me.

"I need some air," he says.

"I'll come with you," I offer.

"No, I'd rather be alone."

I weave my way back through the moving bodies to our table and reclaim the small stool next to Libby.

"Where's Roarke?" Margot asks.

"Outside," I answer.

"Needed to cool off?" she asks conspiratorially.

I hold a glass of ice water to my face.

"Something like that," I say.

———

Roarke does not blow my cover while we are at the club and instead spends the rest of the night getting dancing lessons from Grand Rapids Martha. I know that this does not mean that he has reconsidered. I can see plainly that he does not plan on doing any explaining. He's leaving that job to me. But I am grateful that I will at least get to do it in private and avoid a public scene.

The next day is rainy, but it is not the sort of rain we have at home. Gale-force winds blow down an electrical pole, and the shutters in the hotel library rattle with the gusts. Libby asks if we wouldn't mind rescheduling the interview for tomorrow so that it can be shot outside on the lawn. If it's still raining then, or if the garden has been completely and utterly destroyed by a hurricane, then we'll move to Plan B and shoot it inside, but she needs to scout out locations. Roarke raises his eyebrows and looks at me.

"That's fine," I tell her.

"Why don't we grab some lunch?" Libby suggests, but Roarke is already walking away.

———

The wind dies down a little after three, though it is still raining hard. From the window it looks like a solid sheet of water has enveloped the world outside. Gretchen leaves the billiards room, where we have both been reading, and tells me she's going upstairs to take a nap now that the wind has stopped howling quite so insistently and I am saved the trouble of having to slip away.

The group is supposed to meet for pre-dinner cocktails at five, so there are less than two hours before I need to be back by the time I step out onto the street. I do not bring an umbrella, since I'm certain that it would not survive the smaller gusts of wind that still persist. Instead I pull the hood of my rain jacket up and keep my head bent down and face into the breeze.

The sidewalks are empty and I break into a jog as I turn off the main streets in favor of a narrow alley. I know the way by heart. I memorized it months ago, even before there was a need. Libby's Plan B is an interview inside instead of out and this is mine. This is the plan I made before Roarke said yes, the plan I hoped I would never need, but that I had worried it would come down to all along.

Maritza lives in a second-floor apartment with her grand-mother. She graduated from the New Light School last year and is taking classes at the university. We have been friends since I was ten, the first year we ran the trips to Havana, back before Lissa left and everything changed forever. At thirteen, Maritza was partway between Lissa's age and mine. The three of us were inseparable from that point on. We wrote letters in between our visits and begged Mother to let her come stay with us during our summer holidays, a notion Mother immediately rejected. I have not seen Maritza in nearly a year, but I know that she will help me now—not just because of our friendship but because she knows the truth. Aside from Mother, she is the only one who does.

Her grandmother, who has always insisted I call her Lita, bus-tles around the narrow kitchen. She tells me I am too thin and, without asking if I am hungry, holds out a plate of plantains. I eat without complaining, but Maritza knows why I've come—I called before I left the hotel—and she hurries me outside as soon as she is able.

The rain is still coming down and we splash through puddles

hand in hand for several blocks until she guides me to a doorway and tells me I should stay there. Then she breaks away, pulling her fingers out of mine, and runs into a building across the
way. An eternity passes while I wait and the rain begins to soak
through my jacket at the seams. Soon my back is wet. A car lum-
bers by, its tires rolling through a puddle and throwing up a wall
of water that splashes over my bare legs and the hem of my skirt.
I shiver despite the heat and then Maritza emerges, the package
clutched against her chest for protection.

She does not look in my direction but instead walks back the
way we have just come. I follow half a block behind and wait to
catch up with her until we have left the neighborhood. When we
reach her street, Maritza hugs me close to her, one arm thrown
around my neck while the other guides the brown paper bag up
underneath my jacket. She presses her lips against my cheek.
A taxi honks. Startled, I turn my head and jump back from the
curb. When I look back, my friend is gone.

———

It takes the hot water some time to penetrate my chilled skin.
Maritza's gift sits in its damp brown paper bag beside the bathroom sink. I stand in the shower and try not to think. Instead I
lean forward into the spray and let the scalding jet pour over my
head. I do not hear the knocking until I twist the shower handle
and step onto the bath mat. I dry myself off quickly and squeeze
the water out of my hair and then put on a robe. Roarke is standing at my door when I pull it open.

"You don't have to do this," he says.

"And just what is it that you think I'm doing?" I ask.

"I saw you," he tells me, "outside the pharmacy."

"You have no idea what you saw."

"I can spell it out for you, if that would help, though it would be a shame if Gretchen is snooping from just inside her door."

I hiss at him to be quiet and pull him into the room.

"Why do you care? It doesn't have anything to do with you. You've made that abundantly clear."

"But it's not what you want or else you would have done it already."

I throw my hands up at my sides. "Maybe this is the first chance I had. Maybe this was my plan all along. You were just a bonus, a way to rake in some cash."

"I don't believe that."

"I don't care what you believe."

"You want this baby," Roarke insists. "Or you would have already taken the pills that girl bought for you."

He points through the bathroom door to where the bag sits unopened. I close my eyes and shake my head.

"No," I say. "I don't want this baby."

Roarke sits down on the edge of the bed and leans forward slightly.

"Well, then go ahead and take them. I'll stay with you. You shouldn't have to go through this alone."

"So you'll hold my hand if I do this but not if I decide to keep it?" I say. My voice is bitter.

"That's not fair," he says, and he is right. It is not Roarke that I am angry at.

"I know," I answer and let myself collapse onto the bed beside him.

We are silent for what feels like an eternity and then I offer, "I never wanted it. I never wanted any of this. But taking those pills won't undo what's happened. Taking those pills will just be another thing that I will always be sad about."

"But if you keep it, if you keep the baby . . ." He stops as if piecing something together. "That's why you need the money. It's not just about a cover-up. You need to get away."

I do not even realize that I've reached for Roarke's hand until I feel my fingernails pressing into his skin.

"This child can't grow up in that house," I say desperately. "I have to keep it away from them. I have to keep it safe."

Roarke considers this for a moment. "That's where I came in," he whispers.

I am so exhausted by everything that I actually laugh. "You were perfect," I admit. "One of only ten boys in your graduating class accepted to a school that was out of state, and Columbia, no less. Family in dire financial straits. The gay thing, at first I wasn't sure it would work, but then I realized that you're probably the only person in the entire town who needs to escape as much as I do. More, even."

"How long have you been planning this?" Roarke asks slowly.

"Ever since Lissa left, in one way or another."

"No," Roarke tells me and waves his hand back and forth between us. "How long have you been planning this?"

It does no good to lie, now that everything is ruined anyway, so I tell him, "I've known for a long time that this might happen. I've been watching you for years."

He lets this sink in, then he stands and crosses to the window. Small drops throw themselves against the pane with a steady thud, but I can tell that the storm is passing. The worst is over. It will be sunny by the time morning comes. Then there will be no way to avoid Libby any longer and the truth—or some version of it, anyway—will have to come out once and for all.

Roarke is still looking out the window when he asks me, "Why would you have been watching me even before you knew that you were pregnant?"

I can see that he is rolling this question over in his mind, that there are still holes in the narrative that he has stitched together from all the things I've said. My mouth opens, but no sound comes out. There is no air left inside me; at least not enough to speak. I feel my vision darken and I bite down on the inside of my cheek. By the time I can see properly again, Roarke has turned to face me.

"You wanted out, but they wouldn't have let you get married if there wasn't a baby, would they?" he asks, and I shake my head. "Did you do it on purpose?"

This time my laughter swells until I am nearly in hysterics. I wipe my eyes, not sure if I am laughing anymore or crying.

"No," I tell him finally. "It wasn't on purpose. I never wanted to get pregnant, not like this."

His eyes narrow as he says, "Then why not just use birth control?"

"I couldn't."

"Horseshit," he spits out and points toward the bathroom again. "You have an abortion in a bag in there. You couldn't make your boyfriend buy some condoms?"

"I never had a boyfriend."

Something about the way I say this interrupts Roarke's pacing and he stops in front of me again. I cannot meet his eyes. My throat constricts and I remember how the hands on my neck always squeezed tighter the more I struggled. The harder I fought, the longer it lasted, and so I learned how to be still.

"Essie," he begins and his voice has become gentle as he asks, "who's the father?"

Now I know for sure that the noises coming out of me can only mean that I am crying and I realize that what I want even more than for all of this to be over is to stop feeling so alone. So I tell Roarke why I have spent years watching him, and when I am finished, he takes my hand and leads me to the bed and then lies down beside me and holds me until I fall asleep. Just as I am drifting off, I think I hear a whisper. It's possible that it's only a dream or maybe it's even just the wind, but it's also possible that it's neither of those things, that Roarke is really saying, "We're going to take them for all they've got."

Liberty

The garden is in shambles when we walk through it after breakfast. The storm had been a real gully washer, but by noon the sun has dried the soggy ground. Three gardeners move through the space, plucking out the last of the stray branches that had fallen down into the bushes in the high winds. There had been a hurricane once when they were in Saint John, Essie tells me as she watches the gardeners. Her brothers had teased her for being frightened. They had threatened to lock her outside. Then, while they stood on the patio trying to coax Essie to join them, Lissa slid the door shut and turned the latch. Even though the boys screamed and yelled, their parents couldn't hear them over the howling of the wind. I'm not sure whom I'm meant to feel sorry for as she finishes the story, Essie or her brothers, but presumably someone eventually let them in.

We wait until afternoon, when the light has softened, and then we run through the questions one more time. Roarke is solicitous as we prepare. He hovers over Essie, opening the door for her when we step outside onto the veranda, pulling back her chair. It's not just the well-rehearsed routine they have prepared for the cameras. There is an air of actual concern when she says she's thirsty and wants to take a break. Roarke shoots up out of his chair as if he's just been told the chow line is open and jogs over to a tall dark man at the bar across the way. He returns with three tumblers of ice water but doesn't take his eyes from Essie until she raises the glass to her lips and takes her first sip.

As Margot starts to set up the cameras, I send the youngsters in to change. Roarke emerges a short time later in linen pants and a pressed white shirt with the sleeves rolled up above the wrists to reveal his newly tanned arms. Essie follows not long after. She's wearing red, which is not what we agreed on. From a purely aesthetic standpoint, she looks beautiful: alabaster skin, coral lips, the sort of features that once were hewn by sculptors from blocks of marble. Maybe it should be that simple.

But the color of the dress is a loaded one. Red has always been fraught with hidden meaning. It's the color of blood, which girls have been shamed for or else shamed by throughout the ages, sequestered in menstrual huts or forced to wear a crimson *A* on their chests. It's the color of life but also of death, a thread stitched by our mothers and our grandmothers with careful fingers to hold us fast in time and place. While Sid will recognize none of this, I know he'll see the color and won't be able to help thinking words like harlot or floozy, words thought of as quaint and therefore permissible. I step forward to tell Essie to swap the dress out for another and then stop. Women have been defined by red far more often than they themselves have sought to define it, and in a moment of pique I know I'll regret later, I decide that she should wear any damn color she wants.

I turn instead to Roarke and reach up with both hands to smooth down his collar, then leave my palms pressed lightly against his chest. "You ready for this?" I ask.

He nods and I squeeze his shoulders to offer reassurance before I pull my hands away.

The stylist sets one final curl to rest beneath the curve of Essie's jaw and leads her to her seat. We're arranged in three separate chairs so that we face the hotel and the ocean stretches out behind us. Mama would say that a view like that is proof enough for her that God exists, though she would also say that no proof is needed. The water is far enough away and the sun low enough in the sky that there is no glare coming off the ocean's surface, just an eternity painted in varying shades of blue and gray.

The first question goes to Essie, a softball about the school where they've both been volunteering and the long relationship her family has had with the community there. She tells a story about a girl, Maritza, whom she met when they were both still children, a friend she grew closer to each successive year. She talks about the opportunities that the girl has now, to study at the university, which were made possible by the education she received at the New Light School and by the scholarship program funded by generous donors from all across the United States.

Roarke chimes in then, unprompted, "I know that a lot of my friends back home were surprised when they heard that I was engaged to Essie. I'm not usually a fan of secrets and I know that's how it looked, our not telling anyone that we were dating. I guess we just thought the relationship deserved a little space of its own to grow before we entered into the public eye, some time for us to figure out if it was real. So I get that it was a shock even to those who are my closest friends when they saw me sitting next to Essie on TV, when they heard us announce our engagement that day with you.

"They can't imagine us actually loving each other and at first I found that odd, probably because when you are inside it, falling in love feels like the most natural thing in the world. So I've been thinking a lot about how to explain all of this to my friends, to my family, and what I realized is that even though everyone I know—everyone in the entire country, for that matter—can tell you that Essie's middle name is Anne, they don't see her as an actual real-life person. The same goes for her whole family. Even among the people in our town, I think that there's this tendency to see them just as characters on a TV show, to think that they're always playing a part. People think that maybe there's nothing at all about the Hickses that is real. Not the sort of real that you could fall in love with, anyway. I know this because those were things I used to think myself.

"But now, being here, seeing the work that Essie has done this week, that her family has done over so many years, seeing the lives that they've changed for the better, well, people don't get any more real than that. I just feel honored to be a part of it, to be one of them now, the newest addition to the family."

I permit a breath of silence there, because Roarke has spoken beautifully. The viewers will never suspect that he has memorized these lines. I allow time for Essie to run a finger beneath one eye and it's possible that the tear she wipes away is real. It was a moving speech. Even I half believe that Pastor Hicks is the next Bill Gates until I remember that any Hicks campaign to rid the world of pestilence would probably focus on eliminating "immorality" rather than disease. I press my lips together into a curve that I realize isn't really a smile, but it's the best I can do.

"Back to you now," I tell Essie. "What is it about your time with Roarke that makes you certain that you two will go the distance?"

What she is supposed to say here is that Roarke is the perfect partner, that having him by her side only strengthens her resolve to continue to do the "good works" her family is best known for. We worked on the reply together and it's intended as a segue into our talking about the upcoming wedding, so that we can promote that broadcast ahead of time without really seeming to.

When Essie doesn't answer right away, I'm afraid that she's forgotten her line, but then I see the wrinkle between her eyes that tells me she knows exactly what she's doing.

"I don't know," Essie replies.

"Excuse me?" I say, giving her another chance to get back on script.

Essie shakes her head as if willing herself into action and continues, "I don't know that we'll go the distance. I don't even know what that phrase is supposed to mean. Does it mean being married for fifty years but hating each other after the first ten? Does it mean living in a house you can't afford and working so much that you spend less time together than you do apart? If couples like that are 'going the distance,' I'm not sure that's something I want to aspire to. But I will say that whether Roarke and I last six months or six decades, there is something precious about being seen, about being known, and being accepted for who I truly am. Now that I've finally felt that, it's not something I would ever willingly let go of."

———

"What was that?" I ask when we're finished taping.

Essie meets my eyes and it's clear that she knows exactly what I mean.

"I thought it was good," Roarke interjects, stepping between us. "It sounded honest. It sounded sincere. Isn't that what we're going for?"

"Sure, of course. It was fine." I sigh and put up my hands in surrender, then try again. "It wasn't about what you said, Essie, it was that I didn't know you were going to say it. We have rehearsals for a reason. These scripts have been carefully planned to build at just the right pace, to maximize viewership for when we broadcast the wedding. That's what you want, isn't it? That's what you told me and so that's what we've been working for. I really believe that if we do it my way, we can get at least twenty million pairs of eyes watching live when you walk down the aisle, maybe more. Unless you've changed your mind about what the goal is?"

Her eyes fall.

"No, that's still what I want."

I feel my face soften and I say, "Good. Then it's what I want too. Today's interview was great. Don't worry about anything. Roarke, you especially came through. I know this is all new to you still, but you're a natural in front of the camera. When you look at Essie, it seems like you actually care."

"I do care," he says defensively.

"Of course," I correct myself. "It comes across nicely. That's all that I meant to say." Margot motions to me and I raise my hand to let her know I will be just a minute as I continue, "We're heading out as soon as we pack up the equipment and get the footage sent off. We don't have long before the next taping, though, so I've put together an outline of what we should cover. I'll email it to you both before I leave. Get back to me with any questions. We'll all meet up back in the studio three days after you get home."

"And Lissa too," Essie blurts out.

I nod. "And Lissa too. That's what she said."

I turn to go, but Essie calls after me and I stop. "It wasn't always like this."

"What wasn't?" I ask. Roarke puts a hand on Essie's arm as if to reassure her.

"Before Lissa left, everything was different. Well, not everything, but the important parts. Before she left, the things that felt true at least outweighed everything I knew was false. We weren't perfect. We weren't the people we pretended to be when we were on TV, but we were still . . . I don't know how else to describe it."

"A family?" I ask. I know exactly what she means. Essie breathes out and nods. She looks relieved, so I say, "What were some of the things that were true?"

Her eyes become unfocused and I wonder what she is replaying in her mind. I have spent so many hours watching old episodes of Six for Hicks that it's possible whatever she is remembering is a scene I would recognize. Or, more likely, those memories that are the most precious are the ones that happened when the cameras were absent, when the Hicks family was alone.

"The boys used to come home for dinner on our parents' anniversary. Not their wedding anniversary, which was filmed, but the day they actually met. It was never discussed beforehand and of course there were years when someone was missing because Jacob was living down in Texas or Daniel and Hillary were on their honeymoon. But for the most part everyone who could show up did and they never brought their wives or girlfriends. It was always only us."

She takes a breath as if savoring that thought and then continues, "After dinner, Mother would pull out their old photo albums, the ones from before they moved to town, from the years that they were poor, and when I watched Mother and Daddy laughing over a picture of some tent that had fallen down on top of them while they slept, I knew that there had been a time when they were in love. And I thought that even though it didn't show, that love had to be there somewhere, buried underneath the hair and makeup and all the million ways they spoke to each other that were just the same as if they were reading from a script. If it was there, if they still did love each other, it would make everything else more real."

We are quiet. A peacock staggers by looking vaguely drunk.

Roarke clears his throat. "I think they do. I wouldn't have said that, you know, before, but that day we went to the planetarium, I don't think they heard us when we came in. Your back was turned. Maybe you were closing the door. But your mother was in a chair, just reading, and your father was watching her with this strange expression on his face. He looked happy. I guess I remembered it because at church she's always the one looking at him and this was the other way around. Anyway, it seemed real enough to me."

Essie seems to accept this. I give her one last reassuring smile and then turn away to help Margot break down the set. Within an hour we're ready to leave and Margot asks the front desk to arrange a taxi. All of this goes more smoothly than we had expected, so there's time, on the way to the airport, to pull over and stop alongside a beach. The driver watches, amused, as we unstrap our sandals and step into the foam.

"It seems a shame," I tell Margot, "to come all this way and only just put our toes in."

Margot looks out at the waves and then back at the driver. "I don't think he'd mind if you stripped down and threw yourself under." I splash the water and Margot throws her hands up in surrender. "No? Well, if everything goes according to plan, you and Mike will be able to take a proper beach vacation when all of this is over."

I shrug. "Actually, I don't think I want a vacation. I'm finally doing work that I like. For the first time in a long time, I feel connected to something important."

"You shouldn't confuse fame with importance. You of all people should know that. It's easy to be seduced by a powerful personality. But when it comes down to it, Pastor Hicks is no different than Quentin Ames. Not really. He's better-looking, maybe. Certainly more polished. He's a watered-down version of Ames that's acceptable for mass consumption, but his message is the same."

The mere sound of his name is enough to pull me back

there. The floor is cold, the carpet thin and rolled out over hard cement. I tuck my knees up in the sleeping bag to pull my feet away from the chill and curl myself around Justice. We're seven. Ames says something from across the room. He's calling to us. I keep my eyes closed and pretend not to hear, but Justice slips out from underneath our covers and runs toward his voice. I feel her rough wool socks scratch against my leg, her flannel nightgown brush my cheek. Then she's gone. An hour later, she is dead.

I turn to Margot, and as I do, I feel the warmth flow back into my body. I feel the sand get sucked out from underneath my feet. I say, "It's not Jethro Hicks who's important. It's his daughter."

There is hurt in my voice and anger too.

"I'm sorry," Margot tells me. "I shouldn't have said his name."

She means Quentin Ames, the man who promised us eternal life but got my sister killed instead.

"Don't be. His name doesn't mean anything to me anymore."

Roarke

The day after we fly back, I'm summoned to the rectory. Celia Hicks, whom I've decided I'll never in a million years call Mother or anything of the sort, pours tea and gestures to a plate of freshly baked muffins. As her hand moves through the air, I count the rings on her fingers and think how much the carefully manicured nails look like they belong to a bird of prey.

"Thank you, ma'am," I say and wait for her to protest, to offer some nickname that I should use instead, but she doesn't.

Essie pulls at her sleeve and looks bored.

"I don't think Roarke cares about flower arrangements, Mother. I don't either, come to think of it. Just choose whichever you think will look best."

The corner of Celia Hicks's lip curls down on one side. I nudge Essie's shoe with my foot to tell her that she should be more careful. She sits up straighter in response and crosses her ankles.

"You have such good taste, after all," Essie adds lamely.

There are less than two weeks until Easter, which has been set as the day of the wedding, and Essie and I have one more week off from school. The fact that Easter falls late this year and, as a result, does not line up with the public school vacation was the subject of Pastor Hicks's last sermon, which was broadcast on our flight and is apparently evidence of the nation's war against Christians. Or something. I tuned out most of what he said and instead focused on the back of Mom's head, which was visible in the shot. While we were away, she got her hair cut.

Celia Hicks's eyes flash as she looks at her daughter and then she splits her mouth into a smile.

"I didn't call you both here to talk about flowers," she tells us. "I took care of all that while you were away. There will be lilies, of course, for the holiday. And with any luck, the daffodils outside will have bloomed in time for the ceremony. They should make a nice background as you step out of the church."

"You can't control the weather," Essie reminds her.

"I know that. Don't be foolish. The landscapers have potted daffodils set aside in their greenhouse. They'll plant those on Good Friday if it looks like the gardens are going to be a disappointment."

"So what are we here for then, if it's not about the wedding?" I ask, finding the courage to speak.

"Yes, excellent, best to get down to it," Celia Hicks says. "Roarke, I'm not sure you've met Essie's brother Caleb, but you've probably heard that he's been considering a run for Congress. Bennett Tull has announced that he won't be seeking reelection and Caleb has been asked to run for his seat in the House. Well, of course, rumors have been flying and there have even been polls that show Caleb would be expected to do well against any of the Democratic challengers. But I told Caleb to pray on it first before he decided anything. After all, with a baby on the way, being there for his family should be his first priority, however alluring the spotlight might seem."

Essie snorts and then covers up this sound with a cough.

"What does that have to do with us?" I ask.

Mrs. Hicks lifts her cup from its saucer and sips, then sets the cup down without a sound.

"He's announcing the day after tomorrow at four o'clock. I'd like you both to be there."

Essie shakes her head. "We have an interview."

"Well, certainly this is more important," Celia Hicks counters.

"Not to me. I made a promise to Libby. I intend to keep it."

"My dear, this is hardly worth butting heads over. Besides, I can't imagine the interview will take that long. You can come over to the press conference when you've finished. We'll just need to figure out your wardrobe ahead of time. You can change at the studio before you leave. Politics has grown so twisted, so dirty. People need to see the sort of togetherness that old-fashioned family values brings."

Mrs. Hicks begins to launch into the color scheme and where she envisions each of us standing, but by then Essie is laughing so much that the coughing is not enough of a cover. I nudge her foot again, but this time it has no effect.

"I can't breathe," she manages to gasp as tears begin to wet her cheeks.

Celia Hicks looks at her daughter with thinly veiled disgust.

"Roarke, dear, why don't you take her out back to get some air?"

"Yes, ma'am," I say and stand to pull Essie to her feet.

I drag her through unfamiliar rooms, rooms they must not use for taping, until I find a set of French doors that seem to lead outside. I open them and step out onto a stone patio. It feels like spring and the yard at least I recognize. There is the swing set Lissa climbed to the top of before she fell and broke her leg. The plastic seats are faded, but it looks sturdy enough. The grass is damp and my shoes sink slightly into the spongy ground as I cross the yard and lower myself into a swing. Essie hesitates, still bent over and grabbing at her chest, then follows close behind. She wipes her eyes once more and sits down as well.

"Sorry about that," she says.

I shrug. "Don't be."

"It hit me all at once, just how ridiculous we are. I don't think I ever really saw that until now. I mean, I knew it, but I didn't really *know*. I didn't think about how it looks from the outside."

"Everybody feels embarrassed by their family."

"Sure, but not necessarily on quite so grand, so national, a scale."

"You've been on the national stage your entire life."

Essie shakes her head. "Yes, but that was all for entertainment. Even the church bits. Daddy may want to think they were something else, something that brought people closer to the divine. But entertainment is all it was. This is different. What makes Caleb qualified to run for office? Nothing. He almost flunked out of law school, did you know that? Naomi had to write his papers for him."

I shake my head. "I don't suppose he'll tell the voters that." I pause and lean back to look up at the clouds. "We could say no," I offer, "or just not show up at the press conference at all."

Essie slumps down in the swing and starts to push herself back and forth. The chains creak and then settle into a soothing rhythm.

"What's the point?" she says. "It's hardly worth the risk. We can't do anything that might really anger Mother, not before the marriage certificate is signed. After that, once the money's ours, then we'll be free from them. We'll just have to put up with this freak show of a circus until then."

"It's not much longer," I try to reassure her.

"I know."

"Besides, you should be looking forward to seeing Lissa, right? Not worrying about the campaign."

"I guess."

Essie is looking at her lap. I can't see her face.

"You don't sound so sure."

"I am," she says as she looks up. "I mean, I definitely want to see her, but there's also a part of me that's afraid."

"Afraid of what?"

"That she won't understand the person I've become. No, that's not it. Maybe it's that I'm afraid she will."

"Wait a minute," I say, reaching out to take the chain on her swing and pulling her to a stop. "Wouldn't that actually be a good thing, to have your sister on your side? Don't you want her to understand?"

There's a long pause before Essie finally speaks. "No. I'm not sure that I do."

———

I take the long way home and barely register the route as I turn from one street onto another. At one point I realize that I've missed a turn and drive aimlessly through a cluster of cul-de-sacs I've never been down before, a new development, until I find my way back to a street I recognize and at long last pull up in front of my house. Blake's truck, which he bought used off of Ryan Keane when Ryan's dad upgraded him to an Audi, is parked out front. It still looks new, unlike my sorry excuse for transportation. I glance into the cab, but it's empty. Blake must be inside.

I find him sitting on the couch with Mom, leafing through my baby book. She pulled out all our boxes of photographs from the attic while I was away and has been going through them, looking for the perfect snapshots to give Celia for the rehearsal dinner slideshow.

Blake doesn't look up as I step into the room. Instead he shakes his head and says, "Dude, you had some rolls on you when you were a baby."

"They were for my protection. Mom dropped me a lot when I was little."

My mother swipes a hand in my direction as if to swat me, but I'm too far away to reach. "Stop that. I did nothing of the sort."

"You ready?" Blake asks.

I have no idea what he's asking. "Ready for what?" I say.

"I'm kidnapping you. The guys are meeting us at the lake. Unless of course you'd like to stay here and let me see more of these pictures. Did you even wear clothes before age three?"

He holds up a Polaroid in which I'm wearing a striped T-shirt but am inexplicably without underwear or pants. He waves it in the air.

"I can't. I have an interview and I just found out about this other thing."

"Are either of them tomorrow? Because your mom told me you were free tomorrow. She even packed your bag."

Blake gestures to my camping pack, which is leaning against the post at the bottom of the stairs. My sleeping bag sits beside it, along with a water bottle and a baseball cap.

"They're the day after."

"Good," Blake says and moves to stand. "So you *are* free. We should make good use of that freedom, since you have so little of it left."

He slaps me on the shoulder and moves around the couch to lift my backpack.

"I'll throw this in the truck while you go change into something a little less Six for Hicks," he tells me, gesturing to my button-down shirt and beige pants. "Thanks for the cookies, Mrs. Richards. We'll have him back in time for bed tomorrow. I know he gets cranky when he doesn't get enough sleep."

Blake retrieves my pack without waiting for my approval and throws open the front door.

"Mom?"

She stands, her fingers curling and uncurling nervously at her side.

"Go," she says. "Have fun."

I wait for her to arrange her face into a reassuring smile and then I bound up the stairs. I kick my loafers off into the closet and pull out a stained and dusty pair of boots. Soon I'm back in my own clothes and I marvel at how slipping on my jeans feels in some ways like stepping into my own skin again. I kiss my mother on the cheek and join Blake in his truck, pulling the seat belt across my chest while shooting off a text to let Essie know I may not have reception until the following night. Blake laughs and takes my phone away just as I hit Send.

"Whipped," he says. "You know that's what they call it, don't you?"

"You're one to talk. Didn't Kristin Meyers have you on a pretty tight leash for almost all of junior year?"

"Yeah, well, her brother is a lot bigger than me and he told me he would really mess me up if I ever made his sister mad. I couldn't dump her. In the end, I had to pay Bretton King all of the money I made cutting Mrs. McCluskey's lawn so he'd ask Kristin out and she'd finally break up with me."

"You never told me that," I say. "That's pretty messed up."

"Oh, I don't think you're in any position to judge," he says.

He puts the truck in gear and we back out onto the street.

"It's not a judgment. Just an observation."

"Well, I've got some observations of my own, then."

"Shoot," I tell him.

"You look happy when you're with her. I've been watching you on TV. Don't look at me like that. I know it's lame, but now that you're famous, it's the only way I get to see you. Anyway, at some point during one of your interviews she made you laugh and it was your real laugh, not the one you use when you're pretending something's funny."

"So you buy the whole 'madly in love' thing now?"

"Not so fast. I didn't say that. But if you're happy, that's good enough for me."

I don't answer right away, but when I do I say, "I think that's what I am."

I let the silence stretch again as we pull onto the highway and wait to weave our way into the left lane. I look out the window and watch as the buildings fall away and are replaced by farmland. Blake turns on the radio, but I turn it off again.

"I'm going to get to go to Columbia."

"Huh," he grunts and looks at me sideways before returning his eyes to the road. "So that's it, then?"

"No, that's not it. I'm not going to apologize for wanting to get out of here and I'm not going to deny that it'll be easier with Essie by my side. But I wouldn't be marrying her if I didn't believe in the things she stands for as a person, what we can choose to stand for together."

"What things does she stand for?"

I laugh and turn the radio back on, crank up the volume.

"Everything her family stands against."

———

Reggie White, Ben Matthews, and Zach Lipton are already at the lake when we arrive. That whole piece of land used to be a summer camp—our summer camp—but it closed down a few years ago. It was called Bement. For a while it looked like no one wanted it, then some stockbroker from Chicago made a lowball offer and the bank that had foreclosed on it just wanted to be rid of it, I guess. It was supposed to be some sort of spiritual retreat, or that's what he told Dad when he stopped into the store for a pair of shoelaces. Later that fall, he had someone sell off anything that wasn't nailed down: the canoes, the tables and plastic chairs that were stacked up in the mess hall. But aside from that, nothing else has been done. As far as I know, the man hasn't been back since.

We still camp here when we want to, but it's depressing how deserted and forgotten the place has become. Every time we go, we're half afraid it will be our last visit, but the other half is hoping that the real estate guy has come back to bulldoze over the past. Being trapped in this sort-of in-between is just too sad. Before the camp shut down, the five of us spent every summer together on this lake from the time we were nine until we turned fifteen. Every summer, that is, except for the one when I was sent away. Blake and the other guys think I was on some dude ranch out west, though that's something we never could have afforded. I don't want them to know the truth, so I never said anything about it at all.

In any case, it feels almost like coming home to be back here again. The lock on the gate across the access road has always been easy to pick, so we drive all the way up past the gatehouse and to the dirt lot behind the mess hall, where Ben's car sits empty. The lake is visible through the pines and the gravel crunches beneath our feet as Blake and I cross the clearing where we used to gather before meals and sing songs like "Amazing Grace" or "Johnny Appleseed." From there we jog down a short trail reinforced with railroad ties to reach the grassy beach where we know the others will be waiting. The sand is still visible in places, but without young campers to rake the beach clean throughout the summer, the natural vegetation is reasserting itself in force.

Reggie and Ben are skipping rocks while Zach lies with his

arms spread wide in a sunny spot near the Buddy Board, where the lifeguards used to hang a chip for every child in the water. One time Zach left his chip on the Buddy Board on purpose. He hid behind the changing house while the bell above the mess hall starting ringing and the counselors ran from all over camp to gather at the waterfront. Some made a line to sweep the shallow area while others dove beneath the docks. Zach later admitted to the camp director that he had just wanted a glimpse of Ellen Carpenter in a wet T-shirt and he still maintains that the way her nipples showed through the fabric made it entirely worth getting sent home early that summer.

Blake runs down the last few steps and then jumps on top of the stone wall that flanks the swimming area and raises his arms above his head. Zach catches sight of us first and leaps up.

"The prodigal son returns," he yells, and Blake bends at the waist to take a bow. Zach lobs a pinecone at him and says, "I wasn't talking about you."

I step over the wall and Zach throws his arms around me.

"Congratulations, man."

Even Reggie, who I know hates the Hicks family more than most, gives me a squeeze and says, "They've got you on such a tight schedule, we didn't know if we'd get to give you a proper bachelor party. But since none of us can legally drink, this is probably the best we'd be able to do anyway."

He gestures to a cooler that they've dragged beneath a maple tree to shade it from the sun.

"This is perfect," I tell them. "Thanks."

"Anytime."

Ben hands out the beers and we lean against the cool stones of the wall and look out across the water.

"So," Reggie says finally, "Essie Hicks. Interesting choice."

Blake gives him a warning look, which I catch out of the corner of my eye.

"I think she chose me, not the other way around," I tell him.

"And you just went along with it?" Reggie asks.

"Dude," Blake hisses from between his teeth, "we talked about this."

"No, it's fine. I went along with it. I had no reason not to. My life is better with her in it. That's all I can say."

There's silence and I can tell from the look on Reggie's face that he has more that he would like to add, but he swallows hard and looks away.

"I heard that Aaron Carlberg busted his knee jumping out of a hotel window in Cabo," Ben says, clearly trying to change the subject.

"Do you think he'll lose his scholarship to Baylor?" Blake asks.

"His sister says they'll know more after he's had his surgery, but it doesn't look good."

"What a douche," Zach says. "His parents must be pissed."

"What did they expect, letting him go to Mexico on his own? Besides, they can afford to pay for Baylor even if he never sets foot on a football field again."

Ben stands up as he finishes speaking and walks behind a bush to pee. I finish my beer. The last mouthful is warm and I hold on to it in that space between my lips and my front teeth before I swallow. Ben walks back to where we're sitting and throws himself down on the ground.

The summer we were twelve, Ben and I were in the same cabin and arrived early enough on check-in day to claim two adjacent top bunks. Beneath me slept a boy who refused to shower for the entire camp session. I've forgotten his name, but I still remember the smell. Ben, on the other hand, shared his bunk with our junior counselor Noah, who was the most beautiful thing I'd ever seen. I told myself I just thought Noah was cool; everyone did. But it wasn't that. The following summer was the one I missed.

———

"Where're we sleeping?" Ben asks. "It'll be too cold to stay out here."

He's right. Though it feels almost like summer when we're lying flat in the full sun, by evening the temperature's sure to drop. The cabins aren't heated, but they'll still offer protection. A tent might be warmer, but to even think of bringing one always seemed like some sort of betrayal since the cabins must feel abandoned enough as it is.

"I was thinking Five," Zach says. "Someone or something took a dump in Two and I haven't been able to go back into Three ever since that thing."

"That thing" was the time Zach lost his virginity, which apparently did not go exactly as he planned, though he's never elaborated beyond that.

"One and Six had too much damage in that storm last year," Blake chimes in.

"What about Four?" Ben asks.

"It's haunted," Reggie and I say at once and then begin to laugh.

"Shut up," Blake tells us.

"What?" Ben looks confused.

"Have you seriously never heard what went down in Four?" I say.

"Lakeside Four is where Blake declared his love to Robin Ladoucer only to have her grind his soul, may it rest in peace, into the floor with her steel-toed boots until all that was left was dust."

I raise my eyebrows. "I thought he dropped trou and she couldn't stop laughing."

"Isn't that pretty much the same thing?"

"You guys are the worst," Blake says, but the way he says it I know that he means the opposite.

"Fine," Ben concedes. "Five it is."

———

There are noises in the woods that I never noticed before. We'd cooked hot dogs on sticks over the fire and burned our fingers trying to roast marshmallows for s'mores. Then we swam in the lake on principle, even though by that time the sun was gone and it was far too cold. A watery moon hung just above the tree line and cast a glow on our wet skin.

When we were younger, we used to slip out of our cabins and do the same thing, sneaking down to the water's edge, peeling off our shirts and pajama pants as we went. Sometimes we'd get caught by counselors who were out after their own curfew, hidden in the shadows and sharing long, overly wet kisses or wrestling around on the hard ground. They would send us back to our cabins with a silent understanding that neither group would turn the other in. On the nights we weren't caught, we would make the last part of the run entirely naked and splash into the water with barely a sound, disappearing beneath the dark surface, careful to give no sign that we were there. Sometime around middle school we started leaving our shorts on. I wasn't the first one to do it, but I was relieved when it happened and I felt almost guilty that I had let it go on so long.

Now, staring up at the underside of the cabin roof long after the others have dropped into sleep, I'm struck by the din coming in through the windows. It's not only the steady thrum of the crickets. There are other sounds as well. Frogs noisily broadcast their presence from the tree trunks beyond the clearing, beckoning potential mates closer, like Tinder for amphibians. A few feet from my head, moths throw their bodies against the screen while something louder, something larger, moves heavily across the forest floor outside.

I am struck all at once by how I am a part of all this for the very first time. Life begetting life and all that Old Testament stuff. Not that the baby is mine, not in any biological sense, but it will be mine legally. It will be mine as far as the world is concerned. The tabloids will probably show a shot of the baby alongside one of those photos that Mom is digging out of her boxes. Celia Hicks will see to that, I'm sure. She'll want there to be enough headlines marveling at our family resemblance that her fans never suspect they have had the wool pulled over their eyes. With any luck, this'll take up enough of her attention that she'll never realize that her own daughter has done exactly the same thing, that I've been a willing accomplice, that their secret is no longer theirs alone. It also belongs to me.

The next day we rise early since the cabin's screened windows do little to block out the sun. We have time to hike the entire trail that runs around the lake. We carve our initials into the rafters in Cabin Five. We shout out obscenities across the open surface of the water and wait for the four-letter words to echo back. Ben climbs a tree where he once tied a bandana around a branch and reports that the bark has grown up and around the tightly twisted fabric and claimed the cloth as its own. When at last we pile into the cars and pull past the gatehouse, I look for a long time out the rear window until the lake has entirely disappeared. Blake stays quiet as the truck bounces over the dirt road and I know we're thinking the very same thing: this was the last time. Now that childhood is behind us, we will never come here again.

Esther

It turns out I am more nervous about seeing Lissa than I was about what Mother would say when she found the pregnancy test. I suppose it's because Mother is predictable while Lissa is, after all, essentially a stranger. It has been nearly four years since I last saw her, and when she left, I was a child, knobby-kneed and flat-chested. Aside from being family, we had nothing in common. Even so, when my period came for the first time later that fall, I wished more than anything that Lissa were there to tell. Instead I had to alert Mother, after which there was the requisite speech about becoming a woman and the importance of virtue. I nearly fainted when she started talking and it was not just because I was embarrassed. The whole part about virtue came about six weeks too late.

I look through the pictures I have of Lissa and me together. Not the professional shots, of which there are many, but instead the overexposed prints that we all collected from those disposable cameras you bought at convenience stores, the kind that used actual film. We look happy in the snapshots. Even though I am so much younger than Lissa, it does not look like she is on the swing set next to me because she has to be. She is smiling. She is enjoying herself, ignoring the camera. In only a few of the pictures does she stare right at the lens with the unbridled disdain of a teenager. I flip through these and wonder if that's all it was, her age, or if there was more behind the look than just that.

In one she is holding an inflatable beach ball under one arm. The wind has blown her hair forward and Lissa's third finger is extended, brushing her bangs away from her face. Was it on purpose, the use of that finger in particular? Probably. Lissa specialized in subtle acts of rebellion. There were thirty-four candy bars under her bed, after all. But still, I wonder who was behind the camera. I wonder for whom the obscenity was meant.

Mother watches me from the hall as I sift through the photographs, fanning them out across my bed. I ignore her. I expect her to move on after she reassures herself that I am doing nothing much of interest, but instead she steps forward and into the room. She twists one of the carved wooden finials at the foot of my bed frame and clears her throat.

"What have you got there?" she asks.

I hand her the picture of Lissa and me at the house in Saint John. I was wearing a hat that Lissa had woven out of reeds. It was lopsided and scratchy and the inside rubbed against my forehead, but those things didn't matter. I wore that hat everywhere for the whole rest of that summer and I cried for a day and a half when the wind blew it so far out into the ocean that it was beyond rescuing. I thought that Lissa might blame me, might love me less for not being careful. But Lissa seemed to have forgotten that she'd made the hat in the first place and kept asking why I was so upset. It was Naomi who leaped into the water as I stood crying on the beach and tried to save it, but by the time she got beyond the waves, the tug of the currents had already carried the hat away.

"My goodness, you both look so young," Mother says, and I see her mouth relax into a smile that might almost be natural.

"We *were* young. We'd have to be. She's been gone for so long."

Mother looks genuinely wounded and for the first time in a long while, I remember that this woman is my mother in more than just name, that there might have once been a part of her that actually cared.

"Yes, well, your sister always did have a flair for the dramatic. Did you know I often wondered if she broke her leg on purpose? I don't know why. It just struck me as something she would do. For the attention."

I am angry, though I cannot tell whether it is because the statement is ungenerous or because I have to admit that it is true. Whatever her failings as a parent, my mother knew Lissa well.

"It runs in the family, I guess."

Mother ignores this. Possibly she did not hear me. She has chosen a photograph from Christmas at the lake house and is running a nail along the border.

"It's all of us together," she says.

I look. She is right. Someone else must have taken it, a cook or a nanny or else one of the crew. I watch Mother for a moment, intrigued by the emotions playing out across her face. Does she think there are cameras here in the room with us or is she genuinely remorseful about whatever it was that made Lissa go?

"Do you ever miss her?" I ask finally.

"Don't ask ridiculous questions."

"It's not ridiculous. You never talk about her. What am I supposed to think?"

"It takes commitment, what we do. Elizabeth wasn't strong enough. She wasn't devoted to the cause. We're better off without her."

"You mean the show is better off?"

"I mean we, as a family, are better off letting her follow her own path. And I don't blame her for it. In fact, I'm happy that she's found direction, that she's found peace."

"How could you possibly know anything about her if you haven't spoken with her in three and a half years?"

"I know that if something were really wrong, she would have called. I'm her mother, after all."

"Mom," I say and she looks startled. I have never called her that before. "Why did she leave? What happened?"

Instead of answering, Mother stands and straightens her skirt.

"Lights out in five minutes. We have a big day tomorrow."

I wait, but from her look it is clear that I should not expect an answer. I start to brush a hand across my bedspread to gather up the pictures and put them back into their bin. Mother straightens one of the ceramic horses I keep on a shelf over my desk.

"I miss her every day," she tells me from the hall.

I look up to ask Mother again why Lissa left, but she is already gone.

———

I can't focus during the interview. I don't remember any of the questions and I stumble over the answers we've agreed upon. Roarke holds the narrative together with some help from Libby and they play the whole thing off as wedding nerves. I try to relax and answer questions about flower arrangements and rolled fondant. People want to know the color of the bridesmaids' dresses and whether any of my nieces and nephews will be included in the service. I tell a story about three-year-old Millicent, who was being fitted for a flower girl dress and ran out of the boutique wearing nothing but a pair of Mary Janes and streaked across a busy parking lot. Naomi tripped as she tried to chase her daughter and was nearly hit by a car. The memory of the mortification on my mother's face is enough to distract me for the rest of the taping and I somehow plow through to the end.

I expect Libby to lay into me for making a mess of the interview, but instead she sets aside her note cards and says, "Wait here. I'll go see if she's arrived."

My palms have been sweating since we started the session and I wipe them down the sides of my dress, aware that the curls in my hair are beginning to fall and stick to the back of my neck.

"If I sweat any more, I think I'll dissolve into a puddle like the Wicked Witch," I tell Roarke.

He puts his arm loosely around me.

"It's the lights. They were hotter than usual."

I laugh. "You're a terrible liar. We both know that isn't true."

"I think that what we both know is that I'm not a terrible liar. Otherwise we wouldn't have gotten this far."

"Fair enough."

"You'll be fine," he tries to reassure me. "And with any luck, you'll find out what you need to know."

I swallow hard and try to breathe out slowly. My morning sickness has mostly gone away since we got back from Cuba, but now I feel a surge of nausea. Roarke's look of concern goes out of focus and I blink rapidly as I will myself to remain upright. Fainting would be too cliché. We are interrupted by a loud crack as a metal door swings open and Libby walks back into the studio.

"She's in my dressing room."

I stand motionless, frozen in time, until Roarke asks, "Do you want me to go with you?" and I come back to myself enough to shake my head and follow Libby into the hall. It is the same corridor we walked through just before the interview, but it seems brighter now and longer. The walls and ceiling bleed together and I feel as if I am walking through a tunnel that goes on and on without any end. I do not see the door to Libby's dressing room until I am standing right in front of it, and even then I am confused for a moment until I reach a hand out to touch the wall and the cool granularity of paint rolled over plaster brings things into focus.

"Ready?" Libby asks.

Her pupils widen and I know that she has found my sister for me in no small part because her own sister has been taken to a place where she cannot be found.

"Ready," I echo, hoping that by saying it out loud I can make it true.

Libby turns the knob to open the door and then backs out of the way to let me enter, and because at this point there is no way around it, I walk forward even though I am not at all certain that I have the strength to face the person inside. I hear Libby shut the door behind me as Lissa stands. She looks unsure of herself, which surprises me for some reason. "Leap before you look" had been one of her mottoes. I did not think she was capable of being nervous. She takes a step forward as if to hug me, then stops. Her hair is darker than I remember, longer. "Unkempt" is what Mother would call it, but Lissa looks beautiful and a little wild. She looks like the person she was always meant to be.

I have played this moment out countless times over the years, but in my mind, Lissa was always the one to speak first. She is supposed to say something irreverent or else offer an apology. She is supposed to tousle my hair the way she used to or make a joke about how much I've grown. But instead she just stands there and all of the things I have imagined saying in return slip away and I am left with nothing. I open my mouth and what I produce is something between a giggle and a sob and all of a sudden I am blubbering so much that for a second it seems as if I can't breathe.

Eventually I manage to get out, "How could you leave me all alone?"

And now her arms do wrap around me and I feel her rib cage shaking and I know that she is crying too.

It is a long time before we are able to say anything, and when we do talk, it is not at all how I expected. She wants to know how the remodel turned out in the upstairs bathroom and whether you can take a shower now without freezing or getting burned. She asks what happened to Mrs. Peacham's labradoodle, Roscoe, whom Lissa used to take for walks and who liked to pee in the spot where our own dog, Blister, had been buried, as if making some sort of offering to the dead. It is the little things she seems most interested in and then I realize that it is the little things that she has not been able to find out about on TV.

After a long while, I ask, "Why did you go?"

We are sitting on a narrow couch. Lissa's feet are tucked up beneath her and I am lying with my legs up over the armrest so that my head is on my sister's knee. She smooths my hair back from my face.

"It's complicated," she tells me.

"Isn't it always?"

Lissa leans her head back and looks up at a water mark on the ceiling.

"You know how it is there. I was suffocating."

"So it wasn't anything more than that?"

I feel Lissa's muscles tense, but even so, I know that if she tells me it was just the cameras she was trying to escape from, I'll believe her. That's how much I want it to be true.

Instead of saying no, she asks me, "Why?"

And because this is the entire reason I asked her here to see me, I say, "I'm pregnant."

There is a moment when it is as if the air has gone out of the room because neither of us is breathing, but then it passes and Lissa says, "I was afraid of that."

I sit up and face her, my eyes flashing. Saying it out loud to Lissa, I realize for the first time that I have decided to have this baby. Not by default. Not just because Roarke found me and I didn't take the pills. I have decided that I want it no matter how he or she came to be.

"Aren't you going to ask me who the father is?"

Lissa shakes her head and bites down hard on her lower lip. I can see the blood.

"I don't have to," she whispers finally. "I already know."

———

Candy calls not long after that to make sure we are on schedule for the campaign event. Mother had eventually conceded to announcing Caleb's run at the bandstand in the town park rather than on the church lawn at the insistence of his campaign manager, a classmate from Yale named Ellory Lester who has become a sudden fixture and is now always at Caleb's side. He went on about how the polling shows that Caleb has his work cut out for him with the secular voters in the district while, naturally, he's got the evangelicals in the bag. This is why it is so important that the announcement be made in neutral territory. As a result, Roarke and I have to be ready before we leave the studio since there is nowhere to change once we get to the park.

I slip out of my dress and into a peacock-blue skirt and gold blouse. Roarke carries our bags out to his car while I hug Lissa good-bye.

"I'm glad that you told me," she says. "And I'm relieved that at least from here on out, you'll be safe. I know Roarke will make sure of that. You're lucky to have found him."

"I know."

"It's good that you won't have to do this on your own."

"Like you did?"

"Well, I made a clean break of it. It'll be different for you. You'll have a baby. It will be ratings gold. Mother won't just let you go."

"The way she let you?"

Lissa smirks, "I didn't give her any choice."

"You mean you blackmailed her."

"Maybe just a little. It was hard, though. Final. There was no going back. It will be easier the way you're doing it."

"Which way is that?"

Lissa shrugs. "The way that doesn't start a war."

Her expression almost makes me believe that she knows about the library and what I've hidden there. Suddenly I want to tell her everything. I want to tell Roarke as well, but something stops me. I get into the car, but as Roarke starts the engine, I roll down the window and lean out.

"Wouldn't you say that a war has already been started?"

Lissa smiles sadly but does not answer. She raises a hand, and then we pull away. At first Roarke drives without saying anything, but after a few minutes, he looks at me out of the corner of his eye to say, "I guess that means you found out what you needed to know. Now what are you going to do about it?"

———

I know our cameras are at the campaign event, but they are lost in a sea of reporters. There is a split second when I think I catch sight of the familiar face of one of the show's own cameramen, but then he is swallowed again by the roiling crowd. All the major networks are there and I recognize a few of the local bloggers. Ellory Lester has delivered what he promised. Mother, on the other hand, has produced a good number of Daddy's congregation. If things go according to plan, Caleb may very well have an audience even larger than anything Mother and Daddy have ever been able to wrangle on their own.

Roarke and I wait on the bandstand with the rest of the family for Caleb's car to arrive. Ellory finishes handing out American flags and then, making note of the approaching Land Rover, signals that it is time to raise these flags and cheer. The car stops and Caleb climbs out of the front passenger-side door, waves, and turns to help Naomi and the kids out of the back. Naomi and Millicent are in dresses cut from matching blue fabric, while little Nate wears a white shirt and a red bow tie. Caleb carries him with one arm and waves with the other and together they walk toward the stage. Once there, Caleb hands Nathan to Matty and kisses Naomi on the cheek before taking the podium.

I try to tune out Caleb's speech, but it is punctuated by buzzwords like America and freedom and religious liberty. Every time he says one of these, the crowd cheers and I jump a little, startled by their fervor, by the frenzy with which they whip their little flags in the air above their heads. A breeze picks up, and though it is gentle, it is still enough to make the red, white, and blue balloon arch beneath which Caleb is standing begin to sway to and fro. The crowd subconsciously mimics the movement and soon they are undulating with a force as primal as the tide.

Caleb gestures to Naomi, says something about soul mates, and Roarke reaches out and takes my hand and squeezes it as if to say that this will all be over soon. And it is. Caleb announces his run for the House of Representatives and Bennett Tull himself takes the stage. I look around and try to see where he could have been hiding. He shakes hands with Caleb as if to pass the torch and smiles and waves at his constituents, his hand raised like that of a conductor calling for a crescendo, and he is immediately rewarded as the chorus of shouts begins to swell.

All at once it is finished and we are being swept away. Ellory Lester had been clear on the matter of not allowing interviews. He wants all of the airtime to be filled up by this scene alone and

its meticulously crafted optics. If the networks want to supple-
ment with other shots, they will have to use footage from *Six for
Hicks*, preferably episodes when Caleb was younger. Ellory says
that voters are naturally drawn to those candidates they know
best, and what better way to drive home how well all of America
knows Caleb than to highlight what are essentially home videos
of him growing up before their very eyes?

Caleb shakes the hands that are thrust at him across the temporary barricade. Naomi stands a little to the side with Nathan
on her hip while Millicent hangs on to her skirt. Naomi's teeth
look bright against her dark red lipstick and I wonder if she had
them whitened especially for the occasion and whether she told
the dentist to bill the campaign.

The strobe of the cameras flash like bursts of summer lightning and Millie begins to wail. Naomi, unable to put Nathan
down, pats Millie's head in a way I'm sure is meant to be soothing, but the girl only cries harder. Naomi looks toward Caleb for
help, but his back is turned. Heedless of either his wife or his
daughter, Caleb moves farther away, reaching his hand into the
fray, pumping his arm furiously up and down. He shakes the
hand of a girl not much older than I am and she looks up at him
eagerly. Keeping ahold of her hand, Caleb leans forward so that
his lips practically brush her hair as he whispers something to
her. The girl blushes. Naomi takes a step toward him then, opens
her mouth as if to call his name, but Roarke is already there, lifting up Millicent and rescuing her, spinning her around so that
his body blocks the flashing of the lights, asking her about the
ribbons in her hair. Naomi smiles at me in a conspiratorial way,
a look I find difficult to interpret, but perhaps she only means it
to be kind.

Finally, Ellory signals to Caleb that it is time to leave; Caleb
gives the crowd one last wave and we all turn to walk away. Then,

apparently unaware of Ellory Lester's instructions regarding interviews, the press surges forward to follow us toward the parked cars. Bulky microphones crowd my peripheral vision while reporters call out my brother's name. Roarke charges ahead of them and deposits Millicent safely in her car seat and closes the door to block her from the noise. Naomi gives his hand a grateful squeeze and circles around to the other side of the car and begins the task of buckling Nathan in as well. I feel a hand on my arm and I stop and turn.

"We have no comments at this time, thank you," Mother says brusquely, but it is only Libby and so I grab hold of Mother's hand and pull her to a stop as well, cutting my palm on one of her enormous rings.

"Mother," I say to placate her, "this is Liberty Bell. I'm sure you recognize her from our chats together. I think a formal introduction is long overdue."

Mother collects herself quickly and switches on her smile. "Of course. Liberty, my dear, thank you for all you've done for our darling Esther Anne. We couldn't be more pleased with your coverage. You've really given the public a chance to get to know these two young people and the lovely man and woman they are growing up to be."

"The pleasure has been all mine, Mrs. Hicks, I assure you."

Libby is jostled slightly to one side and Mother pulls my hand to lead me toward the cars. I free it and impulsively reach forward and take Libby's pad of paper out from between her fingers. There is a pen nestled in the spiral binding and I extract it and open the pad to a blank page near the back. I should have done this when we were alone. Maybe I should have done this the first time we met, but for some reason I was not sure I was brave enough until right now. Something about being up in front of all those people, about the way they clapped and cheered with so much hope, and the way that girl looked at my brother, has finally made this necessary.

"You were asking about the old church at the edge of town, the one with the big stone cross out front. I felt so foolish, but when you asked who had founded the parish, my mind went completely blank. I was nervous about the interview, I guess."

Libby tilts her head to one side and her eyebrows come together. Lissa used to look at me like that when I asked her questions she thought I should know the answer to, like where to find Germany on a map or what French-kissing meant.

"Essie, I have no idea—" Libby begins, but I cut her off.

I need her to understand. If I wait until I am home and can text her again, then she will have already left town—and in any case, I am nearly certain that I will lose my nerve. It's happened before. So I continue, "That's really no excuse, though, since Daddy talks about him all the time. He's something of a hero to our family. Before he raised that church's steeple, these parts were entirely populated by heathens, native and European alike. It's completely inexcusable for me to forget his name."

"You must be talking about Livingston James," Mother says. "Esther Anne, we've surely taught you better than that."

I giggle and shake my head from side to side and write down the name.

"Reverend James, of course. How silly of me. My nerves must really be on edge. Mother, don't you think Libby would find the story of the congregation's early years inspiring? Perhaps Daddy has some old diaries or books that she could borrow?"

Mother's smile stiffens and she squeezes my hand so tightly that I wince. However pleased she might be with the Liberty Bell who exists on camera to promote her daughter's sham engagement, she does not want her in our house.

Mother glances down at her watch and says, "The library's

open for a few more hours. They have an entire section of historic documents that deal with the founding of the town. You should stop in and browse through them before you begin your journey home."

"It all sounds very interesting," Libby says, her words coming out slowly.

"Oh, it's fascinating," I agree. "Mother is right. You should absolutely stop in to the library before you get on your way. There are so many wonderful stories from that time, stories that give us a better idea of who we are today. But none of them compare, I think, with really looking into the Reverend James's eyes. They speak volumes, Daddy always said. They open up a doorway to the past."

I am not sure whether I have said too much or not enough, but it's hard to think with Mother watching. Now her tug on my hand becomes more insistent and I can only hope Libby has understood as I am guided to our family's car. Daddy's secretary, Liam, is beside him at the wheel so Mother climbs in back with me. The last thing that I see is Libby's look of confusion. Then Liam pulls the car away.

Liberty

The press mills about for another five minutes and then the crowd thins and I'm left standing in the park almost entirely on my own. I see Margot signaling frantically for my attention from the doorway of the coffee shop where she was hiding during Caleb Hicks's campaign event. I look down toward the corner where Essie's SUV disappeared and give my head a shake as if to clear the fog that has settled over my brain. Mama used to send me out to the barn any time my brain got full up like that. *Go get a wiggle on,* Mama would say, *and don't come back until you've simmered down.* Being around the horses could usually be depended on to settle my thoughts. I shake my head again. It doesn't help.

Reluctantly I cross the street and join Margot at a window table at Common Grounds. I order an espresso, but I know the caffeine won't help me unravel what it was that Essie was trying to say.

"What's wrong?" Margot asks.

I screw up my face, uncertain how to answer.

"I don't know," I finally admit. "Essie introduced me to her mother and then started talking about a Reverend James who lived here back when the town was first founded."

"Livingston James?"

"How did you know that?"

"Because the library is named after him. We drove by it. You can actually see it if you lean this way."

Margot gestures out the window.

"It can't be," I tell Margot.

"What can't be?"

"The library can't be named after Livingston James. If it were, then Essie never would have forgotten his name."

"Maybe she's not the library type," Margot begins. I raise my eyebrows and then she says, "All right. I take it back. She should have known his name. What of it?"

"It didn't make sense for her to bring him up at all. She said I had asked her about his old church, but I never did. And then after Mrs. Hicks reminded Essie of his name, she told me to go to the library to read about the congregation."

"Who did?"

"Well, Mrs. Hicks first, but then Essie seconded it. She said something about how the past informs who it is that we become, which seemed fairly cliché even for her."

"Maybe there's something there that she wants you to see. If so, she couldn't really come right out and say so, not with her mother standing there."

I take another sip of my coffee and feel my teeth begin to buzz. One of the baristas drops a glass and there is a round of applause. She takes an embarrassed bow and begins to sweep up the shards. There is more good-natured laughing and all at once the caffeine kicks in and the faces of the strangers all around me seem to be melting. I blink and force myself to focus.

"We should go," I say and I scrape my chair across the floor and bump the table as I stand.

"We should go," Margot repeats. "Where exactly are we going?"

The bell above the door jingles as I push our way outside and point.

"To the Livingston James Library, of course."

When we enter the library, a stern-looking woman holding court from behind the circulation desk purses her lips with obvious displeasure as we approach. Amazingly she holds this expression without moving even a single muscle while I explain that we would like to learn more about the library's namesake, Livingston James. At this she sighs, as if it is all too much for her, and I get the sense that she is less offended by having to walk us to the back reading room than she is by the notion that there are still people in this world for whom Livingston James is not a household name.

We walk at a snail's pace to the foot of a spiral staircase and she wags her finger to indicate that we should climb. She does not follow.

We are halfway up before she calls after us, "There are some lovely portraits as well as the usual manuscripts, but the bust is my favorite. It was donated to the library by my great-great-grandfather nearly a hundred and fifty years ago."

There are a few snake hisses from the reading room, but these cease as soon as the patrons realize who it is they're shushing. I look up in time to see Margot disappear onto the second floor and I begin to climb up after her.

The room the stairs lead to is circular. We are in the squat tower at the far end of the building that is the only part of the library that rises above ground level. Dark wood beams cross the empty space above our heads, fanning out of the center of the tower like the spokes of a wheel. From the center of the wheel hangs an electric chandelier. Just beneath this there is a large glass case of maps that look to have been hand drawn onto yellowed parchment, with blue ink for rivers, black for roads, and green for the pastures and the wild tangle of forest that encircled the settlement to the north, south, east, and west.

Margot taps a fingernail against the flat surface of the glass. "It wasn't much. Just the church and a handful of farms and houses."

That's all there is in the town where I grew up even now. "It's the same with everything," I say. "It starts out small and either grows or dies out."

"What do you think we're supposed to learn from this?"

"I still don't know."

I move over to the shelves, first pulling volumes out at random and leafing through them, then running my fingers along the bookcases themselves, though what I'm looking for, I can't say. I find a family Bible, the once blank leaves at the very front and back filled with names and dates of births and deaths and baptisms. I open the book to the center, half expecting to find the pages hollowed out in an homage to *The Shawshank Redemption* with some message from Essie hidden inside. But there's only Ezekiel, the part about milk and honey, the pages so thin they are nearly translucent.

Behind me I can hear Margot open a book so old its spine practically creaks in protest. She sets it on a table and turns its pages.

"This one is written by Rosalind James, the reverend's wife. It looks like a diary of the first five years of the church."

I cross the room to join her at the table and say, "Those would qualify as the early years, I guess. Essie mentioned something about that."

Margot leafs through the leather-bound volume and then plants a finger to pin the curling pages down.

"Here," she says.

We both read Rosalind's description of the first Christmas

pageant, the children dressed in real lamb's wool, the angel with her crown of straw. The congregation shared a simple supper in the rectory after the service and Rosalind was particularly proud of how her pudding had turned out.

"There's nothing here," I say after staring at the pages so long my eyes begin to tear. "She can't possibly expect us to read everything from the first few years after the church was founded, can she?"

"I don't know," Margot answers. "What else did she say?"

I try to remember, but for a moment all I can recall is Celia Hicks's smile, the way her makeup made it look as if her face might crack.

"Nothing. The entire exchange couldn't have lasted more than a minute. At first Essie asked her mother if Pastor Hicks might have some books that I could borrow, to learn about the founding of the town, that sort of thing. Then Celia Hicks said I should just go to the library. I think she didn't want to be bothered and I thought Essie might be disappointed, but she agreed so readily that I should visit the library that I figured it must have been what she wanted all along. She just didn't want to be the one to say it."

"And then?"

"And then they left. They walked away. Really, that was the entire exchange."

"So maybe she actually just wanted you to learn some history. Maybe it's no more complicated than that. Judging by the dust, no one else has been up here in ages, even with the impressive bust the librarian's family paid for. Maybe Essie thought someone should give these books another chance."

"What did you say?"

Margot shrugs. "Maybe she felt bad that these books had been forgotten. She's an odd kid. You have to admit that."

"No, the other thing. The bust. Essie said something about looking into Reverend James's eyes."

The bust stands on a pedestal between two shelves. I hurry over to peer at it. Livingston James was a plump man, with very little hair on his head, a deficit he seemed to have thought he could make up for with the tangle of whiskers on either side of his face. Mama would have said he had been hit with the ugly stick, but she wouldn't have said this when she knew I was listening. His milky eyes look hollow. The piece is altogether a little frightening.

"He's hideous." Margot's voice comes from just behind my shoulder and I jump.

"He was a man of the people."

"Which people? He looks more like a monster you would warn children about in a fairy tale."

I lay a hand against the cool marble, then run my fingers over and under the rim of the pedestal and all the way down to the floor. There's nothing there. I stand and brush the dust off my hands, all at once aware of how foolish I have been.

"I guess I was wrong," I say. "There's nothing here after all. Let's go. We have a long drive home."

Margot places Rosalind James's diary back on its shelf and straightens the books around it so that it looks as if we were never here. I give the room one last glance, then throw out my hands in surrender and make my way toward the stairs. I am already partway down when I hear Margot's voice coming from above me.

"Stop."

I jog back up the steps and stand beside her at the entrance to the room. She's examining a portrait of the reverend that is no more appealing than the bust. The canvas is largely covered in various shades of black so that the white collar that supports Livingston James's double chin is in stark contrast to the background. The eyes I'm gazing into are porcine slits perched atop a pair of ruddy cheeks.

I frown. "This isn't any better."

Margot shakes her head. "I know. I'm going to have night-mares about those jowls. But look."

She points at the film of dust that has settled on the frame. There is one place where it has been brushed away, as if some-one had rested a finger on it. Slowly I reach out and put my own thumb into the negative space the absence of dust has created. Using the thumb as an anchor, I can reach around beneath the frame with my other fingers and slip them up behind the painting. I pat blindly, not sure what I hope to find, and then I feel a rough edge of crinkled tape that gives way to something smoother, well-suited for wrapping birthday presents. Scotch was not even a company when this painting was framed. There is no reason for tape of that sort to be stuck to the back of it. I stretch my hand further and then I feel it, a small raised bump, nothing more.

"There's something back here," I tell Margot, "only I can't quite reach it."

"Here," she says and reaches around me to gently pull the cor-ners of the frame ever so slightly forward. I slip my hands up in the space she's created and now I can feel the edges of the object. It's square, an inch or so long at most and flat enough that no one would have noticed it if they hadn't been looking.

Carefully I pry it up and work at the underside of the strip of tape to ease it off the painting's backing. Then all at once it comes free and I'm holding the red square in my hand. I turn the flash drive over and finally close my fist around it.

"What do you think is on there?" Margot asks.

"I haven't the faintest idea."

———

I resist the urge to plug the drive into my laptop right away. Something about the lengths Essie had gone to to hide it makes me want to get out of town as quickly as we can. Margot insists on driving and I don't protest. I'm trembling as I lower myself into the car and it has nothing to do with the espresso. I'm certain now that I was right to worry about Essie all along. No one who is happy to be walking down the aisle hides a flash drive and then sets out a trail of bread crumbs for the only reporter she knows is on her side.

Once the car is parked and Margot has left to meet her wife, I take the stairs to my apartment two at a time. I'm already pulling the drive out of my pocket as I walk in, but I immediately stop short and shove it down again. Mike is blocking the entrance, arms folded, dark eyes narrowed.

"I thought you said you would call her."

I slip off my shoes and stow my bag in the closet in order to avoid the confrontation. When I can delay no longer, I turn around and shut the closet door behind me.

"I will. I promise," I assure him.

"When?" he asks. He is clearly not impressed.

"You know what she wants to talk about."

"I do," he agrees, too quickly. "Quentin Ames is up for parole. Your mother told me. She left messages on your voicemail every day last week, which you ignored, and now she's calling here. I shouldn't have answered, but she called five times in a row and eventually I broke down. I can't be in the middle of this. You know what will happen if I am."

"I'm sorry."

"You don't have to be sorry, but you do have to tell her. Because if you don't, then I will. She has a right to know."

"You don't know what it would do to her."

Mike shakes his head and finally backs up, letting me come farther into the room.

"I do know, remember? Because I watched it happen to you."

I walk past him and throw myself down onto the couch. The truth is, Mike is right and there is no way around it. I should have told her a long time ago. I would have, maybe, if we had still been speaking. It would have just come out—how could it not? In between telling her about the new steak house that opened down the street or why I hate my boss, it would have slipped out, how everything she thought she knew about how her daughter died simply wasn't true.

———

At first it was fun. It was like a sleepover. The younger kids especially were excited, giddy at the change. For Justice and me, though, things felt pretty close to normal, as strange as that might seem. We were in a different place, but we still did chores in the morning and the afternoon and, in between, we had school with Mama. Justice could read much better than I could, I remember that, though she sometimes pretended not to know a word. She would ask me for help and I would make her sound it out, even though I knew her confusion was just an act. Then she would flash a grateful smile and bury her head back in her book.

There were plenty of books to choose from once Ames and Pa and some of the other men broke into the visitor center, though the subject matter was limited to the area's geography and a few volumes of colored illustrations useful for identifying local birds. Before we moved into the visitor center, we prayed and cooked and slept under the stars. Black Rock was still open to tourists then, with twice-daily guided tours through some of the deeper caves. Quentin Ames had printed off some flyers announcing the occupation, but really I think no one in town took him seriously. Three weeks had passed before anyone realized that we were there.

Ames had chosen a small clearing near the perimeter of the park for our initial settlement. There was a cave nearby that he said was sacred and from which he claimed the Messiah would rise again. At the time, I didn't question this. I took everything he said for truth. We came and went as needed through the Laramies' back pastures, which abutted Black Rock near a trail that led almost directly to the camp. It was still warm, but even then it was clear that Ames was preparing for the winter. He himself never left the park grounds, but he would send Pa and Mo Laramie and some of his other most trusted followers back into town to stock up on supplies. Canned goods went into the cave to the right of the one reserved for the Messiah, while guns were kept to the left. By the time a ranger spotted our encampment and called in the Feds, we had enough Spam to last for months.

We moved to the visitor center in stages. The men went first, carrying rifles. By then the tourists had been asked to leave, but additional law enforcement had yet to arrive. The few staff that remained were still inside the visitor center when Pa and Quentin stormed the small shingled building. Pa took the time to pick the lock even though Ames had urged him to skip that part and just break down the door. Pa would be punished for his disobedience, publicly, but Mama whispered to me and Justice that Pa did it because he knew we would need that door later, would need it to keep out the cold.

Ames didn't take hostages. He said he had no use for nonbelievers and that they would only distract from what we had been called to Black Rock to do. To witness. We moved camp quickly while the naturalists, some of whom I recognized from town, scurried off in their matching brown shirts and name tags in the direction of the main road. In the meantime, Ames set up a perimeter that protected the trails back to the cave, claiming that acreage as our own. He barked out orders to the adults and then turned his gaze on us.

Besides Justice and me, there were eight other children, not counting the Niccols boys, who at fourteen and fifteen wanted everyone to believe that they were grown men. Though Ames was laughing and joking loudly with some of the other men when Mama hurried us past them and into the visitor center, she moved furtively and her voice sounded scared. We huddled together in the corner, the older children comforting the younger, when Mama left us so she could return to the caves to fetch more supplies. Mama was still gone when Quentin Ames took five-year-old Virginia Murphy roughly by the hand and led the sobbing girl outside. We followed because we knew we had to and I saw Ames tug Ginny once more by the arm and then let go. He picked up a stick and sliced its pointed end through the dusty ground.

"There," he commanded, "play."

I looked at the ground and saw that Ames had carved the rough outlines of a hopscotch court. Ginny remained frozen, clutching at her wrist where Ames had grabbed it.

"Play," he said again and his voice was dangerous.

"We need a pebble," Justice demanded, apparently unafraid.

"There's no shortage of them here," Ames replied, throwing his arms out to either side. "Find one for yourselves."

Ames sauntered back toward the visitor center, kicking up dust with his boots, and Mo Laramie handed him a rifle. The two men leaned against the building in the shade of the porch and watched Justice. Mo spat out a wad of soggy tobacco into a patch of dry grass. My sister stood with her hand on one hip and surveyed her surroundings. She kept her back toward the men. Then she skipped forward and bent to collect a smooth black stone. She turned it over in her hand, running her fingers across the surface and finally brushing it against her jeans to rub it clean. Justice handed the rock to me.

"You go first," she offered.

I glanced over her shoulder to Quentin Ames.

"Don't mind them," she told me. "Go ahead."

I took the pebble from her and threw it.

We had all gone two or three times at least when the first of the squad cars rolled up. It kept its distance, stopping a ways off where the driveway turned to dirt and the welcome sign was mounted on top of a small rise. Virginia Murphy stood frozen on one foot. It looked like she might start to cry again. We all watched the officer climb out, moving slowly and careful to remain protected by the vehicle. I didn't need to turn around to know that Ames and the other men weren't hiding their guns. The officer waited until three other cars screeched to a halt beside his and then he pulled out a bullhorn.

"Quentin," the voice crackled, "what on God's green earth do you think you're doing?"

The officer took off his hat and wiped a cloth over the top of his head. I recognized him as Derrick Cumberland, who was a few years younger than my father but older than Quentin Ames. Derrick had been the captain of the high school track team the year Uncle Court, Mama's brother, had been a senior and they got all the way to the state championship. Of course, they lost to Nixville, but you would never know it the way Court tells the tale.

So Derrick Cumberland and the men on the porch may not have been friends, but they weren't strangers. There were no strangers in our town, except for the tourists who were only passing through. People kept to themselves. Their children might not go to school. But even so, each one of us was essentially a known quantity. Not Quentin, though. Unlike Pa and Court and Derrick, who had all come up through school together, Quentin Ames was an outsider. He didn't move to town until he was nineteen. His parents had died or else he'd left them: I'd heard it told both ways. Even after the siege had ended and they were writing books about him, the facts were fuzzy. But the man himself never seemed that way when you were standing face-to-face with him. He looked crisp and sharp despite his rumpled shirt and unwashed jeans. He demanded attention. He drew the eye.

The eye of Derrick Cumberland, for instance, never left Quentin Ames as he stepped out of the shade and protection of the porch. There were half a dozen others flanking the entrance to the visitor center, but the officers kept their guns trained on Quentin Ames. He walked forward, his rifle held casually at his side, and stopped in the middle of our forgotten game. He slung the rifle over his shoulder and lifted an arm to place a hand on my head.

"A beautiful day to be enjoying the land, don't you think?"

Ames spoke clearly but softly. Still, it was obvious that Officer Cumberland and the others had heard him well enough.

"This is federal property," Derrick shouted, his bullhorn forgotten at his side.

"This land belongs to the Lord," Quentin Ames countered.

Derrick turned his head slightly to listen to what another one of the officers was saying, then called out, "The United States government would respectfully disagree. You all are going to have to clear out."

Ames stooped over and retrieved our black stone. He handed it to Justice and motioned for the rest of us to back up off the hopscotch court. Justice took the rock and held it in her outstretched hand. She glanced over at Pa. He must have nodded in response to whatever question was in that look because she took a step back and tossed the pebble onto a square. Ames chuckled softly as Justice hopped and then spun around, the stone once again in her hand.

"We're not going anywhere," he said to both no one and everyone all at the same time.

———

I tend to think of this as one of my last memories of Justice, but the truth is, by the time she died, we had been at Black Rock for more than 120 days. Thanksgiving had come and gone and though Quentin Ames led the group in a prayer about all that we had to be thankful for, I was angry to be eating Spam and boiled potatoes instead of turkey smothered in Mama's cranberry sauce, and the sweet potatoes with little marshmallows melted on top. I was more than a little frightened of the cold, which had rolled in with the end of summer and seemed to blow straight through the walls. The snow helped some, when it fell in drifts taller than Justice and me. At least it blocked the wind.

When Ames called out to me, Mama was knitting stockings—I could hear her needles—and although Christmas was just around the corner, the stockings were not for holding presents. They were for our feet. Mo Laramie had nearly lost a toe when a storm started up while he was out hunting. It took him hours to drag himself back through the squall with only a few squirrels to show for all his trouble. Mama made the fire as big as she dared, then heated some water to soak the foot in while Mo cursed and spat and yelled at Lou Ann to be more careful as she pulled off first his boot and then his frozen sock.

I play these memories over in my head every so often because as much as I hate them, I don't want to forget. I try to remember if I was even frightened or if that was just something I added in later, when the shrinks and the social workers handed me crayons and encouraged me to draw pictures that would tell them each of the many ways I was broken deep inside. Knowing that fear was what they expected, I told them how Justice and I had clung together, four arms and four legs all tangled together in our sleeping bag, and cried ourselves to sleep at night. But we didn't. We giggled. We sang songs. We played with our flashlights for ages after we had been told to turn them off. For a long time after the day Quentin drew the hopscotch court, it all seemed like one big game.

Even that last morning, the one when Justice followed orders and I didn't, I wasn't hiding beneath my covers because I was afraid of what might happen if I went to Ames when I was called. I wasn't saved by some sixth sense, some silent warning, some instinct of the forces that had been building up outside. It was because I was cold, it was because I was lazy that I got left behind. I would have gotten up if he had told me to just one more time. But he didn't. For whatever reason, he was satisfied to go with only Justice, and they went outside, the two of them, into the deep drifts of snow. It was my laziness that killed my sister. If there had been two of us, the shooter would have never fired. Pa told me so even before we knew for sure that she was dead.

———

Years later, I went back and saw the black marks on the cement floor where we cooked those squirrels and fried countless cans of Spam and even saved Mo Laramie's pinky toe. A school group stomped into the Black Rock Visitor Center, but the children didn't skirt the scorch marks as I had done. They walked right across them. Two little girls were holding hands and laughing. It made me want to hit them, to scream that this building did not deserve their laughter. I was offended that they weren't saddened by what had taken place there, though they had no reason to be.

There wasn't even a plaque, since that would only encourage other militants. What happened there was just a footnote, a boring history lesson, and nothing more. It was personal only to me.

Except that I know this isn't true. It was personal to Mama too. It was why she wrote letter after letter to the parole board and regularly called the Department of Justice to demand that Ames's case be reviewed. It was why she was calling me now, though we haven't spoken for years, to ask me to write my own letter. Setting Quentin free had become an obsession for Mama. What she really wanted was to have her daughter back, but since that wasn't possible, she would settle for Quentin Ames instead.

Esther

That night I dream of Livingston James, and though I have only flashes of feeling to remember the nightmare by, I know it was about Libby as well. I should have just slipped her a note or found a way to sneak a text from Roarke's phone before she and Margot drove out of town, but in truth I've always felt that there are not many people in this town I can truly trust. With that many of them around, someone might have seen. They are kind to me. They go out of their way to be solicitous. But even without meaning to, they have a tendency to report my every move to the woman from whom I, at times, desperately want to hide. It is like that for every teenager, I suspect. My mother just has more willing spies than most.

The next morning she wakes me by pacing up and down the hall. Mother waits until she hears me turn over in bed before she peers around the door. I prop myself up on one elbow and resist the urge to dig myself deeper under the covers.

"Oh, you're up," she says in mock surprise. "Good. You have a fitting at ten. You'll need to shower. We'll stop off at Lilah's on the way and she'll figure out something to do with your hair."

"I don't see why I have to go. We already know it fits."

My weight has evened out now that my appetite is back to normal and I probably have another month or so before I really start to pack on the pounds. At least that's what Google tells me. Mother sighs and looks at me indulgently.

"The wedding is only a week away. You know they need to air the teaser tomorrow. They'll need some footage of you in the dress."

I sit up and tuck the quilt around my waist, trapping the warmth, and pull the sleeves of my nightgown down over my wrists. I shiver, reluctant to climb fully out of bed.

"It's only a little bit longer, Bug. I know that it all seems overwhelming, but you're almost there. Once the ceremony is over, you won't have to worry about anything ever again."

I start at her use of my old nickname, short for Lovebug, and at her use of the word you instead of we. This is maybe the first time she has given any indication that this is something that is happening to me, not just to her. For a split second I am sorry about everything, not only about where I've tried to lead Libby, but about what I intend to do.

"Was this what it was like when you married Daddy?"

"Goodness no. I think there were barely fifty people at the church that day. We could hardly afford any flowers. I carried a bedraggled bouquet that was mostly baby's breath. It had already begun to rot. I could smell it as I was walking down the aisle. Your father had nothing when I married him. I was the only one who saw the sort of man he had the potential to become."

I wrinkle my forehead. This is not the way she tells the wedding story when the cameras are rolling. I wonder which version is closer to being true.

Impulsively I say, "But you loved him, right? It was more than just his potential. It was love."

Mother looks startled; her smile is brittle. "Yes," she says, "yes, of course. I loved him."

I try to hold her gaze, daring her to admit to some deeper darker truth, but she only repeats her command to shower and then slips away.

Roarke wanted to ask Blake to be his best man, but Mother quashed that idea on the basis that the best man would be in most of the close-ups of the actual ceremony and she didn't want to have to worry about an amateur fidgeting and ruining the shot. Or breaking out with zits and making the whole production look even more like a group of children playing at being adults than was absolutely necessary. In the end, she offered to let Roarke have Blake as one of his groomsmen and looked affronted when Roarke didn't trip over himself to thank her.

Caleb was the superior choice for best man as far as Mother was concerned; she explained her reasoning at length, using the words *chiseled features* and *boyish good looks* more than once. She denied that it had anything to do with increasing his visibility for the campaign, but when I suggested using Matty or Daniel or Jacob instead, she dismissed the idea outright.

So it was that Naomi had been assigned the task of being my matron of honor, since Mother has always been a sucker for symmetry. She and Candy debated for a long time whether it would be appropriate to have a pregnant woman standing beside me at the altar, not seeming to appreciate the irony implicit in the question, and finally decided that it was the perfect symbol of what the purpose of marriage really is. Honor God. Procreate.

Naomi is already in a dusty blue dress when Mother and I arrive at the bridal shop, and she is turning this way and that in front of a mirror made up of three separate panels. The slippery fabric shimmers and accentuates the curve in her lower abdomen. I try not to stare and Mother rushes to embrace her in an expansive hug.

"Naomi, dear, you look lovely," she breathes.

"You don't think it's too much?" my sister-in-law asks meekly.

She has always idolized my mother. Her own parents died shortly before she started dating Caleb and I've always suspected, but never confirmed, that Mother paid for Naomi's last year of college. In my more cynical moments I know it would have been because the relationship was popular with viewers and Mother needed Naomi to stay in school, but when I am feeling generous, I recognize that Mother probably saw something of herself in her future daughter-in-law. Naomi may have grown up poor, but beneath all her fluff and simpering was a shrewdness that had bought her a life she could have never earned all on her own.

Naomi waves a hand in front of her chest, which I take to mean that she is worried about the neckline. Mother tugs on one of the shoulders and lifts Naomi's left breast by an inch.

"Well, it never hurts to err on the side of modesty. But I think bringing this in just a bit will achieve the necessary coverage and not compromise the line at all. Don't you agree?"

I step forward to take a closer look, but as it turns out, Mother is not talking to me. A sturdy-looking older woman scurries out from behind a counter, a line of straight pins held between her thin lips. She extracts one of these small metal daggers and jabs it through the fabric at Naomi's bust. Naomi winces but manages to stand still. Mother steps back to give the woman room to work and glances down at her watch.

"The crew will be here soon. You better go get changed."

The pin-wielding woman, whose name I cannot remember, mutters something while keeping her lips pressed tight. I have no earthly clue as to whether she is even speaking English, her words are so garbled by the pins she is holding, but Mother seems to understand her well enough. She takes my arm and leads me through to the back, where my dress is hanging in the largest of the dressing rooms. I shrug off my sweater and lay it flat on the upholstered bench, then sit to remove my shoes.

Mother stands uncertainly for a moment with her hand on the heavy velvet curtain, not sure whether she should wait inside or out.

"I can't get it on alone," I remind her.

Reluctantly she pulls the curtain and begins to ease the dress out of its bag. The dress is the one thing I chose in this entire wedding—except for Roarke, that is. Mother had originally picked out a gown with a stiff beaded bodice that made me look ten years older than I am, but I told her I couldn't breathe in it and the thought of my passing out on live television was enough to make her relent. In contrast, the dress that Mother is now unwrapping makes me feel light as air. Slipping beneath its layers of tulle is like being wrapped in a cloud that has been backlit by the sun. The delicate beadwork of flowers and vines wends its way over the chest and shoulders and makes me look no more and no less than the seventeen years I am. It is the only honest thing about this entire production and I am surprised to find that I love it. Once I saw my reflection that first time in the mirror, I knew there was no way I could do this wearing anything else.

It is the exact opposite of the sort of dress I used to clip out of magazines and pin to my paper dolls. Those were big pouffy concoctions of satin and lace, with layers of skirt gathered up in rosettes. Lissa never wanted to play at getting married, which was strange because she usually went along good-naturedly with most of my little-girl games. At first I thought it was because she was too old. Later, I began to suspect it was because she thought that getting married meant you turned into someone like our Mother and I could not blame her for wanting to avoid such a fate. Now I know it was more than that.

Mother finishes gathering the layers of the skirt up over her arms as I wriggle into the undergarments I have taken from their own hook. I reach above my head and lean forward and Mother slides the gown from her own arms onto mine. The fabric falls down over my shoulders, and as it does, I feel like I am standing outside during a summer shower, warm and cool at the same time, with the small hairs on my forearms standing to attention. I feel Mother tug at the buttons at my back and then wave her hands in frustration.

"I'll go get Mrs. Riley. She must have a hook of some sort to help with these."

A few minutes pass and Mrs. Riley, mouth now empty of pins, stomps her way back into the dressing room. She uses something that looks like a medieval torture device to thread the small pearl buttons through their loops. When she has finished, she holds the curtain back so I can pass into the hall. The full skirt rustles as I move and brushes against the walls. The cameras are rolling when I walk back into the showroom and Mrs. Riley hustles me over to a small raised dais at the center of the room. Hillary and Lucie have arrived as well and are sitting primly with Naomi, each trying to win the award for best sister-in-law by pretending the sight of me might make her cry. They urge me to twirl and I protest in embarrassment but then give in, letting the air fill my dress and lift the skirt off the floor.

"Not bad," a voice says from behind me.

I feel my heart trip in my chest as I turn to see Lissa standing there.

"What are you doing here?" Mother demands as she charges across the room and then, remembering the cameras, smiles and turns this attack into a stiff embrace.

"Making sure you don't send my baby sister down the aisle looking like a meringue. I needn't have worried, though. She looks just lovely."

Mother squirms, trying to figure out just how closely Lissa

and I have kept in touch, whether we might have been sneaking messages to each other all these years.

"It's only that I never expected you to come, to drive all this way," Mother lets out haltingly. "I thought you were . . . indisposed."

Lissa smiles broadly, enjoying the effect she is having on our mother. "My little sister is getting married. I wouldn't miss this for the world."

The sisters-in-law twitter something about how of course she wouldn't miss the wedding and they all trade kisses and compliment Lissa's hair and say that we really ought to get together more often because it feels like ages since we've all been in the same room. At the periphery of the reunion the cameras circle like predators, zooming in for a close-up of Hillary looking Lissa up and down and telling her she's gotten too thin, of Lucie demanding that Lissa come over soon for a home-cooked meal.

While this goes on, I stand as still as I can to avoid being skewered by Mrs. Riley, who is putting on her own show for the cameras by pinning my dress and then letting it out again. When she has finished, she steps away and throws her hands up with a flourish. There are the expected murmurs of admiration. I try to keep from fidgeting as the cameras zoom in.

"It's perfect. I know that Roarke will love it," Lissa tells me.

"Oh, you've met Roarke?" Naomi says. Her voice is too bright, as if she is trying to cover up for Mother's scowl. She does not wait for Lissa to answer the question before asking another. "Isn't he just a prince? I think if I were ten years younger and single myself, I might try to fight Essie for him."

Naomi giggles, a high-pitched nervous sort of sound. Lissa starts laughing as well, so hard that she has to wipe at her eyes. It's a while before she can catch her breath.

"But then you'd have to give up being married to Caleb. Don't be ridiculous. He's in a class of his own."

Something about Lissa's tone feels dangerous. I have never thought of Naomi as being particularly clever, but even she can sense it. She quickly says, "Of course. I was only joking."

Lissa's smile broadens at this and she echoes, "Of course. I know that, sis."

There's an uncomfortable silence and Mrs. Riley tries to fill it by fluffing out my dress. Hillary rewards her efforts and says, "Essie, you look truly breathtaking."

Mother moves forward to take my hand and then steps back as if relishing this moment. It looks as if she is trying to force a tear. Eventually she gives up, but she dabs at her eyes with a lace handkerchief nonetheless and breathes in sharply through her nose.

"My baby," she croaks helplessly, "is all grown up."

It is all I can do not to punch her, but then she is pulled away as my sisters-in-law surround her and try to soothe her as the four of them embrace. Naomi is crying, which makes me like her more since she is too poor an actress for the tears to not be real. I think it is possible that she is actually a good person and for a moment I am sorry. She will be all right, I know, but there will still be fallout. Collateral damage, that's what they all will be. Still, I tell myself, they have it coming.

Lissa has given up trying to hide her amusement, but at least she has stepped back a little so that she is behind the camera. They will still be able to use this shot. When the snuffling and reassurances have gone on long enough, Lissa steps back into frame. Her timing is perfect. She clearly remembers how this game is played.

"So," she says, causing the group to break up and turn to face her, "where's my bridesmaid's dress?"

A gust of wind rattles the door from outside and there is a faint tinkling from the bell hung over the frame. To Mother's credit, she does not pause for too long before saying, "But you never sent us your measurements, darling. Never mind that now. Let's have Mrs. Riley take them today. I'm sure she can whip something up in time."

Mrs. Riley scurries off to find a measuring tape only to realize eventually that she has one draped about her neck. I step off the small platform and Lissa takes my place. Obediently, she twists and turns and holds her arms out to the side. Mrs. Riley makes note of the size of Lissa's hips and waist and bust, scribbling the numbers down on a pad of paper she has extracted from a hidden pocket.

Lincoln, who is in charge of the camera crew, whispers something to Mother and they pack up to go. While Mrs. Riley finishes up with Lissa, Lucie begins telling Hillary and Naomi a story about how her own wedding dress almost didn't fit, but Mother cuts her off and tells her to take me back to the dressing room and get me out of "that thing." Gamely, Lucie struggles with the buttons and stows my dress back in its bag. She leaves me to change out of the slip and back into my own clothes, and as I do, I hear Lissa casually telling the others about school.

When I come back into the room, Mother makes it clear that she does not want to linger, so I hug everyone and thank them for coming, leaving Lissa for last. She squeezes me tight and then releases me, saying, "I'll see you at the rehearsal."

Mother rolls her eyes and walks out the door. She waits in the car while Mrs. Riley helps me hang my dress in the backseat. There are separate bags for the slip and the veil. The shoes are already at home, though they are not likely to be visible at all. I had argued that I should be allowed to wear sneakers, since they would be more comfortable and I would be less likely to trip and fall, but Mother insisted on heels. Anything else would be unladylike, she said. I wanted to tell her that any chance I had of being ladylike had been taken away a long time ago, but I did not think it would help my cause, so I bit my tongue.

Mother says nothing to me for the whole ride home. I did not really expect her to. There would be too many witnesses. The day has warmed up and Mother has rolled down the car windows. The air smells alive and I prop my arm out of the window to soak in the sun until Mother tells me to bring it back inside and says something about how ridiculous I would look if I got married with a sunburn on one arm. I tell her that the entire car ride is less than ten minutes, but she pretends not to hear and I obediently fold my hands in my lap.

Mother slows the car to wave at Mr. Leonid, who is walking his dog, and then pulls over to compliment Betty Melmer on her geraniums and to ask her to please send over her lemon cake recipe when she finds the time. Mrs. Melmer tells Mother that it was her great-aunt's recipe and promises to copy it out and have it in the mail by the end of the day. We continue to roll slowly through town, with Mother shouting something out of her window every block or so. A woman I don't know rushes over to tell Mother that the Hartnetts might be getting a divorce. Mother nods sagely and then we continue on our way.

Finally, we pull into our driveway. I make no move to get out of the car, assuming that Mother will want to say something to me first, but she opens her door without even looking in my direction and walks toward the house. There will be shouting, then, shouting that she doesn't want anyone to hear. I gather my things and bow my head and follow her inside.

Still, I am somehow unprepared when she fixes me with her eyes and quietly says, "What the hell was that?"

It is not just the swear—a word I have never heard come from her mouth—it is the fact that she does not even trust herself to yell. She is that angry.

"What?" I ask, even though I know it will only make her all the more furious.

Mother practically snarls, "Don't you even try to play dumb with me. What was she doing there?"

"She told you herself. She wanted to see the dress, that's all." I shrug and try to walk away, but Mother grabs my arm, her bony fingers pressing into my flesh.

"Careful," I say evenly. "You wouldn't want any bruises to show up on the live wedding feed."

Mother gasps and takes a step back. I have never talked to her that way before. She looks frightened of me and there is a part of me that wants nothing more than to show her just how frightening I can be, but I also know that I am not yet out of danger and I won't be until the wedding airs.

"Isn't it better this way?" I try instead. "I mean, how exactly were we going to explain it if she didn't even come to the wedding? People may have been satisfied these past three and a half years that she just wanted to concentrate on school, but surely there would be questions if she couldn't manage to make it down from Chicago for something as important as this."

"Yes, but even so, how did she know? How did she know about today?"

I see that I need to calm Mother down, so I say, "Gretchen has been live tweeting everything about the wedding, hasn't she? You asked her to keep the fans informed every step along the way. I'll bet she tweeted something about the fitting. That must be how Lissa knew exactly where we'd be."

Mother's shoulders relax visibly.

"Yes, that must be it."

I should leave it here, I know, but I cannot resist. I kiss Mother on the cheek.

"Thank you for asking her to be a bridesmaid. Thank you for knowing how important that is to me."

I do not give Mother a chance to say that it was Lissa herself who volunteered for the role, who strong-armed Mother into it by doing so on camera. Instead I race up the stairs to my room and turn on the radio. When I am sure that Mother has not followed me, I take out Margot's phone and type a note to Libby.

I hope you found what I left for you. It's every page of every diary I ever kept. The wedding will only be the beginning. People are going to want to know the rest. I trust you.

Once I am sure the message has been delivered, I hide the phone again, then skip lightly back downstairs. Mother looks startled as I enter the kitchen. She is sitting at the counter with her hands wrapped around her favorite coffee cup, the one that Daddy bought her at Hershey Park. She is not doing anything but sitting, which is unusual. She must still be shaken over seeing Lissa.

"I'm famished," I tell her cheerfully. "I think I'll make some French toast. Do you want any?"

"No, thank you," she answers primly and stands to go. Then from the hallway I hear, "Be careful you don't eat too much. Mrs. Riley is a miracle worker, but I don't think she can make your dress get any bigger."

Liberty

The flash drive is on my bedside table where I left it when Mike pulls open the curtains, a towel around his waist and his tooth-brush tucked inside his cheek. He looks down in the direction of the courtyard, grunts, and shuffles back toward the bathroom.

"Mr. Danziger is torturing his dog again," he manages around the toothbrush. I hear him spit, then he says more clearly, "We really ought to call someone."

I tuck my head down underneath the covers so that I'm look-ing at the flash drive as if from within a tunnel.

"Who exactly are we supposed to call? I don't think animal cruelty laws apply to people who dress their pets up like Ewoks."

"Well, they should," Mike proclaims and starts riffling through his closet to find something to wear. "You working from home today?"

I nod, then realize that Mike cannot see my head and reluc-tantly pull back the covers and sit up.

"I have some documents to go through. I really should have started on it last night."

I yawn.

"But you were avoiding calling your mother," Mike says point-edly. "Understood."

After Mike had gone to sleep, I stayed up and binge-watched Netflix with a carton of ice cream to keep me company. Whatever secrets Essie had entrusted me with, I did not want them, at least not yet. My head felt like it was too crowded already and I needed some time to decompress. If I couldn't visit the horses, well, old episodes of *Gilmore Girls* would have to do. When Mike wandered through the living room around two a.m. to get a drink of water, he just rolled his eyes and went back to bed.

Now he pulls on a sweatshirt and begins fishing through his drawer for socks.

"I have study group for dinner. Will you be all right?"

"Sure. It's not as if she's going to come up here and hunt me down."

"That's not what I meant," he says, sitting on the edge of the bed, socks in hand.

"I'll be fine," I reassure him.

He leans across the bed to kiss me and then goes. I stare at the ceiling for a while longer, not yet ready to face the day. Finally, I get up and slip my arms into my robe, drop the flash drive into my pocket, and move in the direction of the kitchen in search of caffeine. Since my espresso yesterday had kept me up half the night, I settle for tea.

Pulling a blanket around my shoulders, I sit on the couch and open up my laptop. But instead of plugging in the flash drive, I find myself on my mother's website, the one dedicated to advocating for the release of Quentin Ames. It's been updated since I last visited it. She must have recruited someone with a fairly decent graphic design background. She was good at that, recruiting. Quentin Ames was why we stayed at Black Rock well into the winter, but Mama was the reason people came in the first place. They trusted her. And if Mama believed that Ames was right about the Second Coming of Christ, they figured they should show up to see for sure. Then, when the Feds arrived, it became more than that; it became an "us versus them" situation. We were up against the world. There was no backing down from that. At least not until Justice was shot.

Mama's website is chock-full of testimonials from those who've been touched by Quentin Ames's ministry. It seems he's continued to preach from within the penitentiary. He writes a weekly sermon and sends it to Mama and then she posts it online. There's a delay, of course, and sometimes his letters are lost. Censored, Mama would say. Other times, he preaches to her directly during their visits and she writes down what he's saying as best she can. She even took a class in shorthand specially, so that what she posts later more accurately reflects what Quentin Ames has said.

Mama isn't the only one who visits him, but she's the only one who's allowed to be a conduit for his word. Most of the testimonials are from women, many of whom have driven hours to see him in person. They write about how it feels to be in his presence and, though I don't want to admit it, I remember and I know that much of what they write is true.

Quentin Ames was—is—a narcissist and probably a sociopath as well. But when he looked at you, the world seemed brighter; the sun shone hotter. Even as a child, I felt it. Even on the worst days we had at Black Rock, the coldest, the ones when there was not enough food to eat or Mo Laramie was in a temper or the ice had gotten up underneath the roof in the back corner of the visitor center and it had started to leak, a look from Quentin Ames could make it all feel worth it.

I remember that Justice had gotten into a fight with one of the Niccols boys about why they didn't bring back more game when they went out hunting. She had taken to counting their bullets in secret and finally came out and accused them of wasting ammunition on target practice or else being terrible shots.

I'm not sure which one she thought was worse, but it had been made clear to the teenagers that if they were to be allowed to go out hunting on their own, there shouldn't be any fooling about. Even then, before the snows, it was getting harder to sneak out to get supplies. Quentin Ames and Pa had both said that bullets needed to be rationed the same as anything else, so what Justice was accusing the Niccols brothers of doing would have repercussions with the grown-ups if any of it were true.

The older boy, whose name I can't remember, said that he shouldn't have to answer to a little girl. Justice's eyes flared. Her chin jutted out and the younger of the brothers laughed and pointed and teased her about looking like she might cry. But he misunderstood her expression, because Justice wasn't a crybaby. The glint in her eye was anger, not the welling up of tears. Without a word, Justice snatched the rifle out of the hand of the closer of the two boys and stormed out of the visitor center. After trading a look of surprise, the Niccols boys chased her outside, with Ginny and me tagging along behind them. But Justice was already gone. She had disappeared into the woods. Not long after, we heard a single shot and Justice appeared a short time later, dragging a wild turkey by its neck. She threw it down at the feet of Niccols the Older and handed back the gun.

She stormed back toward the visitor center without a word and that was when Quentin Ames appeared. He knelt before her and I saw the knots go out of her shoulders, saw her tightly clenched fists relax. Quentin Ames placed his palms on Justice's cheeks. He kissed the top of her head. Then he spun her narrow body around and she walked back to the Niccols boys.

"I shouldn't have taken your rifle without permission. I'm sorry."

Justice never apologized without a lingering note of resentment, but on this occasion there was none. That was what Quentin Ames did. He took all the anger that existed in your body and simply drained it away.

"We're sorry too," one of the Niccols boys replied. "We shouldn't have made fun."

If it had always been like that, then I might have grown up to be like those women who visited Quentin Ames in prison. I might have believed in his goodness too. But what I slowly realized was that every time he did something like he did that day with Justice, every time he soothed and relieved a person of their fury, leaving them with calm, he did not destroy it. Instead he gathered all that bile, that wrath, and held on to it. He was saving it for later. For when the Feds surrounded us. For when he wanted us to be ready for a fight. He wanted to go down in a blaze of glory. He just chickened out in the end.

———

The phone rings and rings and no one answers. Mama got rid of the answering machine after Justice died and they never got another. I should hang up, but for some reason I find the sound comforting and so I let it ring. I can picture it, the phone. It's mounted to the side of the pantry in the kitchen, the wire stapled against the wall and disappearing into the basement through a small hole in the floor. Yellow plastic casing. A real metal bell inside. The sort of spiraling cord that you could pull and stretch and twist between your fingers, could wrap around your wrist and body and then unwrap again. I'm taken by surprise when she does pick up after all that unanswered ringing.

"Hello?"

"It's me," I say. I'm met by silence. I wonder if it's been so long that my mother doesn't recognize my voice. Then, because there's still nothing but the sound of my mother breathing, I venture, "I didn't think anyone was home."

"Your father is just out with Topher running the north fence. Had a storm last week that brought some branches down and the fence didn't fare so well in places. They'll get it fixed up right by nightfall, though, I reckon."

"Is Topher's shoulder still bothering him?"

"It's much better. I mixed him up a salve that seems to have finally got the inflammation down. He tell you about that himself or have you been chatting with Penny again?" I don't answer. Topher's daughter, Penelope, is only one of the ways I keep tabs on my parents and the goings-on at the ranch, and she wasn't actually the source of this particular piece of information. My mother doesn't seem to care, though, because she continues on, "No matter. I'll let him know you asked after him. He'll be tickled. I suppose you're calling to tell me why you don't have time to write a letter to the parole board. You needn't bother. I've seen you on the television. They must have you booked from dawn till dusk. How could you possibly have time to sit down and write one little letter?"

"It's not that," I insist.

"Oh no? Then your little bit of fame must really be getting to your head. Have you forgotten what Quentin has sacrificed for us?"

She's referring to the fact that Ames took the fall for the entire occupation, that he made certain that no one else who was at Black Rock went to jail. It's this selflessness that makes so many women bake him cookies and write him letters. They even send him pairs of their own underwear, or so Mama once let slip before I left for college, her voice dripping with scorn.

"I haven't forgotten," I answer truthfully. As difficult as it is to admit, I know that even though I lost my sister at Black Rock, I could easily have lost both my parents as well.

"Then why would you deny him a few minutes of your time? He would do the same for any one of us."

"No he wouldn't. He killed Justice."

"Oh, honey, no he didn't. The government killed your sister. Quentin was the one who tried to save her. He just wasn't fast enough."

"He pushed her."

"No," Mama says. Her voice is brittle. "He didn't. I won't let you say such a thing."

In the hottest part of summer, Justice and I would sneak down to the creek and climb a tree that curved up over the water. Then we would jump. Each time, until I was falling, I was never sure that I was actually going to go through with it. That's what this feels like, that moment before the fall, but then the words start coming out of me.

"When Ames brought Justice out of the visitor center, there was a protest happening. Birders mad that the park had been closed so long, angry about the damage we must be doing to the birds' breeding grounds. It was being broadcast live on the local news."

I wait for my mother to object to what I have told her, but she is silent and so I take a breath and go on. "It's not what I thought I'd find when I drove over to the station, but I remembered how the cameras had sometimes been out by the entrance. I figured they might have some footage of her, of Justice. Do you remember how Ames used to make us play outside when people were watching? I got it in my head that there might be video of all of us playing hopscotch, and if there was, then finding it would be the closest I would ever get to seeing her alive again.

"That was how I tracked down the tape. It never got picked up nationally. The FBI had taken a copy, of course, in case they ever needed it at trial. But the station still had the original footage. There was no cover-up, no government conspiracy. It was in a closet less than an hour away from where Justice died, less than forty-five minutes from our house. All those years and you never even went looking for answers. It was almost as if you didn't want to know."

I pause again, but my mother is still silent. She's been silent for almost twenty years. "Quentin Ames held Justice up in front of him to stop the bullet. It would have missed her otherwise. He lifted her up when he saw Derrick Cumberland motion to the sniper. And when Justice was hit, he dropped her and left her bleeding. He could have surrendered then, but he didn't. He kept his rifle pointed at the protesters and just stood there and watched her die. Finally, they shot Ames in the shoulder and Derrick rushed forward to put his hands over the hole in Justice's neck."

I stop to catch my breath and listen hard for any sign that my mother is still on the other end. Then I realize that it doesn't matter if she has hung up. I need to say it all. "It took two hundred and thirteen seconds for Derrick to reach Justice and put pressure on the wound. By then the camera wasn't pointed in the right direction. The cameraman must have been getting jostled around. But you can hear the moment when Derrick reached Justice and called out for help. I still wonder sometimes if it wasn't the bullet hole that killed her but those two hundred and thirteen seconds. That's time that Quentin Ames stole from her. Even after he used her body as a shield, it's worse somehow that he couldn't even spare her the decency of taking off the scarf you knitted him to press it against your dying child's neck. I'm sorry, but you're wrong. He didn't try to save her. In fact, it was just the opposite. Please don't ever mention that man's name to me again."

"The FBI agent admitted culpability," Mama says next, but her voice is small.

"His name was Henry Morrison. He was only two weeks away from retirement when Justice died. Taking the blame for Justice's death was something he did to make sure our family got the highest possible settlement from the government. It was something he did for us to try to make things right. I've spoken with him. He's a good man. He's the one you should be sending home-baked cookies to and whose name you should be trying to clear. Not Quentin Ames. Quentin Ames is paying for his sins and he is precisely where he deserves to be. Until you realize that, I don't have anything more to say to you."

I accept the silence on the other end of the line and wait patiently for my mother to process everything I've said.

Minutes pass before she whispers, "I don't believe you."

"I know. And that's all right. I forgive you anyway."

"What for, exactly?"

My eyes well up, and through the prisms of the tears, I see Quentin Ames with his face tilted up in rapture and Mama knitting stockings by the fire. I see Mo Laramie's foot in the pot of water and Justice striding off into the woods with the rifle she stole from the Niccols boy. And then I see the blood, the way it must have looked as it melted craters in the snow. I remember this the most clearly even though it was Agent Morrison who saw it and I accept the memory as a gift that he has given me to make me strong enough to say this single word.

"Everything."

―――――

I am still shaking long after the phone goes dead. I don't move. From the living room window I can see the balcony of the top-floor apartment across the street. The door is open to the inside and a small boy appears, sitting on a wheeled animal of some sort. He coasts forward and bangs against the bars of the railing and then pushes himself back into the shadow of his living room. Over and over again he appears only to vanish. There one minute, the next gone.

When my phone buzzes, I cringe and decide to ignore it. I watch the boy. His head turns as if he's listening to someone speaking from inside. The phone chimes again and this time I glance down and see that there is a text from Essie. I read the message and it is as if the fog that had settled over me since Mike told me that I needed to call Mama has cleared. I feel lighter. Other people's problems can do that, I guess. They don't make anything better, but at least they provide a distraction.

I plug in the flash drive and open a folder of documents. Each is labeled with Essie's name and a number. I open *Esther 9* and read about Essie's ninth birthday party, the chocolate cake and the donkey-shaped piñata. I open *Esther 10* and *Esther 11* and each of them also starts with a birthday celebration. I realize that she must have started a new journal every year. Presumably they were handwritten, probably on rose-colored paper that had pictures of kittens in the bottom corner of each page, and Essie has transcribed them. There are nine documents in total, some of which are several hundred pages long. The last is *Esther 17*, which is short compared to those for the rest of her teenage years, less than twenty pages, but that's probably because it's unfinished. She's living those pages now.

I scroll through the documents at random, wondering what it is that Essie means for me to see. I find it after a few hours of reading, buried a hundred pages into *Esther 12*, the fall that Lissa went away. As my eyes move across the screen, I feel my stomach tighten. I dial without even being aware of what I'm doing, and when Margot answers, I tell her, "You need to come over here right away." I don't wait for a response but instead go straight back to reading.

Twenty minutes later, Margot lets herself in and drops onto the couch beside me.

"What gives?" she asks.

I blink and scroll back through the pages I've just read until I find the passage I'm looking for. I turn the screen toward Margot so that she can see. Her pupils dilate and she says, "Shit. Why do people have to be so predictable?"

———

An hour later, we have printed Essie's journals, put them onto Margot's computer as well, and together are combing through the documents.

"What exactly are we looking for? I presume not just the juicy bits," Margot asks.

"I don't know. The truth, I guess."

"You can't handle the truth." Margot prides herself on her impressions, and her Jack Nicholson is actually pretty good. I smile wanly since she's clearly waiting for a response and throw a balled-up piece of paper at her head. Margot catches it deftly and continues, "What do we do with the truth when we find it? Will she really be willing to go on camera and talk about any of this?"

I shrug. I had been wondering the same thing. Then I remember the first time Essie called me. *I've read your book*, she said as I sat in the stairwell. *I think it may be time to write another.*

"Maybe she wants the truth to be published," I say quietly and even as I say this out loud, I know it's true. "What better way to control the narrative? She even told me what she wanted the day we met, but I didn't understand what she was talking about until just now. She wants me to turn these diaries into a book."

Margot exhales bitterly. "No wonder she needed to get married. She won't be able to live at home after that."

"She didn't mention anything about timing, but there will never be a better time than now. Right after the wedding. The whole country will have tuned in to watch the fairy tale."

"And you want to tear the curtain down."

"How can we not? Especially with the campaign. It's not just gossip anymore. It's bigger than that."

"We have less than a week. That's not enough time."

I fall back and let my head nestle between the couch cushions. "Essie's already done the hard part."

"That's an understatement."

I sit back up and turn toward Margot. "No, I mean she's already written everything down. This is her book, not mine. It should be in her own words. They're all right here; we just have to figure out which ones matter."

"And then?" Margot asks. "We just call up your old editor?"

I shake my head. "We can't. Not without Essie's permission. It's still possible that when we're finished, she'll decide that this manuscript should never see the light of day. If she does want the truth to be out there, we publish it digitally, instantly, the minute she says go."

Margot looks thoughtful and I wait for her to say something. Finally, she says, "Do you think she realizes what this will do to her family?"

"I do. In fact, I think she's counting on it."

———

We divide up the early journal entries and highlight the passages to be included. Not a lot, just enough to lay a framework, to pull the reader in, to remind them of the ways they've been complicit in what happened by watching Essie's family on television all these years.

By the time Mike gets home, Margot is on the floor, her back against the couch and her legs stretched out beneath the coffee table. She's scooping pad Thai into her mouth from a shallow plastic dish while her eyes run across her computer screen. I sit on the couch beside her, a carton of fried rice in one hand.

"What happened here?" Mike asks, gesturing to the empty food containers and the stacks of paper littered across the room. "It looks like a bomb went off."

I think about how best to bring Mike up to speed. Up until now, I've censored what I say to him, mainly just talked about the interviews themselves. I didn't know how to make him understand why I like Essie so much, why I believe she's not just a puppet for her family's brand, but now I have proof that she's different and that I was right.

"Essie wants to publish a book. She's given me all her diary entries since she was nine years old. We're trying to figure out which bits to use."

Mike snorts. "What is it with that family? Is there anything they won't try to monetize? I wouldn't be surprised if they tried to sell their dryer lint."

Mike stops. Whatever each of us may have said about the Hicks family in the past, he can tell by the way that Margot and I are looking at him that we are no longer on his side as far as Esther Hicks is concerned.

"The first time Essie's brother Caleb raped her, she was twelve," Margot says after a long pause. "She bit him, but it was clear that he liked it, so she didn't fight much after that."

Mike lets this sink in. He wipes a hand over his eyes, a gesture that reminds me of my father, and I think how even though none of us really ever escapes our family, Essie has to at least get as far away as she can.

"Fucker," he whispers. "What can I do to help?"

Margot pushes a stack of pages toward him across the coffee table and Mike immediately drops his school bag in a corner, then sits down on the ottoman and starts to read.

"Are you going to finish that?" he asks me after a while, pointing to my rice.

"I thought you ate at study group."

"I did," he answers, "but something tells me that I'm going to need a second wind."

I pass him the rice and we all go back to reading. It's quiet apart from the squeaks of highlighters being drawn across paper, the tap of fingers on laptop keys. Margot shows me a page with a few paragraphs that she's selected and I nod.

After a long while, Mike says, "The relationship with Roarke is a sham."

"I think we all knew that," Margot replies.

"Roarke's family is in a lot of debt. Essie planned to have her mother approach his parents and offer to pay everything off."

"How much are they getting?" I ask.

"It doesn't say. It looks like this was written before she knew for sure the deal would be accepted, but I expect it must be a lot."

I jiggle a pen back and forth between two fingers as I consider this. "That doesn't paint any of them in a good light, does it? They sound like mercenaries."

Essie wouldn't have included this information if she wasn't comfortable with my sharing it. Still, it won't exactly endear her to people. They'll be angry that they were made to believe in a love story that wasn't real. Victim or not, people will say that Essie could have handled it differently. She could have made Caleb stop without sinking to extortion, without dragging Roarke into it as well. She would have been leaving home anyway, so wouldn't she have been safe? Why did she need the money? Why did she need to lie?

I start to speak, but Mike holds up his hand, palm facing out. He runs a finger down the margin of the page.

"Oh, God," he breathes.

"What?" Margot and I both burst out at once.

Mike drops the pages on his lap. The color has drained from his face.

"She's pregnant."

Roarke

Dad wakes me early with a sharp rap on my door and tells me that we're going hunting. It's still dark. I blink at the ceiling, letting my eyes adjust, until I can make out the small wooden airplanes hanging from the light fixture. It's a child's room, but Mom and Dad never had the money to update it. When I turned fifteen, I bought a can of paint myself and covered the walls with what I thought of as a mature gray, but it came out darker than I thought it would and made me feel like I was sleeping in a cave. As soon as I could, I painted it the light shade of green that it still is today.

My ankles crack as my feet hit the floor and I rummage through my closet and pull out my hunting gear. Dad likes to get an early start, but usually he gives me some warning the night before. I grumble as I move around the room, aware that Dad is already downstairs and can't hear. I dress and then, after double-checking the weather, I add another layer. I carry my boots downstairs so I don't wake up Mom and then sit down at the bottom of the staircase to put them on.

Dad hands me a coffee when I reach the kitchen and watches me as I down it. I look at the clock. It's just after five. When I've set the empty mug in the sink, Dad passes me a thermos so that I can have my second cup on the road. The cool air hits me when the door opens and I pull my jacket up around my neck. Dad leaves footprints in the dew as he walks across the driveway and

I see that a few of Mom's tulips must have bloomed without my noticing, though they've closed their cups up tightly overnight.

Dad starts to climb directly into the cab. His truck is already packed. He must've done it the night before, so there's no way this trip is a last-minute whim. I shoot him an accusing glance and he shrugs heavily.

"I was afraid you wouldn't come."

There's no place open this early, so Dad has packed breakfast as well. I gnaw on a bagel as morning bleeds into the sky.

"Where're we headed?" I ask him.

"Someplace new," he answers. "Some private woods. I put the address into the GPS. The others are meeting us there."

"What others?"

"That politician brother of your fiancée's. Probably some folks we haven't met. They told me it would be good for the store. Everyone will be using guns we sell."

"So they'll be filming?"

"That's what they said."

I swallow hard. The wedding is coming up fast. I went along with attending Caleb's campaign event because Essie asked me to, because it seemed like it was just something we had to get through. Then in no time we would be married and once that happened, we would be free of him. We would be free of them all. Now I see that I'm wrong and that the budding politician means to capitalize on the popularity of Essie's and my little love story as much as possible before we earn the right to tell him no. I worry about how I'll make it through the day. Once I was up onstage with Caleb, it was all I could do not to punch him in the face. It probably had something to do with the way he smiled and shook hands with the crowd like a normal person even though he's actually the lowest form of human scum.

I say, "Good for the store? More likely it'll be good for his image to be seen with me. My likability numbers are much higher than his."

"Your likability numbers? That's a thing?"

"When you're in the Hicks family it is. This is what you signed me up for, or don't you remember?"

Dad looks embarrassed and covers up the silence with a cough. He takes a sip from his thermos and fiddles with the radio.

"I hope you know how much I—" Dad starts to say, but I cut him off.

"Don't worry about it. Essie's likability numbers are the highest you can get. It won't be so bad, being saddled with the likes of her."

Dad lets out a "Huh" and concentrates on driving. Though I haven't really been paying attention, I think we're heading in almost the exact opposite direction of the lake. When we reach the town limits, he turns onto a country highway I've never been down and from there onto a one-lane dirt road labeled Private. The cornfields and rows of soy give way to trees. Through the branches ahead, the sky is fading from orange to a thinner yellow light. The ribbon of dirt we bump along seems to go on forever.

"How much land does this guy own?" I wonder aloud.

"Probably half the county. The person I spoke to—I think it was his secretary or else his personal assistant or something—said the camp would be a ways up on the left and that there was no way to miss it."

This turns out to be an understatement, since the camp is really nothing of the sort. It's a compound with a three-story log house at the center that is reached by a crushed-gravel drive. The house sits near the center of a grassy clearing with several other smaller buildings set on either side. A line of Adirondack chairs is visible on a porch and more are scattered across the lawn. Dad lets out a low whistle.

"Is this the sort of place you get when your likability numbers are high?" he asks.

"I think it's the sort of place you get when your net worth is high, regardless of whether you're likable or not."

"I never knew this was back here," he says as the tires begin to crunch over the drive.

"I'm pretty sure that was the idea."

We are greeted, almost immediately, by two lumbering coonhounds who snap and bite at the tires until we've stopped. Then they sit down, tails wagging while they wait for Dad and me to climb out of the truck. I let the dog closest to me sniff at my hand and then give him a scratch behind the ears. The door to the house opens and his head swings around at the sound.

"I see you've met Ringo," a man calls out from the porch. "And that rascal over there is Starr."

Starr looks balefully up at Dad and is rewarded with a perfunctory pat on his head.

"Come on, boys," the man says, and for a few seconds I'm not sure if he's talking to the dogs or to Dad and me. But then Ringo and Starr take off and bolt through the door the man is holding open. He lets it bang shut and then steps heavily off the porch and moves to greet us.

"Welcome. I recognize you, Roarke, from all those interviews you've been doing. I guess that makes you Mr. Richards. I don't think we've met. I'm Gulliver Lester. You can call me Gull. Most everybody does. I'm Ellory's old man. This here's my place. Come on in and I'll introduce you around. I think there are a few people you don't already know."

Gulliver starts back toward the house and we follow. He walks with just a trace of a limp and at one point I almost bump into him when he stops suddenly to hike up his trousers, so I give him kind of a wide berth after that. When we reach the door,

Ringo and Starr are waiting, noses pressed to the screen, but they back off when Gulliver waves them away and retreat to a pair of low cushions next to the stone fireplace. Caleb stands quickly as we enter the room and extends his hand.

"Mr. Richards. It's a pleasure to finally meet you."

He greets my father warmly, then claps me on the back as if we're old friends. I force myself to not pull away from his touch, but he leaves the hand there and so eventually I have to duck across the room. I cover this escape by shaking hands with Ellory and he introduces me to Gulliver's business associate, a severe-looking man named Carl whose eyes are set so far apart that he appears almost cartoonish. I gather that both he and Gulliver have plans to invest heavily in Caleb's campaign and are exploring forming their own political action committee.

"I don't think I'm allowed to be here if you're going to talk strategy," Caleb says, prompting the older men to laugh good-naturedly and look very pleased with themselves.

"You won't get any arguments here," Gulliver answers. "Besides, I think Ellory's pretty much got the strategy worked out. We'll just be here when you need us."

It's clear that Gulliver is proud of his son and while everything about this gathering feels heavily scripted, that emotion strikes me as honest enough. I watch Ellory shrug. Obviously he's used to being adored. He says nothing but instead turns back to my dad and they resume chatting. My father, who in general is shy around new people, actually looks like he's enjoying himself. I eye the large brass clock on the mantel and try to calculate how long I can last without saying something that I will regret. Caleb smiles at me expectantly and I realize that I haven't been listening to whatever he's been saying. I gamble and decide to just smile in response and this appears to satisfy him. He continues on with a story about Ellory behaving badly in Paris, which Gulliver seems to think is a real humdinger based on the number of times he calls it that and smacks his knee.

Soon the camera crew arrives. I don't recognize them. Caleb or Ellory must've hired them directly. Ellory takes them into another room and then reappears a short while later.

"Everyone ready?" he asks.

His father lets out a noise that I suspect is meant to indicate gusto, but it comes out sounding like a belch. Gulliver stands and leads the way outside. There's a small lake or pond behind the house that you couldn't see from the drive. Mist is rising off the water. It's the sort of view that only money can buy. Once all of the men have gathered their gear, they stand around complimenting one another on their choice of firearm. I look on, a little apart from the circle. Caleb passes his shotgun over for my father to examine while the film crew gets some wide shots of the group of us with the water in the background. My father turns the camouflaged weapon over in his hands.

"This is one of mine," he says appraisingly.

"It is," Caleb answers. "Good eye. My father bought that from you when I turned sixteen. I always thought of it as the gun that turned me into a man."

Dad hands the shotgun back to Caleb and then holds out his own.

"This here, now it isn't fancy. But it's served me well. It was a gift from my daddy too. I guess there's something to be said for holding on to the things that matter, even if shinier objects might come your way."

Caleb laughs and slaps my father on the back.

"I like that. Do you mind if I borrow that line?" Dad looks embarrassed and offers a noncommittal grunt in reply. Caleb seems to take this as a yes and looks over at me. "Roarke, your father here is a real gem. I hope you appreciate that."

Gulliver starts in on a description of the property, where the blinds are set up, the clearings where they've seen the most tracks. The turkeys can be heard calling in the distance and the same mist that's coming off the lake is still hugging the shallow hollows in some places. It swirls around Ellory's boots. We head out on foot and disperse, the dogs flanking Gulliver closely. The camera team trails behind us, keeping Caleb in their sights.

I try to fan out to the left, away from Caleb, but he beckons me closer. The cameramen skirt around us, clomping heavily over the uneven terrain. The noise they're making is certain to scare off any birds that are within earshot, but Caleb looks unconcerned. It's more important to look like a hunter than to actually hunt, I suddenly realize. He adjusts his shotgun and then slings it back over his shoulder in a practiced movement. I should've asked Essie if he's a good shot or whether I need to be worried that he might accidentally hit me in the face like that vice president did to his friend a while back, but of course I didn't get the chance.

Caleb points and says, "There's a blind set up right over there."

He guides me toward a spot where the trees thin out. There's a meadow beyond. It's covered with untidy tufts of what looks like tall grass.

"That's some chufa there. The turkeys dig up the tubers." I look attentive for the camera, but really I'm imagining what it would feel like to break Caleb's nose with the barrel of my shotgun as he prattles on. "Gull used to plant corn, but this is much better. This plot here attracts twice the number of birds for a fraction of the work."

I wonder who exactly did that work, since I doubt very much it was Gulliver himself. Maybe Ellory grew up working the land, dirt beneath his fingernails, his back bent beneath the sun. Maybe Gull was one of those rich men who grew up poor and wanted his son to know what that feels like, to know that hunger, not for food necessarily but for a better life, for success, for power. So maybe Gull did send Ellory out here with a hoe and some seed corn when they were setting up this camp, but it's not likely. I think this and then reconsider. I look over at Caleb and remind myself that you never can tell what a family is like from the outside looking in.

He has reached the small shelter and we settle in. He tells me there's a roost not too far off and we listen for the telltale call of a gobbler in search of a mate. Caleb raises a turkey call to his lips and, using his diaphragm, lets out a series of yelps. I scan the area for movement, one hand on my shotgun, aware that the camera crew is blocking the direction I would be most likely to shoot in. From far off in the distance I hear the sharp report of a gun and I wonder who it was that took the shot, knowing there will be no way to avoid a full retelling when we reconvene at the camp in a few hours' time.

Caleb cocks his head but does nothing else to acknowledge the sound. He keeps his eyes on a stand of tall oaks just at the edge of the meadow.

"Your father taught you to hunt, didn't he, Roarke?"

He is leaning comfortably against a tree, pecking out of the blind. He doesn't look at me as he talks. The cameras are close, and in any case, he's probably miked, so I remind myself not to say anything I don't want on tape.

"He did," I reply, keeping my voice low. "How about yours?"

"Goodness no. Daddy is not what you would call rugged. His books, his ideas, that's the world he lives in, not this one. It's how he's able to bring people closer to God, because he lives in that space between the earthly and the divine."

It's a well-thought-out speech and Caleb delivers it easily. It occurs to me that the question about hunting was merely a setup and I've played right into his hand. I can already picture how this scene will be cropped and edited for a commercial. He's praising his father but at the same time setting himself apart. Caleb is offering himself up as the everyman alternative. A grittier, more hands-on version of the man Caleb's would-be constituents already know they love. I'm tempted to pick my nose to ruin the shot, but I keep my hands jammed deep down in my pockets to control them. I've unconsciously balled them into fists while Caleb was speaking. That is why, when the turkey appears, it is Caleb who is ready to pull the trigger. I see it first but am still scrabbling to even raise my gun when Caleb takes the kill.

He looks at me sheepishly and says, "Sorry. I hope you don't mind."

I shrug as if it's nothing, but I'm fuming and it has nothing to do with the turkey. My finger plays over the trigger as Caleb jogs out to examine the bird. It would be so easy, I think. Hunting accidents happen all the time. I see the cameras turn to follow Caleb and I flex my finger, just slightly. No one would know. I could say the gun misfired or that my hand slipped and it went off when it fell. The only problem is that Caleb probably wouldn't die. He would just bleed and it would all be on camera—not my shooting him, but the impact, the birdshot tearing through the fabric of his vest. And once he recovered, he would be like a man risen from the dead. He would forgive me, publicly and with great fanfare, and I would have only succeeded in making him stronger.

I drop my gun to my side.

Then Caleb calls out from the clearing, "He's a real beauty. Do you think you can give me a hand?"

I stand up.

"Sure," I call back. "That's what family's for."

Time passes more quickly after that. Caleb and I separate and I find a tree with a low, inviting branch and lie there for a while, my feet up against the trunk. A gobbler saunters by and I don't even try for my gun. I just watch the way he struts across the forest floor, the light and shadow playing on his feathers. He belongs in this place much more than I do. In other circumstances I would gladly bring him home for dinner, but today it feels like killing things for pride is Caleb's game and it's not a game I want to play.

My watch chirps softly to signal that it's time to head back and reluctantly I lower myself down to the ground and begin to make my way toward camp. I've heard a few other shots while I was waiting for the clock to run out, and as we gather again in the clearing by the house, I see that my father has brought in a turkey not much smaller than the one that I saw. There's the requisite patting of backs and placing bets on just how heavy each of the birds is. Ringo and Starr drink from the pond and then lay their long, sleek bodies down on the part of the dock that hangs over the water.

Finally, Gulliver holds up his hands and announces, "Food will be ready soon. Why don't we all go in to clean up?"

Dad has packed us both a change of clothes and Ellory shows us to a room upstairs with a four-poster bed and an adjacent bathroom where we can change. Unlike the downstairs, which smelled of pine and leather, this guest suite feels airier. There's a bowl of dried purple flowers on the dresser and embroidered throw pillows on the chair. A woman has been here, even if only to decorate. Ellory mentioned as we climbed the stairs that his father had bought this land on his recommendation, after Ellory had visited it with Caleb during their first year of law school. The way he tells it, Gull bought the parcel sight unseen and had the house built after. I wonder if this bowl of flowers is how Ellory's mother approached the matter of her husband having a retreat where she would rarely, if ever, be allowed. If she walked through the house at the beginning, right after the builders had gone and the furniture had been delivered, and left little tokens here and there, evidence of her existence, a reminder to her menfolk that she was never far away.

The table is laid with sandwiches and a candied ham when Dad and I come down from changing. I'm hungry, but I go outside to pack the truck first so that we can make a quick getaway as soon as it's allowed. When I come back inside, Dad and the others have already made up plates and brought their food out back. I pile a plate with ham and potato salad and make my way to the porch. There's a round metal tub of drinks filled to the brim with ice and I fish around for a soda and pull out a Coke.

Gull laughs at this and says, "Don't worry, the cameras have all gone. I think you can have a beer."

I look over at Dad and he nods, whether in agreement or because he doesn't want to make waves I can't tell, but in any case, I shove the Coke back down into the ice and pull out a Miller Lite. The top twists off easily and I drop the bottle cap into a small silver dish that seems to have been put out just for this purpose. I find an empty chair and rest the plate on my lap. The bottled beer tastes mustier than the cheap cans I'm used to and I sip it slowly. Soon Gulliver leads Dad back into the house to show him some painting that he's just bought at auction. Carl stands up to follow them. This leaves only Caleb and me on the porch while Ellory walks up and down the dock below practically yelling into his phone. Caleb switches chairs so he's sitting next to me.

"Thanks for coming today, Roarke," he says. "It really means a lot." What I should say is You're welcome and leave it at that. I almost make myself do it too, but then Caleb continues talking. "You're a lucky man. Luckier than you know."

I hate everything about him in that moment: his straight teeth and his perfect skin but most of all the way his eyes are half closed as if he doesn't think he has to worry that I might use my fork to stab him. I grip the armrests on my chair and feel my chest begin to pound.

"Why did you invite us today?" I ask Caleb. "And don't tell me you care about my family's store."

"I think it's important for us to get to know one another."

Impulsively I say, "Really? I already feel like I know you. Essie has talked about you a lot."

"Has she?" Caleb opens his eyes fully and briefly looks unsettled, but this passes and all too soon his smile has returned. "I know things about you as well."

"Okay," I say, not at all sure what he's hinting at.

"I got sent to Holden Park too. Or did you think you were the only one? We're not as different as you would like to believe."

I feel the color drain from my face and all at once I am back there. I can feel the darkness like something palpable, something you could touch. No, that's not right. Something that was touching you.

I speak slowly and through clenched teeth. "I am nothing like you."

Caleb ignores this and instead says flippantly, "I didn't really care for it there myself. Too much talk, talk, talk. The director going on endlessly about personal goals. It was tiresome."

"Personal goals" was a misnomer, since they were written out ahead of time in bullet points by the staff and by your parents.

"Did you meet them? Your goals?" I say with an edge to my voice.

At this Caleb laughs out loud. "I think you know the answer to that. They didn't really take."

Liberty

By the third day, we have fallen into a sort of rhythm. Mike wakes up first so he can get to campus in time for Torts and tiptoes around the apartment in the dark, bumping into furniture and muttering obscenities. I wake to the sound of him tripping over a pair of shoes he didn't remember to throw into his closet when we finally went to bed three hours ago.

"Sorry," he says and kisses my forehead as I struggle to reenter consciousness.

"Don't be," I tell him. "I need to get back to it. I'll see you after class."

My arms and legs are heavy beneath the covers and I can feel the weight of them pulling me deeper. I'm tempted to shut my eyes for just twenty more minutes, but as I think this, I feel the brush of Justice's nightgown against my cheek and I shiver despite the heat coming off the radiator and force myself to get out of bed. At the sink, I splash water on my face and stare into the mirror, hands flat on the counter, wondering what Justice would look like if she were alive today.

Right after she died, I used to lock myself in the upstairs bathroom of our farmhouse and sit facing the full-length mirror that was hung on the inside of that door. I would tuck my knees beneath my chin and wrap my arms around my legs and stare into that other world behind the glass, the one where Justice's face was looking back. Sometimes I even talked to her, that version of my sister who lived within the mirror's depths, but the walls were thin and I stopped as soon as I realized that Mama could hear because I didn't want to make her sad. No, that's a lie. That's not why I stopped. I stopped because I didn't want Mama to think I was weak. I didn't want her to be reminded that I was the reason Justice died.

I blink and look deeper into the mirror and for a moment I am that girl again, the one who believes in Wonderland.

"What would you do?" I whisper to my reflection. "Would you let her tear apart her family? Would you help Essie burn it to the ground?"

A fly knocks into the bulb above the sink, drawing my eyes upward and breaking the spell. When I look back into the mirror, I see only myself, eyes bloodshot from too much coffee and too little sleep, hair in tangles. I don't look like Justice anymore. I don't even look like the version of myself that graced the inner flap of my book jacket those many years ago. But at least the face that looks back at me is honest. At least now I know exactly who I am.

I shake Margot, who had passed out on the couch, and she growls about all of the different ways she would like to punish me for waking her while I grind beans to make more coffee. There's still half a pot left over from the night before, but I pour it down the sink. We'll need the good stuff to get us going and take Margot's mind off of murdering me outright. I tell her to call her wife, but she's too busy swearing at me to hear.

"I was thinking," I call out from the kitchen, interrupting Margot's description of how I deserve to be run over by a miniature car that has been stuffed full of clowns, "maybe we should move the section about their first trip to Saint John to one of the later chapters."

"Like a sort of flashback, you mean? I guess that could work."

Margot rises from the couch and then slouches against the kitchen counter, eyes on the steady drizzle of coffee sputtering into the pot. "But if we flash back to the years when Essie was young, then where does the story start?"

"It starts now," I say, and I think again of the face I see when I look in the mirror, the one that it took me so long to find. "It starts with the person she's decided to become."

"And who exactly is that?"

I shake my head to clear it, but the thing that had seemed so obvious to me only a few seconds before retreats into the fog. I pull two mugs down from the cupboard and pour out the coffee, take a sip.

"Maybe," I say slowly, "we've been looking at the story all wrong. We've been building up to the rapes as if they justify everything that comes after. As if suffering that sort of violence at the hands of a family member is what drove Essie to fake a relationship with Roarke and try to buy her way to freedom. We've been using the rape to explain away the money those two will be getting for their marriage, for the wedding, for pretending to be something they're not."

"You don't think it does justify all that? You don't think she's entitled to every cent she can get?"

"Sure I do. And screw anyone who says otherwise. But still, this shouldn't be a story about a victim."

"What is it, then?" Margot asks.

"It's a story about a mother."

Margot is silent for a time. She holds her mug between her hands as if drawing warmth directly into her palms. Then, abruptly, she turns and crosses the living room, sets her cup down on the coffee table, and begins to select pieces of paper seemingly at random from the piles arranged on the floor. I follow and stand waiting beside her until she thrusts a stapled section of the diary into my hand and taps the page to indicate a paragraph near the top.

"Here," she says. "This should be chapter one."

She relinquishes the sheaves of paper that are labeled Esther 16 and sits down to wait for my reaction. As soon as I start to read, I know that Margot is right. Essie's story begins right here.

———

When Mother was five, Grandma Lou drove a knife into her husband's left thigh and left him bleeding in a lawn chair while she went inside to call the police. The chair was the kind that folded, with the seat and back woven from plastic tubing that had gone sticky after so many years out in the sun. Mother remembers this because it was her job to hose off the blood after her stepfather had been taken away in an ambulance and Grandma Lou had been placed in handcuffs in the back of the sheriff's car.

Mother was barefoot. She only had one pair of shoes and she couldn't afford to ruin them. As she sprayed down the chair where her stepfather had sat bleeding, the water pooled on top of the dry earth and made a pink frothy puddle that lapped at her toes. It ran past the cinder blocks on which their small house rested and drove away a stray dog who had taken shelter in the shade. Mother felt proud that she had thought to take off her shoes. Her older brother, Cyrus, would not have remembered and then they would have been stained and no longer presentable. Cyrus was always getting beaten for one thing or another and yet he never seemed to learn. Mother, on the other hand, learned early. This was something she prided herself on. I should say here that it wasn't Grandma Lou doing the beating. It was the man in the folding lawn chair, the man Grandma Lou had stabbed. But Mother needn't have worried about getting beaten over a pair of dirty shoes, because she never saw that man again.

Grandma Lou was unshackled and released from the police car without even a trip down to the station. She shook the sheriff's hand and then went into the house to pack. Everything they owned fit in four tattered suitcases, which she had loaded into the back of their secondhand station wagon by the time Cyrus came home from school. They drove for what seemed like three straight days until they ran out of money for gas. Grandma Lou would do odd jobs in whatever town they found themselves in until she made enough to fill up the tank. They slept in parking lots for the better part of a month. What Mother remembers best is crying herself to sleep every night, blaming Grandma Lou for their misfortunes and missing the only home she had ever known.

The point of this story, when Mother tells it, is how Grandma Lou let her temper get the better of her. By then the woman was long dead and could not argue with this assessment. Maybe she wouldn't have. I don't know. I never met her. But I do know that this story was Mother's way of letting us know that everything we had as a family had been built on character. Her character. The character of a woman who prided herself on quiet deliberation and dispassionate logic, on never losing her head. Mother was the sort of woman who often said things like "Let cooler heads prevail" or "Simmer down!" or even, for one mortifying summer, "Take a chill pill." That last one I begged her not to say in public, and lucky for me, it didn't test well with audiences, so she agreed to give it up.

It took me years of hearing Mother tell the tale of how Grandma Lou chose to make her children homeless in a fit of rage to finally ask the obvious question: What had her stepfather done to deserve it? Why had Grandma Lou taken out the kitchen knife and stabbed him? She must have known there would be no taking it back once it was done. So what was it that made it worth all that they would lose?

At this Mother's eyes glazed over and she said, "I really don't remember."

"You must," I insisted, sure that she was hiding something because she remembered everything else there was to remember about that day, right down to the fact that her single pair of shoes was the only thing that they had forgotten, the only thing that got left behind.

"He hit me," she then said reluctantly. "He did that sometimes if we broke something or woke him up when he was sleeping. He whipped us with his belt until our legs or backs were bleeding. But that day I hadn't done anything and he whipped me anyway. That day he beat me just for fun."

That's when I realized that Mother had been telling the story wrong for all those years. Grandma Lou's temper wasn't her fatal flaw, though that was the way Mother always spoke of it. It was her strength and her redemption. She had not acted recklessly. No. She had plunged the knife into his leg as an act of measured caution, to let him know what she would be capable of if he ever struck her child again. To make sure before she took her family away that he had been clearly warned and would not follow.

Mother may have been too close to see it, but Grandma Lou was never the villain. True, she had brewed her fair share of moonshine and even gone to jail for a spell when a police officer made the mistake of trying to blackmail his way into a cut of her profits from the still. Even so, she was never the black sheep of our family. It was just the opposite. She was the hero.

———

Margot and I are in the exact same spots where we've spent much of the previous two days when Mike comes back a few hours later.

"How was class?" I ask without looking up.

"Riveting," he answers with more than a touch of sarcasm and throws himself into a chair. "How are things going here?"

"Pretty well, believe it or not. We've rearranged the early chapters and I think the book reads much better now. I'm beginning to think it might actually be possible to have it ready by the rehearsal dinner so that Essie can take a final look."

"So she's really going to go through with this?"

"It looks that way. And I don't see any reason why she shouldn't."

"I guess you wouldn't," he tells me.

"What is that supposed to mean?" I ask, even though I already know.

Mike shrugs and doesn't answer. It's Margot who says out loud what we're all thinking: "Because you did the same thing and your life is better for it. You're happier without your parents, but who's to say Essie will feel the same when all's said and done? There are ways to get to Caleb but not lose her entire family."

"Maybe she won't lose them."

Now Mike does speak, if only to say, "I think you know better."

They're both right, but it's not something I want to talk about. I'm relieved when my phone rings, even though I don't recognize the number. I shoot Mike a look that I hope is defiant and take my phone into the hall. When I hang up, I stand looking at my phone long after the screen has gone dark, not at all sure what I should do next.

"Who was it?" Mike asks when it becomes clear that I'm not going to volunteer this information.

I don't answer because my mouth has forgotten how to speak. Eventually I manage to say, "It was him. It was Caleb Hicks."

Suddenly Mike and Margot are talking over each other, but I can't understand anything that either of them is saying even though their lips are working furiously. It feels like minutes have passed by the time my ears are able to focus on Margot's voice and I hear her ask, "What in God's name does that asshat want?"

"He wants to take us to dinner," I answer, and from their faces,

I can see that more is expected. "Not you," I tell Margot, "don't worry. Just Mike and me. He and his wife are coming to town for a fund-raiser on Friday night at the Hilton. Something about orphans, or maybe it was refugees. I can't remember. He kind of glossed over the particulars. The point is that he and Naomi bought an entire table and they have two extra seats. Judge Whitmore and her husband will be sitting with them along with two members of the school board. He said he thought Mike might like to meet them."

Mike's eyebrows shoot upward and he sits forward as he says, "Judge Whitmore's clerkship is one of the most competitive summer positions in town. Half of the people in my class have applied."

"You included," I remind him.

Margot rolls her eyes at this. "For some reason I wouldn't be surprised if Caleb Hicks already knows that. Don't tell me you're actually considering telling him you'll go."

"I already said yes," I say. "It just seemed too good an opportunity to pass up."

"Thanks," Mike says.

"Well, in that case," Margot decides, "you'll get a chance to observe the weasel in his natural habitat. There has to be some usefulness in that."

———

By Friday, the manuscript is almost done. I text Essie to tell her that I'll have a copy for her by the rehearsal dinner the following night and that she should wear something with pockets so I can slip her a flash drive. She doesn't text back and I'm seized by a sudden fit of paranoia that she's found out I'm going to the fund-raiser with Caleb and is angry with me. I have to remind myself that most of the time she keeps the phone off and hidden beneath her mattress, so she probably hasn't even gotten the message I just sent.

After googling the fund-raiser, I learn that it's not for orphans or even refugees but for veterans wounded overseas. I try to unravel the thread of memory that's all that's left of my call with Caleb, convinced that I'm so tired that I must have misheard him, but I'm nearly certain that he had said something about Syria and orphaned children. In the end, I decide that he must go to so many fund-raisers that they all start to run together or else he doesn't care enough to try to keep them straight.

Margot insists that I let Farai come over to do my hair and makeup, and I reluctantly agree. Mike is out picking up his rented tux when she arrives, so we have the apartment to ourselves. Farai raises one arched eyebrow at the mess in the living room, where Margot sits eating from yet another takeout container.

"What?" Margot asks with a withering look of her own and Farai turns away to usher me into the bathroom.

She has brought her own lights and mirror and a case of small tubes and brushes as well as other sundry beauty products, products that make me angry when I see them advertised on TV, products that tell our generation of women that to be beautiful, we must transform ourselves into something different from what we are. I balk when it is time to look into the mirror, but I have to admit that when Farai has finished, I still look like myself, only brighter, softer, less careworn. She helps me step into my dress so that it doesn't muss the curls she has so painstakingly conjured from my thin blond hair. Then she steps back and gives me an admiring look.

"I've had to be careful when getting you ready for interviews. It wouldn't do to upstage your guest, whoever she might be. I've never really been able to do you justice until now."

I stiffen at the sound of my sister's name, even though I know that the mention of it was unintentional. Farai grew up near Pretoria. There's no reason for her to know that I was once famous, and even if she does, she probably doesn't care. She has seen much deeper tragedies than mine firsthand. She has traveled a much more dangerous road.

"Thank you," I tell her, stepping back and spinning slowly.

The fabric of my dress, green to match my eyes, lifts away from my legs as I twirl and when I stop, it keeps twisting so it wraps itself around me. It feels cool where it brushes against the backs of my ankles, and though I'm again reminded of the feel of Justice's nightgown, this time I'm able to banish the memory the first time I try. I lean forward to readjust a strap on my left shoe and just then Mike bursts in.

"Five minutes," he says and starts to unzip the bag that contains his tux.

Farai returns to the bathroom to gather her things and I drift into the living room and perch awkwardly on the arm of the chair where Margot sits poring over Essie's manuscript.

"There," I say, and point.

"Yep, got it," Margot answers and cuts and pastes a paragraph from one section to another.

Farai kisses the air in front of my cheeks before she goes, and a few minutes later, Mike emerges from our room. He still looks vaguely flustered, but the tuxedo fits him well.

"You look nice," I tell him.

"You too. Very nice. I'm sorry, I should have said that before."

He pats his pockets to reassure himself that his wallet and phone are where they should be.

"Ready?" I ask, amused at how nervous he looks.

"I think so. Yes. I'm sure I am."

"Enjoy yourself, kids," Margot calls before the door swings shut. "But not too much. And remember your curfew. Be back before you get brainwashed into thinking Caleb Hicks is an actual human being and not a Borg drone."

———

Caleb and Naomi greet us warmly when we arrive and Caleb steers Mike expertly into the open seat closest to Judge Whitmore. Only her husband is between them. He's an authority on extinct languages and has just returned from a monthlong research trip to Papua New Guinea. He looks as if the noise and the lights are a bit too much for him. Mike tells a joke and the man laughs, relieved (it seems) that he remembers how, while Naomi compliments my dress or my hair or some combination of the two. I sit down next to her and am relieved when Caleb immediately falls into conversation with the man on his other side.

Things go on like this for a while, then there are speeches. I try to pay attention, but by the fourth speaker I've started counting the crystals on the chandelier overhead as a way to pass the time. The evening wears on. Mike and Judge Whitmore launch into a heated discussion about the threatened teachers strike and eventually swap seats to be next to each other while Mr. Whitmore regales the woman on his other side with a story about a man he met in Papua New Guinea who hasn't set foot on the ground for more than fifty years, preferring to live out his life on a platform built into the branches of a tree.

Before I know it, I'm being swept back toward the coatroom and Judge Whitmore is handing Mike her card. He waves as she and her husband walk toward the doors and, a few minutes later, the coat check returns our jackets and we follow the stream of bodies exiting onto the street. Caleb says something and I laugh because in that moment it seems funny and then immediately I feel guilty and forget what it was he'd said.

"It looked like you and Judge Whitmore really hit it off," Caleb tells Mike when we've reached the pavement. "I was hoping that you would."

"Yes. Thank you," he says, and I notice the stiffness reenter his body as he remembers that this is a person we are supposed to hate.

I can see this, but I know that Caleb and Naomi would never guess. Mike's coat buzzes faintly and he fishes his phone out of the pocket of the jacket, checks the number, and looks back up at me.

"Excuse me," Mike says, then he moves a few steps away and lifts the cell phone to his ear while Naomi tells me about how her daughter, Millicent, recently took a pair of scissors to her bangs. This means that she'll have to leave her Easter bonnet on for the entire wedding to keep from ruining the pictures, but it won't really matter because Millicent looks so darling in the bonnet that Naomi would have made her leave it on anyway.

Mike rejoins us and something about his face makes Naomi stop midsentence. He takes my wrist and tries to pull me away from Caleb and Naomi, but for some reason I resist. Whatever it is Mike has to say, I don't want to hear it.

"Your mom," he says helplessly, "she's in the hospital. She's unconscious, on a breathing tube. They're still not sure what's wrong. Someone will call when they know more."

"You poor dear."

Before I can object, Naomi's arms are around me and I can feel that the hug is genuine. Her eyes are misty when she pulls away.

"We'll let you go," Caleb says with the same tone of real concern his wife had just used. "But please, let us know if there's anything we can do."

Somehow my feet find their way to the car. Mike pulls the seat belt across my chest. He puts the key into the ignition but doesn't turn it. We sit like that, in silence, until I find the strength to speak.

"Why did he call you?" I ask, meaning my father.

"He was afraid you wouldn't answer."

I feel the panic burn my throat. "This is all my fault," I say.

"How on earth do you come to that conclusion? You think that because you told your mother something she didn't want to hear, her body just gave out? That's not how medicine actually works. You need to stop thinking like that. Just like you need to stop thinking that your father blames you for not being there when Justice died. Maybe he said things right after that he shouldn't have. He was grieving. He had just lost a child. It was the grief itself that said those things, not your father. Your parents love you. Otherwise why would they still be making so much of an effort even after all these years?"

I'm too numb to really consider whether anything Mike has just said is true and so I say, "It doesn't matter. None of it matters now."

Mike drives home and though he turns the radio on at some point, he quickly turns it off again. I watch the streetlights flash by and let my eyes go out of focus until the world is just a blur of light and dark with nothing in between. Even after we've parked and the engine has cooled, Mike makes no move to get out of the car. A raccoon slinks along the fence and disappears from sight. Not long after, there's a clatter as a trash can is knocked over. The noise breaks something inside me and I can no longer bear to be sitting there. I can no longer tolerate Mike's sympathy.

"Well, I'm glad that it happened, in a way." I hear Mike take a breath and hold it. "I mean, I'm glad that it happened now if it was going to happen anyway. Now at least there's still time to make sure I don't make the same mistake again."

"I'm not sure I follow."

"Essie's book. I know she thinks she's thought it through, but she hasn't. I need to make her see that. It's like when you knock over the first domino. Once it topples, you lose control of everything that comes after. There's no way to stop the rest of them from falling down."

Roarke

Blake and I spend Friday driving back and forth from the airport to pick up all my cousins and aunts and uncles who have flown in from out of town for the wedding. By our third trip, we're getting punchy, laughing so hard we can't breathe even though neither of us really knows why and I actually have to stop on the side of the road in order to avoid an accident because my eyes are filled with tears. In midafternoon we pull up late to the curb outside the arrivals level to find my great-aunt Mildred already waiting. She's clutching her suitcase with one hand while wagging her disapproval with the other. Blake swallows his laughter and nimbly jumps out of the passenger side to take her bag and stow it in the trunk, then opens the car door with a flourish and even throws in a chivalrous bow.

Aunt Mildred sniffs in disdain and settles into the backseat, and I wonder for a moment if she has figured out that her impending death, which is supposedly being hastened by an entirely fictitious illness, has been used to justify the timing of the wedding ceremony. I hold my breath, willing her not to blurt out anything incriminating in front of Blake. But though she waits until we have pulled onto the highway before she acknowledges me, when she does, she says, "So, you're selling your soul to the Devil, are you, boy?"

Relieved, I exhale. "Is that what you think of marriage?"

"I didn't say that. It's what I think of this marriage, though."

"I'm sorry to hear that," I say, and when she offers no further explanation, I add, "You know you didn't have to come."

"And miss out on the social event of the year? I don't think so. Lillian Polowy has the room across the hall from me at Kissing Pines and she offered me a thousand dollars to be my date, that's how badly she wants to meet your bride. I told her thank you, but no thank you. I'm not a lesbian, you see. Besides, she smells like old lady. If I were going to bring a date, it would be someone good-looking, maybe someone like you. What's your name, young man?" Blake introduces himself, repeating what he had said back at the airport when they first met. I try to figure out if Aunt Mildred is losing her marbles or if she's simply deaf. "So what are they going to do, exactly? Brand you? Or cut a cross into your chest?"

She is talking to me now, not to Blake. "That seems a little extreme, don't you think?" I say with a nervous laugh. I can't imagine it would be a good idea to admit that she has a point.

"Extreme. I think that's just the right word for it."

"They're not a cult."

"Oh no?"

"Besides," Blake cuts in, "Essie isn't anything like her family. Isn't that what you said?"

I shoot him a look that I hope says *Shut up* and move into the left lane to pass a rusted-out pickup, reasoning that this trip can't go by quickly enough.

"And just what is her family like?" Aunt Mildred asks, leaning forward in her seat.

I glance in the rearview mirror and then move my eyes back onto the road and think how best to answer politely without sounding like I've drunk the Kool-Aid.

"I don't know. They're just people." My aunt's eyebrows come together and I sigh. "Does anyone really like their in-laws?"

For some reason she seems satisfied with this and redirects her gaze to what I can only assume is the back of Blake's head.

"And you, boy, what do you think of the little missus?"

This time I keep my eyes straight ahead, but I feel my shoulders tense as I wait for him to answer.

"Essie?" Blake asks, as if surprised by the question. "She's the best."

———

The following day is the rehearsal dinner, but first there is the rehearsal itself. I'm still unused to being so near the front of the church, so it's doubly strange to be taken by the hand by Jethro Hicks himself and steered up the steps that lead to the altar. I remember how Celia Hicks once said that her husband's eyes were the same shade of blue as her son Caleb's. At the time, I never imagined I'd stand close enough to either of them to tell or that I would even care, but I see now that what she said was true. They are the same, down to the tiny flecks of lavender at their centers.

Pastor Hicks arranges us on the stairs, which are decorated with chips of different-colored stone to form a mosaic. I'm standing with my foot on the head of a serpent, which seems fitting. Caleb's right beside me with Blake on the step below. Early on there had been a plan for Essie and me to be flanked by her brothers and their wives, but a focus group had found this far too kitschy, which goes to show that focus groups sometimes get it right. So next to Blake is Reggie, who has agreed to be here only because I told him that being one of my groomsmen would be like giving the Hicks family the metaphorical finger, and he's wanted to do that for years.

I was allowed two groomsmen of my own, plus Caleb, who was apparently nonnegotiable, to stand opposite Essie's three bridesmaids: Naomi, Hillary, and Lucie. Then, after Lissa crashed the party and volunteered to be Essie's number four, we found ourselves short one young man. Celia Hicks insisted that it be someone from my family and, after reviewing photographs of each of my relatives, she chose my cousin Rand, whom I met once when I was five and who lives with his mother somewhere near Flagstaff. Rand has done some modeling for Abercrombie & Fitch, something I'm guessing Celia Hicks is well aware of. Still, I have to admit that Rand was an excellent choice as he seems to get along well with Blake and Reggie while harboring an instant dislike of Caleb, so I'm happy enough to have him standing by my side.

For some reason this process of deciding just where each of us should stand takes at least twenty minutes, during which all five of the cameras check their angles and the lighting. When Celia and Candy are finally satisfied, they send Gretchen scurrying forward to mark the stairs with different-colored pieces of tape, so when the time comes we'll remember exactly where we should be.

The cameramen for this part of the broadcast are all veterans of Six for Hicks, from what I gather. Margot and Libby will have access beforehand and then again for the grand finale, when Libby interviews Essie and me on the steps of the church just before Essie tosses her bouquet to the waiting crowd. The other networks will be there too, but Essie has said she'll only speak directly to Libby. I guess she means it as a thank-you to Libby for drumming up all the publicity she has, but in any case, it means that they're absent from this rehearsal and I find I almost miss them. I don't know that the Hicks elders have ever laid eyes on Margot or her purple hair. I'm hoping that I get to be around when they do.

After the stairs are taped, Essie and her father practice walking down the center aisle. A photographer snaps some pictures as they make their way forward and I try to imagine on which magazine covers those shots might eventually end up. I work on coming up with pithy headlines to fill the time, since Essie and her father have quite a distance to cover before I can even see them clearly. When they get closer, I notice that Essie is carrying a bouquet of some sort in both hands. It looks like flowers but also not like flowers. I strain my eyes to get a better look.

Somehow Caleb senses my question and says, "Naomi made it for her. First she dyed the paper red and then she cut and glued the pieces to look like roses. She used sheet music from all of the solos that Essie's ever sung in church."

I'm actually touched, and feeling that way because of Caleb makes my skin crawl. I know from Essie that Naomi is an only child but always wanted a sister. It seems to me that this bouquet, if nothing else, is for Essie and not for the cameras. "That's quite a gesture. It must have taken her ages to finish."

"Well, it's not as big as she would have liked. Naomi is not one to do things halfway. If she'd had more time, Essie would have been trailing paper roses."

"Huh. Naomi sounds like quite a woman. That sort of dedication, it's not something you should take for granted."

Caleb looks taken aback by this. "We aren't going to have a problem here, are we?"

He glances down at Blake and Reggie, who are whispering something to Rand and clearly not listening to anything we say.

I raise my eyebrows, enjoying his discomfort. "A problem? Why would we? I only meant to say that Essie is lucky to have someone like Naomi looking out for her."

At this point I have to step forward and wait for Pastor Hicks to place Essie's hand in mine, no doubt to symbolize the transfer of ownership over her or something equally misogynistic, but first he kisses her on the cheek and I'm surprised to see the tears in his eyes. I nod to him gravely and take Essie's hand. Then Pastor Hicks turns his back to us and faces his imaginary congregation. From the floor at the base of the stairs, he says something about how we should be still while he welcomes everyone and has them rise for the first hymn. He stands motionless for a moment, as if running through exactly what he intends to say, arms spread out in the air, and then drops his hands to his side, gives a barely perceptible bow, and walks up the stairs to the left of the altar to face us again, this time from above.

We hurry through the remainder of the ceremony. Essie pledges herself to me. I pantomime slipping a ring on her finger. We kiss. Everyone claps and the sound echoes through the empty vault of the nave, a word I recently learned from Essie. I'm amazed at the noise made by a few pairs of hands being brought together, how each staccato burst ricochets across the emptiness and is amplified without a thousand bodies there to absorb it. I walk Essie back down the aisle while Candy calls after us not to rush, no matter how excited we might be to start our life together. Essie rolls her eyes and walks a little faster, practically dragging me along. I look back at Candy and shrug helplessly and I hear her say, "I guess there's no doubt who's going to wear the pants in that relationship."

Once we reach the back of the church, Essie starts to giggle and I squeeze her hands and start to laugh as well. I can hear Caleb and Naomi, who are next in line to exit the church, closing in on us, their footsteps getting nearer. Impulsively I draw Essie closer and turn her shoulders so we are facing. I touch my lips to hers again, but not the way I had on the steps when her father declared us (almost) husband and wife. This time I really kiss her and I try to make it the sort of kiss that girls write about in their diaries, the sort of kiss we pay to see in movies, the sort of kiss I hope to get someday.

It's not fair, what I'm doing. I know it even as I explore Essie's mouth with my tongue, but I'm thinking only that Caleb will see this and that seeing this will show him that his power over her is finished. Knowing how much this will hurt him feels more right than kissing Essie feels wrong. Beneath my touch, Essie's shoulders tense as I slide one hand up to her chin and then her body relaxes against me. I kiss her until she drops the bouquet of paper roses. It rolls away from us across the floor. Then I pull away.

When we turn, Naomi has picked up the bouquet and is holding it out in one limp hand. It's clear at once that it's ruined, the petals crushed. Some are even torn. The color drains from Essie's face, which only a moment earlier had been flushed.

"Naomi, I'm so sorry. I shouldn't have been so careless," she exclaims.

Naomi tries to hide her hurt, but without success. "No, no. It's fine. It's just this one side. I might be able to fix it."

She blinks quickly and lifts the hand that holds the bouquet to draw an arm across her eyes to dry them. Essie reaches out to touch her shoulder, but Naomi shivers and turns away.

"Don't worry about it, sis," Caleb says to Essie, all the while keeping his eyes on me. "These things happen."

"Sure they do," I answer, making sure to meet his gaze directly. "Especially to things that are so delicate. You let your guard down just for a second and everything you worked so hard to create ends up completely destroyed."

Caleb puts an arm around Naomi, but he doesn't look away. I smirk and take Essie by the hand and pull her toward the stairs. She follows wordlessly as we walk down to the basement and into one of the choir rooms, but I can feel her anger even as we move.

"Fuck you, Roarke!" Essie yells at me when the door has closed behind us.

"Is this about that stupid flower thing?" I say, trying to sound glib.

Essie's face is tearstained. I look at my shoes, abashed. I hadn't heard her crying. I hadn't thought that she would cry. "It's not about the flowers and you know it. You have no right to kiss me like that!"

"He's the one who has no right to kiss you like that," I counter.

"Neither of you do! Don't you see that? Don't you see that how you just treated me isn't any different from how he treats me? I was your prop. I was there to help you make your point. It was about you and what you wanted entirely. It was like I wasn't even there."

"You said that there would be kissing. I gave you kissing. What's the problem?"

I'm being mean and I know it, but I don't care. Essie looks at a loss, but then she says, "Because it felt like you actually meant it. We were supposed to try to fool everyone else, not try to fool each other."

Suddenly all I want is for this fight to be over, even if it means having to admit that I was wrong. I sit down on one of the choir's folding chairs. "You're right. I'm sorry. I just . . ."

"I know," she tells me and sits beside me.

"He has to pay," I answer. "You know he has to pay."

"He will. I have a plan."

———

Essie tells me about the book she's written. Or about the book that Libby has written, or is writing. It seems it's still a work in progress. She tells me about how for the last two years she typed up bits and pieces of her diaries any time she had access to a computer, knowing that her laptop at home was likely being monitored based on something Gretchen once said. Gretchen had echoed part of a line from a poem that Essie had written for English. She had shown the poem to nobody, but she had typed it into her computer, and right then Essie knew that there was nothing private in her life. She had already known this in theory. She had just not known how deep the surveillance went.

Not long after Gretchen's slip, Essie took one of the diaries out of the secret compartment Lissa had helped her cut into the back wall of her closet and smuggled it out of the house wrapped in a dirty soccer shirt. That's when she started transcribing. She worked on it at school or at Lily's house and even once at Caleb and Naomi's when she was babysitting. When she was done with that diary, a thin volume with a unicorn on the cover, she retrieved another. And another. And another. Until she had six years of her life transferred onto a flash drive that she kept ferreted away in a tampon container in the bottom of her backpack. There was another buried in her backyard.

Now she had given one of those flash drives to Libby. Or she had left it somewhere and then Libby had found it. I didn't quite understand that part. But what was important was that the book was ready. She said we should have an electronic copy later that night. All we had to do then was decide to publish it. We, Essie and I.

"I didn't tell you before, because even when I left the flash drive for Libby to find, I wasn't entirely sure I wasn't crazy. It was possible that everything I had written was completely incoherent and I was worried that maybe Libby would read through it all and tell me there was nothing there worth reading, nothing there that anyone outside this family would want to know. I didn't want you to agree to marry me expecting some big reveal to the public, some dramatic moment of truth, and then be left with nothing, be left with only me."

"Let me just make sure I understand you. What's in this book is everything that ever happened? Everything that Caleb did to you?"

"Not in lurid detail, but yes. It's there."

I sit with this for a minute, then I say, "What exactly do you expect will happen when that all goes public? I'm not saying I don't see what the appeal will be for people. They will buy it. Man, will they buy it. And you'll make some money."

"We," she reminds me. "We will make a lot of money. So much more than we have already."

"And that's why you're doing it?"

Essie shakes her head. "No. Of course not. It's never been about the money. Not really."

"What is it about, then? Getting even? Getting out?"

Essie looks thoughtful, draws her bottom lip beneath the top one. "Maybe a little bit of both. But I think that mostly I just want to get to a place in my life when I can say out loud, 'This is what happened,' and not have to hide from it anymore, not have to be ashamed. He's the one who should be ashamed. Not me."

I take Essie's hand and draw it into my lap. There are footsteps out in the hall. They grow louder and then they trail away again. I listen to make sure they're gone, still uncertain what to say. Then, slowly, I offer, "He should be ashamed. We both know that. It's not that I disagree with you. Please don't think that. But I guess I just want to know what you think will happen after everyone buys the book, after they read it, after Caleb raping you becomes all that anyone can talk about, at least for a little while. What happens then? Does he go to jail? Do you press charges? Or does the state, since you're a minor? Do you expect your parents to renounce him? Do you really think they'll be on your side after everything they've always done to keep this quiet?"

"Everything Mother's done, you mean. The things she's said that make it clear she thinks of this as my fault, not his. I shouldn't have tempted Caleb. I should have known how to keep him away. But the wedding was her idea, not my father's. I was eavesdropping when it was decided. Maybe Daddy just went along. Maybe he didn't know," Essie says uncertainly.

"You don't believe that," I tell her gently.

"Well, then they both deserve whatever fire and brimstone comes their way."

"Fine," I say. "Again, it's not that I don't agree with you. It's just that I want to make sure you've thought about it, and not just from your viewpoint or from mine, but from everybody else's. Because if you do this, there will be no going back. It will be out there. Forever. And this baby of yours, of ours, will never be able to escape from that."

Essie stands. "Would you rather that I lie? That we pretend that you're the father?"

I spread out my arms and lean back in my chair. "I thought that was the plan. I thought that was why you needed me."

"That was why I was allowed to need you, at least as far as Mother was concerned. But that wasn't ever what I really wanted."

She crosses to the piano, plunks out a few notes, and pulls the cover over the keys.

I stand and face her, the piano between us, and ask, "So what do you want? And remember, Essie, I will be this child's father, no matter what you choose. I already promised that. Whether or not he or she knows the truth or some other kinder, redacted version of all of this, I'll be there. You just need to decide what it is you want."

She sits down on the piano bench and leans her face against

the instrument, then closes her eyes. I almost don't hear her when she finally speaks. "What if I still don't know?"

––––––

We drive together to the rehearsal dinner, which is basically a pregame wedding reception since all of the out-of-town family and friends have been invited. Essie continues to look troubled on the drive over, twisting her hands in her skirt or tapping her foot against the door. I let her fidget and don't press her to talk.

She seems a little less distant once she's enveloped by a swarm of friends and relations. It seems everyone has come out of the woodwork for this event. Even so, I can tell that her heart's not in it. Her eyes don't really light up again until she spots her cousin Adam, whose late father, Cyrus, was Celia Hicks's brother in that other life she had before. Essie tells me that Adam is a sopho-more at NYU, and he excitedly begins to recite a list of places we have to visit once we're living in New York, where to get the best pizza or the most authentic Ethiopian food, how to wrangle free tickets to plays or musicals or museums. Not long after Essie has introduced us, she excuses herself and heads toward the ladies' room.

Adam asks me what I'm thinking of studying at Columbia and then tells me about one of his professors this semester who seems like he's drunk more often than he's sober, how he once fell off the stage at the front of the lecture hall.

I laugh and then before I have even really finished laughing, Adam tells me, "It's been really nice talking with you. Seriously, man, thanks for playing the gracious host and all, but don't you think you'd better move on? Mingle? I'm fine by myself. You know what they'll think of you if you spend too much time with me."

I try to work out if this is part of the joke about the drunk professor but for the life of me can't figure out what the punch line is supposed to be.

"What will they think of me?"

"Well, it won't be so much a thought as a feeling. You'll be contaminated as far as they're concerned. The stain will pass to you from me."

This isn't really an explanation and I manage a halfhearted chuckle and spread my hands and say, "I honestly have no idea what you're talking about."

"These people are my family, but that doesn't mean I can't call out stupid when I see it. They've been avoiding me ever since I came out, so I was probably only invited because welcoming me back into the fold will make an excellent topic for one of Uncle Jethro's sermons. It'll be about hating the sin and not the sinner, or some such doublespeak."

"Since you're gay," I say, testing out the combination of words as a statement rather than an insult.

He stares at me for a moment as if reconsidering, then says, "Are you sure you got into Columbia? You're not so quick on the uptake."

I must look embarrassed, because Adam quickly claps a hand on my shoulder and says, "It's all right, man. I assumed that Essie had told you. There's no reason you should have known. Our ability to masquerade as straight has allowed us to infiltrate the enemy camp on more than one occasion. It's one of the driving themes of the gay agenda."

"You're joking," I say, though suddenly I'm not entirely sure.

"Of course I am."

My shoulder is warm beneath the weight of Adam's hand and the heat lingers even after he removes it.

"Anyway," he says as he lifts his glass to his lips, "I totally understand if you want to bail. No need to feed the gossip mill."

I scan the room. Celia Hicks is fawning over an older, well-dressed cousin from Florida with a small dog in her purse. Pastor Hicks is not far away, surrounded by a group of women from the parish. He has his back to the wall and it almost looks like he's been trapped by wild animals. A small part of me feels sorry for him. A very small part. Over on the other side of the room, Caleb moves through the crowd, stopping every so often to shake hands as if this is a campaign event. We're so close to the end that I can almost taste it, but all at once I'm tired and I don't have the energy to play their games, not for the next fifteen minutes or so at least. Swallowing hard, I pull out the stool next to Adam's and sit.

"Actually, I'm fine right here."

Esther

I am still angry with Roarke when we walk into the rehearsal dinner. Not as angry as I had been when he was kissing me or in the moments right after we broke apart, but I can still feel it, the resentment, the powerlessness at being touched in a way that was not wanted. Again. It was not the same, not exactly, but it was not really all that different in the end. Roarke at least had apologized. That was something Caleb had never done, not even that first time when he left me bleeding. The closest he ever came to saying he was sorry was when he left a bruise he knew would show, but he did not sound sorry even when he said the word. He sounded defiant. He sounded proud.

I think I would have let the anger linger, I would have wallowed, except that almost as soon as we walk into the function room, I see my cousin Adam. I can tell just from looking at him that he does not want to be here. He does not look uncomfortable. He just looks bored. Bored with all the whispers, the looks, the need for constant vigilance. And who can blame him, really? If I'd had the option, I would have stayed away as well. But he had come anyway because I asked, even though he had planned to let his mother come on her own. So I bring Roarke to Adam and introduce them and then I walk away because I think that what I need is to be alone, even just for a few minutes, to finally let that anger go.

They are laughing when I look back from the other side of the room, their bodies angled toward each other, and for a moment I feel my anger swell again. Then I remind myself that Roarke too is here only because I asked him. I asked and he said yes. He would have been fine all on his own. I'm certain of it. Sure, he would not have been able to afford Columbia, but he would have managed. He would have washed dishes or delivered pizzas or tutored rich high schoolers in order to pay for State. He would have been happy. He would have graduated and become a doctor or a lawyer or an investment banker. He would have made all the money he could ever need entirely on his own. And he would have done it all without ever having to walk into this pit of vipers I have led him to, without risking everything for a girl he barely knew. All at once I realize something and I feel the anger fall away, the kiss entirely forgiven if not forgotten.

Roarke is the first real friend I've ever had, the only one who has ever really known me, and that means something. It means that he never needed me the way that I needed him.

———

Libby is standing just inside the entrance to the function hall when I come out of the bathroom. I catch a glimpse of her through the throng. I cut around the periphery to avoid the bodies and she raises a hand to indicate that she's seen me coming and then ducks back outside.

It is raining, but only just. A sort of mist floats over the parking lot, moving neither up nor down but swirling gently from side to side, illuminated by the lights of a car that is parked nearby. Libby walks toward the car and the lights cut out. A young man climbs from behind the wheel and stands with one hand atop the open door, ready to make a getaway if one is needed. He shifts nervously, his eyes on Libby, which is when I realize just how on edge Libby looks herself. When she leans against the hood of the car to face me, she does not meet my eyes. Her fingers drum on the metal beneath her hips, tapping to some inner melody that I cannot hear.

"What happened? Did someone find out what we're planning?" I do not realize until I hear my own voice how terrified I am.

I remember then how when I was about nine years old, a man had tried to break in through the kitchen window. He had a camera. Daddy was in the papers a lot at that point, even more than now. Some question about his tax returns. Eventually it was buried, but for a brief but memorable span of a few months there was great interest in capturing candid pictures of our unscripted, off-television life. Most of the time the paparazzi left us alone. There were too many pictures of us already out there. Anything extra just wouldn't be likely to sell. But this period of time was different for some reason. They wanted to catch us eating with diamond-encrusted forks, slurping soup with golden spoons. There was a sudden and burning interest in just how we lived, how much we spent, how much was taken from Daddy's various ministries and quietly skimmed off the top. Just as quickly, the press lost interest. But not before the man with the camera climbed through the window over the kitchen sink.

Lissa locked us in an office in the basement and then she called 911. The recording of that call starts as soon as the three numbers were dialed, even before the operator picked up. Later, when the detectives played us the tape, you could hear Lissa's ragged breathing and another sound, a muffled whimper that was me crying from beneath Candy's desk. When the operator did speak, Lissa answered with forced calm, but you could tell that her voice was breaking. It is that voice of Lissa's that I hear when I speak to Libby, worried that we've come this far only to fail, to be found out, the finish line erased now that it is finally in sight.

"No, no," Libby tells me hurriedly, "nothing like that. No one's found out anything. At least they haven't found out from me. But we need to talk about this book you've written."

"You mean it's finished? Can I see it? Do you have it here?"

Libby nods slowly and takes a flash drive from her pocket and holds it out to me.

"I have it and of course you can see it. It's your story, after all. And it's a good one too, as stories go. It has a beginning, a middle, and an end. It has a villain and a heroine. I'm grateful that you shared it with me. I'll even upload it for sale if that's what you ask me to do. But maybe this is where it all should stop."

"I don't understand."

"This will destroy your family, Essie. Not just Caleb. All of them. It will be the end of everything if this ever gets out."

"I know that."

"I don't think you do." Libby holds the flash drive higher and turns it as if to examine the object from all sides. "You think you've thought it through. You think your mind has teased out all of the many potential repercussions, but it's just not possible to do that. It's not possible to predict every eventuality. Or to imagine each of the million tiny ways the people you once cared about will be hurt by what it is you plan to do. So I'm here to give you this, but I'm also here to tell you that I think you should bury it. Put it in the back of your underwear drawer or in a safe-deposit box somewhere. But keep it hidden. The things that are in this story, they aren't things you want the whole world to know."

I stiffen. Then I reach out and snatch the flash drive from Libby's hand.

"It wasn't my fault," I tell her.

Libby looks down. She pulls at the lining of her coat where it has separated from the seam and begun to wear.

"I know," she answers in a small voice. "But that doesn't matter. Sometimes the truth is blamed on whoever was unlucky enough to deliver it. Trust me, I know. If you put this out there, if you make that choice, then everything that comes after, all of that will be on you. Not him."

"It isn't fair," I say, my eyes filling with tears.

Libby straightens and begins to move around to the passenger-side door. "Of course it isn't fair. It was never going to be, from the very beginning. Fair was something Caleb took from you along with everything else. You're fooling yourself if you think there's a way to get that back." She looks across the car at the man standing there, who has not moved at all while we spoke. "We should go," she tells him.

"No," he answers. "Not until you tell her the truth."

The air I suck into my lungs is wet and heavy and makes me feel as if I am drowning.

"What truth?" Libby asks him. Her eyes are flashing.

"The truth about how none of this has anything to do with her or with her family. It has to do with yours."

"That's no one's business," Libby spits. My whole body is trembling and I feel the shaking grow more violent as they fight.

"What? You don't think it's the tiniest bit relevant to the matter at hand? You told the truth and something bad happened and now you blame yourself. But the real truth is bigger than that. The real truth is that there were times that I thought not telling would kill you. That right there is what you're asking her to do. She pays a price whether she buries the book or not."

As he says this, I can practically see Libby's anger melt away and his own furrowed brow gives way to tenderness and worry.

"I wouldn't have let it kill me," she says.

"Maybe not physically, but there are other ways a person can die."

I speak mostly to remind them that I am there, but it is possible that I am talking to myself. "What should I do?"

The man shrugs as if deciding how to answer. "Maybe you can keep this secret forever and not let it eat you up inside. Libby couldn't. I was watching her suffer and I couldn't stand it. The truth had to come out. No matter the consequences. Maybe it would be different for you. Maybe you could walk away and manage to be happy. Maybe you could hold on to the pieces of your past that were good and just let go of all the rest. But that's easier said than done. If the truth will out, so to speak, you might as well get it over with and move on to the real hard part."

"What's that?" I ask him.

"Putting the pieces back together again."

———

I am not conscious of walking back into the function room. I remember being outside. I remember watching the brake lights of Libby's car as it pulled away, so startled that I no longer felt like crying. I splashed water from an ornamental fountain in the garden onto my puffy eyes, patted them dry using my shawl. Then I faced the entrance, knowing that I had to go back to the party but not able to take a step toward the door. Even when I do force myself to go inside, a sort of blur continues to hang around me. Everything feels out of focus. Then Mother takes the microphone and calls out for someone to dim the lights.

"Y'all will have to bear with me," Mother is saying from her place beneath a spotlight. "I'm not really one for public speaking. It should be Jethro up here instead, but he'll have his chance tomorrow. In the meantime, you'll have to make do with me."

There are several shouts of protest, some scattered clapping to reassure my mother that she is adored just as deeply as her husband, which I know is exactly what she wants. She blushes and waves her hand up and down in front of her as if to quiet the crowd, which only makes them cheer all that much louder. Mother laughs and raises the microphone to her lips again.

"Settle down now. Let's save some of this enthusiasm for the reception tomorrow. I'm told it's going to be one heck of a party."

There is more clapping and then the audience, as if on cue, falls silent almost all at once. Mother passes a hand over her eyes to collect herself and then starts to speak again.

"There have been other weddings before this one. Other couples have stood up in front of their families, in front of God Himself, and pledged to carry His light onward together. I've been lucky to watch my own four sons marry four of the most beautiful and supportive women a mother could dream of for her children. I've watched our family grow in love with the birth of each grandchild, and I can truly say that with the passing of each year, we have only become more and more blessed.

"Which brings us to today. I thought I would be up here to talk about Elizabeth long before I had to get ready to say good-bye to Esther Anne, but it seems Our Lord had other plans. It also seems likely that given how adept Elizabeth has become at dodging the cameras, when the time does come for her to tie the knot, she'll do it without letting any of us know." There are a few good-natured snickers at this, and Lissa, who I see now has settled herself next to Roarke and Adam, stands and curtsys primly. The laughter swells and some people start clapping.

"So instead," Mother continues, raising her voice to cut through the applause, "I'm here to talk to you about Esther Anne. The baby of the family, who is not a baby anymore." She waits for the crowd to provide the expected *awww* and then moves on. "And because this is a wedding, I'm also here to talk to you about Roarke, the young man my daughter has chosen to navigate this world alongside, a worthy companion for what I am sure will be an exciting trip. I could not ask for two finer people to honor here tonight. But they were not always the self-assured young adults you'll see exchanging vows tomorrow. And if you'll indulge me for just a few minutes more, I'd like to take you on a journey back in time, a journey through the lives of these two young people I know we've all come to love."

The spotlight cuts out then and a projector illuminates both Mother and the wall behind her. Mother blinks furiously and scurries quickly to the side. Music starts. It is a song I remember Daddy singing when I was young, his voice gentle and drawling, coaxing me to sleep on long car rides or in the hammock out by the lake. There is a slide with our names on it, Roarke's and mine, and then the pictures start to flash before us. Roarke as a tiny scrunched-up ball of brand-new baby; me wearing a christening gown. There are other people in some of the pictures. I recognize younger versions of Roarke's mother and father and some of the relatives I've met today. There are team photos from Little League, a shot of Roarke with several friends wearing matching T-shirts that say Bement that looks to have been taken at a summer camp.

He gets older as the slideshow continues, and so do I. The projector dims and the next picture appears. I am front and center in a group photo of Daniel and Hillary on their wedding day. Both Lissa and I had been flower girls. We wear matching pale pink dresses with puffy sleeves and ruffled trims. I am smiling, and not just for the camera. I remember being happy. It had something to do with the necklace I am wearing in the picture. They are real pearls. It is still one of my favorites. Lissa had been given one as well, but she had refused to wear it to the wedding, which made Mother angry. I was glad, though. I liked having something that made me special, something that made me beautiful, something that made me stand out on my own.

But I see now that I am not the only one wearing that necklace in the picture. Naomi is wearing one as well. And I remember something that I had somehow forgotten. It was Naomi who had given it to me, shyly, the first time that we met. A present for her boyfriend's younger siblings, the girls she hoped to someday call sisters of her own.

After that, all I can seem to focus on are how many of the pictures show me with Naomi. We are riding on a tandem bicycle along the dirt road near the lake house or baking cookies or lying on the beach on sandy towels, a tangle of tanned arms and legs. I am reminded then of how fiercely I had loved her in the time before. Her hair, her smile, everything about her was perfect as far as I was concerned. I made up excuses to sit next to her at family dinners or, in order to put off saying good night, would offer to carry her purse out to their car. Even in the time that came after, there are pictures of me holding Millicent on the day she was born and reading *Blueberries for Sal* to Nate while he fell asleep on my lap. These make me think about what Libby's friend had said before he left, how there was goodness mixed in with all the bad.

When the slideshow has finished, I can still see the afterimage of that rectangle of light when I close my eyes. I sigh. It is one thing to ruin Caleb or even Mother and Daddy. It is another thing entirely to ruin the life of Naomi, someone who loves me, someone who has never done me any harm.

———

When we get home, I tell Mother that I am tired and I go to my bedroom and shut the door. I change quickly and turn off the light. Then I read until my eyes are burning and it is impossible to keep the text in focus as it dances across the screen. It is not until my stomach rumbles that I realize I did not eat anything at the rehearsal dinner. Rubbing at my face, I exhale slowly and close the file, pull out the flash drive and slip it into the pocket of my pajama pants. I crack the door to my room and listen before I venture out into the hall, then head down the stairs.

Before I can make for the kitchen, I hear a noise from the darkened parlor. It is just the whisper of air as it is forced out of a cushion, but it is enough to let me know that someone is there. I stop in the doorway and examine the shadow. Not Mother, which is a relief but still odd, since the parlor is her domain. Instead it is my father sitting there. I try to remember the last time we were alone together and can't.

I consider moving on without saying anything, but somehow I know that even though he has not acknowledged me, he would call after me if I turned away. So I take a step forward and into the room.

"Daddy?" I say softly. "What are you doing down here? Does Mother know you're up?"

He continues to look out the window without answering and I bend over slightly so that I can see what he sees, the streetlight and the clouds parting to reveal the moon.

"Your mother is asleep," he manages finally. "Something about looking fresh for tomorrow. You should follow her lead. You only have one wedding day."

He turns away from the window and I feel his gaze slide over my face as if memorizing it and then his eyes reluctantly break away. He looks sad and I feel the urge to comfort him and immediately the anger from earlier this evening returns, because shouldn't it be the other way around? Shouldn't he be comforting me?

I stay silent, waiting. If ever there were a time for questions, this is it, but I find that there is nothing that I want answered. Or rather, I do not want the answers if it means I have to ask. I do not want to sound like I am begging. I do not want to admit that he has the power here.

Daddy absently twists his wedding band around his finger, looking down at his hands as if surprised to find that they belong to him. Then he looks out the window again.

"Your mother, once she gets her heart set on something, well, there was nothing I could say. She wanted you married, so you're going to be married. Goodness only knows what put that idea in her head, but here we are nonetheless."

He looks truly at a loss and I feel the anger all over again. Even if Mother has not told him directly, how could he fail to guess?

"I'm pregnant," I say in a moment of pique.

Daddy absorbs this as if the revelation is an actual physical blow.

"Jesus," he breathes.

"I don't think Jesus had anything to do with it."

He looks at me again, his eyebrows drawn together. "No, I don't suppose he did."

I do nothing to interrupt the silence but instead lift my chin slightly in what I hope he will register as defiance. But he does not look at me.

"I did my best," he says finally. "I tried to head things off. The summer after you were born there was an incident with a cat. He helped make posters to hang up all around the neighborhood. Elizabeth did as well. But the cat wasn't missing. It was dead. I hoped that might be the worst of it, but we both know what happened next."

I hold my breath, then say, "Lissa. Is that what you mean? Is Lissa what happened next?"

"The director at Holden Park told us we wouldn't have anything else to worry about. Not after he finished out the program there. They promised he was safe."

"He wasn't."

"No. He wasn't."

There are so many things that are left unsaid, but it does not matter. The only thing that matters is that he had known about Caleb all along.

I stand in the door while I pull enough air into my lungs to speak.

"I forgive you," I tell my father.

Then, no longer hungry, I climb the stairs and squeeze the flash drive in one clenched fist as I fall asleep.

Roarke

The suit they buy me to get married in is Armani. I've never felt anything so soft in my entire life. Blake and Reggie strut around the room in the church basement that we've been given to get ready in before the ceremony like they're preparing for the red carpet. Rand rolls up one of the paper programs printed for the service and holds it out to them like it's a microphone and asks them questions about their shoes and hair. Caleb's still off with Naomi somewhere, so we have the room to ourselves and I feel relaxed—excited, even.

There's a knock at the door and I hear my father's voice coming from the hall.

"Is everyone decent?" he calls and forces a chuckle.

The door opens a crack and he peeks inside and then throws it open wider. My mom is standing beside him. She looks unsure of herself, almost as if she's afraid she will be told that she has no right to be here. I open the door fully to let them in, but they take only a few steps inside the room.

"Just wanted to check if you boys were okay," Mom says timidly. "Not too nervous."

She reaches out to brush an invisible piece of lint from my lapel, then touches the tip of one finger to the single white lily fastened there. She considers the flower, lips pressed together thinly, and allows her hand to drift back to her side. It moves as if disconnected from intent, a boat caught up in a current, and it occurs to me that this is how my mother herself must feel. Moving from wave to wave and out to deeper waters without a rudder. Powerless to avoid being smashed up against the rocks. Her wrist turns once, quickly, a spasm, and then falls still again.

"We're fine, ma'am," Blake answers for me. "Aren't we?"

Blake claps a hand on my arm and jostles me back to my senses. I blink and look away from Mom's watery eyes and over toward my father. They are both dressed well for the occasion. The clothes are nicer than anything they would ever buy on their own. Mom's hair has been curled and pinned up in a complicated arrangement upon which sits a small round hat festooned with pieces of netting and feathers dyed to match her dress. I've never seen my mother in this sort of hat before. I wonder if this is by choice or because it never occurred to her. It's probably the latter. But it's also possible that there are pictures of such hats in her box, the one that is filled with magazine clippings of other people's kitchens, other people's children playing in other people's yards, elderly couples lounging on the porch in matching rockers. Maybe this hat is what Mom wanted all along but could never even hope to wish for. Until now.

Dad coughs and I can tell by how he looks at me that we are thinking the same thing.

"I'm proud of you, son," he tells me. "Not just today, but always."

"Thanks, Dad," I answer.

Mom begins to cry.

"Don't," I say. "You'll ruin your makeup."

"Of course," she says and opens her eyes wide and inhales deeply. "You're right. How silly."

They reach out to touch me one more time and I hear the

shutter of a camera sliding open and shut as an unseen photographer captures this moment for posterity and then my parents leave me behind.

———

I spend the next fifteen minutes or so with Libby. It turns out that Blake and Reggie, and Rand as well, have been looking forward to this more than I realized. Liberty Bell is something of a fantasy for them, it seems. They have never met a celebrity whose last name wasn't Hicks. Rand practices some lines of small talk and asks Blake and Reggie how he should stand. As their excitement builds, I feel a sudden urge to protect Libby from this overzealousness, but when she enters the room, Rand is polite. They all are. Their voices are a bit too loud, their faces clownishly animated, but there's nothing gross about the way they look at her and I'm relieved.

Libby asks me how I'm feeling while Margot holds us in frame and zooms in on our faces.

When we're finished, Libby leans in close and whispers, "Have you spoken to Essie?"

I shake my head. "No. Not since last night. Not since the beginning of the party. We sort of lost track of each other after that. Why?"

Libby fumbles with her microphone. She looks unused to holding it. For all of our other interviews we've been miked and we will be today, during the ceremony, but she'll have to use this again when she interviews us outside.

"It's nothing. I said something I shouldn't have, I think. I pushed too hard where it wasn't my place. I was hoping that we would get a chance to talk just now, but the other girls were there. It's all right. I'll find her after."

I nod as if I understand what she's saying, but I don't, not really. "Was Lissa there?" I ask.

Libby laughs and her face clears as if the other thing is forgotten.

"She was there. And she has them all wrapped around her little finger from what I saw. They could hardly stop giggling long enough for Essie to film her segment. Celia Hicks didn't look too pleased by the scene when she came in, which I think only added to Lissa's enjoyment."

"That sounds about right," I say. "Families are complicated like that."

"You're right. It's not just this one," Libby agrees. She looks sad, but it passes quickly and she gives my hand a squeeze and wishes me luck.

Margot comes over then and wraps her arms around me. She holds me tight and for a long time, but it's not uncomfortable. When she pulls away, there are tears in her eyes.

"You're one of the good ones, Roarke Richards. I hope you know that. A prince among men."

Then they're gone.

I blink for a moment at the empty space where Margot and Libby had been and feel a shiver pass through me. Not everyone will feel the same way, I know, if the truth becomes public. For the first time, I consider that the truth is not only about Essie, it's a truth about me as well. Not the whole truth, maybe, but I'm part of the story just the same. A prince, Margot said. Is that how people would see me? As a rescuer? A slayer of dragons? Neither of those seems right, or fair. If there's any rescuing happening, it is Essie who is doing it. She has rescued herself.

"I have to pee," I tell the others, though really what I need to do is walk.

I head down the hall toward the men's room, aware of the

hum of the fluorescent lights, the muffled footfalls moving across the floors upstairs. What's above me? The kitchen alongside the refectory, maybe. I think about the church overhead, a space that has become familiar if not altogether comfortable over the last month. I had always thought of the building as ugly and I still do. It feels more like a sports stadium than a place of worship. There are too many spotlights, too many screens and projectors. They're necessary, I realize, because otherwise Pastor Hicks would be practically invisible to the people in the back rows, the folks like my family, but it cheapens it, I think, the glitz, the glamour.

Spending more time in the church has not changed my mind about that, but I've also been here when the lights are off, when there's just the sun through colored glass to illuminate the space. When that happens, the long strips of carpet that run the aisles are painted in every color imaginable and the vaulted ceiling above me, with its painted cherubs, its golden stars on a backdrop of cobalt, makes me appreciate that people are capable of creating beauty, not just destroying it. Standing just before the altar where the mosaic starts, the tiny chips of stone depicting the Last Supper, I can stand on Jesus's face and look upward toward the crimson- and orange- and lime-tinted glow and experience something close to peace. Something like belonging. Something close to faith.

I pace the hall, willing my body to remember this feeling and slow the pounding in my chest.

"Psst," I hear from somewhere behind me. "Roarke. In here."

I catch a glimpse of Lissa's face, the curve of her arm beckoning me to follow. She disappears back inside the room from which she'd called me. I creep forward, half convinced someone is watching, and then I duck inside.

When I enter the room, I don't even notice Lissa, though she must be somewhere nearby. There is only Essie, standing before me, and I can't look away. She is shimmering. That's the only way to describe it. At first I'm not entirely certain that she's real. She takes a step forward and the soft rustle of fabric is finally enough to convince me.

"You're not supposed to be here," I say too loudly. "I'm not supposed to see you."

Essie laughs and it's the same tinkling sound that first made me think I could trust her. So much has happened since that day, so much has changed, but that laugh has stayed the same. I realize that I love her. I love the girl I am about to marry. Maybe not in the way a man usually loves a woman, but I love her all the same.

"I think that business about not seeing each other before the ceremony only applies to real weddings, don't you?" She doesn't mean this cruelly and I'm surprised to find that I'm at least a little hurt. She must see the disappointment on my face before I can hide it because she moves forward then and brushes her lips against my cheek. "We're above all that is all I meant," she explains.

I try to think how to tell her what I feel, but she's already saying it for me.

"I love you, Roarke. I wanted to say that at least one time without the lights and cameras and people. And it's not just because of what you've given me, not just because of what you're doing for me today. You're the best friend I could ever hope for and I don't ever want that to change."

I put my hands on either side of Essie's face and lean my lips against her forehead. She slides her own hands up to cover mine and we stand like that for a while until I say, "I feel exactly the same way."

"We're running out of time," Lissa says, and I break away from

Essie and see that she has been there all along. "Say what you came to say."

Essie takes a deep breath and starts. "The book. I just don't think I can put it out there. Not anymore."

"Is this because of Libby?" I ask. "She sounded worried that she said something that went too far."

"She reminded me of the truth, that's all. You tried to tell me too. I just wasn't ready to hear it. There are too many people who will be hurt."

"Caleb deserves more than a little hurt," I tell her. "And your parents. I know they weren't right in the room with you, but they still let it happen. That means that they deserve some too."

Essie brushes her hand across her forehead even though there's not a single hair out of place. "It's not just Caleb or my parents who would be hurt by the things that are in the book. There will be questions about Lissa too, about why she left. Isn't it best to leave some things buried? To leave the past behind?"

Lissa raises a hand, palm toward her sister. "Leave me out of this. I don't need protection. I already told you what I think."

"Which is?" I ask.

"That if I had been braver, I would have done what Essie did. But I wasn't. And I ran. What happened to Essie is my fault as much as it is Caleb's. My silence made it possible. Her silence, now, could do the same. He could hurt another girl."

"We don't have any more sisters," Essie protests.

"Do you really think that that will stop him?" Lissa responds.

Essie is silent. Her eyes fall.

"Maybe there's a way for both of you to be right," I say, trying to defuse the tension. "There are other ways, less public ones, to make sure Caleb is dealt with. It doesn't have to be this one."

"Anything having to do with Caleb is public," Lissa answers, "especially now that the campaign is under way."

"Maybe he'd be willing to bow out quietly."

Lissa ignores this and turns to Essie. "Who are you really trying to protect?"

Essie's hands flutter at her side and then bury themselves in the fabric of her dress. "We were a family once. We were happy. It's not just Daddy or Mother or Caleb. The others never asked for this. Think of what it will do to Naomi and to Millie and little Nate. Their entire world will collapse in on them. How do you come back from that?"

"Is it better for Millie to grow up with a child molester in the house?" Lissa asks quietly, and there is a deadness in her voice that is frightening.

"I'm just not ready." Essie sighs. "I'm not brave enough. I thought I was, but now I know I'm not."

"It's fine," Lissa says, taking her sister into her arms. "It's fine. I'm sorry. Don't worry about a thing."

I leave the girls and wander back toward the bathroom. My face in the mirror is jarring in its familiarity. I had expected to look changed somehow. More like my father. It was surprising how quickly I rushed to judgment, how certain I felt that it was impossible for the Hicks family to be worthy of Essie's compassion, her forgiveness. As if how you feel about your family ever makes any sense at all. I should know this better than most. Because forgiveness is exactly what I gave my own parents years ago.

———

The sign at the roadside was welcoming, the stone wall quaint, like something out of a storybook. The farmhouse was visible only after we had turned onto the dirt lane that led away from the main highway. White clapboard. Black shutters and trim.

Only the door was red. There were other buildings as well, but I wouldn't see them until later. I remember that there was a wooden swing hung from the branch of an English oak in the yard beside the house. It looked like a child lived there. It's possible that one did. After that first meeting with the director in his sitting room, I never went back inside. Once Dad left, they took me down the hill, down behind the barn, down where the animals were kept. Even looking back, there was nothing to suggest what was about to happen, nothing I can think of that might have served as a warning. I went in completely blind.

Blake asked me later why I hadn't written to him at camp like I said I would. But I couldn't. I couldn't write down what was happening, but I couldn't pretend it away either. So I just concentrated on surviving, on getting through the days.

The days at least were predictable. Up at six. Muck out stalls. Dig holes for fence posts or for a new latrine. There was some tasteless food, the occasional fight between two of the other boys to break up the monotony. There were the sessions where we were handed baseball bats and encouraged to hit a life-sized dummy. We were supposed to be working through our anger issues. Our hatred toward our fathers. Or something. I recognized that not all of the boys sent to Holden Park were like me. Some were like Caleb, though I wouldn't have put it that way at the time. I only knew that they were not to be trusted. None of them. It was safer that way. Safer, not safe. So yes, the days were predictable. Boring, even. It was the nights when the real learning took place.

The sun set late that time of year, but even so, the rooms where they had us wrap our arms around each other were dark. The physical contact brought an intimacy I found unsettling. Sitting between the legs of a stranger, I would force myself to relax against him, rest my head on his shoulder, allow his arms to encase me completely. I would concentrate on the feel of his heart thudding dully against my shoulder blades and try to slow my breathing. These sessions weren't meant to be sexual, were in fact meant to realign whatever neurons or chakras had gotten out of whack and turned us into the monsters that we were. Still, there were a fair number of erections that would rub against my back during these periods when we were holding or being held. I tried to ignore them. I tried to imagine I was somewhere else.

I must have been doing an all right job of floating through unnoticed, of seeming receptive to the program, because I was never singled out for some of the more intensive sessions, the ones that took place in the barn at night and were witnessed only by the animals. You could hear them when they happened. The thud of a fist hitting soft flesh, the muffled groans, the crying that came after. The dormitory would be silent when the door opened to admit the returning boy. I remember sleeping with my head beneath my pillow. I remember biting down on my tongue to stop from screaming. I remember the taste of my own blood.

Toward the end of the summer, one of the boys snuck out to the barn at night and hanged himself from the rafters. I found the body when I went to get a pitchfork for morning chores. His face was purple, swollen. I couldn't remember his name and in that moment that was the thing that seemed to me the saddest. That he was already starting to be forgotten. I should have yelled for help, but I didn't. Somehow shouting in his presence seemed disrespectful. Also, I didn't want them to see him that way, the counselors, the camp director, the people who had driven him to it.

I found a saw and climbed into the rafters and drew the blade across the thick rope. I worked furiously, but even so, I wasn't fast enough. The others entered the barn just as I was about to slice through the last few rough strands. The director barked at me to freeze. I did. And then the rope gave way. The body fell. There was a sickening thud as it hit the wide pine floor.

"What did you think you were doing?" the director asked me later.

And I had answered, "I was afraid he couldn't breathe," but that was a lie. I knew that he was dead.

They locked the dormitories while the boy's parents came to retrieve the body, but I could see them from the bathroom window. It had rained heavily that morning, but the rain was stopping by the time they pulled their station wagon down the long drive. His mother wore a raspberry-colored coat and rain hat that seemed out of place. They were too bright against the brown grass, the gray puddles in the sandy mud. His father was much older. His back stooped, his face sagging. I was struck by how ordinary they both looked. How completely devoid of dangerousness. They didn't look the way we had all been taught that murderers would appear, wearing hoodies and wielding knives. But they had killed their son just the same.

———

Caleb has joined the others when I get back to the room.

"You get lost?" Reggie asks with a chuckle.

I shake my head. "My stomach," I say. "I guess I'm really nervous."

"It's just about that time," Caleb says. "Nervous or not, we'd better head upstairs."

The tunnel that takes us beneath the church proper is dimly lit. Our shoes click on the painted concrete floor. We wait in the sacristy while Gretchen goes to fetch the microphones. While we loiter, Caleb slides up close beside me and places a hand on my shoulder.

"You've been a good sport about all this, I have to say. I'm not sure I'd have had your patience."

I shrug against the weight of his touch. "It'll all be over soon."

"That's not what I meant. I meant getting saddled with my sister. She's a sweet little thing, but we both know she's damaged."

I look around the room in disbelief. Caleb is not making any effort to keep his voice down. I wonder if he's drunk or just crazy. Or maybe seeing her sold off is harder on him than I would've thought. Who knows what sort of twisted feelings he might have for her, what fantasies are ruined by my being here?

I tell Caleb, "I see Essie for who she is and she sees me, flaws and all. No secrets. It's a more honest relationship than most have. More honest than yours, for instance."

Caleb brings his eyebrows together. "What makes you think I keep secrets from my wife? What sort of husband do you think I am?"

He looks genuinely offended. For a moment I don't realize what he's implying and then the gravity of what he's saying sinks in. I speak slowly and say, "How does that work, exactly?"

Now Caleb begins to smile. "To love, cherish, and obey, isn't that's how the vows go? If you're lucky, your wife will do the same."

I speak before I can stop myself. "Aren't you at all worried? Essie's about to be free of you. She could take you down."

"Maybe," Caleb answers. His tone is even, confident. "But she won't. She's smart. She can't say anything, not without destroying her own life as well. The 'he said, she said' thing never plays out well. She wouldn't want to live through that. Besides, she has no proof."

I raise my eyebrows and force myself to swallow before I say, "Well, then I guess you're safe."

Gretchen comes over with Caleb's microphone. Caleb smirks at me and walks toward the door that leads out to the chancel. I force myself to stand still while Gretchen fastens my own microphone onto my lapel and then, still feeling dizzy, I step into line.

I find my taped mark on the steps before the altar and struggle to remain in place while the organ transitions from its prelude to the "Bridal Chorus." There is more brass than usual. I see Lev Gottlieb in the front row of musicians. He opens the spit valve and gives his trumpet a shake before lifting the instrument to his lips. Then Essie appears at the back of the church. At first I can't make out her features, she is so far away. The crowd turns and there is a flutter of handkerchiefs raised to blot out tears. Ever so slowly, Essie comes into focus and I will her to hurry so I don't have to be up here alone.

Finally, Pastor Hicks is lifting her veil and I step down to meet them. He kisses her cheek and turns to shake my hand. Essie steps up beside me and I place a hand over my microphone and lean toward her.

"Naomi knew," I breathe through my teeth. "She doesn't deserve your protection. None of them do. She knew everything."

Liberty

When we've finished up taping in the church basement, Margot and I claim a pew in the back of the church by a side door so that we can slip out when the recessional starts. We'll meet Roarke and Essie on the front steps for their final interview. Margot takes my phone and starts live tweeting from my account. She tells me my number of followers has tripled since just last week.

"Your followers, you mean," I say.

Margot shrugs. "What they don't know won't hurt them."

She has dyed her hair brown for the occasion, with just a fringe of lavender remaining in her bangs. She called it going undercover, this casting off of her usual purple spikes, but she said it with a grin that showed she realized changing her hair color would never be enough to make her fit in. Not here. She has made an effort, though. She's not wearing an actual dress or anything that extreme, but her slacks and top are light gray. They blend in well enough with the pastel Easter parade.

The crowd filing into the seats is clearly aware of how many people will be watching this on TV. Perhaps I am being unkind. It is a holiday, after all. Even Mama got us a little bit dressed up on Easter. Maybe that's the reason for all the fuss, but in any case, there are an astonishing number of hats and they seem like just the sort of marker that would allow you to recognize yourself from behind if the camera happened to pan over your section of the congregation. There are fresh flowers set upon wide brims but also other fussier concoctions. Tall feathers projecting like spikes from delicate beadwork, satin roses, and even actual painted eggs lying in a nest of crinoline.

I know what Mama would think if she were here. How she'd roll her eyes. She was always dismissive of the sort of pageantry the Hicks family seems to relish, to have perfected. *Getting gussied up in lace gloves and a ridiculous hat won't bring you any closer to God,* Mama would say. *It's hard work that does that, caring for the animals and land that He has entrusted to you that raises you up in His eyes.* Then I would nod obediently and head back to the barn to finish the chores I was hoping she'd let slide.

Mama is awake now, or so the doctors said. Last night after talking to Essie I called the house again even though I didn't really expect anyone to answer. It had become a ritual of sorts, to listen to the ringing, wondering if anyone was home to hear, to imagine the way the sound traveled through the rooms where I had grown up. When the windows in the living room were cracked, you could hear the kitchen phone ringing in the side yard, the one with the seesaw Pa and Topher built and that Justice fell off when she was six, splitting open her chin. It took eight stitches to close the cut and I remember watching the doctor intently, fascinated by the yellow bubbles of fat, the glistening curve of the needle that gave way to a filament so thin it was practically invisible.

"Will it scar?" Mama had asked.

"Every cut scars, at least a little bit. But it came together nicely. Over time, you might not even be able to see that it was ever there."

That night I snuck a pair of scissors. My plan was to cut the stitches out, to open up the wound again and ensure that it would leave a permanent mark. I liked the idea that there could be something physical that distinguished me from my sister, some evidence that I and I alone was me. I had never been one for dressing up in matching outfits, and the year we turned five, I drew a chalk line down the center of our bedroom and forbade Justice from straying over it. I didn't do it to be mean. She was my sister, after all. I loved her fiercely in that way that all siblings love each other, twins in particular: worship laced through with a shard of resentment. I just wanted something that was mine. The night I took the scissors, Mama stopped me before I even got to the stairs. She reclaimed them without asking what I was doing and returned them to the office drawer.

———

I was unprepared when my father's voice came through the receiver. It was the first time he'd picked up since it happened. I wondered then if he'd been at the hospital during all my earlier calls or if I'd simply worn him down. There was a dead silence on the other end of the line when Pa recognized my voice and I was afraid that he might hang up. Then he asked, "Why did you do it?" and I could feel the vibration of those words against my cheek as if he had struck me with his open hand.

Pa wouldn't tell me any more than I already knew. She's awake. She's breathing on her own. That much I had heard from the doctor, who had doled out these updates sparingly, choosing her words so that she revealed what had been agreed upon, careful not to say anything to which my father had not given his blessing. It seems that Topher had been the one to find her. He had folded up his long limbs to bend down beside her and tilted back her chin to breathe air into her lungs. Rolled her on her side. Wiped away the vomit. Halted the slow wind-down of a heart starved for oxygen. He brought her back to life.

"I need to let her go," I told my father, and he knew that I meant Justice. "It hurts so much, even after all these years, and lying about what happened only makes it worse."

He didn't speak, but I could hear his breathing. I could tell that he was listening.

Finally, when I couldn't bear the silence any longer, I whispered, "Don't you miss her?"

This time the breathing stopped and its absence seemed louder than what had gone before it.

"I miss you both," I heard him say.

Then the line went dead.

———

The sun is coming through the stained glass in earnest. There is one section near the top of the window where colors shoot out in all directions in a starburst that looks like I always imagined the beginning of time and the universe would have looked if anyone had been there to see. It is beautiful in the way that such things often are. Once I stare at it long enough, it's less an image and more a feeling. The colors blur and the afterimage leaves a warm glow on the insides of my lids.

Margot fiddles with my phone while the last of the guests find their seats. The organ swells into a grand finale and then dies away, the prelude finished. There's a cough from somewhere to my right and another near the front. The final adjustments are made to the cameras near the altar and then they start broadcasting. Somewhere, I know, before a bank of monitors an executive producer is furiously barking orders into a headset. I relax into my seat, glad to be a spectator for this part at least.

The groomsmen file out to take their places on the stairs. Roarke looks on edge, his shoulders stiff, his chin tilted up unnaturally. Anyone who doesn't know him would just assume that he's nervous, but it's not that. It's Caleb. The air between them is electric, full of static, though that could be my imagination. Still, I can't shake the feeling that Roarke is on the verge of decking his soon-to-be brother-in-law across the jaw. His fists clench and unclench and there's a moment when I think he might actually go through with it, might send Caleb crashing to the floor, but then as one the congregation stands and the moment is forgotten.

Roarke watches Essie walk down the aisle with such a pure sort of yearning that I almost believe they are in love. His eyes do not waver. Even when he steps forward to meet his bride and her father and Caleb claps Roarke on the back with brotherly affection, Roarke keeps his gaze fixed only on her.

Essie looks truly lovely. When we had spoken in the basement, she was still in just her slip and a dressing gown. The bridesmaids fluttered around her, working at the clasp of a bracelet, adjusting the string of pearls that had been a gift from her sister-in-law Naomi so that they nestled upon her collarbone just so. Lucie said something about how people were going to cry when they finally saw Essie in her dress and I had smiled indulgently, but now I see that this is true. In every row, purses are being opened to retrieve Kleenex and real cloth handkerchiefs and even the men are wiping their eyes.

I watch Roarke watching Essie and am reminded of a poem I learned in school that read in part:

> I would like to give you the silver
> branch, the small white flower, the one
> word that will protect you

I realize that whatever it is that is between them, even if it's not love, it is just as real.

The first part of the ceremony goes quickly. Roarke takes Essie's hand and they turn to face the altar. There's a stretch of kneeling followed by some standing solemnly with bowed heads. A choir sings. Pastor Hicks talks about the risen Lord. There are a lot of alleluias. Some Easter hymns. "All the Sacrifice Is Ended," followed by "Christ the Lord Is Risen Today." Then there is "Lift Every Voice and Sing," which was included at Essie's insistence over Celia Hicks's objections, and I watch with amusement as Celia's head wags involuntarily, but the congregation doesn't seem to notice the bit about the blood of the slaughtered.

They sing joyfully and I have to admit that the sheer number of voices is uplifting. I feel my chest expand as the notes climb higher and I remember what it felt like to be part of something that seemed holy, that seemed like it was all that mattered, that seemed true, but then I notice Margot's amused expression at the irony of this hymn in particular, and I break off singing and soon it is time to sit down.

Pastor Hicks gives a sermon before they proceed with the marriage vows. The wedding party have been given chairs to sit in a little off to one side, so that their faces are turned upward toward the pulpit and visible on camera. In many of the broadcasts I've seen, Pastor Hicks preaches from just in front of the altar for at least a portion of his sermon or even steps down toward the congregation. He moves among them and the cameras follow. But now, perhaps because the lighting has been so meticulously planned, he takes up residence in his perch and stays there.

He looks solemn and then he calls out, "Christ is risen, alleluia!" and more than a thousand pairs of hands come together in clapping or are raised up in the air.

Oh! I have slipped the surly bonds of earth
And danced the skies on laughter-silvered wings.

Without looking down at the pages before him, Pastor Hicks recites the rest of John Magee's poem right through to the part about touching the face of God. His eyes stay fixed on his congregants as if he is channeling the voice of the Almighty Himself and speaking His thoughts directly to them.

"That's a beautiful image," he says, "that you or I might touch the face of God, that we might look upon it and know its love and grace. But we don't have to look upon God to see love. We don't have to look upon His countenance to see grace. Oh no. We have only to look at these two young people, to look at Essie and Roarke, and see that He is moving through them. Their love for each other is His love. Their commitment to each other is the same commitment that He shows to each one of us, His chosen people, His beloved children.

"And yes, you may well remind me, one of these young people is not only His child, she is my child as well. I have the bite marks to prove it."

There is warm laughter. Essie lowers her chin and blushes. Roarke reaches out to squeeze her hand. In living rooms across the country, fathers pull their daughters closer, or so I can only assume. That was the intended effect, no doubt. Margot's thumbs fly over the screen of my phone as she posts to Twitter. She winks at me wickedly. She is enjoying this.

Pastor Hicks sighs indulgently and then hushes the crowd.

"So what, you might ask, should a father say when he sends his child out into the world? What did our Heavenly Father say to His Son? What guidance did He offer as Jesus entered the sometimes dark and difficult world that we live in? Did He tell him to look both ways before crossing the street, as I know all of you have when raising your own sons and daughters? Perhaps He told him not to stay out past eleven. That's also good advice. Or maybe, just maybe, He said, 'Be brave.' Just that. Such a simple directive and yet so hard to manage. 'Be brave,' our Father might have said, and we would have done well to listen."

He stops and looks at Essie tenderly. She meets his gaze and it's Pastor Hicks who turns away, who drops his head to shuffle his papers before moving on to talk about the resurrection and the light.

When he's finished, Roarke and Essie face each other before the altar and promise to honor each other in word and deed. They promise to make a life together that is filled with faith and love and grace. When Roarke slips the ring onto Essie's finger, even Margot tears up. He keeps hold of her hand while Pastor Hicks blesses their union and proclaims them man and wife. Then Roarke leans forward and kisses Essie and a collective sigh is heaved by the entire congregation. Cheers break out toward the back of the church and soon everyone is clapping and throwing confetti into the air. Roarke and Essie laugh as they head down the aisle, the tiny paper hearts fluttering over and around them and landing in their hair. Margot has to pull me away and toward the exit so that we can get outside in time to meet them.

———

On the landing out in front we have cordoned off a small space for the final interview. Just below this, the rest of the press have set up behind a metal barrier. They are milling about aimlessly when we burst out of the side doors—some are even sitting on the pavement—but they jump to attention at this sign that the moment is approaching. A bank of cameras begins shooting when Essie and Roarke emerge. They stop to breathe and shake the confetti out of Essie's dress and then make their way past the velvet ropes that have been hung around our space. Both Essie and Roarke embrace Margot and me and we all stand in a circle holding hands until the rest of the wedding party and the guests begin to pour out of the church. We nod at one another and move to our places.

"Thank you for tuning in," I say into my microphone. "I'm Liberty Bell and I'm reporting live outside the New Light Church, where I'm joined by the newly married Esther and Roarke for their first interview as husband and wife. It was a beautiful wedding, as I'm sure many of our viewers know firsthand, having attended the ceremony remotely, so to speak, through the earlier part of this broadcast. I have to admit that it was emotional for me to watch, but it must have been all the more so for you two, who were living it. Roarke, we'll let you start. How did it feel to finally marry the woman you're standing next to?"

Roarke grins boyishly and I am reminded of how young they are, but he sounds composed when he begins speaking. "You're right, Libby, it was very emotional. I had trouble holding it together up there during some bits."

"Well, you couldn't tell from where I was sitting, though I will say that I was way in back and this is an enormous space, isn't it?"

"It is," Essie offers, "but the one thing I was always amazed at growing up is that even though the church is so big, it never makes you feel small, not while you're inside it. And I was grateful for the space today. We both were. Grateful that it allowed so many of the people we love to be here with us. What better way to start our life together than with this resounding demonstration of love from our families and our community?"

I tilt the microphone back toward myself and say, "There's one last thing to do, though, am I right?"

Roarke nods. "There is. But I think we're ready to take care of that right now. I see my father-in-law coming over with the marriage certificate. We'll sign it and then it'll be official. We'll be married."

Pastor Hicks places a piece of paper on a small table behind Roarke and Essie and they bend to sign it. They keep their bodies turned away so Margot can capture the moment and then Essie hands the marriage certificate to me.

"I think I'll give this to you, Libby, for safekeeping. We've all got a party to get to. You're invited, of course, but maybe you would be good enough to drop it in the mail on your way?"

I laugh as if this is unexpected and take the paper and its envelope. Pastor Hicks has moved away and is standing next to Celia. They're in the shot behind Roarke and Essie along with the rest of the wedding party. People continue to file out of the church, but the steps are crowded now. The guests are taking in the spectacle or else waiting for Essie to throw the bouquet.

I'm about to say something to wrap up the segment when I see Essie look back to Roarke. A barely perceptible nod passes between them. She turns to face me and I feel my stomach drop. I know what's coming.

My mouth is dry, but I manage to croak, "Is there anything else that either of you would like to share?"

Essie looks pointedly at the microphone and I force myself to bend it toward her.

"There is, actually, and it's something that I've been thinking long and hard about because it's not easy to say. I want to tell you all, everyone watching, how lucky—just how incredibly and breathtakingly lucky—I feel to be here with Roarke today.

There's been a lot of lead-up to this moment. There's been a lot of talk about flowers and dresses and my hair. And I understand the fun in that. It's every girl's dream to be a princess for a day. I got to have that. And it was magical.

"But to be honest, what was most special to me about this day is that I thought it would never come. I appreciate how odd that sounds, coming from someone my age, someone a lot of people out there think is too young to be married, too young to make such a big decision, a forever decision. But to me, this decision was the easiest one I've ever had to make. And the fact that Roarke was so generous as to open up his heart and make this day happen for me, happen for us both, well, for that I owe him more than I can say."

Roarke's lips turn up slightly as he accepts this compliment, or perhaps it's a look of determination, of encouragement.

"It was hard," Essie continues, "to believe that I deserved a day like this. I used to think no one would ever love me. I used to think I was unlovable. I used to think that everything that happened to me was my fault, that I deserved it. 'Be brave,' my father said during the ceremony. It's hard to be brave, but I know I have to try. That's why I want to say to every young girl who is out there listening, no one asks to be raped. I didn't. I didn't ask for it when I was twelve and I didn't ask for it two months ago when, after years of abuse, my rapist got me pregnant. I didn't deserve to be hurt that way, to be violated. That's why I've written a book about everything that happened to me. Because if I'm going to try to be brave, it means I can't be silent anymore."

There's a scream and then I'm knocked to the ground as Margot and her camera tumble down on top of me. The crowd surges and Essie and Roarke are pulled away. I fumble for my phone, then realize that Margot still has it. My hand is shaking when she hands it back so I can dial Mike.

"Did you see?" I gasp, cupping the phone close to my mouth, the pounding of blood in my ears louder even than the crowd. "I can't believe she did that. Did you hear what she said? Upload the manuscript."

Mike's voice comes to me as if through a long tunnel.

"I already did."

Esther

The first thing that happens when I finish talking is that there is a scream and then Mother hits the ground. She has fainted, possibly, or else she is faking. Trying to divert attention. It doesn't work. Reporters actually step over her fallen body to get closer, the metal barricade forgotten, knocked over on its side. I am vaguely aware of the annoyed look on Mother's face as Lucie helps her up. When I look back, Margot and Libby are on the ground. Caleb is close behind them. I did not see him push Margot and her camera over, but even so, I know it happened. I am jostled backward and Roarke holds tight to my hand, but the press of the bodies is too much and we are dragged apart. I feel his fingers twist around my own, trying to find purchase, and then he is gone.

The flashing lights from the horde of cameras make it impossible to see clearly, but I am aware of the closeness of the crowd. It has spilled down the steps and over much of the church lawn. The daffodils are getting trampled. Those farther back could not have heard what I was saying, but they already seem to know. Word has traveled back in a game of telephone. Like a wave traveling across the surface of still water, their smiles are replaced by something else. Even those onlookers at the periphery who had been making for their cars in an attempt to beat the traffic turn back at the commotion. Naomi emerges from one of the church's side exits. She is holding Nate and has Millicent by the hand. We lock gazes and I see her take in the noise, the confusion, the hot flashes of anger, then she turns and runs.

The reporters are shouting questions, but I cannot hear anything distinctly. Someone grabs my arm and I almost fall, but I am held upright by the bodies pressing in around me. I am thrust back again and this time it is hard to breathe. My dress is getting stepped on and the weight of other people's feet tugging at the fabric threatens to pull me down. Then there is an arm around me and Blake throws his jacket over both our heads, shielding us from the lenses of the cameras. Together we break free and move forward and miraculously the sea of bodies parts to allow us through. Blake opens the door of a limousine and follows me inside. The door slams shut and muffles the shouting.

He is panting.

"I've got to hand it to you, Esther Anne, you sure know how to put on a show." His face softens and then he says, "I'm sorry."

I swallow hard, unable to answer. For a moment I am worried that I might throw up. Instinctively I reach out to roll down the window, but then I remember what is going on outside and stop. I see now that Roarke is pressed up against the pane of glass and I worry that he is trapped and won't be able to open the door. I realize how stupid I have been, that people can die in crowds like this. It happens at stadiums and movie theaters. People are trampled when someone yells Fire and that's exactly what I've just done. I told myself a spectacle was what was necessary, that they would have been able to cover things up if I didn't reveal the truth in such a public way. But that's not the only reason I did it. I did it because I am selfish. I did it because I wanted to see the looks on their faces the moment that I took everything away.

I swallow the rising contents of my stomach and again lean toward the window, thinking that maybe if I open it, we will be able to pull Roarke through before anyone else can poke their head inside. Then someone—an arm only; I cannot see the face—pushes a reporter back and gives Roarke just enough time to pull the door partway open. He slams it shut once he is in. His hair is standing straight up and his shirt has come untucked.

"I almost didn't get out of there alive," he says. "The rest of them are hiding inside. I'm not sure what they're trying to accomplish. These people aren't going anywhere. They might be trapped in there for hours. Thanks for getting her out safe, man."

"No problem," Blake answers. "It's all part of the job description."

The boys stare at each other and it is clear to me that something is being communicated in this. I just don't know what it is.

"Look," Roarke says carefully, "if you want to say 'I told you so,' that's fair. I deserve it. I know you never really bought the whole fairy-tale act. So say something if you want to, but do it now or else drop it forever. I just want things to go back to normal."

Blake looks like he wants to answer right away, but he stops himself. His gaze swings like a pendulum from Roarke's face to mine and back again. "I don't think going back to normal fixes anything. It's not as if we were being honest with each other even then, and it always hurt that you didn't trust me. I just don't want there to be any more lies between us." I see Roarke take in what Blake is really saying. He looks paralyzed and just about as nauseated as I still feel. Finally, Blake takes Roarke's shoulder and squeezes it. "Relax, man," he says. "I'm still the same guy I always was and I know that you are too."

Suddenly I begin to cry. The tears are streaming down my face, but the moment I feel them coming I know that I am not only crying, I am also laughing uncontrollably. My body is shaking so much that my sides hurt and the center of my chest begins to burn. A hundred years ago, women would have been diagnosed with hysteria and locked up, out of sight, as a penalty for such emotion. But this is not a hundred years or even a week ago and for the first time, I feel just a glimmer of what it would be like to be free. When I wipe the tears from my eyes, I see that Roarke and Blake are staring at me, shocked, uncertain what to do. Then the door of the limo opens and Reggie White scrambles inside to sit across from me and we are aware once again of the shouts of the reporters through the glass. The vehicle trembles slightly as they jostle against the door.

"It's getting a little dangerous out there," he says, "and I think we all know which one of us that crowd would consider the most expendable, so I vote that we blow out of here as soon as humanly possible."

"I'm sorry for dragging you into this," Roarke tells him.

"Are you kidding? That was maybe the most amazing thing I've ever witnessed. I just wish you had warned me first. Then I would have had an exit strategy planned. Seriously, though, Essie, I don't know what to say. All this time I thought you were judging me, and it turns out I was judging you right back. I should have known better."

"Thanks," I say.

A slow smile spreads across Reggie's face before he continues. "So, is the reception still on? Because I could really go for some of those tiny hot dogs right about now."

It occurs to me that in all my scheming, I had never actually thought this far ahead. My imagination had only gotten me to the point when Thelma and Louise go off the cliff, or Carrie stands on the gym stage at her prom. I had not dared to think of what happens after. There will be a crash, certainly, but before that . . . well, there's that moment when you feel like you can fly.

I look at Roarke and he shrugs. "Why not? We got married, didn't we?"

"We did," I tell him, sounding almost surprised. I wipe my

hands across my face again. I still feel a little sick, but it is passing. And I realize that at the very least we need someplace to go until we can figure out what happens next. We can't sit in the back of a limousine forever. So I say to Reggie, "I think we can probably find you enough mini hot dogs that you're never going to want to eat another one for your entire life."

"That, my friend, is how you know you're throwing an epic party."

"Well, then let's go," Roarke says.

He taps on the glass separating us from the driver and the limo begins to pull away through the crowd.

———

It didn't end there, of course. For a while we were like fugitives, Roarke and I, always on the run. We graduated high school without ever setting foot in Woodside. Instead we took our exams in a hotel room while the principal paced anxiously to and fro or peeked out between the curtains to see if there were any press below. Roarke was valedictorian, but since he was unavailable, they asked the runner-up, Veronica Richter, to give a speech instead. She ended up talking about how everyone in the town had been complicit in what was done to me and promptly got escorted off the stage.

The stage where Roarke should have given his speech is not so different from the one where I sit now. My name is printed on a folded piece of cardboard set in front of me. There are other name cards on the long narrow table; six in all. When I heard the list of people on the panel, I was confused about why the organizers had asked me. Compared with these other women, I have done nothing. Next to me sits an obstetrician who repairs fistulas for girls in Ethiopia. Two seats down is a young woman who was shot in Pakistan on her way home from school. I am surrounded on all sides by heroes. At home as well. As far as I'm concerned, Roarke is a hero too.

When Libby and Margot decided to film a documentary about Holden Park, the first interview they did was with Roarke. He had told them about the program after Libby quit her job and was looking for something to do next. Be brave, my father had said. Roarke said this was a good motto, and since we were now a married couple, he needed to do his part. I watched him describe finding a boy who had killed himself that summer, and when he did, it was as if I was right there with him. I could practically hear the sound the body made as it was cut down and crumpled onto the floor.

A member of the audience stands and is handed a microphone. Her question is for me. She wants to know what has happened to my family since my parents fled the country, since Caleb was locked up and denied bail. You can tell from the way she speaks that she believes in justice, which makes sense, because justice is what this panel on breaking the cycle of violence against women is really all about. But the truth is, I do not know if Caleb will be convicted when the case eventually goes to trial. I do not know if justice will prevail.

Even though I was technically below the age of consent when the baby was conceived, other rapists have been let off with even more damning evidence against them. Men convicted of forcing themselves on women in college dorm rooms or parked cars or behind dumpsters, men whose crimes were witnessed by other men still walked away with a light tap on the wrist, a shake of the head, a Boys will be boys, a warning to be more careful where they put their penises, to be smart enough to know which girls won't talk. The justice system has bent over backward to avoid denying these men their bright futures, has spent too much time considering their suffering, their heartache, instead of seeing them as the predators they are.

Caleb, on the other hand, won't necessarily be able to depend on the old boys' club for sympathy. After all, incest is harder to dismiss. Lissa has said she will come forward if she needs to, but for now she is staying where she's been happiest, out of the spotlight. She told me that Mother struck her hard across the face when they were still barricaded in the church, blamed her for everything that happened, accused her of putting me up to it. My sister hit Mother back. Lissa was surprised at how shocked Mother was by the blow, but later she realized that this must have been the moment Mother knew for certain that she had lost control of it all.

I tell the girl as much of this as I am able, trying to explain how it was the groundswell of public outrage that led to Caleb's arrest despite my parents' best efforts to make it all go away, to shift the narrative, blame the victim, imply that I had somehow orchestrated it all. I tell the audience that these smears very well may have been successful had it not been for people just like them, who refused to look away, to pretend they did not see. And I thank them. I thank them for being here today and I thank them for being there for one another even after we have all gone our separate ways.

———

When the session lets out, I shake hands and pose for pictures. I am also given a surprising number of hugs. On my way home, I stop to pick up the dress I will be wearing to Libby and Mike's wedding and then climb back into my cab. When the taxi stops again, I overtip the driver and step out onto the pavement outside our building, trying not to let the thin plastic bag around my dress drag on the ground. The sidewalks are still slushy and I am not wearing the right shoes, but I can just detect the first breath of spring in the air. I pick my way carefully between the gray puddles and, as I do, I take in the tall buildings, the general bustle of the city, the constant motion that has begun to feel like home.

I am anonymous here in a way I would not have been able to hope for in any other place, except maybe overseas. We tried that for a little while, the summer after the wedding. We climbed the Eiffel Tower, explored the Louvre, then took the Chunnel and visited Windsor Castle and ate scones in a crooked teahouse just next door. A few people recognized us, but on the whole it was refreshing to be in a part of the world where stories like mine, like ours, seem like a tiny blip compared with the drama their royal families have wrought over the centuries. Now this city is home, is mine in a way I never expected to feel a place might belong to me and I to it. This city is where my daughter was born. We named her Louisa after my grandmother. She is ours, Roarke's and mine, no matter what a paternity test might say. She is beautiful and she is loved.

I stand outside our building and pause to let the sounds of the neighborhood wash over me. Then I go inside. We have a loft not far from campus. I walk there with Louisa sometimes to meet up with Roarke in between his classes. Other times I walk there on my own. I think about applying to college the way I always assumed that I was supposed to. I think about the other things I might do instead. The freedom of having a choice and of that choice being entirely mine seems like a miracle. I still don't know what I will do.

I open the door to our apartment quietly. I like to watch my new family in those few moments before they know that I am there. It's one of the things that gives me the most comfort, knowing that Louisa is all right even when I am away. From the doorway I can see the life that we have made together: the mismatched furniture, the scattered plastic toys, the large framed black-and-white photo of a papier-mâché Liberty Bell that hangs above the couch.

Roarke turns and I see that he is holding Louisa. She is wearing a smocked dress that his mother sewed by hand. Louisa's hair falls in soft curls around her face as Roarke buries his face in her belly and she throws her head back and erupts in a fit of shrieking, her face wet with spit, and the room is filled with the sound of laughter. Adam emerges from Roarke's bedroom and checks a pot on the stove. He leans over and inhales the steam and reaches into the cupboard for some seasoning. Roarke puts Louisa down onto a play mat and begins to pull plates off a shelf to set the table. Adam joins him with the silverware and kisses him lightly on the cheek.

Despite my best efforts to shield him, Roarke is a media darling. His parents are beloved as well. After all, unlike my parents, they raised a hero, not a rapist. Roarke has his own flock of paparazzi, and it turns out that he and Adam are more popular as a couple than he and I could have ever hoped to be. That sort of attention has opened him up to a torrent of online abuse, but he ignores it. In any case, his fans are fiercely protective and more than happy to fight his battles for him. They are fiercely protective of us all. It may be silly, but it gives me hope, this army of strangers that have sworn to stand up against slut-shaming and homophobia and bigotry. That have promised to parse right from wrong.

Some nights I still lie awake and wonder if I made the right decision. I go back over everything and try to work out what I could have done differently, how I might have saved Louisa from being marked by the publicity of how she came to be. But anything less and Caleb probably would have walked away unscathed, and I couldn't risk that—not only for Louisa's sake but also for the sake of whatever girl Caleb set his sights on next. So these days when people ask me why I did it, I tell them that it was no more complicated than this: I wanted a safe place to raise my daughter, both in this apartment and later when she has to face the world. That's all any of us ever want, but we won't get there unless we refuse to stay silent. Somehow I knew that it would feel that simple even before she was born. The money, finally standing up to my family, those were just a bonus. Louisa's safety was all that ever mattered all along. I step across the threshold and Roarke and Adam turn and smile as I pick up my daughter. I press my lips against her head and I know that I am home.

ACKNOWLEDGMENTS

I am beyond indebted to my editor, Jenny Jackson, and her colleagues at Knopf. Their insight and endless enthusiasm have made this book better than I ever hoped it could be. Innumerable thanks to my agent, Kirby Kim, for remembering me after a decade of silence, and to Brenna English-Loeb and the rest of the team at Janklow & Nesbit.

My thanks to Laura Certain, physician scientist and grammarian, for her early and careful reading of this text. To Lindsey Fitzharris for forging the path and giving encouragement. Thank you to Sardiaa Leney, in advance and in writing, for all future safari adventures. My gratitude to Terri Becker, Karen Gruskin, Rich Bachur, and my colleagues at Boston Children's and Beverly Hospitals for their support. To Ellen, for making it in Mozambique and beyond. To Lucie, fellow PK and the closest thing to a big sister I will ever get. Next, I would not be the person I am without Mark Rourke and Holly Dolan and the rest of my Bement family. Thank you for knowing me before I knew myself.

Thanks to my mother, Jan, for not being anything like Celia Hicks and my father, Dan, for being the sort of priest allowed to have children. To Matty, Marnie, and Timothy as well. To Uncle David. Thanks, finally and most importantly, to Daryl Achilles, a prince among men, and to our two children, Emmaline and Gideon, who deserve a safer, kinder world than this one.